Praise for the novels of
LJ Cohen

DERELICT

"Cohen has real talent with character development and interaction, and prickly, defensive Ro is a sympathetic and interesting heroine."
—*Publishers Weekly*

"LJ Cohen deftly weaves together realistic teenage characters, futuristic technology, and big stakes for a real page turner."
—*Wen Spencer, Award winning SF&F novelist, author of the* Ukiah Oregon *and* Elfhome *series*

"Get on board Derelict, and you'll take an edgy, nonstop flight into an audacious SF future with unremitting danger as your pilot—and thrilling adventure your destination."
—*Lynn Viehl, NYT best selling author of the* Stardoc *and* Darkyn *series*

"Intricate plotting melded seamlessly with delightful characterizations kept me turning pages as fast as I could go in an attempt to keep up with the unfolding story. A cracking yarn set in a lush future I'm hoping we'll hear more of."
—*Nathan Lowell, Creator of the* Golden Age of the Solar Clipper *and the* Tanyth Fairport Adventures

ITHAKA RISING, book 2 of Halcyone Space

"As the story unfolds and the pieces come together, the inexorable pressure of fine story telling, smooth characters, and compelling action rocket the reader into jump space where anything can—and probably will—happen."

—*Nathan Lowell, Creator of the* Golden Age of the Solar Clipper *and the* Tanyth Fairport Adventures

DREADNOUGHT AND SHUTTLE, book 3 of Halcyone Space

". . . engaging characters and a believable universe . . . The admirably brave and übercompetent Dev shines as a stellar addition to the genre. . ."

—*Publishers Weekly*

"If you love the kind of space story where ordinary people with flaws and fears are the heroes, and good people need to make choices in a messy and uncertain world, then DREADNOUGHT AND SHUTTLE is the kind of book you'll want to clear your evening for."

—*Audrey Faye, author of* The KarmaCorp Novels

"A fabulous and phenomenal tale! Cohen has delivered us an exhilarating one-two punch in this third book of her Halcyone Space series. Sci-fi lovers will geek out over all the techy-goodness. And for us adventure-seekers, there's a thrilling (and romantic) chase through space that will leave you happily satisfied!"

—*Janet B Taylor, author of* Into the Dim

"A fitting third installment to the Halcyone Space series, LJ Cohen's Dreadnought And Shuttle brings together again the team we learned to love in Derelict and Ithaka Rising, for a rollicking adventure of rescue and justice."

—Lou J Berger, author of "Leaving Bordeaux" and other short fiction

THE BETWEEN

". . .a moving tale of heroism and compassion. . . Lydia is a young woman utterly unprepared for the world she's about to enter—but she learns fast. She's a character you'll want to meet again, from a writer you'll want to read again. Take good note: LJ Cohen is a new voice to follow."

—Jeffrey A. Carver, author of The Chaos Chronicles

PARALLAX

Also by LJ Cohen

Halcyone Space
Derelict (book 1)
Ithaka Rising (book 2)
Dreadnought and Shuttle (book 3)

Changeling's Choice
The Between (book 1)
Time and Tithe (book 2)

Future Tense

Short Stories
Stranger Worlds than These

PARALLAX
Halcyone Space, Book 4
LJ Cohen

Interrobang Books

Newton, MA

Published by Interrobang Books
Newton, MA

www.interrobangbooks.com

First print edition: June, 2017

ISBN-10: 1-942851-05-7
ISBN-13: 978-1-942851-05-9

For my story-whisperer:

you earned your keep on this one.

Chapter 1

TUGGING HER FINGERS THROUGH sleep-tangled hair, Dev stared at her barricaded door and wondered if Micah was awake too. She reached for the micro he'd gotten her. It was hard not to resent the easy access to funds that made the expenditure an afterthought to him.

The time glowed dimly on its display, nearly washed out by the brightness of the artificial light in her room.

Zero three fucking fifty.

It was no use trying to get back to sleep. Dev reached beneath her pillow for the polymer knife she'd made when she had been a prisoner aboard Maldonado's ship. The reflection of the blade in the bathroom mirror comforted her as she washed up and got dressed. Its weight in her pocket felt even better.

Her generic bedroom could have been aboard any ship or even back home in Midlant. The dorms were prefab construction, little modules bolted together and piled on top of one another. It was just one step above the temporary shelters refugees had built out of the containers that used to deliver supplies and food to the settlements. But this room was hers.

And she'd made it as secure as she could with a mechanical latch freshly bolted into her side of the door. Housing would be pissed, but that was their problem.

Dev walked to the window and yanked the blackout curtains aside. Below her, a twinkle of blue lights marked the emergency beacons on the artfully curved paths cut through the University's grounds. Even the Commonwealth Officer Training Corps first-years wouldn't be up for their daily run for another hour or so.

Now that she was awake, she felt safer turning off all the room lights. Standing in the abrupt darkness, she knew it didn't make a lot of sense. The days were usually easier than the nights, but even then Dev would make sure to get to classes early so she could claim a seat at the end of a row, closest to the door.

It was only when a smear of pink muddied the eastern horizon that Dev realized she'd been standing by the window for over an hour. She swore and dropped her new micro in the pocket with her knife before striding to the door and unbolting it.

Micah stood just outside her room with a cup of coffee in one hand, his other lifted to knock. By the time Dev's sleep-deprived brain had processed it, she'd already barreled into her roommate. The cup tumbled from his grip, spilling coffee all over him. She stood in stunned silence as the polymer cup bounced and rolled across the gray utilitarian carpet.

"Shit!" Micah stumbled back, brushing coffee from his shirt and pants.

Dev dropped her gaze to the floor and stared at his scarred bare feet, the now empty cup, and the dark stain spreading between them. "Crap. I'm sorry," she whispered.

"Good thing I made a pot, then," Micah said. "Help yourself.

Just leave me some. I need to change."

She glanced up in time to see him hobble across their quarters. "I'm sorry," she repeated, even though he'd already disappeared behind his door. Retreating into her room, she grabbed a towel from the closet and tossed it on the spill. The coffee turned the off-white material a dark, uneven brown. The earthy scent permeated their apartment. It was the real stuff. From Micah's private stash.

Damn it.

Sighing, Dev crossed to the small galley and poured herself more. She was still standing by the sink, cradling the cup in her hands when Micah reappeared, this time in his clunky shoes, wearing a clean shirt and pants.

"You're not going to dump that on me, are you?" he asked, leaning against the counter.

Dev flinched and some of the coffee sloshed over the side of the cup onto her hand. It wasn't as hot as the cup he'd spilled which meant she'd lost time again. Shit. "Stuff's too good to waste," she said, and took a large sip to cover her unease.

Micah made no move to pour himself some of the expensive brew. Instead, he studied her in the silent apartment. "If it's any consolation, I'm not sleeping too well, either."

By some unspoken agreement, after they had hidden their "borrowed" ship in a private hangar paid for with Micah's father's blood money, and after they'd returned to campus with cover stories both their advisers seemed to accept without comment, neither of them had talked about Dev's abduction.

She knew damned well why she didn't want to go there, but could only guess that Micah's guilt was what kept him silent. Which may have explained the new micro and the gift of morning coffee. "It wasn't your fault."

"If it hadn't been for me, he wouldn't have come here and found you."

He. Alain Maldonado. An image of her captor's narrowed green eyes superimposed itself over Micah's worried blue ones for a moment and Dev's hands shook. She glanced at his shoes, envisioning the damaged feet they protected. Micah had more reason to hate the man than she did. "He's gone. He can't hurt you anymore."

"I could say the same to you, but it wouldn't matter. He left his mark on both of us." Micah looked down. "Literally and figuratively."

She covered the uncomfortable silence that followed with a clatter of dishes, dropping her empty cup into the sink.

"Dev." Micah's voice startled her.

"What?"

"Have you talked to your brothers?"

She refused to meet his gaze. What was there to say to them? *Hey, how's things? Guess what, I was kidnapped and threatened and got someone killed who was trying to help me.* There wasn't anything any of her brothers could say that would ease the roiling mix of anger, guilt, and fear that she'd been battling since the trip back. It wasn't like she could take a leave from Uni. Not and keep her position and her scholarship. She was her family's last chance. Her brothers needed her to cope. Which is what she'd learned to do as a young child in Midlant. Cope.

"You should. Talk to them."

"Thanks for the family advice, now shut up." Dev winced at how sarcastic she sounded. Micah had every right to call her on it, but the only thing he did was raise an eyebrow.

"You promised to take me there."

Dev looked Micah up and down. He would fit in at the settlement about as well as she had on a spaceship. His casual clothes were clearly customized, and his stance showed both his spacer history and an ironic grace from years spent playing the very public role of Senator Rotherwood's son. "My brothers would hate you."

"Sorry?"

Damn. She hadn't realized she'd said that aloud. "Look at you."

He glanced down at himself, frowning. "What do you mean?"

Even his scowl looked posed. It was as if he was always ready for a holo. Always controlled. Composed. The only times she'd seen him unguarded were in the biodome during his panic attack and when he'd walked into the bridge on Taro Odachi's small ship to find Dev alive after she'd escaped Maldonado. The naked relief on Micah's face had unnerved her. "It's just that ..."

"What?"

"Dressed like that? You'll be pegged as either a spacer or a city boy for sure."

Except that's not what they'd call him. They'd mock him as a voidhopper, which was definitely better than a highsider. Young highsiders still liked to take their chances slumming in the settlements. The ones that brought their own security details lived to brag about it.

"Then I'll wear something else."

Dev pushed past him and into the common room. "Why?"

"Why what?"

"Why do you want to go to Midlant?"

Micah's uneven footfalls sounded behind her. They both stared out the window to the campus below. The blue emergency lights paled as the sun rose and a few early risers were crossing the well-manicured paths. "Because you're right. I don't understand. All I know of the settlements was what I learned in school. And that was filtered through the Commonwealth."

"It's not my job to enlighten you." Dev's face heated up. It wasn't Micah she was mad at. Not really. It was the way her adviser was surprised that she'd come back after disappearing. It was the way her teachers never expected her to work as hard as she did or do as well. It was the way her classmates avoided certain subjects when she was around, or were overly apologetic when they talked about anything related to the settlements. It didn't take long for Dev to drop every vestige of the Midlant dialect at Uni. But she never got over the anger that would blaze inside when one of her fellow students would take great pains to say, "Not you, Dev. You're not Settlement at all."

She thought for sure Micah would get angry and clomp away. Part of her even wanted him to. But the minutes passed and he stood next to her silently. Dev's breathing slowed and the tension in her shoulders eased. "I'm sorry. That was out of line."

"No, it wasn't." Micah retreated to the galley area and dragged over one of the high stools. He sighed quietly as he sat and Dev felt a pang of guilt. "Look, I spent most of my childhood having my life scripted for me for the sake of political expediency. Now both my parents are dead, I don't know what it's like to even have a family, and I never had much of a chance to make my own friends.

"Not until Halcyone. And not until you." He shifted his micro from hand to hand. "You don't want me to apologize anymore.

Fine. I'll stop apologizing. But what happened out there? On Maldonado's ship? It links us, whether you like it or not. Besides, you made a promise." He looked up, then, and smiled. There was both a warmth in Micah's face and a practiced intensity.

"And did your father keep all his promises?" Dev winced. She was having a hard time holding on to the filters that kept her from being too conspicuous in the world beyond the settlements.

Micah shrugged. "No. And the consequences eventually caught up with him. Even halfway across the cosmos."

Dev had been so desperate to know that Ithaka truly existed —that somewhere out in the void there were some who refused to crack under Commonwealth control—she'd promised to take Micah to Midlant in return for knowing the truth. And he'd told her. Now either keeping her promise or breaking it would have consequences. Dev wasn't sure which would be worse.

*

Ro opened her eyes to an empty bed again and swore softly.

"Sorry. Didn't mean to wake you." From where she stood in the galley, Nomi dropped her gaze to the floor.

"What time is it?" Ro could just as easily have grabbed her micro or queried Daedalus Station, but it was a way to keep Nomi from withdrawing even more than she already had.

"Zero six seventeen."

"Did you get any sleep at all?"

Nomi turned away and heated the water for coffee.

It had been barely a week since Ro had returned to Daedalus Station. A week since Alain Maldonado—her own father—had triggered a supernova's worth of chaos, including Nomi's arrest and interrogation. At least he'd managed to get himself killed in the process. There was some consolation in that.

Ro got up and washed up in the small head. Nomi had left the seal open on a packet of analgesics. It was the only thing out of place in the organized minimalism of the woman's life and it spoke volumes. Sighing, she slid the meds in the empty slot in the recessed cabinet. When Ro emerged to change, the bed was already made and a full cup of coffee sat on the night table. She sipped at it as she tried to figure out what to say.

Nomi's silence was like a new vibration in an engine. Left uncalibrated, it would shake the delicate mechanism of her girlfriend's psyche apart.

Setting down her coffee, Ro walked across their quarters to where Nomi sat on the end of the sofa staring past her micro. Her unfocused gaze flicked up at Ro and then away again.

A faded and pilled quilt lay folded neatly across the back of the sofa. Unsure of what else to do, Ro sat and tucked the relic from her childhood around both of them. Nomi hugged her.

Ro waited, stroking the smooth dark wave of Nomi's hair. It felt like eons before she muffled some indistinct words into Ro's collarbone.

"Hmm?"

"I'm a mess. I'm sorry."

"Hey. No apologies. Okay?" Ro pulled free of their embrace and tipped Nomi's chin up. Her eyes were bloodshot. The dark circles beneath them were the color of a bruise. "That would be my job."

"I have to get ready for work." Nomi pulled away from Ro's gentle hold and frowned. "And before you ask, I haven't been able to speak privately to Simon since..." She gestured at the small room.

Since she'd been placed in house arrest and Simon Marchand, the now acting comms supervisor, had risked a charge of treason to send her a message.

"It seems like he's making sure we're never on shift together."

Was he avoiding contact for Nomi's sake or for his own? "Has he said anything to you at all?"

"Oh, he's the same perfectly jovial Cajun food-obsessed man he's always been. But other than complain about his unexpected promotion screwing up his official retirement? Not a thing."

Everyone on station was busy speculating about what had happened to Daedalus's previous comms supervisor. Lowell vanished not long after Nomi and Jem had uncovered evidence he was being paid covertly by the Commonwealth's Commander Targill. There wasn't enough data to know what he'd been spying on, but they had a good idea. And it certainly wasn't officially sanctioned by the Commonwealth.

Aside from Ro and her crew, no one else knew the truth, except for Mendez, their station commander and she had been avoiding them as well.

It was too late to worry about trusting Commander Mendez. She already had enough evidence to have them all arrested. That she hadn't bothered Ro more than she would admit. Simon Marchand and his dubious loyalty was another matter.

What was he after? Simon was in the perfect position to communicate with Nomi if he chose to. So why hadn't he?

Nomi yanked off the blanket, stood, and paced the narrow space between the couch and the galley. Her micro tumbled to the floor. "I don't … This isn't … I'm not good at this shit. I do communications. Send packets in a clear path between one ansible and another. This? This is all static."

Static that Ro had brought to Nomi's life. Static that kept getting louder and louder with every orbit.

"And don't you dare apologize!" Nomi whirled toward her, brown eyes blazing.

Ro smiled up at her. "You know you're like destabilized aduronium when you're angry."

"Volatile and dangerous?"

"Bright and powerful."

Nomi blushed nearly purple and looked down, letting her hair swing forward to hide her face.

"Hey." Ro picked up Nomi's micro and glanced down at the display. "You're going to be late for comms if you don't get moving."

"Will you be on Halcyone today?" There was an edge to Nomi's voice that had never been there before.

"Probably not. I have to chase down a problem in the power-plant subsystems. Ping me when you take your break. I can meet you for lunch."

"I don't need a babysitter."

Ro flinched. She was the sarcastic one, the one whose temper lay close to the surface.

Nomi reached for Ro's hand and gave it a gentle squeeze. "That was out of line. Will you meet me in hydroponics later? A walk would do me good."

Taking a break and getting out of the cramped access corridors beneath the space station would be good for her, too. Nomi had taught her that. "Of course." It would also be a safer place to talk than their quarters or Halcyone. The running water masked low conversations almost as well as the comms blockers Ro had installed on the ship.

"Guess we can't just power up Halcyone and ask her to jump us somewhere no one can find us." Nomi smoothed the top of her uniform before retrieving her micro and slipping it into a pocket.

"I wish," Ro whispered, as Nomi headed out of their quarters and into the corridors of Daedalus Station. You couldn't outjump fear. She knew that now.

Chapter 2

Hɪs ᴍɪᴄʀᴏ ʙᴜᴢᴢᴇᴅ, vibrating the metal posts of Barre's bunk. He swatted at it and tried to go back to sleep. It tumbled from the edge of the desk, hitting the floor with a clang. Confused dream images tangled with the echo of the bright sound that his mind identified as a B-flat. It was too early for music. Too early to be awake.

He pulled the thin cover over his head and curled onto his side. The temporal foam shifted with him, cushioning his hip and shoulder on the narrow bed. His micro buzzed again. Barre linked his neural to the little computer and sent the signal to power the annoying thing down. His room fell silent. Barre let his head sink into the pillow. If Ro needed him, she'd damned well wait until a decent hour.

Halcyone's alert tone reverberated in his small quarters and blasted through his mind simultaneously. Barre yelped and jerked upright, hitting his head on the upper bunk.

"Halcyone! What the fuck?"

The sound cut out so fast, Barre's ears rang. He rubbed the spot on the side of his head where he'd struck the metal support.

"Halcyone?"

The AI was silent. Barre got the feeling she was sulking. He wasn't as skilled in reading the ship's physical state as Ro, but he quickly scanned the basics: They were still safely tethered to Daedalus Station. Life support was operational. No one was trying to hack her systems. So what was the alarm all about?

"Halcyone?"

She wasn't even answering his direct query. Fine. The ship wanted him up? He was up. Barre untangled the blanket from his legs. He shivered as his bare feet hit the floor.

"Priority message. Text only."

Halcyone's voice seemed sharper and more clipped than usual. Damned personality subroutines. It was hard enough dealing with Ro. Now he had a touchy AI to contend with. He was going to have to teach it what "not a morning person" meant.

"Fine. Be that way." He leaned forward and picked up his micro. Definitely not awake enough to use his neural. As soon as he turned the device screen-side up, words started scrolling across it.

/She won't respond to my messages. What's her status?/

No greeting. No idents. And it traveled via the same secure messaging program Ro had enabled. There was only one person it could be from: Ada May. Which explained Halcyone's sudden mood shift.

/She's stable. My folks took her out of the induced coma three days ago./

He didn't know why Lieutenant Commander Gutierrez hadn't contacted May, but obviously she hadn't. The soldier had a lot of healing yet to do, and judging by their brief conversations after she'd been injured, most of it wasn't going to be the physical stuff.

/Can you talk to her?/

Barre was surprised to get May's reply so quickly. Either ansible conditions were extremely favorable, or she had some additional tricks to subvert Commonwealth comms that she hadn't shared with Ro. He was betting on the latter.

/Please./

He could just about hear May's soft voice in his head. It was practically the only thing soft about the old rogue scientist. But now that Taro Odachi—the man who had taken on the role of Charon, Ithaka's Ferryman—was dead and Gutierrez was refusing contact, May must be feeling vulnerable. While she had to have other supporters scattered through the cosmos, it was pretty clear that Ada May, Charon, and Gutierrez had a shared history. Maybe someday the lieutenant commander would even tell him about it.

/I'll do what I can. But it'll be hard to see her without attracting attention./

There was absolutely no reason he could invent for visiting the injured LC in medical. Barre couldn't admit he'd given her emergency care on Charon's ship after the Ferryman sacrificed himself to save her. Officially, Halcyone had been getting some refit work on Eurydice Station at the time and was nowhere near them when Gutierrez and Charon had gone after Ro's father and his stolen ship.

Barre set the micro down and leaned forward, shaking his head. His dreads slipped forward to hang in his face. What a supernova this mess was. He supposed he could visit medical when Jem was there for his scans, but that still didn't give him an excuse to talk to Gutierrez and anything that brought attention to the LC could endanger both Ithaka and her role in safeguarding it. Not that there was any guarantee she'd even be willing to talk to him.

Still, he was a better choice than Ro. She and the LC were aduronium and a quasi-quantum field. Barre yawned and glanced back at his bunk, but he was already awake. Maybe he could harass his little brother for a change.

"Good morning!" He let a few bars of what he considered Jem's theme play through his mind. If the link between them worked, Barre would get revenge for all the times his perky little brother used to wake him up.

"I hate you."

A triumphant anthem echoed through the link between them. Then it was as if a blast door sealed shut and the contact ended.

He grabbed his micro and typed a quick note to Jem.

/Need to talk. Come by when you're up./

Barre sidestepped between the bed and his instruments to reach the cramped head. He could probably find storage space for everything, but having it all here with him made the utilitarian room home. He stripped off the baggy drawstring pants he slept in and tossed them toward the bed before sealing the transparent walls of the retractable shower. The facilities on Daedalus were far more spacious, but this belonged to him.

By the time he'd toweled dry and changed, the door chime sounded. Barre triggered the release. Jem stood in the ship's corridor, two mugs of coffee in hand. His little brother looked wrecked and Barre immediately felt guilty for waking him, but kept silent. Jem hated when Barre fussed over him. He tied his dreads back with a small cord before taking one of the mugs.

"This had better be important."

He gulped down the bitter, black drink. "It is." Unless Jem wanted to climb up to the top bunk, there wasn't enough room for both of them in Barre's quarters. He ushered his little brother back into the corridor and headed to engineering. The largest single space on Halcyone, it had become their de facto meeting place.

Even knowing Halcyone was as safe as both the AI and Ro could make it, and even after the door sealed behind them, Barre was still concerned about speaking openly about Ada May and Ithaka—the hidden base of her anti-commonwealth insurgency. But until he and Jem had worked out all the bugs from their accidental and unreliable neural link, this would have to do.

"What gives?"

"Ada May messaged me. The LC isn't talking to her."

Jem sighed as he settled into one of the engineering station seats. "Well, Gutierrez certainly can't communicate freely from the middle of medical."

"I suppose not." Though surely May had ways to encrypt and secure comms. "She asked me to talk to her."

His brother lifted an eyebrow. It was nearly exactly the same look of cynical amusement that their mother often gave the medical staff. "Even if Mom and Dad let you loiter around their patients, what makes you think Gutierrez would talk to you?"

Barre shrugged. He had saved her life. But personal gratitude aside, there was absolutely no reason for the station's lieutenant commander to speak with the unranked adult son of the station's doctors. Even visiting her would raise questions they couldn't risk. But Jem was in and out of medical all the time, thanks to their parents' scrutiny. And Jem was good at not being noticed, at constantly being underestimated. "I was thinking it should be you."

"Fine," Jem said. "It's not like she can order me to leave."

There were advantages to being a minor. And Jem was a good choice apart from that. "Don't let her intimidate you. I think she could use a friend." The LC's worst wounds weren't the ones his parents were treating.

"I don't think I'm that person."

"And someone she can talk to about Charon."

"Barre, I really don't think I'm that person."

"There isn't anyone else, Jem." After barely escaping the trap Ro's father had set, Emmaline Gutierrez had been as vulnerable as Barre had ever seen her. It didn't take a trained psychiatrist to know that Charon's death had hit her hard. It was a loss that was tangled up in the complications of her secret past as well as her own guilt at surviving. If she wouldn't talk to May and she couldn't talk to any official on Daedalus, maybe Jem was the logical choice. Barre finished his coffee and set the empty cup down carefully. "Just do the best you can."

*

The silent bulk of the University's biodomes surrounded Micah. Each one contained a carefully controlled atmosphere and soil ecology, protected by biometric security and full-on biohazard-style double airlocks and decontamination procedures. Small robots skittered around alien landscapes, monitored by vigilant AIs, carrying out their careful experimental programming.

These sophisticated environments were a far cry from the hydroponics setup Micah had cobbled together on Halcyone for his experiments on the ubiquitous hallucinogen grown and distributed by the drug cartels. With the use of one of the domes, Micah could control every aspect of the frustrating plant's growth—from its genetic code to its soil conditions. But Doctor Parrish had essentially demoted him to a beginning student and the classes he'd been assigned to didn't grant him access to the biodomes.

Instead, he had years of failed data, Parrish's buggy growth-modeling program, and a long-forgotten glorified greenhouse.

Parrish didn't matter; the work did. Micah wasn't about to let a petty academic bureaucrat sideline him. It had been easy to slip back into the role of the diligent student. His teachers had made the appropriate sympathetic noises and excused his absence when he had disclosed the severity of his burns, and if he limped a little more than when he'd first arrived at Uni, it was as much expressing the reality of the constant low-level pain as it was deliberate theater.

How much of his father's persona had been that mix of truth and subterfuge? Micah stumbled to a stop, sweating in the late afternoon heat, uncomfortable with where that line of thought led. His father wasn't the reason he was here. His mother was. And it was for her sake and in her memory that he was returning to his work on bittergreen.

Micah pushed his way through the overgrown hedges that had hidden the equally overgrown dome from its more advanced fellows. Squashing a pang of guilt, he punched in the code Dev had shared with him and waited as the outer door swung open. Yes, he was going to use it as a study space and a refuge, as Dev did. And he was also going to figure out how to grow nonsterile bittergreen here.

The outer door sealed, holding him inside the small airlock. There was no decontamination routine, but he didn't know if that was because the last experiments were run here before that was automated, or the routines just no longer worked. Another thing he'd have to figure out. Bittergreen wasn't finicky about where it grew and Micah would have to make sure there wasn't any microbial contamination from soil tracked in from outside. That was one variable he hadn't had to worry about on Halcyone.

He hit the inner door release and was slammed with a blast of heat and humidity. Perfect growing conditions for the riot of weeds that over-spilled the neat lines of formerly organized raised beds. Weeds that would need to be completely cleared out, down to the last rootling and seed head if he was to get anywhere with the bittergreen.

For now, he needed to assess the dome's neglected controls. An access panel was mounted against the side wall of the biodome. As Micah studied the mostly unlabeled buttons, he wondered how long it had been since anyone had actually used the space.

He'd have to engineer a hard frost. Then clean out the beds and sterilize the soil. But to do that, he'd have to trace all the sensors back to the access panel that formed the central data hub of the dome. If he was lucky, he'd be able to pair his micro to the very basic user interface and control it remotely. It was more like Halcyone's life support modules than her higher cognitive processes.

That was probably why this dome had escaped anyone's

notice.

As Micah lurched his way across the tangle of vegetation, following conduit and testing its integrity, he sighed, wishing Ro were here. She was much better at this than he was. In the time it had taken Micah to follow the water lines and locate the soil sensors, she would probably have programmed several drones to do the mapping.

He wiped sweat from his forehead and sat down at the edge of one of the raised beds. A low hiss was all the warning he had before the ground-level sprinklers turned on and soaked him. The startling laughter that followed made him tumble backward into the weedy and now damp bed.

Dev stood over him, still laughing, ignoring the water that sprayed up at her. She extended a tanned arm to help him up. Micah glared at the broken hose that was still spurting water straight up to the ceiling of the dome, three and a half meters overhead. He was going to have to install pressure regulators.

"It does that. Sorry."

It was good to hear her laugh again. Even if it was at his expense.

She leaned down to pick up his micro from the puddle it had fallen into and studied the crude schematic he'd been drawing. "Looking to reclaim this mess?"

He grabbed the device from her. "Once a botanist, always a botanist," he said, shrugging. It was her space. Or at least she had a stronger claim to it than he did. He should have asked, but what would he have done if she'd said no?

"The water will turn off in eleven minutes. I could never find a way to change the programming. You just have to avoid that spot four times a day."

"Thanks for the warning."

"I didn't know you were setting up shop here."

Micah felt his face burn. He should have asked. But then she would have wanted to know what he was growing. And why. "Is it okay? Do you mind? I have some experiments I need to finish and Parrish won't authorize me for my own space." He sounded whiny to his own ears. Maybe she wouldn't take it that way.

"It's a biodome. If you can use it, sure. Go ahead." She paused, met his eyes and looked away. "Can I help?" Now it was her turn to sound tight and awkward.

Micah looked at the tangle of conduit left to trace. There was nothing at this stage that would reveal his plan to grow bittergreen. He wouldn't have to lie to her. Yet. And her assistance would make the work go much more quickly. It was good to see her out of their apartment, too.

They worked in comfortable silence for the next few hours, until twilight fell and the interior of the dome turned a deep purple.

"Well, that's a good start," Micah said, brushing dirt from his pants. "Thank you."

She looked up and smiled at him. "Now you look proper Settlement."

"Still think your brothers would hate me?"

"Do you really want to find out?"

Micah stiffened, blinking in the stillness. Her face was lost to darkness; if the dome had artificial lights, he didn't know which buttons controlled them. He could use his micro as a lamp, but there was a quiet intimacy with the two of them standing side by side, draped in shadows. "So you talked to them?"

Dev sighed. "Yes. Giles told me I was being an ass."

Giles. Tanner. Vic. When Dev had been taken, Micah had found her brothers' contact information and had prepared a message to autosend in case he didn't make it back with her. He had quietly recalled the message and deleted it.

Micah sat on the edge of one of the raised beds. "What was it like?"

Dev joined him, sitting close enough for him to feel the heat from her body. "Growing up with three older brothers?"

He nodded, though she probably couldn't see him.

"Complicated."

She fell silent again. If she wanted to talk about her past, she would. Micah understood complicated. His relationship with the late senator was the very definition of the word.

Night fell. It was as dark as it was going to get. Micah looked up at the transparent dome overhead. No stars showed through the smear of light from the University and the cities nearby. And even if the grid were to fail, it would take a generation before the sky would clear enough for anyone to see more than a few bright planets and suns.

Somewhere out there, Daedalus Station kept watch over an insignificant wormhole. It was a miserable place. He should have been glad to have gotten away.

His feet were starting to throb. He'd been out since early this morning and hadn't had a chance to elevate them. Barre would lecture him if he were here. Micah sighed and turned to Dev. "You never told me what happened on Maldonado's ship."

"The bastard drugged me. I woke up in a stripped-down galley. What's there to tell?"

Micah knew there was more than that. The way her hand was never far from the slim, translucent blade she'd crafted was the biggest tell. But there were others, too. Maybe it was enough that she'd agreed to take him to Midlant. He shifted his weight forward and tried to ease some of the stiffness in his feet. "You hungry?"

"Why, you cooking?"

"Buying. Much safer that way."

"Deal."

There was a hint of a smile in her voice. It was a start.

Chapter 3

Nomi's comms shift passed swiftly. There was just enough traffic to keep her busy and her mind mostly occupied. Yizhi Chen sat in the command chair and was her usual model of efficiency. Quiet and competent, she had been part of Lowell's "two-crew" along with Simon Marchand for more than a year. Once Marchand had been promoted, she'd been moved up to the first-shift supervisor. Was she part of the conspiracy, too?

There were too many moving parts for Nomi to get a sense of the whole. The missing Cam Lowell was or wasn't a Commonwealth informant. Jem's hack had at least exposed a link and a money trail between him and Commander Targill.

He might be a Commonwealth war hero and decorated ship's captain, but he was someone Commander Mendez didn't trust. Someone who was far too interested in what Ro knew about Ithaka and who seemed to show up on Daedalus Station far too conveniently.

Lieutenant Commander Gutierrez didn't trust anyone. Well, that wasn't strictly true, but she certainly didn't trust Lowell.

She'd spent the better part of her career keeping him under close surveillance. Had she known Targill had been pulling Lowell's strings?

But why?

Everything circled back to Targill.

And then there was Simon Marchand, who wanted to protect her from him.

"Ensign."

Nomi jerked her head up. "Sorry?"

"Your break started three minutes ago."

"Yes, sir." She signed out her terminal and set her headset down. Twenty-seven minutes until she needed to be back. She set her micro for twenty, pinged Ro, and left comms. What were the chances that Ro would actually be able to break away from her work and meet Nomi in hydroponics? There was a time that would have frustrated her, but Nomi knew Ro's infuriating ability to hyperfocus was part of who she was, part of what made her so relentlessly competent.

Not that understanding made it easy to live with, but she remembered her grandmother complaining about the same traits in her grandfather. And they managed a marriage that spanned more than half a century as they traveled across the cosmos. For now, it was enough that she and Ro were together. That Nomi knew Ro loved her. That she loved Ro. Conspiracies and conflicts notwithstanding.

Nomi nodded and smiled to station personnel on autopilot as she headed to the large parklike hydroponics bay. She spent time here every day. Sometimes alone, sometimes with Ro when she could pry the engineer away from her work. Nomi's favorite spot also happened to be the safest place to have a quiet conversation—a bench next to the small waterfall that was part of the water reclamation system on Daedalus. She was grateful for the careful attention to the aesthetics of the place as much as she was for the privacy.

She set her micro down and stared at the churning water.

"May I?"

Nomi's heart sped up. Simon Marchand stood before her. His thick eyebrows highlighted deep brown eyes that always seemed amused and matched the boyish smile set in his weathered face. "Lieutenant." Her body stiffened but her voice was even and steady as she waved him to the seat next to her.

"Simon. Please. After all, we're not on duty."

"Simon. What can I do for you?" Nomi kept her gaze on the pool in front of her and her hands clasped in her lap to keep them from shaking.

"I seriously underestimated you. I won't make that mistake again."

His voice was quiet, conversational, but the words held a subtle threat. Or was Nomi confusing artifact for signal?

"Whatever you think you've accomplished, Targill will be back for you."

She drew her breath in sharply. "I'm an officer of the Commonwealth of Planets. He's bound by the laws, the same as I am." If he'd had any sort of solid proof of her data mining, she'd already have been arrested.

"And you're completely certain of that?"

She struggled for something to say and Ro's question jumped into her mind. "Who's side are you on?"

"That depends on how you define the sides."

The Commonwealth. Ithaka. Two sides and the silent war

between them. A simple equation. But where did that leave Targill? And then there was Simon. Who was he working for?

Nomi wished Ro were here. She would be better at this real-time game of 'nought and shuttle. "You risked a lot to try and help me. Why?"

"And you haven't thrown me under the afterburners. Why not?"

She glanced over at the man who'd befriended her when she first got placed on Daedalus Station. "Are you even from New Louisiana?"

"Born and bred. You've had my gumbo." His expression of faux hurt was so sincere and so dramatic at the same time, Nomi couldn't help but laugh. "I need that data," he said, his voice just as light as if he'd invited her to dinner or told one of his long shaggy dog tales.

It wasn't worth denying what she and Jem had hacked. Too many people already knew about it. "Why?" Nomi glanced around. There were at least a dozen station personnel wandering the hydroponics bay. She could get up and leave and Marchand couldn't stop her. Couldn't threaten her.

"You've unbalanced a set of equations that have been carefully balanced for decades."

"But whose side are you on?" Nomi asked again.

"Think. Who already has the information you stole? Do you really want to give them the advantage? If I can protect you from Targill, I will, but I can't do it without your intel on Lowell. Whether you understand it or not, I'm your friend." He paused to shrug. "Or at least I'm not your enemy. That may be the best you're going to get."

"Nomi?" Ro's voice called out from the other side of

hydroponics.

Nomi closed her eyes briefly in thanks to a deity she wasn't even sure her grandfather really believed in.

Marchand stood as Ro walked toward them. "Ro. Nomi. You know where to find me."

"What was that all about?"

"I have no idea."

Frowning, Ro sat down beside her. She took Nomi's hands in both of hers. "You're freezing."

Her micro's alarm startled them both. "I have to be back in comms in seven minutes." She had no idea how she was going to get through the rest of her shift now.

Ro stared in the direction Marchand had left. "I'll walk you there."

*

If Lieutenant Commander Gutierrez had still been in intensive care, it wouldn't have mattered that Jem was the child of the station's doctors. But since she'd been upgraded to serious, but stable condition, she was no longer in isolation. Which meant—at least theoretically—Jem could visit her.

There was still the matter of what possible reason he had and why she would agree, but those were wormholes Jem would jump when he got there.

He entered medical and stood by the door, watching. His mother was on duty, which meant his father was probably asleep in their quarters. She moved with a calm efficiency that belied the intensity Jem knew was always simmering just below the surface. An intensity that seemed to burn through her control whenever Barre was concerned. At least it only used to be with Barre. Ever since Jem had gotten his neural implant, her emotions always seemed to be in turmoil around him, too. Or maybe he was just able to see them now that his damaged brain and the black-market device had wired his senses together.

One of the technicians flagged her down and she strode across medical to confer with him over a remote terminal. While she was otherwise occupied, Jem nodded to the daytime receptionist and walked in as he'd done thousands of times before in all the places his parents had been posted. He and Barre were practically raised in medical bays just like this one. At an early age, they had been taught where they were and weren't allowed to go; it never occurred to either of his parents that they would ever abuse their privilege.

Gutierrez had been moved to the step-down area. Thin scrims separated the beds. From inside, patients couldn't see through them, but from the angle of the monitoring station they were transparent. Not that it mattered. Gutierrez was the only patient housed there. Jem slipped through the opening and sat in the chair near the LC's bed.

She was alive, which given how bad she'd looked when they brought her in was astounding. They had had to detach her prosthesis. While Jem had spent his lifetime around injuries, he still had to turn away from the mass of decades-old burns-scars on her chest and left shoulder that told a vivid story of her amputation. Her newer injuries, including the gash along her right arm, were healing well. Her lower half was covered so he couldn't assess the state of her recent burns, but his parents were good at their work. Barre's emergency care had given the LC a fighting chance. Gutierrez would survive.

"I didn't realize the Durbins came as a package deal," she said. "What's your specialty?"

"I —" Now that he was here, Jem realized he had no idea what to say to her. "I'm sorry. People ... people are worried about you." People. She would know who that meant.

Gutierrez closed her eyes and turned her head away. But she made no move to hit the call button.

"They could build you a new arm." An image of the maker space Ada May had nurtured and hidden on Ithaka flashed through his mind. He was sure Dr. Land would be able to help her the way he had helped Jem.

"Why are you here?"

Jem flinched. Even though her voice was subdued, it still held the sharpness of the woman's accustomed command. He sifted through a number of possible replies, but none of them felt right and he was afraid he might give something away about Ithaka or Ada May where Commonwealth ears could hear them.

As the silence lengthened, Gutierrez turned back to stare at him.

Deep circles darkened the skin beneath her eyes. Her short hair lay matted against her head. Without her prosthesis and her crisp uniform, she seemed small, lost. Something in her expression reminded him of how he had felt lying on a similar bed after the emergency surgery to release the pressure of his brain bleed. "I thought you might need a friend."

"A friend," she repeated. There was little tone or emotion in her voice. It was clear ice shot through with ash and it chilled Jem more than her anger would have.

He drew his legs up onto the chair and circled them with his arms. "I'm sorry. About Taro."

Gutierrez stared at him without blinking. "The Ferryman made his choice. He knew the cost."

Jem took a deep breath. "It doesn't make it any easier."

"For him or for me?" Her lips twisted into a half-smirk.

"Both."

"How old are you?"

"Does that matter?" He was old enough to know that sometimes even the clearest jump landed you in null-space.

"I suppose not."

"Do you want to talk about it?"

"No." Gutierrez glanced at the opaque scrim but still didn't signal the call bell.

"Do you want me to leave?" Barre would have been better at this.

"Stay if you like. It doesn't matter."

Jem forced himself to look at the remnants of her left arm. It ended in a mass of capped scar tissue just beneath the shoulder. Conduit as thin as a human hair that had served as artificial brachial plexus and additional peripheral nerves would have to be completely replaced along with the purely mechanical elements of the prosthesis. "You haven't talked to her."

They both knew he wasn't referring to Dr. Leta Durbin.

"There's nothing to say. When I'm declared fit for duty, I'll return to work." Gutierrez shrugged. The scars on her left shoulder rippled in a way that made him flinch.

"And if you can't? Who will take your place?" It was going to be hard enough for Ada May without the man called Charon—her Ferryman. But what if she lost Gutierrez, too?

"I'm just one old soldier. As replaceable as my arm." Orange highlighted the words with the worry she refused to express.

"I don't believe that."

"I'm tired, Jem. And maybe there are some fights you can't win." She shifted in the narrow bed and winced. The whine of the autoinjector filled the cubicle. Her eyes fluttered, then half-closed as the pain meds raced through her. "Tell her that. There are some fights you can't win." Her voice slurred and she trailed off.

"That's not ... You should ..." Before Jem could even begin to sort out what to say, she'd fallen asleep. "Great. Just seismic," he muttered to himself as he crossed the medical bay to sit and wait outside his parents' office.

"I don't have time to run your scans now, Jeremy."

His mother's voice startled him. She stood in front of him, a pressed lab coat over her jumpsuit. He glanced up at her familiar scowl, not sure if it was meant for him or not.

"It's fine. I can come back." It would give him another excuse to talk to the LC.

"When was your last neo-benzo dose?" She glanced between him and her micro.

"Zero six hundred."

She held his gaze for a long moment. As he returned her stare, he realized it had been months since he'd been able to hold his eyes steady like this. Maybe there would come a time when he didn't need the meds anymore. It wasn't perfect, but it was better than it had been.

"Your father believes you can be trusted to monitor your own dosing schedule." There was a bitterness in her expression that tasted like burned polymer.

He expected her to be glaring at him with the same intensity that she had turned on Barre when she'd discovered him using bittergreen the first time. But she was looking past him, her eyes fixed on something far beyond the familiar and generic medical bay. There was a time Jem would have translated her reaction as anger, but he was sure it was fear. What in the cosmos would Dr. Leta Durbin be afraid of?

First Gutierrez, and now his mother. He suppressed a shudder. "It's okay, Mom. I can come in to get them."

"It's better this way." She nodded slowly, still not looking at him.

Better. Better for who?

Reaching into a pocket, she pulled out a portable med dispenser and unlocked it with a swipe of her hand. "Now you."

Jem coded in his hand print without asking the questions crowding his thoughts. Why the controlled dispenser for the mild sedatives? They could be addictive, but they were easily reversed. There were far more dangerous drugs his parents handled routinely without the secured delivery system. And why now? She'd been giving him his neo-benzos for weeks.

"The techs will be able to access this if your father or I am not here."

Did she think he was diverting his meds to Barre? As far as Jem knew, Barre hadn't used in months—not since he'd gotten sick on the tainted bittergreen from Hadria. That was before Halcyone. Now Barre had the ship and his music and his freedom. He didn't need bittergreen anymore.

"Sure, Mom." The little device delivered two sealed tablets into his waiting palm.

His mother waited while he opened the package and let the drug dissolve beneath his tongue in a burst of sour before slipping the dispenser back into her pocket. "Good. I should have time for your scans before shift change. You're welcome to wait in my office."

He needed to clear his head. "I'll come back. If that's okay."

"Fine."

Her voice was stiff and formal, but she couldn't hide the tinge of yellow that highlighted her uncomfortable emotions. Jem wasn't sure which of the two conversations was more unnerving.

Chapter 4

Barre sat in the silence of Halcyone's engineering bay considering the message Jem had just sent him. At least Gutierrez hadn't refused to talk to him. It was a start, anyway.

Ada May was expecting an answer. Well, she wasn't going to like the answer she got.

Using a mix of musical phrases and words, Barre asked Halcyone to send a secure message by way of Lethe, the AI Dr. May had programmed to help safeguard Ithaka. Halcyone acknowledged with a brief fanfare.

Even if the Commonwealth had hackers skilled enough to monitor the ship's AI, Barre was fairly confident the language he'd created out of fear, necessity, and his musical ability would be nearly impossible to crack. Even Ro couldn't communicate with Halcyone the way he could.

And he doubted that anyone could hack Lethe from the outside. It had taken his and Ro's combined abilities along with Halcyone's help to do it, and it only worked—even briefly— because they had physically been on Ithaka. He was confident

May had sealed even that way in.

A cheery whistle from Halcyone interrupted Barre's thoughts. A headerless text message unspooled in his mind's eye directly through his neural. It wasn't the same as the mind-to-mind communication he and Jem shared sometimes, but it was efficient and left less of a physical trace than pushing the messages through to his micro.

/How is she?/ He read it to himself in Ada May's voice.

Barre wished he had better news for her. It was probably best to be as direct as possible. Like his mother. The irony didn't escape him. */Her physical injuries are healing. But she's depressed. Isolated. Discouraged./*

/I need to speak to her./

/Even if that were possible, I don't advise it./ And it wasn't possible. Of course May knew that. There was far too great a risk of discovery and too many lives at stake. Including Gutierrez's. Including theirs. */She said to tell you there were some fights you can't win./*

/I don't believe that. The Emmaline I know doesn't believe that, either./

It was still odd to hear someone using the LC's given name. */She needs time to heal./* That was the only thing Barre felt comfortable saying. Maybe it was even true. But that was up to Gutierrez. */I'm sorry. But you have to let her be./*

There was a long pause and Barre wondered if the connection had snapped.

/It's not that simple. With Charon gone, I need her more than ever./

Barre had no answer for her. Surely with all the resources at May's disposal, she could find another set of eyes within the

Commonwealth.

/She's going to need to do extensive rehab. We have medical staff loyal to us scattered through the cosmos. If we hack her orders, will you transport her?/

/And if she refuses to go?/

The space between messages was long enough for Barre to fear the connection had dropped, but then May continued. */I still need someone I can trust to ferry important cargo./*

/Wait. You want me to take over Charon's job??/

/Yes. Await further contact./

The connection dropped with a high-pitched whine from Halcyone.

"Well, space me," Barre muttered. He stood and paced through engineering. With the ship docked, the controls were dark. As he walked, he moved in and out of the shadows created by the soft lighting along the narrow runway. Await further contact. Await further contact. As if it was already settled. Who in the cosmos did she think she was?

Barre stopped short, nearly slamming into the edge of a console. She was Ada-freaking-May, co-creator of the SIREN source code that made true AIs possible and the presumed-dead leader of a hidden rebellion against the Commonwealth.

And he was what? The disappointing scion of the famous Doctors Durbin. A musician stuck in the outer fringes of the galaxy with little credit to his name and a little brother he wouldn't leave. Crew on a ship that didn't belong to him and never would.

Halcyone sent a ping through his neural for an incoming message.

"What?" he snapped, just as he recognized the AI's musical

tag for Ro.

"Barre? You okay?"

He collapsed into a nearby seat and let his dreads fall forward to cover his face. "We have to talk."

"No shit. Where are you?"

She could have just as easily tracked him with her ghost program. That she hadn't said a lot about how much Ro had changed in the past several months. "Aboard Halcyone. Engineering."

"Good. Is Jem with you?"

"No."

"Tell him to meet us there. Nomi and I are on our way."

Ro dropped the connection before Barre could reply. Halcyone was her ship, no matter how skilled Barre was in communicating with the AI. And if it came down to a confrontation between Ro and May over the future of the little freighter, he wasn't really sure which of them would prevail. He only knew that he'd rather be stuck in an escape pod with a kilo of unstable aduronium.

*

Ro and Nomi reached Halcyone's airlock just behind Jem. The AI greeted them all by name and opened the door before Ro could trigger the release. Even though she was the one who had programmed and uploaded the AI enhancements, the rate at which Halcyone evolved still surprised her.

"Thank you," Nomi said.

"You are welcome, Konomi Nakamura."

Ro didn't see the sense in offering such niceties to a program, no matter how humanistic it seemed. Programmers had created these meaningless interactions to make people more comfortable. AIs were designed for complex problem-solving and making judgments in data-rich environments—nothing more, nothing less—not for putting humans at ease.

Nomi took her hand as they walked through the airlock. There wasn't enough data for a thousand Halcyones to process and come up with a solution that would tell them who to trust and what to do next. Ro only hoped that Barre would have some insight or angle she hadn't considered.

Ro squeezed Nomi's hand, trying to transmit a confidence and assurance she certainly didn't feel. Even Jem was uncharacteristically quiet. Well, they would have enough to talk about in a few minutes.

The door to engineering slid open. Barre sat in the dimly lit room, his eyes staring at an invisible point ahead of him.

"Halcyone, lights up thirty percent," Ro said.

He blinked as the space brightened. "Good. You're here." Barre looked as fatigued as Ro felt. His shoulders were rounded and he slouched in the chief engineer's chair. "I heard from —"

"We need to —"

Barre's words merged with Ro's and they both stopped.

Nomi dropped into a chair across the aisle from Barre. Ro sat on the floor and leaned against Nomi's legs. Jem jumped up to perch on one of the consoles.

"Let's try that again." Ro glanced up at Barre. "You said we needed to talk. So talk."

"We're as secure as you can make us?"

There was a time she would have resented him for that. But it was less a slight against her programming abilities than his concern about their safety. Concern she shared. She double-checked the security protocols and nodded.

"It's Gutierrez. She's shut Ada out. Won't even answer her messages. I asked Jem to check on her."

"And?"

Jem shrugged. "I did the best I could. She told me to tell Dr. May that there were some fights you couldn't win."

"So she's lost her guard dog and her ferryman."

Barre sighed.

"What?" Ro demanded.

"You're not going to like it."

"There's already nothing about any of this I like. So commit to the jump, already," Ro said. Nomi placed her hand gently on her shoulder, part comfort, part warning.

"She wants me to take over for Charon. To transport Gutierrez to a friendly clinic, for starters."

Ro shifted her weight forward. "Using what ship?" But she already knew. Charon's ship was docked on Earth with Micah. Halcyone was the only other ship they knew of that could access the hidden maps and get to Ithaka and its protected holdings. "And when, exactly, was she going to ask me?"

"It's Ada May." Barre shrugged. "Why are you at all surprised?"

"What did you tell her?"

"I didn't. She just pretty much assumed I was going along with the program."

"I don't think you'll be able to convince Gutierrez to go anywhere," Jem said, frowning. "No matter what Ada wants."

"Honestly? May and Gutierrez are the least of our concerns right now." The only way May was going to get her hands on

Halcyone was over Ro's dead body and the ship's cold engines. Ro glanced up at Nomi. "We have more than enough static close to home."

Nomi tucked her hair behind her ears. The dark strands slipped forward again even before she started speaking. "Simon Marchand wants a copy of the worm's data."

"How did he find out about it?" Jem asked.

"I have no idea," Ro answered, frowning.

"How do we know we can trust him?" Barre asked.

"We don't. I thought he was my friend. Now I'm not sure. But he isn't working with Lowell, and maybe that's enough."

Ro reached up to take Nomi's hand. "We may as well just broadcast it through the ansible grid. There will be fewer people who don't have access to it than who do."

"Maybe that's not such a bad idea, Ro," Jem said. "Not the data part, but at least word that we're looking for him. That way, if he shows up anywhere, someone will make noise."

At this point, Lowell was probably wanted by Commonwealth forces, Commander Targill, the cartels, and the smugglers. Ro was willing to bet Ada May would like to get her hands on him, as well. "And likely get him killed in the process. We need information, not a literal dead end." She stood and ran her hand along one of Halcyone's consoles. It was warm, alive with checked power and possibility. Would she have still risked waking the ship if she'd known what a clusterfuck it was going to lead to? Her fingers tightened on the polymer. This was her ship and nothing was going to change that.

"I think Jem's right. There's still Micah's dad's money left. We offer a reward for his capture," Barre said. "Get the word out through Ithaka's black-market channels. Set up a dead drop for messages. I'm not sure we have a whole lot to lose here. Targill is probably out there looking for him. And if he finds Lowell first, he'll bury the man so deep we'll need a terraforming rig to dig him out."

Ro relaxed her grip. "I don't know. If we fuck up, not only are we exposed, but so is Ithaka."

"I'm sorry, but I think that ship has already jumped."

Barre was right, but that didn't make it any easier for Ro to accept. When they went after Jem and stumbled onto Ithaka, she and Barre ended up committing to its safety. Nomi hadn't had the chance to make her own choice and Ro's decisions kept putting her at risk. Hell, they'd gotten her arrested. "Nomi? This is as much your call as ours."

Nomi rested her head in her hands for a long moment. Then she stood and set her micro on a free console. "Look." She pulled up a blank window and with her careful hand, wrote the names of the major players across the top: Dominic Targill. Simon Marchand. Ada May. Celia Mendez. Next to Mendez, she added Commonwealth with a question mark in parentheses. Next to Marchand, and Targill, just question marks.

"We have two main sources of intel—what Jem and I dug out of Lowell's files and the cube you liberated from your father." Nomi nodded in Ro's direction. Across the bottom of the window, Nomi wrote "Lowell's data" and "Maldonado's data." Choosing a line tool, she drew a solid red line from Lowell to Mendez. Then she swapped red for yellow and also connected Maldonado to Mendez. "Who else knows what?" she asked softly.

They'd had no choice but to give everything they had to Mendez. It had been the only way to ensure Nomi's freedom.

What the commander was going to do with it was an open question, and one that made Ro uneasy. "I sent copies of both to May," Ro said. She expected at least Barre to give her pushback about it, but he kept silent, frowning.

Nomi added one of each color line to represent the information Ithaka had.

"Don't forget Gutierrez. She has the original cube," Barre said.

"But she's still off the playing field. Besides, she doesn't know how to access it and she doesn't have my DNA."

Jem jumped off the console and stood close to Nomi's virtual window. "So who else knows what?"

Ro followed the red lines to their destinations. "We're presuming since Targill was Lowell's handler, he already knows what's in the files you scraped."

Nomi nodded as she added a red line between Lowell and Targill. "Okay, then, what do we do about Simon?"

That Nomi called him by his first name said a lot. He had risked his own safety to help her when she'd been arrested. Ro wasn't in the habit of trusting, but she trusted Nomi's instincts. "We give him the data on Lowell. But that's all. We still haven't fully examined what was on my father's memory cube. Bad enough we gave Mendez an unencrypted copy."

Ro looked at her three companions. Each of them nodded, though this time Nomi was frowning.

"If Mendez has your father's data, we have to assume the Commonwealth has it as well."

"But what part of the Commonwealth? We still don't know what Targill's doing." Ro paced the narrow corridor through engineering. It was easier to think when she was moving.

"Commander Mendez is smart and she wants off this rock. We know she already suspected Targill long before you gave her the worm data." Otherwise why assign Nomi to Targill's ship during that first search for Halcyone? Otherwise why arrange to speak privately with Nomi when she was under house arrest and then act as if it hadn't happened when Targill came to question her?

"We assumed it was the Commonwealth versus Ithaka." Nomi's face paled. "'It depends on how you define the sides.' That's what Simon told me. And if it's a choice between Mendez and Targill, I have to go with our commander."

"This is just getting better and better," Ro said.

"Assuming Mendez is playing this close to her p-suit, we're only safe as long as she doesn't discover enough to use for her own benefit," Barre said. "If she thinks we're still her best conduit to intel, she'll let us take the wormhole first."

"Then we need to stay at least one jump ahead of her."

"We need to take apart your father's data," Nomi said. "Figure out if there's anything we can use before Mendez does. That's more important than Lowell right now."

"I'm not comfortable doing that here. Think about it. There are four copies of the information on that cube and three of them are on Daedalus Station. Gutierrez has the original. Mendez and I have unencrypted clones and so does Ithaka. As much as Ada May is our ally, I'd still feel better if the data were somewhere I had access to and away from Commonwealth eyes."

"You need to leave the station."

Ro, Nomi, and Barre turned to Jem.

"You're right. There's too much scrutiny here. And too many of us who know too much about Ithaka in one place. It's an unacceptable risk. Gutierrez won't leave. I can't leave. But you can."

There was a desperate edge in Jem's voice that made Ro want to reassure him, even as she understood his fear. "This is my place." Halcyone was Ro's ship, by legal right and earned by blood and sacrifice, but home was the small room she shared with the gentle, dark-haired communications officer.

Jem moved to block her restless pacing and grasped both her arms. "And if you stay, what's to prevent Mendez from arresting Nomi again? And this time taking her off-station? Or say Targill comes back. As long as you and the data are here, Nomi is vulnerable. Take the intel somewhere the Commonwealth can't control it. The sooner you analyze it, the better position you'll be in to bargain."

"Bargain with what?" Ro slipped from Jem's grasp. "Mendez already has the clear data."

"But she doesn't know your father." Nomi collapsed the virtual window and leaned against the console. "Jem's right. You know he is. If there's anything useful in there, you're in the best position to make sense of it."

"I'm not leaving you."

"You don't have to. At least not in the short run." Barre nodded to Nomi. "You're still owed bereavement leave. Commonwealth policy. Five days plus travel. Go pay your respects to your grandfather. Lucky for you, you have a friend with a jump-enabled ship."

"And what about May's little job for you?" Ro couldn't believe she was even considering what the rogue programmer wanted. But a weak Ithaka was not in their best interests, and with Charon dead and Gutierrez injured, May was clearly vulnerable.

"Maybe Halcyone can pull double duty," Barre said. "We file

a flight plan to Nomi's colony. Then use the Ithaka nav program to disappear from Commonwealth eyes, run whatever transport May needs us to run. Pick up Nomi on the way back."

A flash of pain moved through Nomi's eyes. Her grandfather's death had shaken her and Ro had felt helpless in the face of such grief. "Halcyone doesn't need both of us to fly." It felt like a giant hand was squeezing her heart. As if she had suddenly hit high g's without acceleration foam. "I'll stay with Nomi. Come back for both of us when you're done playing the Ferryman."

Nomi blinked at Ro, her eyes shiny.

"Are you sure?" Barre asked.

"No." Then she turned to Nomi. "Yes. Besides, it'll give me time to comb through my father's data without any distractions."

"Won't it look suspicious when all three of us leave the station together?" Nomi asked.

Barre shrugged. "The two of you need to file a flight plan, but I'm neither crew nor station staff. I don't even have official quarters on Daedalus anymore. I'm as close to invisible as we're going to get."

Jem smiled. "You're our secret weapon. Who suspects a musician of conspiring against the galactic government?"

Ro had to stop herself from checking their security again. It was as tight as she could make it—which was pretty damned near vacuum-proof, between her skills and Ada May's. And if the Commonwealth was listening, they had already said enough to implicate themselves ten times over. Still, hearing it so bluntly from Jem's voice sent a shiver through her.

"What will you tell Mom and Dad?"

Jem sighed. "Do you think they'll even ask?"

Ro winced on Barre's behalf.

Nomi pulled Barre into a hug. "My parents will be honored to meet you." She glanced over at Ro. "Both of you."

Ro's face burned and she stared down at her feet. Would they welcome her? Truly?

Chapter 5

IT WAS AFTER FOUR this time when Dev woke up, blinking in the artificial lighting of her room. She'd take that as a victory. At least she'd only have a few hours of wondering what the fuck she had gotten herself into promising to take Micah to Midlant. Then they would be on their way and there would be no turning back.

Michael Chase—the entitled student who'd shown up a few weeks ago—would never belong in Midlant. But the Micah she'd watched work to clear up the abandoned biodome was a different person entirely. One she hadn't really seen before.

He'd been so focused on the watering infrastructure, he never even noticed her. It was the kind of intensity and concentration Dev had on a dig-site. And Micah was just as unconcerned by his wet and dirty clothes as she would have been. Their time working together in the darkening dome was peaceful in a way Dev hadn't expected. Certainly, it had been the first time since her kidnapping that she hadn't been hyper-aware of her surroundings and of the sharp blade in her pocket.

She changed and dimmed the lights before opening the door into the common room. Micah was already dressed, sitting with his feet propped up on the coffee table. It was all too easy to imagine the rawness of his self-inflicted burns and his shaking hands on the plasma gun.

"Are you sure about this?" he asked.

He was wearing dark, heavy-duty work pants with multiple cargo pockets and a bronze shirt that set off his light hair and tanned skin. At least he wasn't spacer-pale. Chances were an even fifty-fifty whether his senator father had paid for skin-tone alterations or his time under full spectrums with his plants had given him the color naturally.

Despite the glow of his skin, he still looked tired. Dev wondered if her eyes had that same sunken look. She'd avoided looking in the mirror since she got back.

"It doesn't matter. I made a promise."

The one thing a Midlanter always had was their word. Maybe it was the only thing they could claim and not have taken from them.

"We can do this another time, Dev. Really. It's okay."

"No. It's not." He didn't understand. He couldn't. Highsiders lied. In the settlements, breaking faith got you killed. "Besides, my brothers want to meet you."

"That's what I was afraid of." Micah smiled weakly.

He still looked like something for the vids. Dev sighed. Even in his casual clothes, Micah looked too polished. Too highside. This was not going to go well. But Micah had gone after Maldonado. Her brothers would accept him for that, no matter what. That was Midlant and you took care of your own. If he wandered the settlement on his own, it would be a different matter. He would be a target. For theft alone, if he was lucky.

She glanced back at his feet. He'd burned them to escape Maldonado. He could handle Midlant.

"Can I make you coffee?"

Dev shook her head. Her stomach was queasy enough. "We need to be at the spaceport by six."

"I still don't see why we can't just take Charon's ship. It's atmo rated and I had the reg beacon altered."

It would have made the trip faster and more comfortable, but aside from Dev's discomfort of having a dead man's ship, it would attract too much notice. By himself, Micah would do a good enough job of that. "Are you packed?"

"Fine." He put his feet on the floor and levered himself to standing. "I just need to get my shoes on and I'll put myself into your capable hands."

She stared at him as he hobbled into his room, unsure if there was any mockery in his voice. "Fine," she echoed in the silent apartment.

He didn't take long. When he returned, his walk was much smoother. If she hadn't known how bad his feet were, she might not even have noticed the slight hesitancy of his footfalls.

They took a transpod across the silent campus to the spaceport. It was a Commonwealth holiday, and classes were canceled in lieu of some school-wide celebration. It gave them three free days. They would be headed into the thick of the semester after this. There wouldn't be another chance to get away until the term ended.

Once inside the spaceport, Micah gestured for her micro and bumped her ticket over. He had insisted on paying for both of them, and although it made her uncomfortable, she hadn't refused.

"Courtesy of the senator," he said, shrugging.

Dev couldn't imagine living a life where invisible credit was always waiting at the other end of a micro. She even owed the device she held to Micah and his father's spoils. Though, if it weren't for Micah, she wouldn't have been taken by Maldonado and her own micro wouldn't be elemental space dust now—her micro, along with her abductor, his ship, and Taro Odachi.

She slipped her hand in her pocket, seeking the comforting presence of her blade. She'd crafted a sheath for it and between the material and the shape, it would read as a data stick to security. It was definitely not the kind of application of her research Dr. Sellen would approve of, but Dev was willing to bet Sellen hadn't been raised in a settlement.

Micah seemed more nervous moving through security than she did. His charming smile never wavered, but something in the set of his shoulders and the way he shifted on the balls of his feet gave it away. At least to her. The bored Commonwealth soldier barely glanced at his credentials and his travel authorization before waving him through.

Predictably, it took Dev a lot longer.

The soldier took her time examining Dev's credentials, scrutinizing the holographic photo. "Reason for travel?"

Dev set her jaw and blanked her annoyed expression. "Visiting family."

"In Midlant?" The soldier's voice hadn't changed, but Dev could hear the disdain in it anyway.

"Yes."

"Returning in three days?"

"Yes, sir." Adding that "sir" grated.

"University ident." It wasn't a request.

From beyond the security barrier, Dev saw Micah step toward her. She glared at him and warned him off with a shake of her head before calling up her Uni ident on her micro. It wasn't as if this didn't happen every time she traveled. It was just less humiliating when she traveled alone.

Finally, Dev was waved through, though she felt the soldier's gaze on her all the way up the jet way.

"What was that all about?"

"Get used to it, space-man." Dev tried to keep her tone light and forced herself to smile.

"I —"

Dev cut him off with a sharp look. Micah frowned and fell silent.

His silence continued as they boarded the small transport and found their seats. Micah waved her to the window. They buckled in and Dev flashed to when Micah helped her secure the webbing on the co-pilot's seat on Taro's ship. He didn't deserve her anger.

Dev sighed and rested her head against the viewport.

"Does that happen every time?"

"Yes." It would be even worse leaving the settlement.

"Fuck. I'm sorry."

"It's nothing. I'm used to it." Dev lied to herself as much as to him.

"It's not fair. I wish —"

She interrupted him again. "Well, you can't wish the waters down." It was an expression her grandmother used whenever Dev had complained about something as a child.

Whatever Micah was going to say next was drowned out first by the holographic safety briefing and then by the whine of the engines engaging. They were on a direct flight. If Micah's money and privilege couldn't shield her from her past, at least it would get them to Midlant without further scrutiny.

For the brief flight, Dev pretended to be asleep. There were so many things she should have told him about Midlant, about her brothers, but there really was no way to prepare someone for the settlement. It even took her by surprise on her brief and infrequent visits home, as if her time at Uni had smoothed her edges and blunted the memories. Her Midlant roots and her Commonwealth education marked her as an outsider in both worlds in ways she still didn't fully understand.

Maybe Micah would get it, but this wasn't the time or the place to have that conversation.

She opened her eyes and sat up as they began their descent into the spaceport. As they disembarked, passengers queued up in two lines—one for Midlant, one for everywhere else. Here Micah would have his chance to "enjoy" the extra scrutiny. A settlement border was like a semi-permeable membrane: certain molecules could easily enter and others could easily leave. Just not the same ones.

Dev waved him in front of her in case she needed to intervene on his behalf. She needn't have worried. Apparently Micah had inherited the art of looking comfortable and relaxed in any situation from his father. Their travel authorization linked him as her guest, which probably helped too. Still, the security guard gave her a curious look as he passed them through.

It wouldn't be the first such look Dev would get with Micah at her side. "Stay close," she whispered. "Make sure your bag has its security seal."

He raised an eyebrow, but didn't argue as they threaded their way through the crowded terminal. A young mother corralled three small children into a corner while she changed her infant's diaper on the floor. A gang of teens roamed the arrivals area trying to hustle jobs carrying travelers' bags. Anyone unwise enough to hand their luggage over would most likely find it significantly lightened when they got to their destination. A man in a stained coverall was arguing with the gate agent. Something about a mismatch between his travel authorization and his ident.

The guard tapped an impatient finger against his holster. Several additional security agents turned toward the gate. If the old Midlanter didn't back down, he was going to find himself stunned or arrested or both. Dev was surprised he didn't know better.

Micah slowed and frowned at the developing confrontation. Dev tugged at his sleeve. "We don't want to be here when this finishes."

The first guard unholstered his weapon. Micah gasped.

"I told you." Dev pulled Micah away as the unfortunate Midlanter was forced to the ground and his arms and legs bound.

"But he didn't do anything wrong."

"Welcome to my world," Dev said, shrugging. "Now move before they include us in their sphere of interest."

Micah paused to give Dev a look she couldn't interpret before he matched her pace and walked away. She certainly wasn't going to tell him how many times she'd been detained and questioned on her way to or from anywhere. Commonwealth security never needed a reason.

At least, once in Midlant proper, security wouldn't be a problem. Or rather the lack of it might. Dev put her free hand in her pocket and slid her blade from its sheath. She thought of her grandmother's collection of knives and was perversely comforted in knowing some things never changed.

*

Jem sat in the patient lounge waiting for his father to finish his rounds. It shouldn't have taken long. Gutierrez was the only inpatient.

The senior tech apologized. "I can ask him for the med dispenser, if you need to get out of here."

"I'm okay. Got nothing but time." Jem hated the taste of bitterness in his own voice. He was the one who suggested that Barre, Ro, and Nomi leave the station. It wasn't their fault he was stuck here. Besides, he wanted to get a look at his scans from the other day and he didn't think his folks would be too happy if he started perusing his own records.

"Can I get you something to drink?"

"Nah." If he needed anything, he could just get something from his parents' office. It was strange being both the child of the station's doctors and their patient. It made the boundaries between him and the medical staff awkward in a way it had never been all the years of his growing up. Even when he'd been sick before, it hadn't changed the balance of power the way his head injury and neural implant had.

It still felt like his parents were punishing him for getting it, though Jem knew if he confronted them, they would be outraged at the accusation.

He closed his eyes and listened to the colors of the sounds around him. There was the reassuring green hum of machinery ready for any emergency and the cool blue of the tech's voices doing routine inventory. It was familiar and comforting as much as it was also still something Jem was getting used to.

Regardless of his parents' beliefs or how long it was taking to integrate the device and the strange sensory world it had brought, Jem didn't regret getting the implant for a nanosecond.

Raised voices smeared the air burnt orange. Jem bolted upright in the chair and opened his eyes.

"You're in no condition to leave." His father backed out from Gutierrez's curtained cubicle, in full-on Dr. Kristoff Durbin mode, his shoulders squared, his jaw set, his expression firm, but kind. For every step he retreated, she advanced until they both stood in the center of medical.

"And you have no right to make me stay." Gutierrez's voice was a rusty blade sawing through his father's practiced reasonableness. Without her arm prosthesis, she looked off-balance, as if she would tilt to the right. Jem jumped up, but he didn't think she would accept his help even if he knew how to offer it.

There was nothing off-balance about her anger and her determination to leave.

"My uniform and my sidearm, Doctor."

The asteroid and the tractor beam. While he'd seen both of his parents stare down actively hostile and dangerous patients, this asteroid was Lieutenant Commander Emmaline Gutierrez and his father didn't stand a chance of pulling her off course.

He just didn't know that yet.

Jem stood against the wall and watched as he first tried to be logical. "You're not cleared for duty, Lieutenant Commander. Right now, I'm the one who will do that assessment. The sooner you get back to my telemetry, the sooner we can return you to full health."

"You've done all you can. I know my body far better than you ever will and what it needs is time. Time I will not waste sleeping in medical."

Then he tried empathy. "It must be frustrating and difficult to be without your arm. As soon as you're stronger, we can send you off-station for a new limb."

"I managed one-handed long before you were learning to crawl, Doctor." Her dark eyes narrowed. If it had been Jem standing beneath their gaze, he would have flinched. His father didn't move. Good for him. "The sooner I can return to my quarters, the sooner I can rebuild my prosthesis."

"I don't think it can be salvaged." He put his hands in the pockets of his lab coat. "Be reasonable. Your burns are still healing. Your right arm doesn't have its full strength back."

"No."

"No?" His father was beginning to lose his temper. Jem could see it in the rigidity of his shoulders and in the way his words were tinged with red.

"I wish to sign out AMA. You can try to keep me here against my will, but I wouldn't recommend it."

Even one-armed, with her face drawn and her skin sallow, swaying slightly in bare feet and barely covered by a thin knee-length gown, Gutierrez was an intimidating force. If Barre hadn't exaggerated, she'd been half-dead on Charon's little ship and still managed to pilot herself and Dev to safety.

"I don't advise it, Lieutenant Commander."

"Does it look like I'm asking for your advice?"

She looked exhausted and if this standoff didn't end soon, Jem was worried she'd end up on the floor. But surely his father could see it, too.

"I could declare you a risk to yourself."

She spoke so quietly, Jem had to strain to hear her reply. "You have no idea, Kristoff."

His father's face reddened. "Fine. You're right. I can't force you to stay. I can only ask you to reconsider."

They stood barely a half meter apart in strained silence. Jem held his breath. Gutierrez kept her dark gaze steady.

His father swore softly. "Fine. At least give me a few minutes to get you a fresh uniform."

"Fine," Gutierrez answered and staggered back to her bed.

"And you'll need to sign releases," he called over his shoulder.

Muttering to himself, his father stomped toward the chief tech. Jem knew he would delay the discharge process as long as he could in the hopes that Gutierrez would either change her mind or be too weary to leave today.

"Good luck with that," he whispered and slipped behind the scrim and into Gutierrez's cubicle.

"Are you here to reason with me too?" She had collapsed back into the bed, and the telemetry was decidedly unhappy about her vitals.

"You think?"

She laughed harshly. "No. I suppose not."

He forced himself to study the residual limb and the cap sealing off the nerve access. "My father is right about one thing."

The look she gave him lit up his brain in harsh, bright colors.

"It's going to be hard to fix your arm one-handed."

"I'll manage."

"You could go off-station. There are dozens of places that could patch you up. She would see to that."

"I'm sure she would." Gutierrez's reply was subdued and her gaze shifted to something only she could see.

Jem sighed. "I could help you."

Now it was her turn to sigh.

"I'm good with machines. I mean, software is more fun, but I can fix anything. Ask Ro."

She turned to stare at him with unblinking, dark eyes. Maybe invoking Ro's name had been a mistake.

"Look, I'm not here to convince you of anything. What you do next? It's your choice. Not hers. Not mine. But you need help and I'm a steady set of hands."

"When you aren't reeling with dizziness or disabled by headaches."

"How do you know about all that?"

"I'm the station's second in command. I know about all Daedalus's inhabitants. Besides, I went through some of that, too." She shrugged her intact shoulder.

So she did have a first-gen neural! "I'm much better now. I've figured out ways to damp down the vestibular activation."

"Huh. It took me almost a year."

Was that a compliment? Jem looked directly at the LC and gave one last try. The worst that could happen was she would throw him out. "So, will you let me help you? Please? At least until you get your arm working."

She returned his stare. Her expression was eerily blank, as if there was no human emotion behind the mask of her face.

Jem squirmed on the hard chair at her bedside. Even his new synesthesia gave him nothing useful. He was aware of the moments flowing by and that his father or the tech would return any time now with a uniform for Gutierrez and her discharge authorizations. It would be hard to justify his presence here.

Her silence made him want to say something. Anything. Gutierrez would make a hell of an interrogator. Even without the sharp claw hand, she radiated strength and danger.

She wasn't going to answer.

His father's voice—raised and angry—reverberated through medical. Jem felt sorry for the techs who would bear the brunt of Kristoff Durbin's frustration today. And it was time for Jem to leave. He'd tried. It wasn't like he could force her to accept his help any more than his father could force her to stay in medical.

The chair scraped softly against the floor as he stood up. Gutierrez turned to the opaque curtain and then back to Jem.

"Fine. But when I tell you to leave, you leave. No questions."

Jem exhaled heavily. "Deal."

"Now leave. I'll contact you."

"Yes, sir."

Chapter 6

"THIS WAY," DEV SAID, looking back over her shoulder.

Micah followed her through the spaceport. She seemed to have an almost uncanny ability to predict where a path would open up in the crush of people crowding the terminal. Being among so many of his fellow humans made him uneasy. The Uni campus had been bad enough. This was almost as overstimulating and chaotic as a wormhole jump.

The terminal was alive, not just with movement and color, but with the smells of too many bodies after too many hours of travel. Dozens of different cuisines melded into a funk of stale grease and cheap calories. And in addition to Standard, he heard more dialects than he thought still existed on Earth.

He hustled to keep up with her quick pace and rapid changes of direction, but he stumbled, stubbing his right toes against the hard floor. Even with the cushioned shoes, the pain shocked through him. "Fuck." He danced around on his left leg, waiting for the nerves in his right to stop singing. When he glanced up,

Dev had vanished and he was the only still point in a swirling mass of moving people.

"Fuck," he repeated again, softly. He could ping her on his micro, but that would be admitting defeat. For the moment, the mass of humanity shifted past him in all its colorful array. It looked like a holo Micah had seen once of a resurrected reef and a school of bright fish wheeling around some underwater obstacle.

But his anonymity wouldn't last for long. He checked the security seal on his bag before pulling his micro out of his pocket. Fine. Defeat it was. Or at least acknowledging that this was Dev's home territory, not his. Not by any measure.

A hand grabbed his arm.

Micah jerked backward and lost his balance again. Before he could fall, the arm steadied him.

"Sorry. Didn't realize you were having trouble keeping up." Dev loosened her grip. "You good?"

Relief shocked through him. "Yeah. I'm good. How much more walking?"

Dev frowned. "I knew this was a mistake."

"Fine. Let's go." People were starting to turn and stare at them. They were a disruption in the flow of the current and the last thing Micah wanted was to be noticed. Well, maybe the second to last thing. If he had his preference, he'd be traveling in a transport of some kind. Preferably one with noise canceling features and air filtration.

He ignored his throbbing feet. They were likely as healed as they were ever going to get. Better get used to that now than hold out for some unrealistic fix. He got the sense that settlement life didn't condone whining.

Dev started walking again, but this time she slowed her pace a little and kept glancing back to make sure he was still following. There was no way Micah was going to let himself fall behind.

When they reached the main exit, Dev stopped and waited for him to catch up. It was quieter here. Most of the people who had been on their shuttle had already left the spaceport and they must have been in a brief window between launches. "How far is Midlant?" Micah asked, catching his breath.

"That depends." Dev stared out the glass doors, frowning.

"On what?"

"On whether or not Giles was able to get a transport."

"You should have said something. I would have rented us one."

The look she threw him could have withered bittergreen. "Rental companies won't permit their vehicles in Midlant. And most Midlanters don't have their own, either."

Micah set his jaw, determined not to let Dev see his frustration. Some kind of public transport, then. More crowds. More jostling. More walking. "Well, then, what's our next adventure? Loop? Underground?"

"Funny. Really funny," Dev said.

"I don't understand."

"You really think the Commonwealth would give the settlements that kind of direct access?"

"Why not? Infrastructure. That's what a government is supposed to do." Even his father at his most self-aggrandizing and self-centered knew that. Supported that for his constituents, even as he bilked money from every level of a public works project.

"You really are that naive." Dev stared at him until he had to look away. "Go book yourself a ticket back to Uni. If you rush, you can probably make the next flight."

His face heated, but he stood his ground. "I'm sorry. I'm a spacer. I've spent more time planet-side since I got to Uni than in my entire life beforehand put together. I can tell you about mortality rates on asteroid mining operations or radiation limits on commercial pilots without even looking at my micro, but this? This is all new. So play out some tether, okay?"

"Okay." Dev looked away, but not before Micah saw her cheeks redden.

"I'm a quick study. With all the places my father was posted at, I've had to be. Tell me what I need to know."

"Here's the short version." Dev's voice was clipped. "The settlements are a cross between a refugee camp, an internment center, and a colony outpost. The Commonwealth administers them, but what that really means is it keeps them—keeps us— isolated from the lucky and the connected."

"I don't understand. It's been, what, sixty, sixty-five years since the Drowning? And there's still all kinds of money that gets earmarked for settlement programs." He remembered his father complaining about the continuing income stipends when Micah was too young to realize the senator's politics were a simple matter of fighting for the largest share of power, influence, and credit.

That comment earned him another scathing look.

"You'll see. Can you walk?"

"Sure."

They walked out of the spaceport into the searing light of what was going to be a hot day. Sweat had already started to bead on Micah's forehead and drip down the back of his neck. He refused to ask how far they had to go. Once clear of the vehicle loading area, the density of people decreased even more. Micah called up a map on his micro, then glanced around trying to orient himself. Midlant was eighteen klicks or so due north of the spaceport. Not far as the flitter flew.

And there was plenty of flitter traffic. Ground vehicles, too. Nearly all moving south or west. An occasional transport or private car rumbled past them, headed northward. Each time she heard one, Dev paused to wait, but none of them even slowed down.

She checked her micro, frowned, and kept walking.

Already the spaceport looked like some hulking mirage in the heat shimmer. A shuttle screamed across the sky. Micah could've been on that shuttle. He blinked as the contrail faded before he turned back to the road. Two travel lanes stretched out in each direction. A tangle of greenery rose up on either side, threatening the dark surface. Roots from tall trees had already broken up the hard-packed material of the shoulder. Micah had to watch where he stepped. It was going to be a long walk.

Another car sped past them, kicking up dust and small pebbles. It slowed to a stop, paused, and reversed course.

"Don't say anything."

"What?"

"Just keep your mouth shut." She paused to look him up and down. "Please."

Then the car was next to them and Micah didn't have a chance to answer her.

It was an old model and looked heavily modified with surplus military-grade armor. The front screen and windows were opaque. At least it would be cooler inside. The electrical engine whined softly as the car idled. Dev stood patiently on the shoulder, looking straight ahead. What were they waiting for?

The window opened. A driver sat in the left-hand seat and leaned across the center console, peering out at them. He was the only person in the semi-autonomous vehicle. Definitely an older model. The car and the driver.

The man was deeply tanned, his cheeks stubbled, but his head was shiny and shaved. His short sleeves revealed arms completely covered in geometric tattoos. It was hard to guess at his height, but he was slim, with a long, narrow face. He was content to sit and watch the two of them as the moments slid by. Micah shifted his weight from foot to foot.

"Oi. Melt 'nuff?"

"Oi. Vray that."

Dev's speech was accented with a kind of nasal twang that he'd never heard before.

"What corner?"

"Nines and sevens. Old Town."

The man nodded. "I live. I drive. Worth a pocket?"

"How heavy?"

Micah swiveled his head between the two of them, trying to make sense of the strange conversation. It was a mix of words in Standard and sounds that seemed like words, but Micah didn't have a clue about their meaning. So few words passed between them, yet Dev seemed to understand exactly what the old man was saying. He cocked his head and gave Micah a look he couldn't interpret.

"Heavy enough. Fair share from the hopper's fair share?"

Dev's expression darkened. She glared at Micah and sighed.

"No. His share's a handshake."

"Vray?"

"Vray."

"So both? To nines and sevens?" He paused to glance at Micah again. "Hoppers rare meat in Old Town."

That Micah understood. There was no way he could hide his spacer background. Or anything else, if this man was any indication. Without Dev to translate, he probably wouldn't be able to function in Midlant at any level.

"Handshake counts for all."

"Vray." He turned to Micah. "Hopper, you best learn to count."

Micah didn't know how to respond, so he kept silent.

"Fine then? Both to Old Town for a light pocket." He paused to laugh. "My light pocket. A tenner for each."

Micah took a step closer to the car. Dev held him back. His feet were slick with sweat and all he wanted to do was sit.

"Tenner for each? Each? Oi, see me highsiding? No, deep, tenner for both."

"I drive. I live. Food don't fall from trucks now. Tenner and half or it's feet."

Dev looked over at Micah again and sighed. "Good handshake. Pair or paper?"

"Oi, pair. Use virt for some needfuls. Better for the hopper, no?"

"Vray." She pulled Micah closer to the car. "Slide in. Pair your micro to his and pay him ten credits upfront. We can do the rest once we're in Midlant."

It was strange hearing her slip in and out of the dialect their driver spoke. How was Micah ever going to manage in this place if they didn't speak Standard? He settled in the hard seat and rested his head back, listening to Dev and the driver talk in a language that flowed past him like water.

*

Opening Halcyone's airlock, Ro ushered Nomi inside. "All set?" she asked, not letting her nervousness show. While Nomi had been on board more times than Ro could count, this felt different somehow. Nomi was trusting her to fly them across the galaxy, practically turn them all inside out, and get them back again whole. Yes, Ro had piloted Barre, Jem, and Micah, but that first journey had been accidental. None of them had chosen to come aboard. Nomi had.

"I guess. We have our flight clearance. Simon has what he needs." Nomi hitched her overnight bag higher on her shoulder. "You really didn't need to meet me here. I think I know my way around the ship."

"I know... I just ..."

Nomi leaned over and kissed her on the cheek. "You're so cute when you're flustered. Barre already on board?"

"He's doing pre-flight. Come on. I want to make sure he doesn't screw anything up." On the way to the bridge they stopped to toss Nomi's bag into Ro's quarters, even smaller than the tiny room they shared on Daedalus. At least the trip to Sasurau was relatively short, even with conservative burns and reasonable acceleration.

At the entrance to the bridge, Nomi paused and frowned at the permanently open and partially melted doors.

"It's on the repair list," Ro said. "But she's safe to fly."

"I know. I was just thinking of Micah."

The bridge had been pretty well destroyed during the war, but the door was a more recent addition, thanks to him. Ro still didn't know how he'd managed to hobble to the bridge after burning his feet free of the shock cuffs her father had shackled him in. Even with the ones still on his wrists, he'd blasted through the door to free her and Barre. It was an act of incredible bravery she wasn't sure she could ever match. She hoped he and Dev were doing all right back at Uni.

"Welcome aboard, Nomi!" Barre's booming voice filled the bridge. He strode over to the door in a handful of long strides and wrapped her in a big hug.

"You're in a good mood," Ro said.

He set Nomi down and smiled. "Hey, this may be the first time we've taken off on a normal flight. No panic, no emergency. Just a regular flight plan to a perfectly ordinary destination. I think that's worth celebrating."

A short fanfare played through the speakers. Halcyone was welcoming Nomi aboard, too. She patted the top of one of the consoles. "Thanks, Halcyone."

"Now that we're all happy spacers, can we get going?"

"Will you do the honors?" Barre stepped back, blocking out most of the viewscreen.

"Everyone take a seat." Ro waited until the two of them buckled in before strapping herself in the command chair. "Halcyone, open a channel to Daedalus traffic control."

"Channel opened."

"This is Captain Maldonado of the freighter Halcyone. Requesting permission to take off." Ro's cheeks burned and she didn't want to meet either of her friend's eyes.

"Halcyone, you are cleared for takeoff."

"Thank you, Daedalus."

She kept her focus on the virtual window above her console as she sent the command to retract the docking clamps. Halcyone rocked slightly when her thrusters engaged. Monitoring the ship's position, Ro eased them away from the station toward the flat rock formation where she could safely engage the interstitial engines to escape the asteroid's gravity well.

Once she started the flight sequence, Ro's jitters fell away. The ship responded with Ro's own eagerness. Leaping into space never got old. As soon as Halcyone settled into a stable orbit around Daedalus, she turned to Nomi and Barre and flashed them a wide smile.

"Nice job, Captain," Nomi said.

Her cheeks warmed, but not with embarrassment this time. "Ready to fly?"

"Ready to go home."

Home. The room they shared on Daedalus was the first place Ro had ever considered home. While Nomi still had most of three years left on what she owed the Commonwealth for her education, suddenly those three years felt very brief and very temporary. "Okay, then. Time to get squared away for a jump."

"It would be a lot more efficient if we invested in at least a few jump-rated chairs," Barre said.

"I know." They had had that conversation more than once. Even two of the temporal-damping seats would wipe out a decent chunk of the money Micah had left. And if they had them delivered to Daedalus, someone would notice and ask questions Ro didn't want to have to answer. "It's on the list." After the bridge doors. And replacing the two escape pods they were down. And getting a new viewscreen.

Ro glanced up at the display. She had almost gotten used to the crack that ran across its face.

Nomi unlatched the flight harness. "I don't know. She has a certain charm."

Barre followed suit and stood, shaking his dreads free. "Wait till you experience the jump cushioning."

"It does the job."

"Aye, aye, Captain."

Lucky for Barre, he slipped from the bridge and into the corridor before Ro could swat at him. She turned to Nomi. "Ready?"

"Aye, aye, Captain."

They walked hand in hand to Ro's quarters to prepare for the first of several jumps that would take Nomi home. Ro thought she'd rather face an uncharted wormhole than her girlfriend's family.

Nomi broke the silence at the door to the captain's quarters. "It'll be fine. They're going to like you."

The door slid open and Halcyone interrupted Ro's confused thoughts before she could answer.

"Confirm flight parameters alpha and beta."

Ro glanced down at her micro. It was a familiar program. There was only one wormhole in this sector of space—the one Daedalus orbited and her Commonwealth crew controlled. The equations were basic enough Ro could have run them in her head, but she still checked the numbers. "Flight parameters alpha and beta confirmed."

"Burn of one-third g for twenty-nine seconds in two minutes.

Countdown required?"

They could easily walk around the ship during a burn that shallow. "Negative. Jump countdown only, one-minute warning, notify every ten seconds."

"Affirmative, Captain Maldonado."

"Let's get secure." Ro waved Nomi into the compact room.

Nomi put her hand on Ro's arm. "This isn't my first transit."

"It is on my ship."

"Fair enough."

The single bunk was only slightly wider than a standard single unit. By freighter standards, a luxury. The temporal-damping foam that Ada May had given them was another luxury. After they stowed their boots, Ro signaled for Nomi to take the inside spot on the bed. It was the safer position, given the added stability of the wall's vertical referent. As Nomi settled into the conforming foam, Halcyone's engines vibrated gently and Ro's feet pressed a little more firmly into the floor. The ship was accelerating softly toward the wormhole. They would glide at their cruising speed for a few minutes until they got close enough to jump.

Ro climbed in beside the taller girl. Their legs pressed together for a moment of silent comfort, before they untangled themselves. Their bodies needed to be separate for the jump, each of them carefully nestled into the foam. She stowed her micro in the webbing directly over her head. Nomi did the same. It wasn't optimal, but the small devices would give them a focal point. Someday, Ro would be able to bring Halcyone to modern standards. It would take more than all the money Micah had given them. For now, Ro was simply grateful for the old ship and the freedom it represented.

"One minute to jump."

"All set?"

Nomi reached over and gave Ro's hand a squeeze.

Ro triggered Halcyone's internal comms. "Barre, you secure?"

"Aye, aye, Cap. See you on the other side."

No jump was routine, but Ro had done everything she could to safeguard her ship and her crew. The rest was up to Halcyone and the AI's ability to judge, then counter the temporal distortion as they moved through the wormhole. Before Dauber and May had made that possible, more than half of the early pilots developed jump-sickness. To this day, no one knew what made someone susceptible, but given the odds, Ro was grateful for Halcyone's dynamic shielding. She tried not to think about how tenuous that shielding was.

"Ten seconds to jump."

Ro shook herself back to attention. Beside her, Nomi was counting down softly from ten to zero. There was a moment when Ro felt the warmth of Nomi's body and then all sensory feedback scrambled into a swirl of weight, color, and pressure. She kept her gaze straight ahead, staring at the target in the center of her micro's display.

Time during a jump ceased to have any meaning. There was no way to keep track of it until the ship materialized into interstitial space again, but Ro always had a sense that some jumps were longer than others, even jumps through the same wormhole. Which both did and didn't make sense.

This jump seemed to take a lifetime, as if the universe somehow sensed Ro's reluctance to travel this particular flight plan and held her suspended in a place of endless waiting.

Trapped between one heartbeat and the next, she didn't even feel as if she had a breath to hold. Didn't feel as if she had a body that could breathe. She was a mélange of memory and sensation as short-circuited as how she imagined Jem's daily battle with synesthesia must feel.

Her conscious mind knew if she could turn her head, Nomi would be there, but in this altered reality, each of them was isolated in her own pocket universe. There was nothing to do but wait and even that was an impossible concept when she was outside the flow of measurable time.

Ro couldn't move.

The pressure to move was unbearable.

Then she heard a gasp and had ears again. Her chest rose and fell in an easy rhythm as if nothing at all had happened.

And according to Halcyone's calculation of elapsed subjective time as opposed to galactic time, almost nothing had.

There was a rustle beside her. Nomi shifted to her side and brushed her hand across Ro's face. "That wasn't too bad."

Tears leaked from the corners of Ro's eyes as she laughed and was unable to stop.

Nomi frowned at her. "What? What did I say?"

Getting herself under control, Ro rolled off the bed, and stood in the compact compartment looking down at the puzzled Nomi. "Relative. It's all relative." She shook her head, staving off a return of the laughter. "Never mind. Let's check in with Barre. We have a bit of a haul before the second jump."

Chapter 7

THE CAR TRUNDLED ALONG the rutted road. Dev stared straight ahead, avoiding Micah's glance.

"Long hours with the English?" the driver asked.

"Hours plenty," Dev answered. There would never be enough time away from Midlant for her to feel anything other than alien in the outside world. No matter how flawless her Standard. No matter how hard she worked. Slipping into the rhythms of the Midlant patois was uncomfortably effortless. She wondered what Micah was thinking.

But she'd told him to keep his mouth shut, and he complied. She was both grateful and annoyed.

The driver kept up a steady stream of questions and amused comments—many of them directed toward Micah— even as she wished he'd just let them ride in silence. But that wasn't the Midlant way. Gossip and innuendo were.

"Hopper have a tale?" He stared at her through the rear-view mirror, his eyes lit with amusement. The car rumbled along without much supervision and this stretch of road was in pretty good shape.

"Long hours to spin."

"Vray?"

"Vray." It would only make him more curious, but Micah's story, even what she knew of it, wasn't hers to tell.

Judging by his age, the driver had been a young child herded into the settlement along with his family by armed Commonwealth soldiers. He probably spoke Standard well enough—it was likely his cradle language after all—but with so many people from so many different heritages crammed into the original refugee camps, the polyglot that emerged became the dominant language almost from the start.

Even her grandparents had rarely spoken Standard around Dev and her brothers, and they'd been in their teens when the coastal cities were abandoned and their lives uprooted by the Drowning. Dev had learned at a very young age to hide her facility with Standard around other kids in Midlant, but only after several nasty beatings. The schools in the settlement—such as they were—taught only in Standard. Using the common patois was the surest way to being expelled from class. And plenty of her age-mates deliberately did that. But not Dev.

Now she wondered if, in her drive to get out and succeed, she'd just swapped another set of impossibilities for the ones that waited for her in Midlant.

The car slowed. Micah shot her a questioning look.

"Another hour. Give or take."

He raised his eyebrows.

The driver laughed. He'd been watching their brief interaction. "Soon enough, Hopper. Too soon, maybe, for your deep lady?"

Dev's face heated, but nothing she could say to their driver would convince him Micah wasn't paying her for sex. "Not filling pockets with tales, deep." At least that might get him to stop talking, even if her dark look wouldn't.

Her micro pinged.

/is he saying what I think he's saying?/

/maybe— what do you think he's saying?/

/that we're involved/

Involved. What a polite, distant, and sanitized way of saying it.

/not quite/ Dev stared straight ahead as the car turned off the relatively smooth main spaceport road and onto the side road that traversed the last few klicks to the settlement gate. It would take them as long to go this short distance as it had the rest, put together.

/so—what does deep mean?/

She owed him that much, at least, or he'd think it was some weird sexual term.

/deep—it's slang—from d.p. Displaced Person/

/oh/

This time it was Micah's turn to be embarrassed. He turned away, his cheeks blazing, and fell silent. Dev hoped he, too, would stop talking. But her micro pinged again.

/you call yourselves that? why?/

/better to claim it then let the highsiders use it as an insult/

/highsiders?/

/wealthy outsiders—look, i'm exhausted—can we do the whole dictionary thing later?/

Micah gave her a long look before slipping his micro back

into a pocket. Dev cringed inwardly, but it was too late to apologize for her abrupt dismissal. He turned to look out the window on his side of the car. Dev stared at the rolling hills of what had once been central Pennsylvania farm land and was now an overgrown buffer between polite civilization and the Midlant Settlement. The carcass of a few old barns poked out from new-growth forest. It wouldn't be long before even they were erased, along with the history of the place.

"Dev?" Micah's soft voice startled her in the silence of the car. "Is that bittergreen?" He jerked his chin toward the tall, fernlike plant that grew wild along the side of the road.

"Yeah. It strangles everything it touches." Someone had thought the genetically engineered plant would make a good anchor for the soil. Which it did, but inelegantly and by crowding out the native plants in the process. There was definitely a metaphor in that, which said a lot about the Commonwealth in its dealings with the settlements.

Micah made an inarticulate sound, deep in the back of his throat.

Dev wondered what his story was, but what right did she have to dig when she'd cut him off so effectively?

The rest of the trip passed in tense silence, but it was better than juggling the driver's curiosity and Micah's endless questions. The former was self-limiting. The latter she would have to deal with. Especially when he met her brothers. Dev wasn't sure which was going to be worse—Micah's settlement education or her brothers' scrutiny and criticism.

For the hundredth time, Dev cursed herself for the promises she'd made and the rigid honor that made them impossible not to fulfill.

"Would empty a heavy pocket for the tale of a hopper and a deep," the driver said.

He only smiled when Dev glared at his reflection in the rearview mirror.

*

Hopper. Deep. Vray. Micah was going to have to be the quick study he prided himself being or start getting used to this feeling of being utterly lost and powerless.

He honored Dev's request for silence through the rest of the trip, not knowing what to say, anyway. There was more bittergreen here, running wild on the side of the road, than he'd seen in a lifetime. No one cultivated it. It didn't look like anyone even harvested it. And it clearly self-seeded. He didn't know if he wanted to laugh or cry or hit his head on the car's window repeatedly.

All of his years of work trying to reverse engineer bittergreen that didn't set sterile seeds, and it was here all along. On the road to the settlement. Growing like the weed it was.

He'd have to find a way to analyze some samples with only the tools in his micro. Somehow Micah didn't think he'd find a state-of-the-art botany lab anywhere in Midlant, even if he could tell Dev what he was doing. And he couldn't risk taking samples back with him to Uni.

Could he?

Leaning his head back in the seat, Micah closed his eyes thinking of how he might use the biodome to grow this wild variety. He'd have to test it for its hallucinogenic compounds to find out how similar it was to the bittergreen the cartels controlled. It could be the root stock. Or maybe the strains just shared a common ancestor.

All issues Micah couldn't untangle without a lot more equipment and time than he had here. The motion of the car lulled him into a quasi-meditative state and he was startled when Dev broke the silence.

"We're here."

He opened his eyes as the car slowed to a stop in front of a metal gate set in a two-meter-high fence.

"Done and done," the driver said.

"Not nines and sevens, deep," Dev said, frowning.

"Pocket not heavy enough to pay the troll."

Micah was starting to make sense of the weird mix of Standard and slang. It was clear enough the driver didn't want to take them all the way to Dev's house. At least not without being paid more. Fine. He had money. That's what it was for. And a fine fuck you very much to his father. He pulled out his micro.

Dev put a warning hand on his wrist. "We had a shake."

"Tides shift." The driver shrugged one shoulder.

"When the water rises, all swimmers drown." Dev's words were clipped and cold.

"Not all swimmers," he said.

She turned to Micah, her voice steady, but the hand she placed on the door shook. "We're leaving."

He glanced down at his micro. They still owed the driver the balance.

"Now."

The driver stared at them through his mirror as they left the car. He shifted to watch Dev through his window and continued to idle there for several minutes.

"You shake like a highsider," she said.

Anger twisted the driver's features, but he said nothing. After a few more moments, he shifted his car into reverse and left. Dev watched until a curve in the rutted road hid him and the hum of the electric motor died away.

"Dev?" Micah stood close to her and waited for the tension to break. Wind sighed through the tangle of overgrown greenery. Bittergreen leaves fluttered in the breeze. "Are you okay?"

She turned to glare at him. "Fine. Let's go."

Micah frowned at the closed gate. Were there guards? Would they give him the same kind of hard time he'd gotten at the spaceport?

There was a data-pad set into the concrete next to the gate. It was as out of place here as he was. A symbol of the outside—no—highside world, juxtaposed with ancient and crumbling concrete and rusted metal.

The gate was less a security feature than a reminder of the divide between the settlement and the rest of the Commonwealth. A divide that Dev had bridged. He looked between her and the remnants of the border and wondered at what cost.

She strode up to the unattended gate and shoved her micro at it. It beeped cheerfully. "You're my guest," she said. Her voice was stripped of her characteristic droll tone. "Confirm your ident."

Micah waved his micro at the data-pad. His Commonwealth identity was as firm as it was ever going to be. If Maldonado had found him, others could. He couldn't spend a lot of time worrying about that now. Besides, Maldonado was dead.

The gate creaked open, slowly, reluctantly. Just inside the

gate, a large metal sign greeted them. The official Commonwealth seal had faded lettering layered on top of it. Micah peered closer to read it. Mid-Atlantic Refugee Camp. Commonwealth Authority. Emergency order 87/73/section 37 A.

Beneath it, scratched into the metal, he traced the words, "welcome to the drowning." Dev's words to the driver echoed in his mind. When the water rises, all swimmers drown. Except it wasn't true. Not for the highsiders. Not for the voidjumpers. Not for people like his father. Not for people like Micah.

His face flushed again and he turned away from Dev's scrutiny, finally understanding her reluctance to bring him here.

She set out along the weed-encrusted road and Micah followed, his hand brushing the impossible shape of bittergreen leaves as they walked. He refused to complain or even ask how long it would take to reach her place. His silence was the least he could offer her.

After they had walked three or four hundred meters, she paused to look back. The gate and the fence were lost in a thick buffer of greenery. Ahead, the road was an uneven ribbon of black. "It's about another half klick to the settlement proper. Then we should be able to hire another ride. But if we can't, can you make it? Maybe one more klick total."

Micah glared down at his traitorous feet. "I'll make it."

He knew he was slowing her down, but she didn't complain. And she didn't press his pace, either. It was only ten minutes, but it felt like far longer when they reached the outskirts of the settlement proper. Micah stopped and stared at the jumble of rusting shipping containers forming haphazard towers in front of them. "How do we get through?"

"What do you mean?"

"I don't see a gate. Where's the security?"

She pointed to the nearest containers. "That's not a wall. Those are people's homes."

He frowned and took a few stumbling steps forward over the uneven ground. What he had taken for the fluttering of trash wedged between the large rectangles were curtains over crude windows cut into the corrugated metal. Narrow steps welded to the walls reminded Micah of emergency access ladders on a spaceship. As he watched, a young child spidered up first one level and then a second before disappearing into a doorway. "Homes? They made apartment buildings from shipping containers?"

"They? You mean the Commonwealth Guard?" Dev looked as if she'd swallowed something caustic. "No. The Guard left the survivors a city of tents and primitive latrines and not much else. These containers came later. They're what supplies were dropped in from a government just glad it didn't have to do much else."

"I'm sorry. I didn't know."

"Why should you? The Commonwealth is happy to let the settlements fend for themselves. Whatever happens here, stays here. But Midlanters built this. My grandparents helped build this." Her voice contained both pride and anger.

"You grew up in one of those?"

"Surprised that I'm house-trained?"

Her tone was amused; her gaze burned. Micah struggled to find something to say that would ease the tension, but there was nothing. She wasn't mad at him. It was a deep and secret shame, and he understood what that felt like. "Come on. Take me to your place."

She led Micah through what felt like a maze of random paths through the stacked containers. There were streets wide enough to drive a compact vehicle or a large trundle through, but they took tight turns and rarely ran more than the length of two or three of the rectangular "buildings." "Your city planner must have been drunk."

He must have said the wrong thing again because Dev picked up her pace.

"What?"

There was no reply. Micah forced himself to a slow jog, ignoring the pull of the scars along his feet.

"Okay. We know I'm an idiot. Let's agree and move on."

She stopped, but didn't turn around. It was a start. Micah halted beside her, looking straight ahead. A group of kids played in an empty courtyard sheltered on three sides by double-stacked units. In the late afternoon, the space was deeply shadowed. A young girl ran in and out of a narrow slice of sunlight, flashing like a quasar, her laughter echoing off the metal. The rest of the group chased after her. That had been Dev, once.

"Look. I need a flight plan, here."

"The roads. They were laid out like this on purpose. So there would be no sight lines. So the Commonwealth Guard couldn't send tanks through. Not easily. Not without a fight."

"Oh."

"Look up at the topmost containers."

He followed her pointing finger. There was a decorative looping fence along the front-facing sides. "Okay. What am I looking at?"

"Lookouts. Like the battlements of a castle."

The skin between his shoulder blades itched. Were they being watched? Slowly, Micah turned in a complete circle, looking at the constructed neighborhood with different eyes. It was a fortified city. Without Dev, he'd have been hopelessly lost.

He realized that he hadn't seen any other people but the children, who now stood at the edge of the courtyard staring at them. Not them. Him. Micah smiled and waved. They laughed and scattered, disappearing into different containers, leaving him and Dev isolated in the center of the brooding buildings. He shivered. This wasn't his place and Midlant knew it.

Highsider. Voidhopper. Micah glanced up to the nearest container's roof, certain he'd seen a flash of light, but nothing moved. "So where is everybody?" He tried to keep his voice casual, but it was hard to suppress his unease.

"You mean, do they know we're here?" Dev gave him a look that was at least a little bit amused. "They know. No secrets in Midlant."

That he doubted. There were secrets everywhere. He learned that from his father.

"Come on. It's just a little farther and you can rest your feet."

There was no way Micah was going to admit how good that sounded. As they walked past the cluster of buildings, he swore he heard the murmur of curious voices, but he wasn't going to turn around if Dev didn't.

He had no idea how she navigated the tangle of crowded neighborhoods. Every cluster of containers looked alike. There were no street signs or numbers, but Dev walked with complete confidence. She stopped short. Micah nearly bumped into her.

"We're here."

"Ready or not."

"Well, up you go," Dev said, pointing to a rusting ladder.

"After you. I insist."

She snorted. "Probably for the best. If you fall, at least you won't take me down with you."

"Thanks for the vote of confidence."

"Any time."

Dev gripped the sides of the ladder and scampered up easily. Micah hitched his bag higher on his shoulder and followed, not nearly as graceful, his hands slick with sweat. Well, he'd been the one who insisted on this trip.

No reverse in a wormhole.

"Welcome to Midlant," she said.

Micah glanced up. Dev stood in an open doorway, silhouetted by light from inside the container. He gripped her offered hand and gasped as she yanked him off the ladder and through the door. As they stumbled deeper into the container, he fell against her to a chorus of wolf whistles and deep laughter. She grabbed his shoulders to steady him.

"You good?"

Her strength was shaped by this place and by her fierce will to thrive. It was a strength he would have to rely on. "Yeah." She waited until he got his feet stabilized beneath him before letting go.

"And that's enough from you lot."

Her brothers. Micah squared his shoulders and looked past her. Three tall men sat watching him.

Chapter 8

"DAD?" JEM WALKED INTO his parents' dark and silent office where his father sat brooding after being outflanked by Gutierrez. He actually felt a little sorry for him.

He looked up from his desk, pinching the bridge of his nose. "I'll talk to your mother about the meds if you'd like."

"It's okay. It's not such a big deal and if she's better this way, I can live with it."

"Thank you, Jeremy."

"Look. If this is a bad time, I can come back. But I'd really like to review my most recent scans."

"It's fine. Sit down." His father set his micro on the desk between them. He fumbled getting the virtual window at the right size and position so they could both see it and Jem had to resist the urge to fix it for him. Jem had seen him perform emergency surgery with an improvised blade on a mess hall table, but the basics of a 3d rendering sometimes eluded him.

"Your mother will probably hate to admit this, or she'll

attribute it to time and rest, but your brain is actually healing. What is your sense from the inside, so to speak?"

Jem grinned. "Yeah. I'm better. It's not perfect, but the nausea is a lot more manageable."

"And the integration?"

"It's still tiring, but I can link with my micro pretty reliably now." He didn't mention his infuriatingly random ability to speak directly neural to neural with Barre. There was exactly nothing in the literature about it and judging by Ada May's reaction, it could make them targets for all kinds of attention that neither of them wanted.

Maybe it was a quirk of his injured brain or an artifact of how Dr. Land had to do the placement, or maybe something to do with the fact that he and Barre were genetically related. More likely, it was also due to Barre's weird musical brain. No matter, it wasn't going to be easily replicated, especially since even he and Barre couldn't figure it out.

"Can you clone these? I'd like to have a chance to go over them later."

"I'll make it even easier than that. I'll grant you read-only access to all your test results. How's that?"

"That's great, Dad, really."

"As far as your mother is concerned ... " His dad sighed and pressed the heels of his hands to his eyes.

"Yeah, well, it's Mom. What are you going to do?"

"She means well, Jem." He laughed, but it was tinged with weariness.

Jem could pretty much fill in the blanks, but there wasn't much he could change and she loved him, loved Barre, too, even when she couldn't show it. It was an old conversation and one not likely to play any differently any time soon.

"I've also overridden the setting on the dispenser. It only requires your credentials now. Your mother will get the notifications when you authorize your dose. Just ask whoever is on call for it, okay?"

It hurt Jem that his mother couldn't trust him, but he knew it was the best he was likely to get. "I can live with that."

His father gave him a rare, unguarded look. One with a flash of fear bright in it. "I'm glad," he said, softly, almost as if he were talking to himself.

Jem left his father in the silent office, got his meds, and walked out of medical, still puzzling over his father's strange despondent mood. His micro buzzed just as the doors closed behind him. He sighed. Was his mother going to overrule his father about the meds? Jem just wanted them to figure out what worked for both of them and leave him out of it.

He waited until he got halfway to the nexus before accessing his micro and stopped short in the middle of the corridor. The message was from Gutierrez.

/*Need assistance*/

Jem didn't expect the thrill that shot through him. It was an equal mix of fear and excitement. Yes, this was what he wanted, but still. Gutierrez was as volatile as Ro in many ways, and given the LC's history, also likely far more explosive. /*OMW*/

As usual, no one paid him the least bit of attention as he moved through the station and toward the officers' housing section. The door to Gutierrez's quarters opened as soon as Jem arrived. He stepped inside, not sure what to expect, but the sight of the LC in civvies definitely wasn't it.

She stood in the center of the living area, looking uncertain.

The left sleeve of her tunic was pinned up at the shoulder. The oversized top reached nearly to the knees of slim leggings, but it was her bare feet that made her seem so vulnerable.

The door sealed behind him. Jem looked around the room, his hands in his pockets, as he waited for her to say something. The mix of bright reds and golds of the furnishings along with the smooth lines of the long, low wood table in the center of the space somehow suited the LC. At least she seemed less guarded here: less the station's lieutenant commander and more Emmaline Gutierrez. Her damaged prosthesis lay on the table surrounded by delicate tools and spools of wire, in stark, mechanical contrast to the well-polished wood grain.

"It seems I need two hands, after all." Her voice was low and nearly colorless, as if she had somehow desaturated all of her emotions. Jem heard the hint of fear and need, but only because he understood that kind of desperation.

"I'll do the best I can. I'm good with basic bioelectronics and mechanicals, but I've never worked with prosthetics before."

One of her eyebrows lifted, but otherwise her expression remained passive. "So there's something you're not already an expert in? How refreshing."

Jem shrugged. It wasn't as if he didn't have to deal with sarcasm from Ro on a daily basis. "Where do you want me to start?"

She turned her back on him and paced the room, her bare footsteps silent on the soft carpeting. "About half the components need to be swapped out and most of the wiring rerun."

"You know, you'd probably have an easier job just getting a new prosthesis."

"No." She didn't even turn around. Her voice was void black. It brooked no further discussion.

"Okay, then." He moved fully into the room, carefully keeping the table between them. Avoiding the deep red sofa, Jem sat cross-legged on the floor to examine the artificial arm more closely. It looked like it had been charred by a laser torch before being crushed beneath a trash compactor. Only the hook at the end seemed untouched and as shiny and deadly as ever. Jem sighed. This was going to be a lot harder than he'd anticipated. "Do you have the schematics?"

Gutierrez sat down and set her micro beside her on the sofa and manipulated the small device with her right hand. Jem's micro pinged. "Schematics."

He opened them in a virtual window next to the prosthesis, orienting the readout to match how the arm was lying on the table. The plans were heavily annotated. "Not the original specs, I take it."

"No."

No wonder she didn't want a new one. How many decades had she tinkered with and enhanced this limb? Jem gave a long, low whistle. "You're good."

"No. She is." Gutierrez laughed. Jem would have tasted the bitterness in it even without his synesthesia.

He returned to the schematics and shifted to the exploded view. The sheer number of components contained in the crude-looking arm astonished him. "A lot of these aren't stock."

"No."

"Look. If we're going to work together, you're going to have to do better than monosyllabic answers."

"Fine."

Jem sighed again. It was going to be a long day. "I was thinking I could strip out the fried wiring and at least start to work on the brachial plexus." That was where the artificial nerves would interface with her remaining intact biologic ones. Once he got that working, they could do some basic testing to make sure the limb was going to function before they spent a lot of time on the downstream components.

"An appropriate strategy."

So, she could say more than a single word. Holding back a smile, Jem focused on the schematic. He exploded the diagram of the wiring harness and traced the complex braiding of the cybernetic nerves. It was going to take hours to do this right.

Gutierrez's micro buzzed and before she could reach it, it had vibrated itself off the table. Jem reached down to pick it up.

Snatching it from him, she said, "I'm one-handed. Not helpless."

Jem was surprised that she took the call sitting in the living area with him, rather than retreat into her bedroom. She did turn partially away, angling the virtual window so it was edge on to Jem and impossible to see. The voice coming from the micro was indistinct, but he could hear Gutierrez's side of the conversation.

It was brief. Her voice held an uncomfortable brightness with an orange edge. "Yes, sir. I understand." Then a long pause before she continued. "Yes, you will have my full cooperation. Sir. Yes, sir."

Jem tried to catch her gaze, but she turned away, leaving his curiosity unsatisfied.

Chapter 9

"OI! LOST TIDES AND HIGHSIDES," Giles said, laughing, as he stood from the rectangular table in the center of the kitchen area. There were three mismatched and empty glasses upended on it. Her two older brothers, Vic and Tanner, were leaning back in their chairs, both with their feet propped up.

"Thirsty, nuff?" Tanner asked. He waved an empty wine bottle.

They'd been drinking for hours, and far more than one bottle by the looks of it.

Dev glanced at Micah who stood silently by her side before she dropped her bag on the worn rug that her grandmother had braided. In a way, she'd been the family's original materials scientist, learning to repurpose anything that came her way. That's how she'd survived and it's what she taught her children and grandchildren.

She would have been furious. Not so much at the unswept floor and the random piles of trash, but at the serious lack of hospitality. No matter how meager their stores, Grandmama would have had food and drink prepared. Even if it meant she didn't eat.

"We have a guest. And you speak Standard as well as I do." Dev ignored Giles's open arms and pushed Tanner's feet off the table. Vic slid his down before she could reach him. "I'm going to show Micah to his room." She glared at each brother, in turn. "I'm assuming he does have a place to sleep."

"Vray." Giles smiled. "Sorry. I mean, yeah, sure. He can have my bed. I'll bunk with Tan and Vic." He waved his arm in a broad, sweeping motion that nearly knocked down the wall hangings their grandmother had made. "Welcome, Micah, our homestead is yours."

"I don't mean to kick you out of your place. I can sleep wherever. It's no problem."

"You are our guest," Dev said, emphasizing each of the words in a cold, harsh tone as she glared at her brothers. That meant something, no matter that Micah didn't understand. Her brothers knew better.

Tanner and Vic scrambled to their feet. Tanner nearly tripped over the chair he'd just vacated. How much had they been drinking?

"You can rest a bit before dinner." She glanced over her shoulder at her brothers one more time before leading Micah through the long, rectangular space that had been Dev's only home. The twelve-meter-long container had been divided into four rooms by heavy curtains. Today they were all tied back for airflow. Micah followed silently as Dev moved into the first of the three tiny bedrooms carved from the back half of the container.

The first room was bare of anything but a small bed and an empty set of shelves. It had been her room; everything that mattered to her was now in her apartment at Uni. At least Giles hadn't turned it into the garbage heap. What had once been her brothers' room was now a cluttered mess of sealed cartons and piles of dirty clothes. Dev wrinkled her nose at the stale, mildewed odor.

The last room had been her grandparents'. When their grandmother had died, Vic had initially claimed it for his own. Then when Giles had washed out of school and returned home, Vic and Connor moved out of Old Town and into their own place.

At least it was reasonably clean. A double bed took up most of the space. A large storage locker, stenciled with Red Cross in block letters, sat at the foot of the bed. The faded rug had once been the sacks that flour and rice had come in, torn into strips, braided, rolled, and sewn into a large oval. There were long rents in the seams now that her grandmother wasn't there to mend it.

Dev gathered up the thin blanket from the bed and turned to Micah. "Stay here." She didn't wait for his response before stomping back through the container to the front room. Her brothers were attempting to clean the living space. Dev ignored them, opened the front door, and shook out the blanket. There was something satisfying in the snap of the fabric and the cloud of dust that rose from it. She left her brothers arguing over something in rapid-fire patois and returned to the end room to find Micah standing exactly where she'd left him.

"What?"

"We don't have to stay."

"The hell we don't."

"Look. I didn't mean to cause a problem with your family. It's okay."

Her face heated as she whipped the blanket back over the bed. When she faced him, her hands were empty and looking for something to throw or break. It didn't much matter. She had to do something with her restless anger, so she shoved him toward the bed. "Rest your damned feet before you hurt yourself again."

Micah collapsed onto the soft surface, bouncing slightly, laughter and surprise fighting for dominance in his expression. Laughter won. "You're as bad as Ro."

"Feet. Up."

"Fine. You win." He grimaced as he unlaced his shoes.

"Do you need help?"

He gave her a look she couldn't interpret. "I may not know about siblings, but I know about avoiding family. And you're avoiding yours."

It was hard to avoid family in a house that was essentially one big room. Dev could hear her brothers continuing their argument. It was probably about her. She frowned, listening more closely and made out the words "hopper" and "highsider." "I'm going to have to tell them something about you. Who you are. Why you helped me." Why she even got caught up in his mess in the first place.

"Dev, I —"

She held her hands up as he started to sit up. "I know. If it's not your story to tell, it's definitely not mine. I'll try not to betray any confidences, but I have to tell them something." And it had to be close to the truth. At least the truth as she understood it. "I need to make sure they don't burn down the place. Hang out here. I'll come get you when dinner's ready." Dev sighed as she glanced around the room. Next to their apartment at Uni, it was a hovel. Next to anything Micah must have been used to? What was worse than a hovel? "I'm sorry about the room."

"It's fine, Dev." Micah shifted his legs and relaxed into the pillow. "Really. I've crashed in a lot worse."

What was that supposed to mean? She stopped herself from snapping at him and returned to the front room to deal with her brothers. Giles was sweeping the dust and detritus out the front door. Vic was pumping water into the barrel they used as their storage tank from the cistern this cluster of containers shared. She would have to show Micah how to trigger the water heater in the head.

"Where's Tanner?"

Vic jerked his chin toward the door. "Hopper hungry, vray?"

Dev struggled to rein in her temper. "Yes, Micah's probably hungry. I'm hungry. We've been traveling all day. And unlike the three of you, we'd like something other than whatever swill was in those empty bottles."

"Oi! That's high-test swill. Methinks you be needful." He handed her a glass full of the amber liquid.

"Three drunk Morningstars are quite enough, thank you." It was one thing to hear their cabbie use the Midlant patois, but hearing her brothers use it made Dev cringe.

"Too highside for us, sister?" Giles grabbed the glass and downed it in one gulp.

"That's not fair!" It wasn't Dev's fault that Giles had dropped out. She hated having to be the shining example of the Commonwealth's largess, their token settlement success. Most of all, she hated the envy and the despair in her brother's voice.

Vic studied her with his dark gaze, his lips set in a hard line.

He looked so much like the pictures of their father at that age. Dev hardly remembered either of her parents. They had shipped out to the colonies when she was small, leaving all the Morningstar kids with a newly widowed grandmama and promising to send back money which rarely came. After a while, no word came, either. They were swallowed up by the void both literally and figuratively.

"Midlant is proud. Midlant is fierce. No shame in our share. Unless you boost it."

Dev turned away so Vic couldn't see her face blaze. "No shame here." She was the one who should be ashamed. But it was so hard to be what everyone wanted her to be and still find a space where she was just Dev.

"So what's the jumper's tale?" Giles asked.

"Long, thirsty hours," Dev said. "Will spin it once, over full plates, vray?"

Vic locked the pump handle and came over to embrace her. "So you do remember where you're from."

His stubble tickled her face and he smelled like sweat and alcohol, tinged with the local flowers used to flavor the wine, but his strong arms wrapped around her and for a long moment, Dev was just his little sister again. Safe. Loved. Teased. Tears burned in her eyes and she blinked them back. "Deep, deep down," she whispered and there was pride in it. Pride in her grandmother's strength sent through the generations to her and her brothers.

"Oi! Who's hungry?" The smell of chicken wafted through the container even before Tanner swung himself through its door.

Dev's mouth watered. "From Hoeppner's?"

"Vray. Last call, too."

"Nice catch!" Grace Hoeppner made the best chicken and dumplings in all of Midlant. They usually sold out long before nightfall. Micah was in for a treat.

"Go get your friend. We'll set the table," Vic said. "And don't worry. We'll be gentle."

They clearly didn't know Micah. He was as tough as any deep she'd ever met.

She walked back toward the rear bedroom feeling at least less inclined to deck each of her brothers. They were idiots, but they were her idiots. Full night had fallen and a breeze moved through all the open windows in the container, but it was still warmer than the temperature controlled apartment back at Uni. Micah was a shadowed lump on the bed in the darkness.

"Micah?"

The bed creaked as he shifted, but he didn't respond.

Dev sat on the edge and gently shook his shoulder. Micah bolted upright and clamped his hand on her arm tight enough to grind the bones of her wrist together.

Her free hand slipped into her pocket and nearly drew out the blade before she realized what she was doing. "Micah!"

His hand released. "Shit. Dev. I'm sorry! I must have been dreaming."

She rubbed her wrist, all too familiar with the kinds of nightmares he might be having. The two of them really were a pair. "You can wash up in there." She pointed to the small cubicle walled off from the square room. "There's a switch under the sink for the water heater. Just remember to turn it off when you're done."

Micah nodded before retreating to the head.

"And dinner's ready. I hope you're hungry."

He paused at the door. "Your brothers okay with me being here?"

"It's my home as much as it is theirs. And yes." She wanted to warn him not to say anything stupid, but of course he would. Being in Midlant was like being a visitor to another universe. One he had no guidebook for. And whose fault was that? Dev could have better prepared him, but they hadn't really had the time and if she were being truthful to herself, she hadn't wanted him to really know where she'd come from. There was that shame again.

Well, a bellyful of Hoeppner's chicken and dumplings was nothing to be ashamed of. She'd even enjoy some of the so-called wine her brothers were drinking. It was a homecoming, after all.

After washing up, Micah followed her through the container, a noticeable limp to his step. He hadn't complained about all the walking, the crude facilities, or the primitive container. He was certainly as proud and fierce as any Midlanter.

She hoped her brothers would see that.

They had actually set the table with Grandmama's hand-embroidered tablecloth. The five place settings didn't match. That had never bothered Dev before.

Her brothers all stood waiting. Micah halted beside the table.

She paused for a moment before deciding to introduce him with the name he'd taken at Uni. "Michael Chase, these are my brothers. Giles, Vic, and Tanner."

They each nodded in turn. No one made a move to sit. That was the settlement way—the guest chose first. But Micah didn't know that.

"It's an honor to meet you."

Dev frowned at how highside Micah sounded. Is that what

her brothers heard when she spoke Standard?

They all stood there as the food steamed on the table, her brothers waiting for Micah to make a move, Micah waiting for someone to tell him what to do. If it wasn't so clearly and ridiculously awkward, Dev would have laughed. Instead she waved him to a seat at the head of the table. The rest of them sat around him and started reaching for the food.

Giles barged in with his usual tact. "You're not very pale for a jumper."

Her two older brothers were too busy shoveling large helpings of stew onto their plates. If Grandmama had still been alive, she would've rapped them across the knuckles with her big wooden spoon for serving themselves before their guest.

Micah sat stiffly on the edge of the hard chair. "I don't know how much Dev's told you about me. I'm a botanist. Lots of time under grow lights."

"A plant guy. Huh." Giles reached halfway across the table to pour Micah some wine. "Grapes are grown here. Midlant's finest!"

When Micah picked up the glass, Giles, Tanner, and Vic all raised theirs. "To our sister's jumper friend," Vic said. "From the void to the deep. Welcome."

He shot Dev a brief questioning look before taking a sip of the wine. Her brothers emptied their glasses smoothly.

"Well, then," Micah said before tossing back the rest of his drink. "Thank you."

Giles nodded his approval and poured another round.

Before they could get to her glass, Dev upended it on the table. "One of us has to remain functional." She thought about warning Micah, but decided he would deserve the hangover. So would her brothers. They passed the serving bowl to her and she handed it to Micah. Her brothers may have forgotten their manners, but she hadn't.

He stared into the bowl, set it down, and drained his wine glass again before taking a small portion. Most of what he'd put on his plate was dumplings and gravy with a very small piece of chicken that had fallen off the bone. Then he slid the serving bowl back toward her.

Her brothers were too busy stuffing their faces to notice how Micah picked at the food. Dev hadn't thought to ask him if he had any restrictions or allergies. In Midlant, you ate what you had. Luckily for them, tonight they had Hoeppner's.

Dev dug into her meal, reveling in the familiar and comforting flavors of home. If Micah didn't like it, he'd be a hungry jumper tomorrow. If they got up early enough, they could make the bakery before the bread sold out. If he managed to wake up while it was still morning.

Tanner opened a fresh bottle of Midlant's finest. Finest turpentine, more like it. Her brothers had managed to make quick work of the huge portion of stew Tanner had bought. Micah had managed to clear most of his plate. She'd lost count of the times his glass had been refilled, but there was a bright flush to his cheeks. Her brothers would continue drinking until there were no more bottles to open.

Another quaint Midlant tradition.

"No, don't get up. I'll clear the kitchen," Dev said, rolling her eyes as Giles tried to push back from the table. Like as not, they'd trip and fall giving her broken dishware along with chicken bones to clean.

"So tell your tale, jumper." Vic had likely downed more than his share of the empty bottles, but her eldest brother was as shrewd and sharp as ever, drunk or sober. "It's a rare shake between deeps and highsiders."

Dev kept her mouth shut. This was a test and Micah had to float or drown on his own. It would also give him the chance to frame their story. She hoped he was sober enough to figure that out. As Dev moved around the table stacking dishes, she had a flashback from her early childhood helping Grandmama clear dinner while a group of Midlant men sat drinking and talking. She'd complained about her brothers not doing their fair share and her grandmother just smiled.

It wasn't until Dev was much older that she realized how her grandmother knew everything about anything happening in Midlant. The kitchen—if it could even be called that—was close enough to the table that she could reach out from the sink and tip Tanner's chair backward. Of course, he would end up in the water barrel and they'd flood the container, but that wasn't the point. Dev smirked and set the dishes on the counter top before pulling out the large plastic wash tub.

And listened.

She was surprised how close to the truth Micah held. But then again, it was a lot easier that way. Less to remember who you told what to. When he got to the part when Maldonado had sent him the video of her captive on his ship, Giles whistled long and low and turned to her.

"Jumper got the jump on you?" he asked, laughing. "Leave the muck. You must be needful." He turned her glass right side up and emptied the last of the wine in it.

Giles was definitely the drunkest of her brothers. He always slipped deeply into dialect when he drank.

"Fine. But you lot get to finish cleaning up, then." Dev sat and twirled her glass between her hands, staring at the amber liquid. "Bastard drugged me. Didn't see it coming."

"Midlant blades dull on the highside," Vic said.

Dev glanced down at the pocket where hers was concealed. Not anymore.

"He was using me to get to Micah. He thought ..." Dev shook her head. "I don't care what he thought. I trashed his ship and got out. He didn't."

It wasn't as simple as that and it left out Emma Gutierrez flying her to safety and Taro Odachi dying to save them.

"Are you important, highsider?" Vic asked.

A chill moved through Dev in the warm and close container. Important. Influential. Wealthy. That's what Vic was asking and the way he asked meant he wanted some advantage. Micah looked at her, his eyes narrowed.

The container fell silent. The open windows brought the sound of distant shouting and the barking of dogs. Muffled laughter came from the container below them.

"Only to the wrong people," Micah said softly.

Giles leaned forward, an eager light in his eyes.

"Oi!" Dev interrupted and tossed back the entire glass of wine. It burned down her throat, but she didn't sputter or cough. "Guest counts for all. Morningstars owe the tab and twice over." She slammed the empty glass on the table, shocking Micah and her brothers to silence. "Go drown yourselves. This tale is closed."

As she stood, her chair tipped back with a crash. Their downstairs neighbors shouted. Dev shouted something incoherent back before grabbing Micah's arm and hauling him to his feet.

She marched Micah to the end of the container, pulled the curtain between his room and the rest of the space before curling up on the bare mattress in what had once been her room.

*

Even after Jem had left Gutierrez's quarters, he'd pored over her arm's schematics for hours. When his vision blurred and his queasiness threatened the dinner he'd hastily eaten, he linked his micro to the neural and let his mind float through the information.

It was too much to take in and he fell asleep in his clothes, his micro beside him on the bed.

He woke to a brightening room and a pounding headache. "Daedalus, local time?"

"Zero six hundred."

It was too early, even for him. Jem lay back and put a pillow over his face. As soon as the external world vanished, Gutierrez's schematics rose up around him in layers and layers of complexity.

"It's definitely way too early for this." If he was going to be able to do any work today, he needed food and his morning dose of neo-benzos. Probably not in that order. He linked to his micro and collapsed the 3-d rendering of the plans. An alert tone blared through his mind and he lost the connection.

When he opened his eyes, the room spun. Jem swore and closed them again. His micro repeated the same alert.

"Cool your afterburners." Whoever it was would just have to wait until he showered and got dressed.

Jem staggered to the head, left his clothes in a pile on the floor, and stepped into the shower. Bracing his arms against the walls, he let the spill of the hot water relax him. He closed his eyes and practiced some of the mind techniques that helped ease the vertigo and strengthen the neural integration. The tension in his neck and shoulders released and he no longer felt like he was stuck mid-jump.

Maybe he would be able to eat first, after all.

His micro was still buzzing with incoming messages when he finished getting dressed. Jem frowned, considering the device. Integrating tired him out, but staring at the small screen triggered the head injury symptoms. Either result limited how much work he could do in a given day. Sighing, he reached for the micro. Whatever stamina he had for using the neural would be dedicated to Gutierrez's schematics.

Close to a dozen messages scrolled across the screen. All anonymous. All insistent. All asking about Gutierrez.

All from Ada May. They disappeared as he scanned through the list. "Gee, Barre, thanks for the heads-up," he thought as he shook his head and typed a quick reply. */How do you think she is? She signed out of medical AMA/* Slipping the micro into his pocket, he decided to try the commissary before going for his meds. He'd feel the vibration when Ada messaged back.

It was silent in his family quarters. His mother was probably already in medical and his father was likely still sleeping. With another half hour or so until shift change, the corridors were fairly empty as well. The commissary was crowded with sleepy crew getting ready for work. On any other morning, Jem would have saved a seat for Nomi. They were only gone a day and already, Daedalus felt empty.

Jem grabbed two slices of plain bread and a glass of some kind of nondescript, sweet juice before looking for somewhere to sit. His micro buzzed and he halted, mid-step.

"Need a hand?"

Startled by Simon Marchand's soft drawl, Jem nearly dropped his tray.

"Have you heard from your friend recently?"

For a millisecond, Jem thought he must mean Ada May and he was grateful that his dark skin didn't easily flush. "They're probably still en route," he said, recovering his balance and stabilizing the covered cup.

"Here. There's room for both of us." Marchand guided Jem over to an empty table.

As he sat, his micro buzzed again. He tucked it down more snugly in his pocket—Ada would just have to wait. Marchand was a more urgent and present concern. Did he know that Jem was the source of Lowell's stolen info? It would be safer just to play the naive child others took him for, even if Marchand suspected otherwise.

"It must be interesting to be the child of the station's docs."

Interesting? Well, true, but that wasn't the word Jem would use. He shrugged, not knowing where Marchand was going with this, and nibbled at the edge of the bread. Having something in his stomach made the meds behave better.

"I bet you've seen all sorts of things over the years."

"I guess." Why was Marchand chatting him up? In all the time Jem had been on Daedalus, he didn't even think the man had ever glanced at him once. His micro buzzed again. He was going to have to excuse himself so he could read Ada's messages in private.

"Speaking of interesting." Marchand gestured in the direction of the commissary door just as the entire room fell silent.

Jem followed his gaze and stared, his mouth gaping open. Emmaline Gutierrez stood inside the doorway in full uniform with its left sleeve pinned to the shoulder. She must have had a hell of a struggle getting her boots on one-handed.

There was no way in the cosmos either of his parents would have cleared her for active duty yet, so what was she doing here and in uniform, looking like she wanted to shoot something or someone?

She strode through the commissary as if nothing had changed, her expression practically daring anyone to ask her how she was. As she reached the back of the room, the far table silently emptied of its occupants. The LC sat in her usual spot, her back to the wall, and surveyed the room.

One of the mess hall staff brought over a black coffee. Gutierrez nodded her thanks, took a sip, and returned to her quiet surveillance. Jem was probably the only one who noticed the slight tremor in her right arm and the way her body leaned a little left, as if overcompensating for the weight imbalance.

Well, he'd have a few things to tell Ada May at least.

Simon Marchand stood and bused the empty dishes from the table. "I thought she was on medical leave. But I guess with Commander Targill running the station ..."

Jem's mouth fell open. "Targill? Where's Commander Mendez?"

"Recalled to central command, I'd expect," he said. It was disconcerting. Marchand's voice had no discernible emotional overlay. To the ear, it sounded easy and conversational, but it was a uniform beige to his mind. "Oh, and I'm covering for Nomi this morning. If you speak to her, give her my regards. Ro as well."

"Yes, s-sir." Jem's mind raced. The call the LC had gotten when he'd been in her quarters the other day must have been from Targill. Targill was here. Just after they'd released the information Nomi and Jem had hacked. So Commander Mendez was gone. Was she reporting to her superiors or was she under arrest? Was Targill her ally or a rogue Commonwealth agent? What they'd discovered about Lowell pointed to the latter.

The acting comms officer never looked away from Gutierrez. Who did Marchand owe his allegiance to? Gutierrez's neutral expression didn't change as her gaze swept over the departing man, but her lips pressed together in a tight line as she noticed Jem.

As he stood to leave, she narrowed her eyes and leaned forward.

As if he would risk coming over to talk with her in such a public venue. With Targill on board the station, Jem would have to be very, very careful to stay unnoticed.

The next time he headed over to Gutierrez's quarters to work, he would have to enable Ro's ghost program. If his parents discovered where he was, they'd have questions that would be complicated to answer. Marchand's friendliness was a new kind of threat, and triggering Targill's suspicions could land Jem and his friends in a universe of hurt.

He slipped his hand into his pocket to silence his micro. Everyone was just going to have to park in a holding orbit. Ada was going to have to stop communicating with him. And he was going to have to warn Ro about Targill.

First things first.

Shift change meant crowded corridors. Jem hugged the right-hand side and headed for medical, hoping his mother would be too busy orienting the incoming staff to want to talk to him. Unfortunately, it was empty and she noticed him as soon as he stepped inside. It was too much to hope for something like a nice bout of station-wide food poisoning right about now.

"Here, I want to do a quick exam," she said, herding him into one of the private rooms.

He wanted to tell her that nothing had changed since yesterday, but kept his mouth shut. The eye roll was involuntary. Unfortunately, she'd never misinterpret it for nystagmus.

She pulled out a small pen light and had him follow it, first with one eye covered, then the other, then neither. With all the sophisticated scanning devices and tests, there was no substitute for the basics and a good mind to interpret them. His mother, for all her faults, was an excellent doctor. Jem just wished he wasn't her patient.

To be honest, he didn't want to be anyone's patient and he understood completely what Gutierrez was going through, but at least her doctors weren't also family.

His mother, quiet to begin with, had fallen completely silent and Jem glanced up at her, startled. She was looking past him, her eyes unfocused. "Is everything okay, Mom?"

"Oh, sorry." She turned back to him. "Your eye tracking looks good."

He hadn't been worried about himself—his own experience and his scans showed clear improvement—but the vulnerability in her expression frightened him.

"Your father was right." She paused. Jem wondered what she

was thinking about. "I've been too harsh on you. I'm sorry. Here." She handed him the dispenser with strangely unsteady hands. "It has a week's supply. It's unlocked. I'll want to reassess the dose as you continue to integrate."

"Are you ..."

Her cheeks flushed and she backed away until she hit the curtain.

"Sure, Mom. Thank you."

But she'd ducked out of the exam room. Jem frowned after her, turning over the medicine dispenser in his hands. He wasn't sure what was more unnerving—Gutierrez sitting in the commissary, pretending nothing had happened; Mendez disappearing abruptly and being replaced by Targill; or his mother admitting she had been wrong. He wouldn't be surprised if gravity suddenly stopped working.

Chapter 10

"You good?" Ro asked as she rolled off the edge of the bunk.

Nomi scooted to the outside and sat up, letting the universe settle for a moment. As jumps went, these two hadn't been too hard, which was surprising given the very basic conditions aboard Halcyone and the age of the ship. "Better than you, I suspect." Ro's normally pale face had a gray cast to it. "Do jumps always affect you like this?"

"It depends."

"Would coffee help?"

"It depends," Ro said, again. This time a fleeting smile eased the tightness of her face.

"Well, it's not going to be the stuff Micah could score, but there are few situations that a jolt of caffeine can't make better."

This time Ro laughed. "Wasn't sure I'd ever find someone more of an addict than me."

"See? We're a perfect match." She stood and threw her arms around Ro's slender shoulders. Ro stiffened slightly before relaxing into the embrace. Nomi wondered if there would ever be a time her skittish girlfriend would be able to let the fear go.

Barre's voice broke through the internal comms. "Meet me on the bridge? I have something akin to coffee and food."

"Sold," Nomi said.

His laugh had a hint of music behind it. She wasn't sure if that was Barre or Halcyone. Or maybe both.

"Be right there," Ro said. She slipped out of Nomi's loose embrace and took her hands instead.

Nomi canted her head.

"So, what did you tell your family about me?"

"Oh, the usual." As if there was anything usual about Ro.

"Nomi, I need a tether, here!"

Sighing, Nomi steered them both to sit on the edge of the bed. "My brother will be an obnoxious brat, but don't take it personally. My mother will be overly polite, but that's because she's always afraid of saying the wrong thing. My father? He'll try to get you to overhaul all the house computer systems and he'll want to cook for you."

"Oh."

She squeezed Ro's hands, examining the squared-off nails and the callused fingers. "Just relax. They will like you because I like you." That was true enough, though that wouldn't stop their curiosity. At least they would reserve any questions they had until Ro was otherwise occupied. "They're going to want to know about your family. Your upbringing. But they won't ask directly. That would be rude."

No, they would talk about food and traditions and tell slightly mortifying family stories. Which would be awkward for Ro and awkward for her parents. Nomi sighed. It would be awkward for her, too.

"There's a lot we can't talk about."

"I know." They both fell silent for a moment. "But you can tell them all about Halcyone."

Ro smiled. "Not everything."

"No." Anything that veered toward Ithaka and Ada May was obviously off the flight path. But how Ro wrote the AI enhancements and how she and Jem figured out how to hook them into the original damaged program? That was clear skies.

It was going to be okay. It had to be.

"Come on," Nomi said. "The insti-synth is bad enough when it's hot."

"You get used to it after a while."

There were too many things Ro had had to get used to. If Nomi had anything to say about it, that was going to change. She stood up and tugged Ro after her and out of their quarters. "Come on. I want to see where we are."

The scent of the near-coffee wafted out into the corridor. At least it smelled like the real stuff. Barre handed them each a covered cup and Nomi inhaled deeply, savoring the moment before she took her first sip and broke the illusion.

Ro just took a large slug and set the cup down on a nearby console before conferring with Barre. "Halcyone, display current position."

The forward screen blinked to life with a starscape that reminded Nomi of the ansible display on Daedalus. She could well imagine each star as a lone node waiting for signal.

"Display Sasurau Prime. Scale out as needed to map course. Indicate current position and destination."

Ro's communication with Halcyone always seemed curt,

where Barre seemed to chat with the ship like it was just one of the crew. Nomi wondered if Halcyone felt the difference. Her grandfather would have said so. The screen flared momentarily as it recentered and redrew. A blinking yellow light in the upper right-hand corner of the screen made Nomi smile. Home.

It would be the first time her grandfather wouldn't be waiting at the spaceport to greet her since her first trip off-planet years ago. He had stopped taking jump flights decades before, convinced that he'd used up all his luck in the early days before temporal shielding had been perfected. It didn't matter that he was a brilliant engineer and had worked on the technology. Nor did it matter that he seemed to be one of the lucky ones who wasn't susceptible to jump-sickness.

He had always insisted on making sure she was whole and unscrambled, as he called it, when she disembarked.

"What's our ETA?"

Ro pressed her lips together and looked up at the display, though her gaze seemed to slide right through it.

"We need to decel and match orbit," Barre said.

The technical details of space travel flowed effortlessly from him, now. She smiled at the gifted musician who was also so much more than that.

"Probably thirty or less to touchdown."

A half hour for Ro to turn herself inside out with worry. Nomi curled into one of the command seats and contemplated her coffee while Ro checked the equations for the final leg of their journey. Nomi knew enough about navigation to know this trip wasn't anything Halcyone couldn't handle easily on her own, but it kept Ro occupied. She glanced up at Barre and he shrugged. There was nothing either of them could do for Ro, anyway. No matter how many crew were on board, every jump was one you took alone.

*

Halcyone followed a standard glide path to the tiny spaceport below, leaving Ro free to brood. The old freighter barely rocked as the docking clamps engaged. It switched over to port power and the lights in the bridge brightened to daylight standard.

"Look. If it's any consolation, the last thing I want is to be ferrying passengers all over the cosmos for our friend. You're the one who loves to fly. But you're also the only one who can sort through your father's data, and we need any advantage we can get."

Barre was right. And she still didn't like it.

Nomi stepped onto the bridge and Ro's dark mood evaporated. "Wow." She had changed out of her usual off-duty attire and into a floor-length kimono tied with a black sash. The dark floral print contrasted with her pale skin and highlighted the shine of her glossy hair. "You look amazing." Ro glanced down at her coverall and wiped at the dark stains she didn't remember getting.

"It's the only formal kimono I took with me to Daedalus. I didn't expect to need mourning clothes." Nomi's brown eyes welled up with tears.

"I think your grandfather would have understood," Barre said softly. "You ready?"

That should have been her saying all of that.

"You ready, Ro?" He was wearing a clean tunic and dark pants. His dreads were tied back in a neat bundle. Ro looked down at her grubby clothes again. When had he changed? And why hadn't he said anything to her sooner?

"Wait for me by the airlock. I'll just be a few minutes." Ro sprinted to her quarters and pulled out the few pieces of clothing she'd shoved into her bag. She stripped off the dirty coverall and stood in her underwear, frowning at the wrinkled shirts and pants strewn across the bed.

The door slid open.

"It doesn't matter what you wear," Nomi said. Her cheeks were red and she was out of breath. "They will honor you for bringing me home. For standing beside me. For supporting me."

Ro dressed in silence before stuffing her things back in the bag. At least there would be no random grease stains or rips in what she had on.

Nomi silently took Ro's hand as they headed to meet Barre at the airlock. Ro tried to slip free before they stepped off Halcyone, but Nomi shook her head and gripped tighter. Barre snickered behind them.

An automated kiosk just inside an airlock led into the spaceport proper. If it could even be called that on a colony this small. Barre checked them in and the door irised opened onto a small waiting area that was practically all windows. A handful of bays were arranged in a hub and spoke pattern and most of them were empty. Sunlight poured in from huge skylights overhead and Ro blinked furiously to accommodate to the brightness.

Several armed guards in Commonwealth military uniforms ignored a group of colonists across the waiting area who were queued up for a small passenger shuttle. Ro sucked in her breath when one of the guards glanced their way, but he looked past her in professional disinterest. It seemed overkill to even have soldiers in this sleepy port town.

"Did you tell your family we were coming?"

"Yes." Nomi's voice was very small.

"Hey!"

Ro pulled free of Nomi and whirled around, her heart pounding. A boy a little taller than Jem stood behind them smirking. He had wide, brown eyes and dark hair in a spacer's short brush cut. His outfit was nearly identical to Barre's, rather than the traditional Japanese outfit Nomi had worn.

"Gotcha!"

"Daisuke!" Nomi threw her arms around her little brother and squeezed him until he complained and squirmed loose.

"Mom! Dad! Found them!" His voice filled the waiting area. The guards looked their way and past again.

Ro wanted to hide back on Halcyone.

"You must be her girlfriend." Daisuke stared up at her with narrowed eyes. "You don't look like an engineer."

"You should see her after a day in the station's subsystems," Barre said, laughing before Ro could sputter her way through a response.

"And you're the musician. Cool!" The boy darted off, running halfway across the room to tug Nomi's parents toward them.

"Told you he was a pain," Nomi said, smiling.

"I didn't think anyone could be more annoying than Jem."

Nomi and Barre shared an amused look. "Gotta love little brothers," he said.

Then there was no more time for talking as Nomi's parents reached them, sweeping their daughter, Ro, and Barre into a whirlwind of greetings and hugs. Ro had to force herself not to pull away. She took slow, measured breaths and thought of the silence of interstitial space and the stillness of Halcyone's bridge at night.

At least no one seemed to notice her not talking, especially since Daisuke spoke enough for all of them. But Nomi's mother finally silenced her son with a stern look. The woman took both of Ro's hands in hers and bowed. She was wearing simple, casual clothing, but managed to imbue her actions with a sense of formality that made Ro feel small and grubby in comparison.

"Be welcome, Rosalen. Konomi has spoken very highly of you."

"It's a pleasure to meet you, Nakamura-sama."

The woman glanced at Nomi and raised an eyebrow and in the expression, Ro saw the striking similarity between mother and daughter.

Nomi matched her expression perfectly. "Don't blame me. That's all Ro."

"Please. We're certainly not that formal. I'm Azuki. My husband is Paul."

"Paul?"

"My wife's father—Nomi's late grandfather—was the traditional one," Paul Nakamura said. "I was raised on Earth. My family probably played ten generations of genetic roulette between my last full Japanese ancestor and me. Azuki puts up with me anyway." He had rounder eyes and a narrower face than his wife or his children did and a spray of freckles across his nose.

"I'm sure you're tired," Azuki said. "We have lunch waiting and then we'll show you your rooms."

"A delayed interrogation? How considerate." Nomi's eyes

nearly disappeared when she smiled and it made Ro smile in response.

"Thank you for your hospitality, but I won't be staying," Barre said. "I have a time-sensitive errand to run, but I'll be back to pick up Ro and Nomi in a few days."

He'd better be. If Barre let anything happen to Halcyone, she'd fly through a wormhole in a flitter to find him and make him pay.

"At least let us feed you," Paul said. "Azuki has had me chained in the kitchen all day. Besides, we're only a short ride from the spaceport. One of us can drop you back here whenever you're ready to leave."

"Better than three days of emergency rations," Nomi said. "If you're suitably appreciative, my dad'll even pack you leftovers."

"I'd definitely like that."

Nomi's parents and brother kept up a constant stream of casual conversation that Ro didn't even bother to try and follow. She watched Nomi stare out the transport's window. "You okay?"

"I'm glad you're here," Nomi said. "Will you come to my grandfather's shrine with me?"

No one close to Ro had ever died, until her father had blown up in a stolen ship. There had been an accident on one of the places he had been posted to long before Daedalus and two of the engineers had died. There hadn't been much of a ceremony. Their bodies had been cremated and their ashes jettisoned into space. She wasn't sure what to expect, but if Nomi needed her, Ro would be there.

"Here we are," Azuki said.

Ro stood beside the parked transport and stared at the house

Nomi had grown up in. No wonder she loved the hydroponics bays on Daedalus. A riot of greenery surrounded a snug, two-story home. Flowering vines twined around the railing along its wide, open porch. Ro closed her eyes on the bright colors and confusion for a moment, imagining herself back in the controlled environment of Daedalus Station with its moderated temperature and air.

The buzz of a drone swept past her ear and she opened her eyes to track it, before shaking her head. Of course it wasn't a drone. This was a planet. These were live pollinators. For all the efficiency of mechanical solutions, there was something powerful about watching the bees stagger from bloom to bloom.

"Home. Come on. Let me show you." Nomi snatched Ro's hand and pulled her off balance.

The Nakamura's house was fairly compact, but it was larger than any place Ro had ever lived. Filled with personal mementos, art, and family holos, it made her feel both envious and utterly out of place. The only things she owned, other than Halcyone, were a few changes of clothes, her micro, and the worn quilt she'd stubbornly kept with her since childhood.

Azuki pulled her away from Nomi's impromptu tour and handed her the bag she'd left in the transport. "You probably want to wash up. There's a WC through there and you can toss your bag in Nomi's old room." She turned to her daughter. "Help your father." Despite the woman's soft voice, it wasn't a request.

"I'll be in the kitchen if you need me." She held Ro's gaze for a moment before disappearing down the hallway.

"Nomi told me about your father."

Ro stiffened. Surely she hadn't told her folks that Alain Maldonado had been a sadistic misanthrope who kept his only child isolated and dependent on him her whole life. That she was glad he was dead.

"I'm sorry. Loss can be complicated."

There was a faraway look in Azuki's eyes and Ro realized she must be thinking about the recent loss of her own father. But Nomi had idolized her grandfather. Surely, there was nothing in the least complicated about the relationship in such a caring family. "Yes, it can be. My condolences."

"I'm glad Nomi has someone to lean on." Azuki opened the door to her daughter's childhood room and waved Ro inside. "She works hard to be self-sufficient, but she's always been close to her grandfather. It was difficult for both of them to be so far apart."

Ro was trying to figure out if there was a rebuke in Azuki's voice. Her first instinct was to snap back something about how if they'd been able to afford Nomi's University tuition, she'd never have had to sign on to the Commonwealth.

"I wanted her to stay in system, but my daughter has her grandfather's stubbornness. I'm sure you've noticed."

Nomi? Stubborn? Ro laughed. "She really hasn't told you much about me, has she?"

Azuki sat down on the bed and patted the blanket beside her. Ro would have preferred to stay standing on the opposite side of the room, but that would have been rude.

"I know she cares for you or she wouldn't have brought you here. Tell me about your family."

So much for Nomi's assurance that her mother would be overly polite. She sighed and glanced up at the open door, but there wasn't going to be any rescue. "Growing up, I didn't have any of this." Ro waved her hand, trying to take in the room, the house, Nomi's family. "I'm not an easy person to be around. But I couldn't scare Nomi away. Trust me. I tried."

She couldn't look at Azuki, afraid of seeing anger or disappointment in her expression. Digging her fingers into the soft green blanket, Ro thought of her quilt and how easily Nomi had smoothed it over her bed. Like it was nothing special. But it was everything to Ro.

"I'm saying this all wrong. My father was an abusive man." There. She said it. No hedging or equivocating. "He made me think I wasn't worth caring about."

Azuki drew a soft breath.

"Nomi taught me otherwise. And I would jump through an uncharted wormhole without a p-suit for her."

The woman patted Ro's arm, gently. "I think that will do." She stood up, the bed creaking. "Meet us in the dining room when you're ready. I hope you're hungry. Paul made a mountain of food."

"Thank you." But Azuki had already left the room, leaving Ro shaking with fear and relief.

Chapter 11

MICAH WAS SURE HE WASN'T going to be able to sleep in what was essentially a large metal box without any functioning air supply. The anemic breeze that blew warm air through the windows also brought dust, allergens, and toxic byproducts of combustion from all across the settlement. Halcyone wasn't much more than a metal box about as ancient as Dev's home, and even her life support systems were better than that.

How could people live like this?

How did Dev live like this?

He struggled to find a position on the thin mattress that didn't make his back ache, but that wasn't going to happen either. His stomach rumbled and he really hoped he wouldn't have to use the primitive head in the corner of the curtained off room. As far as he could tell, it was the only sanitary facility in the whole container which meant if anyone needed to relieve themselves, they would have to walk through the sleeping area.

It was going to be a long night.

Dev's brothers argued long after she had marched him back here and left to find her own rest. Or at least he thought it was an argument. It was hard to tell if the raised voices were from anger or just the aftereffects of alcohol. His focus wasn't all too clear, but even if he'd been fully sober, he wouldn't have been able to parse the foreign patois the brothers kept slipping in and out of.

The music of it finally lulled him into an uneasy sleep. He woke to bright sun pouring through the window, a full bladder, and a brutal headache blooming behind his eyes. The rhythmic buzz of snoring carried through the container. He checked his micro. Zero five hundred local time. Micah needed about another week of sleep before he'd be ready to face Midlant again. And an I.V. And a ship's hold full of coffee.

Groaning, he rolled to his side and slowly forced himself upright. The room spun a few times. His stomach heaved. He took several deep breaths through his mouth, waiting for everything to settle before shuffling to the head.

He sat to empty his bladder and leaned against the counter beside the toilet. The head was as small as the ones on Halcyone, but primitive. There was, at least, rudimentary plumbing and the water tap worked. He could hear the flow in the exposed pipes overhead. They must have had a small pump that moved the water from the barrel in the kitchen. Watching Dev's brother hand-pump water to fill it last night had been like something out of a history vid.

"Oi! Finish up in there!" one of Dev's brothers shouted from the other side of the thin pocket door. He hadn't yet figured out how to tell Tanner apart from Vic. Giles looked a lot like Dev, so it was easier, but he hadn't sorted out their voices.

"Sorry. I'll just be a minute." Micah splashed the lukewarm water on his face and rinsed out his dry mouth. His toiletries were still packed and he would have to sneak back here to clean up properly. "All yours." He opened the door to find Giles squatting by his bed, looking through his travel bag.

It wasn't as if there was anything in there of value or that warranted privacy, and his micro was locked to anyone shy of Ro's hacking skills, but that wasn't the point. Just as he was about to confront Giles, Dev came barreling in through the half-opened curtain and smacked the back of her brother's head. He overbalanced and went sprawling on the threadbare rug.

"Get out. Now."

"But I need to use the head!"

"Go piss in a patch of poison ivy."

"Fine." He scrambled to his feet and shrugged. "Jumper's got sleek cover. Worth a heavy pocket at the market."

Dev stood, her spine rigid, pointing to the door. "He's our guest and you are an idiot."

They both waited as Giles stomped out of the container. Micah wanted to apologize, but he wasn't sure why or for what.

"About my brothers —"

"It's okay."

"The hell it is!" Dev whirled to face him, picked up his bag, and threw it at him. "Pack up. I'm taking you back to school."

"Excuse me?" He had pushed her to talk to her brothers. And he was the one who forced her to keep her promise and take him here. The thought of an air-conditioned, filtered transport and a quick ride back to civilization should have had him practically salivating, but two things were clear: she had unfinished business with her family, and Micah wasn't going to leave without getting bittergreen samples. "Can't take a little rudeness? I didn't think anything made Dev Morningstar back down."

She paced the length of the small sectioned-off room. Like Micah, she had fallen asleep in yesterday's travel clothes. Her hair was a spiky mess and her eyes were red-rimmed. "This isn't my place anymore."

"That's bullshit. You make whatever place you're in yours. I learned that as a kid. And you know it even better than I do. Look at what you've done at Uni."

"Yeah. I'm a good little statistic for our esteemed institution. I even talk fluent Standard. Aren't I special? Settlement girl makes good. Well, I'm sick and tired of being someone else's public-relations pawn."

"And what does fleeing Midlant prove?"

"How dare you lecture me. You've been running away from your past faster and harder than I ever could." Her face was as red as if she'd been out working in the heat of midday. "You're hiding from money and power and influence. Everything anyone unlucky enough to be born in a settlement would kill to have." She stepped up to him and poked him in the chest. "You wouldn't have lasted a day growing up here."

"You're probably right." And that wasn't the point. This wasn't about him. He got that now. Coming here had little to do with his need to understand settlement life and everything to do with understanding Dev.

He set his bag down on the bed and sat beside it. "Look. I feel like I came out of the wrong side of a jump. Can we argue about this later?"

"Fine." Dev strode past him and into the head.

Micah changed quickly while she was cleaning up and was tying his shoes when she emerged rubbing damp hair with a towel. "Do you need me to wait outside while you change?"

She glanced at him sideways. "I grew up here. With three brothers and no privacy. I think I can manage."

They had led such different lives. As an only child, Micah always had his privacy. A room of his own. Plenty of solitude. He resisted the impulse to look away as Dev slipped her shirt off and walked back to her room. Her deeply tanned shoulders contrasted with the white fabric of her tank top. The thin straps revealed her well-muscled back and arms.

"I don't have the kind of strength you do."

Dev paused, but didn't turn around.

"But I do understand complicated families." He dragged his hands through his short hair. "Your brothers love you. No matter what you think. Sometimes, the people closest to you can't tell you that." He thought about his father. The late senator had loved Micah, in his strange, selfish way.

Micah grabbed his toiletries and, after washing up, waited on the edge of the bed for Dev to finish changing.

"So you want us to stay." She stood in front of him, hands on her hips.

"Yes."

"Here, in the Settlement."

"Yes."

"With my brothers."

"Yes."

"Fine." There was the slightest upturn at the corners of her lips.

"Fine." He struggled to match the exact tone of her reply and not to laugh, but he couldn't keep a straight face. Her laughter joined his.

"I was wrong about you, Micah. You probably would have gotten yourself elected mayor of Midlant if you'd grown up here."

He fell silent and stared past her toward the window. She wasn't the only one with unfinished family business, but at least she had family still alive. "Yeah, well, we already had one Rotherwood in public office and it was more than the cosmos should've had to deal with."

At least she had the consideration not to push any further.

"If we're staying, we should track down some breakfast."

He followed her through the container toward the door. Giles was still out and would stay away for a while, if he was smart. Micah was betting he was smart. There was no sign of Dev's other brothers. There was also no sign of the half dozen or so empty bottles from the wine they'd gone through last night.

Micah winced when Dev opened the door and light flooded in.

"No sympathy. Next time you won't try to keep up with my brothers." She stepped off the makeshift porch and scampered down the ladder as Micah waited, wiping his damp hands on the fabric of his pants. The ability to feel through his feet hadn't completely returned. Both Dr. Durbins had warned him that his sensation might always be impaired. Walking on level ground wasn't a problem, but there was no way he could descend gracefully. He gripped the handrails and carefully watched where he placed each foot. By the time he'd touched ground, Micah was dizzy and sweating. Up had definitely not been as difficult.

But then again, yesterday he hadn't been hungover.

Dev only smiled "Come on. I know where to get the best bread in Midlant."

"What about coffee?"

"I'll see what I can do."

She led them on what to Micah was an incomprehensible route. He pulled up a mapping application on his micro and wasn't terribly surprised to see a blurred outline of Midlant and nothing more.

"How do you find your way anywhere?"

"I could tell you, but then I'd have to kill you."

Micah kept swiveling his head from side to side, not because he had any hope of retracing their steps, but because he wanted to take it all in. And he still couldn't believe bittergreen just grew wild on the sides of the road and in any empty lot.

"Why doesn't anyone sell it?"

"Bittergreen? It's everywhere. There's no market here."

He stopped short and fanned his hand over the spiky leaves. Could he tell her? "Dev, there's a fortune in that hedge if someone could smuggle it out of the settlement. Unless it's not potent. Wait. Is it the cartels? Are people afraid of the cartels?"

"Afraid?" She narrowed her eyes, but in confusion, not anger. "Why would we be afraid of the cartels?"

Micah could think of a hundred reasons, and too many of them had connections to the guns his father and Ro's had been attempting to smuggle on Halcyone.

"No one's afraid of the cartels here. Hell, they hand out the high-grade bittergreen for free."

"Wait. What?"

The scent of freshly baked bread made Micah's mouth water.

He could guess which of the containers was the bakery, but there was no need. A queue of people wrapped around it to the street behind.

"Come on!" Dev tugged at his hand, pulling him to the back of the line. "We got here early enough. They haven't run out yet."

"It's not even oh six hundred!"

"But it's Stoltzfus's bread."

Within a minute, there were other people lining up behind them, chatting to one another in the Midlant dialect. Micah could pick out one word in maybe five. And even for the words he understood, he lacked enough context. He wanted to press Dev for more information about the cartels. About bittergreen. But it was too public here.

The queue moved slowly, but steadily. The smell of the bread made Micah's mouth water and his stomach rumble.

Dev laughed. "Worth it."

"Vray," he answered. One of the words he'd figured out. She nodded her approval.

Then it was their turn. Micah reached for his micro to pay for the two loaves of bread Dev bought, but she shook her head. She passed several slips of paper currency to the woman standing between the container and a large, rickety table heaped with unwrapped loaves of bread before pulling him out of the line.

She tore off a hunk and handed it to him. "Here."

It was still warm. Micah hesitated, even as his stomach growled again. The bread had been exposed to who knows how many microbes and pathogens. The container. The table. The woman's hands. Midlant itself. It had been a struggle to finish last night's meal as soon as he realized it wasn't vat-grown chicken he was eating. The shape of the wing and the gusto with which the Morningstars had attacked the meal had unnerved him.

But this was bread. Not a living animal that was slaughtered to feed him. He took the piece from Dev's hand. The crust crackled as he took a bite, and the bread had a slightly sour tang he couldn't place. But it was delicious. Better than anything they served at Uni. Better than anything he'd eaten on Daedalus.

"Wow," he said, stopping short in the middle of the street.

Smiling, Dev tugged him across to an empty lot with some scattered benches. "Stoltzfus's sourdough. It's famous across all of Midlant."

They sat and finished one loaf and most of the second. Micah still wanted coffee, but for now, it was pleasant to sit here in the early morning sun, while the air was still cool.

"So. The cartels. Are they active here? What about Commonwealth patrols?" It didn't make a lot of sense. If they weren't selling bittergreen, there was no reason for them to have a presence. And why would they give the drug away?

She gave him a puzzled look. "You still don't get it, do you."

"Get what?"

"This isn't the Commonwealth. This is Midlant. Where do you think the cartels started?"

"What do you mean?"

"Look around you. This. Is. Not. The. Commonwealth." Dev paused and relaxed her hiked-up shoulders. Started again. "Yes, officially, we exist within the Commonwealth. But the reality is, each settlement acts as a sovereign space. With its own ways of keeping the peace.

"After the Commonwealth Guard initially set up the first tent cities, it was stretched too thin to do anything more than protect food and water shipments."

Micah couldn't imagine how chaotic that must have been. "And your grandparents were settled here?"

"If by settled, you mean forced into a tent at gunpoint? Then yes."

"Fuck." That was definitely not the story he had learned.

"They were lucky. Midlant ended up being one of the better organized settlements. There was a large contingent of Pennsylvania Dutch here who suddenly found their skills in high demand." Dev shrugged. "But the inhabitants needed a hell of a lot more than what a bunch of plain farmers or the Commonwealth could provide. So they organized. Formed mutual protection societies."

"The cartels?"

"Yes."

Micah stood and paced. "But they're drug dealers. Gun smugglers." Among other things. They had trapped his father in a web of illegal activities that stretched across the galaxy and ultimately led to his death.

"Who do you think funded the schools? Made sure widows and orphans got enough to eat? Kept looting and hording to a manageable minimum? Organized food disbursements? It sure as shit wasn't the Commonwealth.

"And later, they formed the clearinghouses for temp work off-settlement. Sure, they took a cut, but they also kept the employers honest and mediated any disputes."

"And the bittergreen?"

Dev canted her head. "I wouldn't have pegged you as a user. Why the fascination?"

He walked to the fence line of the empty lot and yanked one

of the leggy plants out of the ground. Dirt trailed in clumps from the exposed roots. "This shit ruined my life."

It was such a simple plant. A weed that grew quickly and under any number of growing conditions, producing a leaf that when roasted and steeped in hot water had mild hallucinogenic, pain relieving, and anxiolitic properties.

"You do know they discovered the drug part by accident, right?"

He shook his head.

"The Commonwealth initially developed it to prevent soil erosion. They planted it in the settlements to see what it would do. And then it took over everywhere, but there was no way to effectively get rid of it, short of a scorched earth campaign. So the folks here started figuring out ways to use it."

"Space me." A fucking accident. The drug he'd gotten for his dying mother. The drug that gave the cartels a way in to blackmail his father. A fucking accident.

"Waste not, want not. The Settlement way."

Micah tore apart the bittergreen stalk and ground the leaves under his feet. Then he sat down and rested his head in his hands. They smelled of greenery and dirt. Familiar smells. Comforting smells.

"What's wrong?"

And he told her. In a muffled and halting voice he told her about his mother, in unremitting pain from the disease that ultimately killed her. And how as a young boy, he bought bittergreen to ease her suffering, but he'd been recognized and the cartel chief had trapped his father in a web of illegal activity. Because of him. All for a drug that grew wild here, everywhere he looked.

"I've spent my whole life trying to reverse engineer commercial bittergreen to break the cartel's monopoly on the drug." He lifted his head, but didn't want to meet Dev's gaze. "It's why I became a botanist. It's why I wanted the biodome. I wanted to hurt them the only way I knew how. I'm an idiot."

"Oh, Micah."

He stared past her, not wanting her pity.

"You do realize that bittergreen is the smallest part of the cartel's income stream. They control the contracts between the settlements and any organization that might want to hire its labor—municipalities, corporations, mining colonies, you name it."

Of course it was. Part of him probably always knew it.

"There are finite ways of getting out of the settlement and the cartels directly control almost all of them."

Micah ticked them off on imaginary fingers: temp work on planet, temp work off-planet, bittergreen production, and smuggling. "Which ones don't they control?"

"Getting a scholarship or dying."

For several long minutes, they sat together silently. Micah brushed off his hands and stood. "Well, what should we do next?"

*

Jem's micro buzzed for the umpteenth time this morning. It was time to deal with Ada May and this was as private a place as any. Unless there was some kind of medical crisis, no one would kick him out of the exam room and there was little chance Targill would come here.

He sent a brief update to Ro, Nomi, and Barre through the secure messaging program. Not that they could do anything about it, but they needed to know. Then he glanced at the increasingly agitated messages from Ada May.

He didn't know what to tell her. If the LC didn't want to communicate, nothing Jem could say was going to change that. Ada would be better off giving the woman space to heal and to grieve. But he was just a kid. What did he know? And even if her messages were as secure as she could make them, there was always a risk of discovery, particularly the more of them she sent.

The last message in the queue was from Gutierrez.

/Are you available?/

Well, at least it was a request. And it would give him a chance to sound her out about Targill. Available. Jem was nothing but available. His parents still wouldn't release him to begin school again.

/Yes/

He swallowed his morning dose of the neo-benzos and engaged Ro's ghost protocol before heading from medical to Gutierrez's quarters. Even if anyone pinged Daedalus for his location, it wouldn't betray his presence. Ro would probably be amused that he was using it on the LC's behalf.

Now that shift change was over, the corridors were quiet once more. He glanced around, but the few people traveling through the station weren't paying him any attention. As before, as soon as he reached Gutierrez's door, it slid open.

She was still wearing her uniform, but had removed her sidearm. It lay on the table in its holster next to her damaged limb. Gutierrez sat sideways, her long legs draped over the chair's arms in what looked like relaxation, but was silent vigilance. Her booted feet swung with the precision of one of Barre's metronomes.

"What's the plan for today?" Jem asked as he sank into the couch opposite her.

"What did Marchand say to you?" Nothing changed in her body or her position, but there was an orange cast to her voice that hadn't been there before.

Jem didn't think that was the important question. "Why is Targill on-station?"

"What did Marchand want?"

"Your guess is as good as mine." As she glared at him, he added, "Sir." It was easier being here when Gutierrez wasn't in her Commonwealth uniform.

"What is your best guess?" With each swing, her boot heels drummed on the side of her chair as if counting out seconds of his silence.

He wished Ro were here so he could ask her what to say. What to do. "That it had something to do with the data we gathered on Lowell." Which led right to Targill. A shiver moved through him.

Gutierrez's eyes narrowed and she looked even more like some kind of hunting cat. "Data. Explain."

Space me. He was sure she already knew about that. But she'd been in bad shape on Charon's ship when he and Nomi had released the worm into the comms computer, and she'd been in medical recovering ever since. How much trouble would he be in with Ro now? And worse, what did Targill know? Why was he here?

"We were looking into connections between Lowell and Ro's

dad. We found them."

Gutierrez moved with the grace of a dancer, or a trained soldier, despite the missing arm. Leaning forward in the chair now, she locked her gaze on Jem. "But that's not all you found."

He sighed. "No. But you're not going to like it."

"I already don't like it."

There was nothing to be gained from holding back. Gutierrez was an ally. A reluctant one, to be sure, but an ally. "Lowell was patrolling both sides of the wormhole. While he was trading intelligence with Maldonado and flirting with the smugglers, he was also getting paid ..." He swallowed hard. "By our friend Targill."

She drew her breath in sharply. "Are you certain?"

"Yes."

"And Marchand? What's his interest?"

"We gave him a copy of what we found."

"Fuck." Her voice got dangerously low. "And why would you do that?"

Jem fiddled with his micro, flipping it over and over as he thought. If he kept her in the dark, then it was as if they trusted Marchand more than Gutierrez. Gutierrez worked with Ada May. That meant they were on the same side. Right? He glanced down at the floor and took a deep breath.

"Because he tried to help Nomi when the commander had her arrested. Because he doesn't trust Lowell either. Because the Commonwealth either already knows about Lowell's spying, or is complicit in it and we need all the help we can get." He drew his legs up on the sofa. What a cosmic mess. "I was figuring Marchand was connected with you. With her." With Ithaka, though Jem didn't like naming it out loud. Not in the station proper.

"He's not one of ours."

"Then which side is he on?"

For a brief second, Gutierrez's guarded expression shifted to an uncharacteristic uncertainty. "You're assuming there are only two sides."

He rubbed his forehead, hoping to stave off an incipient headache.

"I need a copy of that information, Jem. I really do." Her voice was gentle. A request, rather than a demand.

She already had the original of Ro's father's memory cube, even if she didn't have the key to unlock it. Jem couldn't think of any reason not to share what they had on Lowell with her. Hell, Mendez had a copy. Jem drew his breath in sharply. Was that why she'd disappeared and Targill came to take over her command? Had she triggered the wrong ansible node? "Fine. I can bump it to you."

When she nodded, Jem picked up his micro and pushed the data-file to her machine. It buzzed again with another message from Ada May.

"You can't avoid talking to her forever."

Gutierrez glared at him but said nothing.

"At least tell her you're okay. If you don't, she'll just keep messaging me. Every contact is risky. You know that. Especially now."

"Tell her ... Tell her I'll contact her when I'm ready." Gutierrez's soft voice vibrated with a blur of colors.

"You need to tell her. Yourself." Jem didn't understand their history. He only knew that Gutierrez, May, and Odachi had been together at the start. That there was some old bad blood between the LC and the man they called the Ferryman. Barre was right— she needed to talk to someone, but Jem knew she wouldn't. She would hold all her hurt and grief in and one day, her containment field would fail and it would all explode.

His parents had taught him well. He could bind wounds and soothe burns and provide more than basic life support, but he was just a kid and Gutierrez needed help he didn't know how to give.

She didn't acknowledge his refusal, but she scooped up her micro and set it in her lap. While she composed a note, Jem called up the prosthetic's schematic and let it fill his mind's eye. Of all the problems orbiting them, this was one he could solve, or at least come close to solving. He pushed aside his worry about Targill and Marchand for now while he matched the schematic to the limb stretched out on the table so he could create an overlay.

The access trigger had burned out along with almost all the other relays, so he had to use the magnifying loupes and find the smallest screwdriver to work the manual release. The top compartment of the forearm opened with a soft click. Jem straightened out the elbow and worked on the upper arm. Once the entire limb was splayed open, he returned to the schematic.

Even after they had run new filament, there was so much left to do. Entire microcircuit boards were going to need to be swapped out; if she'd done as much customization as Jem suspected, they were going to have to craft new ones.

When Gutierrez finally broke the silence, Jem started, nearly dropping the tiny tools he was holding.

"I'm sorry. Don't worry about Targill. He's not your concern."

"Does that mean he's yours?"

Gutierrez gave him a sharp look. There had to be a reason she'd been tracking Cam Lowell all this time. Was finding Targill the reason? Jem didn't want to talk about this any more than she did. "If I have to make all new components, this is going to take a lot longer than I thought."

Silence again. Followed by the smallest of sighs. He didn't know if it was relief or disappointment. Gutierrez leaned over the table. "The joint gimbals are stock and so is the neural link transmitter. We can start with those."

"What about the kinesthetic stabilizers?"

"Custom. As are the input/output modules."

Jem removed the loupe and put down the tools. "I think we're doing this the wrong way."

"So you are suddenly an expert in cutting-edge prosthetics. Good to know."

"Save the sarcasm. I'm trying to help you."

Gutierrez turned aside and Jem had to clench his teeth to avoid apologizing.

"Look. You're the expert here. Not me. I'm just an extra set of hands." He glanced up, hoping to catch her gaze. "Literally."

She didn't turn back, but her shoulders relaxed.

"And I really need both of yours to make this work. So here's my idea. I replace all the damaged parts with stock ones. We reconnect the limb." Though he suspected they'd need his parents' help with that. She probably wasn't going to be happy. "Then you reintegrate. Once you have two functioning arms, you can help with the fabrication and we replace the relevant components piecemeal."

This time she did meet his gaze. The circles beneath her eyes looked like bruises. "Do you have any idea how hard it is to start from scratch?"

He traced the scar buried in his thick short-cropped hair with his right hand. "Actually, I do."

"Point taken. Fine. Let's get to work."

Using her knowledge and the parts diagram on the schematic, they made a list of what they needed. Some of the components she already had in an old repair kit. Others were universal and Jem could swipe them from medical. A few they had to order. He let Gutierrez handle that, since there'd be a record.

After about an hour, Jem's left eye began to twitch. He filed the schematic away and let his mind go blank. "I think that's all I got for now. Sorry."

Again, Gutierrez let the silence build up between them. Her gaze was distant and her face unreadable. "You have nothing to apologize for, Jem."

He straightened up their work space and resealed the limb's compartments, feeling guilty for his lack of stamina. Her gratitude was harder to accept than her curt orders or her disappointment.

As he rose to leave, she stood to follow him to the door. "Be careful of Marchand. He's never shown up on my sensors before."

Jem had no doubt that the man would register on them now. He almost felt sorry for him. "I'll raid medical after my mother leaves."

"Good."

That could have been agreement with Jem's plans, or acknowledgment that his mother was a formidable opponent. Maybe both. As he headed back to his quarters, he wondered if

Leta Durbin would have let the LC leave AMA. It was probably a good thing these two strong women hadn't gone head to head.

Chapter 12

After lunch, while Nomi's father was packing him food, Barre pulled Ro aside. She had been quiet and polite through the excellent meal. He knew her well enough to know how far off course all of this had knocked her.

"She's your ship. She'll always be your ship," he said, as the two of them walked through the small garden behind the house.

"I know that. And I trust you. It's just …" She shook her head.

They walked along a path traced out with small stones that took them in and out of the shadows of small trees. Ro kept her face averted, but it wasn't hard to read the tension in her rigid spine and her heavy footfalls.

"Just bring her back in one piece, okay?"

"I'll do my best." He guided them to a bench beside a small created waterfall. "This isn't a job I asked for."

"I know."

Barre could trace the course of every single choice he'd made from the day he drank the tainted bittergreen and his parents' very real threat of mandatory rehab, to Jem hiding him on Halcyone, to where they were today—front and center in a conspiracy that had started decades before any of them were born. But that didn't make his new role and his new life any easier to understand. He was a musician. Now he had to be a covert operative in a war no one admitted was being waged.

Ro placed a hand, small and light, on his forearm. "Be careful. I know May isn't our enemy, but if it comes down to a choice between us and Ithaka ..."

"She's as close to a friend as we've got out there, Ro." The cosmos was turning out to be a far more complicated place than he'd ever imagined.

"Go get your care package and get out of here. The sooner you finish May's errand, the sooner you get back here and the sooner we get home."

She was staring back at the house. Barre smiled. "I think you'd rather explore uncharted wormholes than go back in there."

She just shrugged.

"Well, keep me posted about your dad's files."

"Don't let May bully you."

As Paul Nakamura drove him back to the spaceport, Barre mulled over Ro's warning. Ada May was their ally, but the old computer scientist was also using them for her own ends. He wished he knew what they were.

There was security in the little spaceport, but the officers seemed bored by their jobs. One armed man waved him through to the transient berths and toward the automated kiosk that had checked them in. That seemed lax, but Barre had no doubt the Commonwealth knew who and where they were. He only hoped his leaving wouldn't trigger anyone's curiosity. He'd already laid in a sham course that had him buying some repair components for Halcyone. Given that she was such an old ship, that wasn't unusual.

The AI opened the airlock for him and welcomed him back with a brief musical fanfare before he signaled her. He patted the bulkhead next to the door. "Glad to be back, too."

The door sealed with a click. Barre stowed his care package in the galley before walking to the bridge. His footfalls echoed in the corridor. It was strange being here alone. It wasn't that he didn't work on board solo all the time, but usually Ro or Nomi or Jem were a ping away.

"Well, it's just you and me, this time," he said, looking at the dark bridge display, its crack a vivid reminder of Halcyone's violent past.

He completed the pre-flight check, creating a flight plan to the nearest stable wormhole. Once he got off-world, he could run the Ithaka nav hack and contact Ada May to find out where in the cosmos she needed him to go. And why. If she would actually tell him.

As he busied himself with the now routine work of piloting the ship, he let his thoughts drift back to the enigmatic scientist. Her blue eyes sparkled with intelligence. A clever and creative mind lived in her slight frame. She had survived the war that had nearly destroyed Halcyone forty years ago. That war had martyred Charles Dauber, her friend and partner in creating the SIREN source code that made the first true AIs possible.

She had been responsible for the birth of artificial intelligences and also nearly for their death, coding a kill virus for the Commonwealth during the war. That she had crippled it and sabotaged the supposed immunity of the Commonwealth computers was not known, outside of Halcyone's crew. Nor did most of the universe know she was very much alive and the leader of a quietly subversive rebellion.

Ro didn't trust her, even as she wanted to idolize her. In his little brother's eyes, she was a supernova. Barre wanted to believe May was on their side. He'd seen the real woman behind the legend. Had understood her sadness and regret.

Halcyone broke into his thoughts with a quiet melody. The forward screen glowed with a star chart. They were orbiting their target wormhole.

Barre played a musical trigger directly to Halcyone through his neural. She requested confirmation to reboot the nav system and he gave it. The ship's lights dimmed slightly; the screen redrew.

"Navigation ready."

Time to contact Ada May.

He pulled up a virtual window from his micro and composed a message. Some things were still simpler to do the old fashioned way.

/Halcyone and I are at your service. What's the plan?/

The ship settled into a wide orbit around the wormhole and as they waited, Barre pushed the last piece he'd been composing to the bridge speakers. Hearing the music resonate through the air made it less lonely somehow than playing it through his neural. At least Halcyone was listening with him.

The music stuttered. Barre blinked. That wasn't supposed to happen.

"Halcyone, run diagnostic on ..."

Without any warning, the forward display winked off and on

again, but instead of recalibrating and showing him the starscape outside, Ada May appeared in the center.

"This will definitely be simpler," she said, smiling.

"Dr. May!"

"Guilty as charged." It looked like she was sitting in her room on Ithaka, nearly swallowed up by the large, high-backed chair. "If we're going to be working together, we need a way to talk in real time. So I took the liberty of making a connection between Lethe and Halcyone using the ansible network."

"Hijacking it, you mean."

"Technicalities, young man."

She winked at him and Barre had to laugh.

May was like a future version of Ro. Which probably explained a lot about their relationship.

"A caveat. It has several limitations." As May leaned forward, her hair glinted silver in the reading light's glow. "It can only be triggered after you've enabled the Ithaka nav program, and you need to ping me with a text first. Otherwise, Lethe can't track you."

Ro would likely have something to say about that, but she wasn't here and May's hack would make it easier to get this over with. "And you're certain we're secure?"

May raised an eyebrow. Barre shrugged. He had to ask. Even of her. That was the level of paranoia they'd been forced to live with.

"Fine. So what in the cosmos is so important that you needed me to risk Ro's fury?" He tried to keep his tone light, but some of his frustration probably leaked through.

After a brief silence, May nodded. "First, I appreciate your efforts on Emma's behalf. She is alive because of you. You have my thanks."

He was his parents' son—what else could he have done?

"We are in your debt."

Her use of "we" felt very formal.

"Now, as to your errand." May rested back against the chair, her face falling into shadow. "I have a set of coordinates that should be familiar to you. I need you to go there and act as our ferryman." Her voice softened. The Ferryman—Taro Odachi—had died saving Gutierrez and Dev. Barre had only met the enigmatic man once and briefly at that, but he and Gutierrez had been with Ada May from the start of Ithaka's covert insurrection.

"I'm not him," Barre said gently.

"I know. But you're here and I trust you."

Barre exhaled heavily. "I'll do my best."

"Of course you will." She paused to access her micro. "I'm transmitting the information directly to Halcyone. I don't need to tell you to be careful. To be discreet."

No, but she reminded him, anyway.

"Don't attempt to initiate communication with me when you're en route, unless it's a dire emergency. Especially once your passenger is on board."

That was interesting.

"And Barre?"

He looked into her bright blue eyes as she leaned forward into the light again.

"I was right about you, young man. You are remarkable."

Barre's cheeks warmed at the compliment, but before he could say anything, the screen blanked briefly and was replaced by the starscape outside. "Okay, Halcyone, let's see where our friend is sending us. How about you plot a course and show me."

A ripple of light moved through the display as Halcyone replaced the external view with the map view. The wormhole near Sasurau was circled at the left of the screen. Her proposed course would take them through three additional jumps, each with interstitial burns connecting them. At the top right-hand corner was their destination. Barre narrowed his eyes and stepped closer.

"Halcyone, show coordinates of destination."

A set of numbers glowed next to the circled system.

"Holy mother of the cosmos."

They were the same numbers Ro had received from May before. He was certain of it. The coordinates led to a smuggler's base—and the last time they'd been there, they had to threaten to blast their way free. May couldn't be serious.

"Halcyone, did Ada May send any other data with the coordinates?"

After a small beep of acknowledgment, a text file showed up on his micro. It consisted of two words. Just a name. And no explanation.

Cameron Lowell.

Barre swore at the glowing words and then looked back at the flight plan. This was turning into a clusterfuck of galactic proportions.

*

After Barre left, Ro continued to sit on the bench staring at the fountain. The burble of water and the buzz of insects helped her mind stay safely blank. Going inside meant risking more conversation with Nomi's mother and facing the fact that Barre had taken her ship.

She only realized Nomi had come to sit beside her when she felt a light touch on her arm.

"You okay?"

"Your family is very kind." Ro understood why Nomi was so eager to come home.

"I told you they'd like you."

"Grease stains and all?" She wanted to keep things light for Nomi's sake.

"Yes. But you clean up nice." Nomi interlaced her long fingers in Ro's more squared-off ones before lifting their joined hands to her lips.

There were so many things Ro wanted to say: That she didn't deserve this kind of love. That Nomi deserved better. But that was old programming. Junk code Nomi was helping her to rewrite.

"Do you need to rest for a while?"

There was a tightness to Nomi's voice that meant more than the casual words. Ro studied her face, noticed the distant look in her normally sparkling eyes.

"No. Is there something ... what do you need?" Ro cringed at how blunt and direct she sounded.

"I want to say goodbye to my grandfather."

"I'm sorry I didn't get a chance to meet him."

"So am I." She stood and pulled Ro up after her.

"Wait. Should I change?" If Nomi said yes, Ro wasn't sure she had anything suitable to change in to, but asking felt like the right thing to do.

"You're fine. My folks aren't hung up on traditional ways. Neither was Sofu, really. But he did hold on to some things."

Nomi smoothed the front of her kimono. She leaned down to pick a few bright purple flowers before walking Ro back inside the house, past the open kitchen and into a living area Ro hadn't yet seen. If she could ignore the natural sunlight pouring through the large windows, Ro could have been in any of the living spaces on Daedalus. A sofa and two chairs faced a small closed cabinet nestled between two windows.

"You can sit here," Nomi said. She bit her lower lip as she glanced across the room.

"What?"

"It's probably going to seem weird to you. That's our family shrine." She sighed. "My grandparents didn't really follow Buddhist practices. Not strictly, anyway. But along with the traditional names, Sofu wanted us to have a shrine. His ashes are inside. In a truly Buddhist household, there would be incense burning and flowers." Nomi glanced at the blooms in her hands.

Ro stood and took one of the stems.

Nomi smiled, blinking back tears, and opened the cabinet doors. Inside was a carved statue overlooking a wide shelf. On a white cloth covering the shelf sat a plain metal urn.

"Oh, Sofu," she whispered. Then she bowed and placed the flowers beside her grandfather's ashes. Ro did the same.

What would it have been like to have had a family? To have grandparents and siblings and parents to care for? Her father had taken all that from her, before she even had known what was possible. It didn't matter that she had never known Nomi's grandfather. It mattered even less that she didn't know how to grieve. She would wait for as long as Nomi needed her.

"Thank you," Nomi said, softly. She closed the shrine's doors before sighing. "I'm going to miss him."

Ro didn't know what to say, so she kept silent. Until now, she had never thought about anyone missing her, mourning her. It was an uncomfortable idea. A shiver moved through her, as if she'd stepped from the sun side to the night side of Daedalus.

"Are you okay?"

"Hey, I'm supposed to ask you that," Ro said, forcing a smile on her face.

"Come on. Enough sadness. I need to change out of these formal clothes and I want to show you around."

"Around where?"

Nomi's smile gave nothing away. "Around. I thought you'd be curious about where I grew up."

This was more than a social trip. Ro tapped her fingers against the hard surface of the micro tucked in a pocket. Her father's data was waiting for her to make some sense out of it. And she was hoping to enlist Nomi in the task.

"It's just a walk. How often do you have a chance at real sunshine and real air?" Nomi's voice held a quiet teasing, but there was also an edge to it.

"Sorry."

"Stop that," Nomi said. "Look. Just wait for me in the kitchen. There's coffee on. Real stuff."

Ro swore to herself, hating how easily she slipped back into being her father's daughter.

There was coffee in the kitchen, and Nomi's mother, too. Ro stood at the threshold wondering if the one was worth risking the other.

"Come in, my dear," Azuki Nakamura said. She sat on a high stool by the counter. A micro projected several virtual windows at her eye level. Steam from the cup beside her turned the displays into patterns of light and shadow. "Help yourself to some coffee."

"Thank you." Ro was glad Azuki didn't get up to serve her.

"Cream is in the chiller. Do you sweeten it?"

Ro shook her head and poured herself a cup.

"I hope you don't mind—I'm in the middle of something." She gestured at the displays with graceful hands. Hands just like Nomi's.

"Not at all. I'm just waiting for Nomi to change."

Azuki had already turned back to her work, completely ignoring her. Ro smiled. For the first time since coming here, she felt at home.

"Ready?" Nomi had slipped into the kitchen behind her and wrapped her arms around Ro's shoulders.

Nodding, Ro set the cup in the sink. Nomi's mother didn't look up from where she was frowning at the overlapping windows. Ro found that strangely comforting.

As they stepped out of the house, Nomi's little brother came running up to them. "Hey! Where you going? Can I come?"

"Nowhere and no," Nomi said.

"Come on, Nomi. You promised to tell me all about the station and Halcyone. I have a model of that exact freighter." He turned to Ro without taking a breath. "Do you want to see my collection? I have every class of ship from the first experimental jumpers to modern dreadnoughts."

"Daisuke. Go. Away."

Ro couldn't help it. She laughed. Seeing Nomi so annoyed with her little brother reminded her of how Ro had tried to keep Jem away. How much his enthusiasm made Ro want to stuff him outside the nearest airlock on more occasions than she could count.

While Nomi glared at her, Ro got her amusement under control. "I'd be happy to, Daisuke. But I think your sister already has plans for this afternoon."

The boy sighed and his shoulders slumped. "It's just that I missed you and you promised and you're going to leave again in a few days."

"It's okay, Nomi. We can walk after dinner."

Her eyes widened and then she smiled. "Fine. Go make sure your room is habitable. We'll be up in a few minutes."

As he thundered back through the house, Nomi turned to Ro and opened her mouth to speak. Ro put up her hand to stop her. "If he's anything like Jem, putting him off will only make it worse."

"I was trying to keep him from pestering you."

"Too late. Besides, there's only so much unmediated weather this spacer can handle."

"Fine. We'll humor Daisuke. Then I guess I'll have to humor you."

"Excuse me?"

"Like I don't know all you want to do is dig into your father's data."

Ro's face flushed. "It's not the only reason I came here, but Nomi, it may be the only advantage we have."

She sighed. "I know. Let's get my brother out of the way and then I'll help you with those files."

Ro slipped her arm through Nomi's and smiled.

Chapter 13

DEV FOLLOWED MICAH'S GAZE as he stared at all the wild bittergreen. The cartels were more complicated than her quick and dirty summary had made it seem. Her brothers were connected, Vic more directly than Tanner or Giles, but that's just how it was in Midlant. Everything filtered into the settlement through the cartels. She wasn't sure Micah would understand. "Well, you wanted to see where I grew up, right?"

He glanced around, nodding.

"Come on. Let's go for a ride." She led him through the maze of Midlant's streets to a locked storage shed at the far edge of the settlement. As it opened to her palm print, Dev's shoulders relaxed. It took a moment for her eyes to adjust to the unlit space, but all her things were still there, untouched.

"What is this place?"

"As soon as I was old enough to walk, I used to follow my brothers to the abandoned towns around here. They would try to lose me, but I could always find them." There was one day where

Dev wandered into the skeleton of an old house and found that the kitchen had been almost perfectly intact. She'd spent the afternoon poking around the shelves and the closets, piecing together the way people had lived before the Great Drowning had caused everything to change. Her brothers had been frantic when she hadn't found them, convinced that she'd been lost or killed.

From that day on, they never hid from her again, but she also found something more compelling than following them to where they drank or did drugs.

"That's when I started to range farther and farther away from Midlant, looking for places to explore. I liberated a broken trundle and modified it." She pulled the tarp from the ungainly looking thing. "It'll manage our weight. It just won't be fast."

The place she wanted to take him was about six klicks away, but even if he could manage the distance, it would still be hell on his feet.

"Climb in." She rummaged on the shelves for some of her tools and her carryall. It was made from the same tough fibers her grandmother had woven their rugs from; its familiar weight slung across her shoulders, along with the jingle of metal tools, was a comfort. As was the polymer blade in her pocket.

Standing here felt right—felt like home in a way the home she grew up in hadn't. For the first time in a long time, Dev didn't feel the need to check the edge on that blade.

"You want me to ride in that?" Micah asked. He stood at the threshold of the shed.

"Unless you'd rather walk. And the road—if you could call it that—isn't exactly in good shape."

"It's a glorified luggage cart."

"It doesn't look like much, but it has a dual solar/waste oil engine and the wheels are salvaged from a Commonwealth Guard ATV." Neither of which anyone would see just looking at it. Which was the point. "Trust me. She's reliable."

"You built it, right?"

She had. It had taken her most of a summer and all the money she could scrounge from odd jobs and selling bits and bobs she'd found in abandoned places.

He helped her roll it out of the shed and waited as she locked the door.

"Shall we?" She triggered the bubble top, waved him to the far side of the bench inside, and squeezed in next to him. Their legs touched. As she raised her hands to the steering column, she brushed his arm. The top latched with a loud click, sealing them inside. "It'll take about an hour to get to where we're going." She kept her voice low, not exactly uncomfortable with the strange intimacy of having him so close.

Dev wanted to ask him if he was okay. He kept saying he wanted to understand who she was. Well, this was it. Exploring the small abandoned towns around Midlant was what had kept her happy and sane through her childhood. She pressed her thumbs into the little ident pads on the steering column and the trundle whined to a start. At least there would be enough sunlight to use the solar engine; they wouldn't smell like stale fried food before they arrived.

Between the rutted road and the hard tires, it was too noisy to really do much talking. Micah spent most of the trip staring out at the remnants of what had been an old undivided highway with two lanes in each direction. The dirt berm in the center was now a two-meter-high hedge of bittergreen. There were still a few exit signs, but they were either faded and unreadable or shot full of holes and unreadable.

Several off ramps could still be traced through the bracken and trees, but they didn't lead anywhere useful. Most of the small towns had been raided and dismantled a long time ago.

Dev checked her micro's mapping function and the time. They should be getting to their turn-off soon. At least the trundle was slow enough that she wouldn't miss it. It had been more than a year since she'd last been here and she was worried that the road had vanished. Micah placed a hand on her arm.

"Almost there," she shouted over the whistle of wind noise and vibration.

He nodded.

The remnants of a large road sign lay across the left lane and into the berm. That was her landmark. She turned just past the sign onto a road she knew was there, even if she couldn't see the entrance.

Once on the exit road, it was just another half klick to the little neighborhood she'd spent so much time poking around in. Very little had changed since her last trip here, but a few seasons of growth showed in the height of the canopy, the thickness of the weeds, and the penetrance of roots breaking up the roadbed.

The trundle bumped its slow way onto a narrower road and after a few more turns, they were there. She stopped in a patch of open ground surrounded by tall trees and popped the bubble.

"Here?"

"The trundle needs to charge its batteries. It's just a short walk through there." The little neighborhood was hidden on the other side of the thicket, which was probably why it hadn't been looted as badly as the other nearby areas.

Their footsteps were muffled by layers of dirt and leaves. Birdsong rose around them. It was a kind of silence she couldn't really find in the settlement.

"This isn't anywhere near the coast."

"No. We're pretty far inland. This used to be central Pennsylvania."

"But things weren't drowned here. Why were all the towns abandoned?"

Dev sighed. "Another decision, courtesy of your Commonwealth. So many people were displaced. All over the country. All over the world. Resources were stretched too thin. There wasn't enough to support the infrastructure of all these small communities, so they moved everyone to the new cities."

"Except the people in the settlements."

"Well, everyone with money or influence. Plus it was a way to keep the settlements more or less contained. It wouldn't do to have us pushing out into civilization." The Commonwealth wanted to keep them far enough away so that the rest of society could keep their fiction of prosperity, but close enough to exploit the cheap and desperate labor. Only a lucky few, like her, got the kind of education that let someone from a settlement make it on the highside.

Micah fell silent as they pushed through the last few trees and reached what Dev had come to think of as her private little town. Even though it hadn't been stripped too badly, the sixty-five or so years of neglect and exposure to the elements hadn't been kind. Most of the buildings along the main street had collapsed, helped along by the creeping tree roots from the elms and maples that had lined the now broken sidewalks on both sides of the road.

"Come on. There's a great house I want to show you." It was her favorite place in the entire town—a three-story stone farmhouse. The windows were all long broken and years of weather had swept through the inside, ruining the plaster walls and warping the wide wood boards of the floors, but it was otherwise more or less intact.

She tugged him over to the front door, which was miraculously still standing.

"Is it safe?"

"Is anything?"

"Point taken."

"This place is close to four hundred years old. Isn't that amazing?" It took both hands and all of Dev's strength to move the swollen door against its rusty hinges. She pulled out the flashlight from her gear bag and flicked it on. They kicked through a pile of dried leaves in the entry, moving through the slanted light and into shadow.

The room to their right had probably been a living room, complete with an ornate fireplace and carved mantel. Other than the detritus of leaves and trash, it was empty. All the rooms were empty. Whatever furniture had once been here must have gotten moved with the occupants.

Dev had explored other homes in other towns where it had been clear that the people had left hastily and what had been abandoned had been either looted, dragged away to burn, or just deliberately trashed. This house had been carefully emptied. There were discolored rectangles on the walls where art had once hung. She couldn't imagine having enough money and resources to display something designed only for aesthetics.

The wall hangings and rugs in her container in Midlant

functioned as sound dampening and insulation. While they weren't strictly utilitarian, they weren't anything she'd call art.

Micah probably grew up with useless decorations on his walls.

"There's nothing in here," he said.

"Come on. I'm not going to risk taking you up the stairs, but we can explore down here." She ran her hand along the mantel trying to imagine a winter's night with a fire in the fireplace. There were so many rooms. Four downstairs alone. Upstairs there were four huge, private bedrooms, each with its own sanitary facilities. There was another floor above that, but she hadn't been up there in years. Not since a storm had come through and ripped a hole in the roof.

A house this size could hold practically a whole stack of containers from Midlant.

She led Micah through the kitchen. Her favorite room in the house, it had large windows on two sides. The one over the sink faced what had once probably been open fields, but was now a tangle of vine-choked trees and weeds as tall as a person.

"I used to pretend I lived here. Especially when I couldn't stand to be around my brothers anymore. It was the only place that felt like it really belonged to me."

Micah leaned on the worn wooden counter. "This room is bigger than some of the quarters we got assigned."

Dev lifted an eyebrow.

"Well, at least bigger than any kitchen I've ever seen. It's a pretty wasteful allotment of space, though."

"I guess." She shouldn't have expected Micah to feel the same attachment to the place that she did, but it still disappointed her. "Come on."

He followed her out the back door, blinking in the bright light. The back porch was shaded by the tall trees and they could sit for a while before they would need to head back.

Micah reached over and carefully pulled up a bittergreen plant. Then he tossed it aside. "Old habits die hard. I can't believe I've spent all this time planning a revenge that has no meaning at all. I just wanted to beat the cartels at their own game." He shook his head. "How ridiculous is that?"

"Play stupid games, win stupid prizes," Dev said, shrugging.

"Thanks. You're such a comfort."

While it was likely getting hot in Midlant, here, between the breeze and the shade, it was still pleasant. People had lived here once. They enjoyed the view from their back stoops. Maybe they even farmed the vast overgrown meadow that stretched out in front of them.

"Will you come back to Midlant when you're finished at Uni?"

The settlement was a dead end. She knew it. Her brothers knew it. They pushed her to succeed, even as they resented her for having a way out. She sighed. Sending money from the outside was the only way to get ahead in Midlant. It was what had driven her own parents off-world. "My brothers need me and we take care of our own."

"What happened to your parents?"

"Morningstars don't belong in the void." Her grandmother's words were as true now as they were when her parents vanished. "They signed on for a mining gig on a colony. For a while, they sent home money. Life got a little easier for us. But it didn't last."

Sometimes the credit transfers would arrive. Other times, they would be mysteriously lost in transit. The mining corporation would offer proof of transmission. The Commonwealth-controlled bank would insist nothing had been received. After a while, her grandmother just expected a certain amount of diversion. Which was why it had taken them a few months to realize both her mother and her father had just disappeared. "We never got any official notification from the mining company. All they would say was my folks were no longer employees. The Commonwealth refused to investigate."

"I'm sorry."

Dev shrugged. "Can't hold back the water."

"Is that another folksy Midlant saying?"

"Folksy? Seriously?" Dev stood and brushed the dirt from her pants. "Where were your forebears during the Drowning?"

"Likely somewhere high and dry. At least on my father's side."

Micah stared past Dev, his expression blank. The way it always was when he talked about his father.

"Fortunately for the sake of his political career, the late Senator Rotherwood was lucky enough to have a tragic family backstory. When he was in his twenties, his parents both died in some freak accident doing development work on a colony world."

"So we both lost family to the void."

"Yeah, well, his inheritance funded his first political race, so it would have been a lot better for the galaxy had my grandparents never left Earth either."

"Was he that terrible?"

"Corwin Rotherwood? Probably not in the grand scheme of graft, greed, and corruption in the cosmos."

Dev couldn't remember him ever referring to the man as his

father. "And your mother?"

"I wish I knew why she married him. She was an amazing woman. Smart. Kind. Generous. Everything the senator was not." He shrugged. "The rest you already know."

A rustling in the trees caught her attention and Dev peered into the shadows around the dense greenery. There was an abundance of small animal life around here that didn't pose much of a threat to them. But there were the many-times offspring of abandoned family pets—feral cats and dogs that roamed the area. The cats typically stayed hidden, but the dogs could be aggressive. She reached into her pocket for her knife.

"Dev? Is everything okay?" Micah stood beside her and peered in the direction of the woods.

The sound died away and all there was left was birdsong and the wind through leaves.

"It's all good." She took her hand out of her pocket. "We should head back."

*

Nomi sat on the floor of her old room, her back resting against the sleeping platform. Nothing had changed in the more than five years since she'd left home, including the colors of the walls. Her parents had sprung for the nanotech paint and she'd programmed each of the four walls to display a different shade of green from the palest almost gray to a deep emerald. She was surprised her brother hadn't messed with it. "You do realize that you're never, ever going to be able to rid yourself of Daisuke."

Ro laughed and it was a pure sound of amusement, free of her usual guarded emotions. "He's not so bad. A little spaceship-obsessed, maybe. Honestly? I was probably like that at his age." Her smile vanished, her gaze suddenly far away. "Maybe things would have been different if someone had been willing to listen to me."

"Thank you. For paying attention to him." Maybe it would help fill the hole in Ro's life to give what she hadn't received.

Her face reddened. "It wasn't a big deal," she mumbled.

But it was, and they both knew it. "Come on. Let's start digging through your father's files." It was going to take longer than the few days they had here. With the sheer amount of data to process, it might even take months. But they could at least make a start by the time Barre and Halcyone returned. And maybe they'd find something they could use.

Ro settled beside Nomi on the floor, their legs touching. "Okay. Can I use your micro to set up an ad hoc?"

It wasn't a huge amount of computing power, but it would help split the load. "Sure." Nomi smiled as she handed her device over, surprised that Ro had actually asked.

"See? I can learn." Ro blushed again before turning her attention on both micros.

Chaining them together would allow them to both divvy up the files and cross reference any significant findings. Ro worked fast, her fingers flicking the air in front of her device and pulling virtual windows up all around them. "I'm going to do a chronological initial sort, then organize by file type for a first go-round. Sound good?"

"Yup."

Data flashed across the screens too fast for Nomi to process, but Ro seemed to know what she was looking at. "Huh," she said. "That's odd."

"What?"

"There's a whole archive of image files here and it's passcode-locked." She tugged her fingers through her hair and frowned at the flickering windows.

"But that doesn't make sense. Your father already protected the entire device with your DNA."

"It's my father. Sense doesn't enter the equation." Ro halted the flow of data before tossing a bunch of screens toward Nomi. "Why don't you take this chunk of text files. I'll ponder my father's devious mind for a while."

If anyone could figure it out, Ro could. Not because she was like her father, but because she had had to survive him. "What am I looking for?"

"I wish I knew. When I first cracked the damned thing, Micah, Barre, and I did some poking around. We were looking for any mention of Lowell, but didn't find much of anything. Micah's father was in there, though. And guess whose father was going to sell him out?"

"Yours?"

"Got it in one."

Nomi squeezed Ro's shoulder. "Hey. It's okay. You can borrow my folks. They have a ridiculous need to take in strays."

"Is that what I am?" Ro's eyes sparkled, giving lie to the frown.

"Well you did show up at my doorstep and I did let you in. I guess I take after my parents."

"Pretty pleased with yourself."

Nomi leaned over to kiss her and felt Ro's lips curve into a smile. "Yup."

Ro rested her forehead against Nomi's. "You are the best

thing that's ever happened to me."

"Better than Halcyone?" There was a catch in Nomi's voice that she hadn't intended. It was supposed to be a light tease and truly, she didn't begrudge Ro her beloved ship.

"Yes."

Nomi exhaled softly. "That was out of line."

"No, it wasn't. And I don't tell you how important you are anywhere near enough." This time, Ro kissed her. First on her forehead, then the tip of her nose, and then her lips. "Okay. Time to get to work."

Tingling and flushed, Nomi turned to her micro and the multiple windows of data Ro had tossed her way. If she spent time scanning every file, the system's primary would go cold before she got halfway through. Her work with ansible traffic was all about patterns, seeing enough of the metadata to make a prediction and route the traffic appropriately. She'd have to do the same with Maldonado's files.

She and Ro worked quietly, comfortably, sitting side by side. They hadn't ever done this before and Nomi was surprised as how easy it was.

Without stopping to overanalyze, Nomi sorted the files, flicking ones that felt similar into groups. After each group held over fifty files, she stopped to see what she'd gotten.

In one virtual pile, there were dozens and dozens of what looked like notations in code. Nomi set all the other groups aside and took a closer look. Each document had just a few lines of text: an alphanumeric grouping in two or three clumps, exactly thirteen numbers, and what looked like a single line of binary.

"Ro? Take a look at this."

"Hmm?" Ro blinked up at Nomi from where she'd been

staring at a single window projected above her micro. With an angry swipe of her hand, she sent the display tumbling. It vanished, popping like a soap bubble. "What do you have?"

"I'm not sure, but there are too many of them for it to be irrelevant." Nomi circled her neck to work out the kinks before fanning out the windows like a deck of playing cards. "Some kind of program, stored in discrete lines?"

"How retro." After studying the files with narrowed eyes, Ro shook her head. "I don't think so." Her hands sliced across the air in front of her micro. The windows shuffled themselves into a different order, displaying in an offset stack so Ro could see several at a time.

She growled softly to herself and reshuffled. Nomi couldn't figure out how Ro was sorting the files, but it clearly made some kind of sense to her. Three more times in quick succession, Ro reorganized them. She had an almost AI-like ability to see the data and analyze it in one glance.

Finally, she leaned back, clasping her hands around the back of her neck. "Huh."

"What?"

"The middle line is all dates in numerical notation: day, month, year. But he was tricky. Whatever events he was tracking, he didn't record them on the date in the file or even chronologically. But there were enough of them clustered that when I sorted by creation date, a partial pattern stood out. See?"

Now that Ro had pointed it out, Nomi could see the march of dates. "Some of these go back nearly twenty-five years, Ro." She did a quick calculation. "He started this—whatever it is—when he was your age."

"What were you tracking, you son of a bitch?" Ro asked the

glowing screens.

Nomi thought back to the data she and Jem had discovered in the public records. He would have been in Chicago then, a young, hot-shot hacker pulled from a subsistence life in the NorPac Settlement and dropped into the academic pressure-cooker that was UCom-NW. It likely hadn't gone well. "Did he ever say anything about his Uni days?"

Ro snorted. "Other than his utter disdain anytime I brought up going? No."

"The records didn't say why he scrubbed out."

"And that surprises you because ... ?"

Nomi sighed.

"My father fucked up everything he ever touched. Every job. Every posting. Everything." Ro's face blazed red. "Even me."

"That is simply not true." Nomi was glad Maldonado was now elemental gasses and particles spread across an entire sector. Couldn't have happened to a nicer guy.

"Keep going. You're good at this."

Nomi returned to her task. Ro was going to have to come to terms with her father in her own time and in her own way. They continued in silence for another hour, but Nomi wasn't able to find any other clear patterns in the rest of the files. There were basic text documents, partial schematics, incomplete programs, and old job offers. It was as if Maldonado had just kept copies of every note he'd ever taken for any reason, all jumbled up together without any apparent organizational structure. There were thousands and thousands of individual files and the only way they were going to assess them all was with the help of an AI's processing power.

"Son of a bitch," Ro shouted. She scrambled to her feet and

threw her micro across the room so hard it took a notch out of the far wall. The golden green of an entire section of paint flickered and turned a neutral gray.

"Ro? Ro, what's wrong?" Nomi stood and quickly crossed the room to where Ro stood, her shoulders shaking.

"I'm sorry. I'm sorry." She tried to smooth the gouge in the wall, but it stayed stubbornly gray.

Nomi gripped Ro's arms and gently turned her around. Her girlfriend's green eyes were bright with tears and her cheeks were red and splotchy. "What did you find?" Nomi asked softly.

Shaking herself free, Ro leaned down and picked up her micro. "He kept them from me. He kept her from me." Her hands shook as she handed it to Nomi.

She triggered a virtual window then drew her breath in sharply as the display filled with images of a young Maldonado, a woman Nomi didn't recognize, and a baby that had to have been Ro. "You have your mother's face." But Alain Maldonado's piercing green eyes. "Do you remember her at all?"

"No." Ro sighed. "They split when I was under a year old. He never talked about her and judging by how little he cared for or about me, I still have no idea why he took custody. He was a vindictive bastard. She probably wanted me and he couldn't stand it."

She swiped the tears from her eyes.

"It doesn't matter. My mother vanished somewhere in the cosmos and my father is dead."

"Ro? Why did he have these images doubly locked?"

"Why the hell did he have them in the first place?"

Nomi had no answers for Ro. People kept the strangest things for the strangest reasons. She tried to lighten the mood.

"Now you have something more of hers than that ratty old quilt you drag around everywhere," she said, smiling.

Ro frowned and stared at the images, her eyes narrowed.

Chapter 14

Ro got through dinner with Nomi's family on autopilot. Fortunately, Daisuke was more than up to the task of talking for all of them. Or talking at all of them. His constant chatter was almost comforting—like the background hum of Halcyone's life support.

Sighing, she glanced at her micro, but there were no messages from Barre. Not that she'd expected anything yet—it had only been a few hours since he'd taken off.

Her thoughts kept circling back to the images she'd unlocked from her father's data. Alain Maldonado had to have been the most unsentimental individual in the cosmos. He never kept anything from move to move, other than utilitarian items like work clothes and tools. He had never understood her attachment to the quilt that had been her mother's, but at least he respected her need to hold onto it. Either that, or he didn't want to have to deal with her tantrum when it disappeared.

"Ro?" Azuki asked, "would you like to retire for the evening?"

She glanced up at the empty table. "I'm sorry. I was thinking about something."

"Yes, I see."

At least the woman was amused, rather than annoyed. Ro forced a smile for her. "Where's Nomi?"

"Cleaning up."

Ro pushed back her chair and stood. "I should help."

"I don't think there's room for you in the kitchen with both Paul and Daisuke there. Besides, you're our guest. Nomi told me you have a problem to solve. Go. I'll send her up with some tea later."

"Thank you." Words seemed so inadequate. She'd had no experience in dealing with someone so gracious, so understanding. Until she'd met Nomi.

"You are quite welcome, my dear."

Nomi's voice rang out from the kitchen in mock outrage at something Daisuke said or did. Ro smiled and headed back to their room, but as soon as her thoughts slid back to her father, her mood sobered.

Displaying the unlocked photos on several virtual screens, she surrounded herself with images of a fiction: a mother, father, and baby looking for all the cosmos like a happy little triad.

The more she studied the photos, the more subtle signs of tension she noticed. Her father never looked at the infant Ro and when the camera did catch his expression, it was the same dangerous, cold stare she remembered all too well.

Her mother was a puzzle. It was hard to assess from the pictures, but she seemed very young. She. Helene was her name. And along with having Ro the traditional way, she had also taken the Maldonado surname. She wore her blonde hair long, the way Ro did. Ro wondered if she'd somehow remembered that deep in her subconscious. Helene—Ro couldn't really think of her as her mother—had the same shape face as hers as well. Looking at the woman was like looking into an alternate version of herself, except for Ro's green eye color, which was her father's genetic contribution.

Ro had no idea what had happened to her, only that Alain had divorced her and had gotten full custody.

Why? Why would he do that? She stared at the clearest image of him in the bank of photos. It was also the only one in which he was holding her. His body language nearly shouted disinterest. The quilt wrapped around her tiny body had been less shabby then, but it seemed like that was the only thing that had changed.

There was no reason Ro could imagine that explained why Alain Maldonado had not only saved these photos, but had gone to the trouble of locking them behind two layers of protection. It made no sense.

Sighing, Ro swept the images aside.

"You take after her." Nomi was sitting at the small desk in her sleeping clothes, holding one of the promised cups of tea.

"Oh! How long have you been sitting there?"

"Long enough to finish mine and for yours to get cold." She yawned and leaned forward to set her cup down on the tray. "I didn't want to interrupt you."

"You should have. My brain is on vapor lock."

"Then close it down for now. Get some sleep. Start fresh tomorrow."

Fresh or not, Ro didn't see how she was going to figure her

father out, but she didn't voice her doubts to Nomi. She washed and changed and by the time she got to the bed, Nomi was already asleep. Her black hair fanned out over the white pillow. Her eyes were shifting back and forth beneath closed lids. Ro wondered what she was dreaming about. Her own dreams of late treated Ro to a horror show of jumps going wrong and lost ships in unfamiliar space.

It didn't take a trained clinician to interpret those kinds of images.

She slipped under the covers beside Nomi in the narrow bed, seeking her partner's warmth. Nomi didn't stir. The rhythmic flow of her breathing usually helped Ro fall asleep, but not tonight.

The bed was too small. The frame squeaked every time Ro shifted. Her mind refused to quiet even though her body was exhausted and she finally got up. If she couldn't sleep, she could work. She always did her best work late into third shift anyway, when most of the station was silent.

The virtual screens from their paired micros gave enough light to work with. Ro pulled up the images once more, but this time, she wasn't looking at the depictions of herself and her parents. She was looking at them as data.

Her father never did anything without a reason. He had saved and safeguarded these images. Images were densely packed information. So what did that information mean? How could she analyze it?

Her hacking toolkit had plenty of programs she could adapt. And if she was back on Halcyone, she'd have the power of the AI to help. Even using both her and Nomi's micros together wouldn't give her enough cycles to make sense of the code behind the images, but Nomi's home AI might.

In the blue light of her virtual screens, Ro glanced over at the sleeping woman and then back to their paired micros. Quelling the pang of uncertainty, she opened the networking app in Nomi's device. It was already passively connected to the house AI, receiving basic info including her family's calendar and the environmental controls. Ro extended the data handshake to full active mode so she could access its unused processor power to run her analysis hacks.

Now, for what to throw at the images.

Ro paced the small open area beside the bed, walking through and disrupting the displays while she considered the tools she'd built over the years. Probably the first pass would be the most basic—and the one least likely to achieve any sort of results, but she certainly wouldn't figure out anything unless she was systematic. Even a lack of a pattern would tell her something.

She accessed an old file type comparison routine and tossed it at the image file folder. If there were hidden files in there, her program would find them.

There was a familiar comfort in working by the flickering light of the displays while everyone around her was asleep. Nomi would chide her for avoiding people, but the truth was, Ro had more people in her life now than she had ever imagined possible.

All of those connections with Nomi, Barre, Jem, and Micah were like open programs using resources. And yet, she didn't want to return to her prior life. It might have been more efficient, but it was also a lot lonelier.

A soft beep alerted Ro to the finished program. Using gestural commands so she wouldn't wake Nomi, Ro had the micro list the results in a fresh window. As she'd figured, nothing there but images.

Alain Maldonado one, Ro, zero.

She returned to the archive view so she could sort the images in a variety of ways. Maybe there would be a pattern. She tapped the file name and the folder displayed the images in alphabetical order. They were named according to the default of whatever camera app had been used to record them. If there was a message hidden there, she wasn't clever enough to find it.

"Date taken" didn't reveal any specific information either, only that the initial image was taken when her mother was still pregnant with her and the final one, when Ro was still a baby.

She searched through the "date modified" column, but there was no evidence that the images had been altered in any way.

Two more dead ends.

Scrolling across the screen, she glanced at all the remaining metadata, but nothing caught her eye. Except "file size." It was one of the last columns and it was problematic in an interesting way. Each of the thirty-six photographs had about ten times the data it should have had. Even for the highest resolution images.

Gotcha.

There was something hidden in the image files. But what kind of something? Figuring that out and extracting the data was going to take a different kind of analysis.

She opened her toolkit and looked through all her image hacks. Hiding programs or even other images in an image was old tech. But it was still effective, especially if the original image wasn't available for comparison.

If her father had hidden another level of information in these photos, then the key to unhide them had died with him. Without that key, Ro just had to do things a little more creatively.

Son of a bitch was crafty—she had to give him that. Even if someone had been able to brute-force his memory cube and unlock the archive, unless they really knew Alain Maldonado, they wouldn't realize the photographs were just a decoy. They would waste their energy on the other documents. But Ro suspected that without whatever was in the images, those files would remain innocuous collections of text.

She would definitely need the computing power of Nomi's house AI for this. Each image contained an enormous amount of information stored in eight-by-eight matrices. Every single matrix would need to be examined for extraneous data hidden in its lower-order bits. Her father could have stored any number of things that way, without the resulting images showing any signs of degradation. If she found a pattern, she'd have to analyze it and try to reverse engineer his process.

It was going to be a long night. Nomi sighed in her sleep and rolled over. Ro shivered, as much from fatigue as cold, and contemplated setting the analyzer running and curling up next to her. But Ro didn't trust her father not to have set up booby traps for the unwary hacker. A sleepless night wouldn't kill her, but not knowing what Alain Maldonado had hidden might.

*

After leaving Gutierrez, Jem headed back to his quarters. He hated how much rest he still required in order to simply function. Yes, it was better. Yes, it got a little better every week, but his progress was still maddeningly slow.

He checked his messages, but there was nothing yet from Ro,

Nomi, or Barre. He sent another message, just to be sure. Then he slept. For far more hours than he'd anticipated. But when he woke, his headache had finally faded and he figured it was a good time to go shopping for prosthetic parts. Raiding medical was something he'd done since he was a little kid, though it had been insta-plaster and quick-set polymer he'd taken to build with, then. This was going to be a bit different.

There was little outward sign of the change of command on the station. Personnel moved through the corridors, ignoring Jem as usual, though that could be because of the lateness of the hour. More importantly, there seemed to be no additional staff members that he could tell. He checked the docking bays. Either Hephaestus had dropped Targill off here and left for other duties, or she was orbiting the station. There was no way for him to figure out which without attracting their new commander's attention.

It was just into third shift, and his mother should have been long gone from medical. The doors whooshed open and Jem walked inside. He wasn't trying to hide his presence. If anything, he'd spent so much time in and out of medical in the past weeks, the staff had pretty much stopped noticing him.

He nodded to the receptionist and headed to the supply bay. No one stopped him. Why would they?

Once inside, he closed the door and pulled up the parts list he'd organized. No matter that Daedalus Station was a tiny outpost with a small staff, his mother insisted on keeping medical fully stocked with the equivalent of an active battle-station assignment. He thanked the cosmos for her thoroughness.

It was hard not to feel like he was stealing. But in reality, this was for Gutierrez. And she was the station's second in command. Besides, anything he took would be noted by the station's inventory control system and reordered, so it wasn't like anyone would miss the components. At least not for long.

What he had would probably keep him busy until the custom parts the LC needed to order arrived. He carefully nestled the microelectronics in his bag before stepping out of the supply bay —and right into the formidable presence of his mother.

"Jem. I didn't expect to see you here."

"Um. Hey, Mom." *Shit.* He wasn't going to tell her the same. What was she doing here?

"You do know we don't keep drugs in there." Her eyes were narrowed and her voice colorless and cold.

Did they have to go through this again? Why was she so convinced he was on his way to being an addict? "I really don't know what to tell you. I'm not stealing drugs. I'm not taking drugs, but if I was, I certainly wouldn't be diverting them from here." He stepped around her, but she caught his arm in a grip that was as strong as Gutierrez's prosthetic one.

"I need to check your bag."

Jem sighed. "Can we move to your office?" If he had to betray the LC's confidence, he didn't want to do it in the relatively public area of the medical bay. Even during the skeleton shift.

His mother gave him a long, appraising look before nodding and leading him there. She didn't let go of his arm until they were in her office, behind a sealed door.

Jem stepped to her desk and upended his bag. The sealed components tumbled out. "No drugs. Satisfied?"

But she wouldn't be satisfied, not until she had pulled the whole story from him.

"These are for Lieutenant Commander Gutierrez. She asked me to help her rebuild her prosthetic. You could try trusting me once in a while."

"You could have asked for the parts. She could have requisitioned them."

That was stupid. Of course they could have. Why hadn't he? This thing with Ro and Ithaka and the Commonwealth had gotten them seeing conspiracies in every corridor. "You keep telling me I have to rest my brain. I thought you'd be mad." That was true, as far as it went.

"Oh, Jem, I just want what's best for you." Her voice vibrated like a bell and cracked.

"What are you so afraid of?"

Her face grayed. She stumbled back several steps until she hit a chair and collapsed into it. Jem had to strain to hear her in the otherwise silent room. "I don't want you to make the same mistakes I made."

"Mom. Please." But he didn't know what he was asking from her. Her fear and her shame flooded him. It was too much. He put up his hands as if to hold back anything else she might say.

Tears glittered in her brown eyes and she suddenly looked so unbearably weary.

"It's okay. I can put the parts back. I'll ask the LC to requisition them officially. If you don't want me to help her, I'll —"

"No." She took a deep breath, and was once more the strong woman who commanded the entirety of a medical bay with the force of her personality and confidence. "Go finish what you started. She needs someone's help. It might as well be yours."

Jem leaned against the desk, grateful for the gift of being

annoyed with his mother again. "Well, thanks for the vote of confidence."

She stood, crossed the room, and hugged him. Jem's chin tucked into her shoulder. It wouldn't be all that many months before he was as tall as her. It made him uncomfortable in the same way that seeing her raw emotions did. "You don't need me to tell you how good you are. It's my job to worry about you. And if you're going to be working with the LC, at least you can relay how she's progressing."

"Isn't that kind of confidential?"

"You're part of her care team now, and your father and I are still her physicians of record."

Well, that made sense. He was going to tell the LC, though. There was a limit to the number of secrets he could juggle.

His mother released him and was silently repacking the pile of components when her micro sounded her pager tone. "No rest for the wicked."

Jem smiled as she smoothed her lab coat and headed out of her office—Dr. Leta Durbin, in control again. As difficult as it was to have grown up under her stern supervision, seeing her this way was strangely comforting.

He finished filling his bag and paused at the door. His mother's voice was raised in uncharacteristic anger. The male voice opposing her wasn't one he recognized. He triggered the door release and slipped into the main medical bay. In the center of the room, near the receptionist's kiosk, his mother was squared off against Commander Targill.

Jem had only met the man briefly, when he was recuperating on Hephaestus after his rescue from Halcyone. The tall man with the silver buzz cut and the nasty scar across his right temple was unforgettable. And formidable. Especially considering he'd been committing treason all these years and in plain sight.

"I am ordering you to release the lieutenant commander for duty."

Jem frowned. He thought Gutierrez was already cleared. Otherwise what had she been doing in her uniform in the commissary?

"And I am countermanding that order. Sir."

The Commonwealth war hero towered over his mother, but if Targill thought he could use either his size or his authority to intimidate her, he was in for a surprise. "Doctor, I really believe you should reconsider your position."

"What position would that be, Commander? My main job is to safeguard the health and safety of every member of the staff and their dependents. Including you. If you are ordering me to place your convenience over the well-being of one of my patients, then that, sir, is an illegal order."

That was the Leta Durbin Jem knew.

Targill leaned forward and lowered his voice. Jem couldn't hear what he was saying, but his mother drew her breath in sharply.

"Those records are sealed. Sir." The dark skin on her cheeks flushed. She took a step forward, forcing Targill to retreat. "And I don't appreciate being threatened."

Jem took a step back and hit the wall by her office.

Targill's scar was a livid purple against the red of his face. His mother didn't shift a muscle and stood glaring up at him. That was the look that had tamed generations of young doctors and medical staff, and if Jem was honest, him and his brother. He gave Targill full marks for standing there a good two minutes before he turned and walked out.

That he walked calmly and with measured steps made Jem nervous. He was glad the man was up against his mother, and not him.

She held her ground for several long minutes after Targill left as the silent staff returned to their routines and their work, ignoring the dramatic scene that had just played out around them. Then she sagged against the receptionist's desk.

"Mom?" Jem walked over to her, but stood a few steps away, not knowing whether he should give her a hug or let her have her space. "You okay?"

She gave him a smile that didn't reach her eyes. "I'm not a fan of bullies. If you can help the LC, do it."

Jem would have helped her even if she hadn't been tied to Ithaka and Ada May. Now, he had to warn the LC about Targill, though it was a good bet she already knew.

He queried his micro for the time. It was definitely too late to show up on her doorstep, but he could leave her an urgent message. It was somewhat ambiguous, but he didn't want to name Targill, not even with Ada May's messaging program. Gutierrez was smart enough to figure it out.

He turned back at the medical entrance, but his mom hadn't followed him. "You coming home?" It was rare for either of his parents to do overnight shifts outside of an emergency.

"Go ahead. I'll be along in a bit." Her voice rang with a false cheerfulness that jangled Jem's ears and flooded his mouth with a bitter taste.

"Mom?" He took a step closer.

Gone was the vulnerability and the momentary openness. "I don't need a minder, Jeremy."

Perhaps she needed a friend every bit as much as Gutierrez did. Jem sighed and headed back into the silent corridors of Daedalus Station, the bag of prosthetics parts and circuits not nearly as heavy as the unaccustomed worry for his mother.

Chapter 15

"Halcyone? What's the local time?" Barre asked.

"Zero seven eighteen galactic standard time."

He rolled out of his bunk, tied back his dreads, and washed up at the small sink. He had instructed Halcyone to bring them to the far side of the volcanic planet orbited by the smuggler's moon. The electromagnetic interference would keep the ship from being noticed until Barre was ready to be noticed.

It had been an uneventful trip and the two long interstitial segments around the final jump had given Barre plenty of time to ruminate on his misgivings. He didn't want to risk sending Ro a message. Not from here.

What the hell was Ada May thinking sending him to pick up Cam Fucking Lowell?

Their former comms chief had been obsessed with finding Ithaka to the point of it becoming a joke among Daedalus's staff. Now he was being escorted directly there. It was too convenient. If he'd been Targill's agent, why had he fled the station instead of calling on the commander's protection? Unless Lowell was using his apparent disgrace to infiltrate Ithaka. And Ada May was letting him.

Of course she suspected the man's clandestine connections. She'd been playing 'nought and shuttle with the Commonwealth for a lot longer than Barre'd been alive. Not only did she have the data Jem had hacked, but a lifetime of context and history to draw on. Lowell had to be a wealth of intel, if he was willing to cooperate.

But that was a big if and even with Ithaka's protections, bringing Lowell there was a risk Barre didn't want to take.

He didn't feel ready to play the role of Ithaka's Ferryman, but he had made a promise to Ada May. At least Larson, the bartender-cum-smuggler Ro and Micah dealt with last time they were here, wouldn't recognize him. Though Lowell would. That could be problematic.

The smuggler's planet would certainly remember the ship. And its captain. Barre snorted in the silence of his cabin. Ro had that effect on people.

He changed into loose-fitting black pants and a black shirt—clothes he could comfortably move in if he had to get out fast—before heading to the bridge. When he stepped through the ruined doors, Halcyone automatically dialed up the lights and displayed their current position on the forward screen.

They were in a stable orbit around the volcanic planet. Pleasant place. He was glad they wouldn't have to visit, though the dangers on the surface were ones he understood better than those waiting for him at the smuggler's bar.

This wasn't a job for a musician. If things went poorly, what was he going to do? Serenade them? Halcyone carried no weapons, and even if she did, Barre wasn't sure he'd be comfortable arming himself.

Halcyone played a dissonant fanfare through their neural link. She seemed to sense his moods and the intent behind his thoughts more and more easily. Ro would have mocked him for imagining things, but he knew better.

The AI was reminding him that sound could be a weapon.

"Yeah, but at this point, the only person you could blast would be me." Even if they could program some kind of auditory barrage he could play through his micro, it would affect him as well. Unless he could figure out how to program his neural to filter out specific sound frequencies.

Huh. It actually should be possible, but Barre didn't have the time or the resources to design it before he had to rendezvous with Lowell. Something to explore with Ro's and Jem's help, perhaps.

"Well, just stay connected in the background, okay? I may need you to fire the engines in a hurry."

Halcyone played her confirmation tones.

He gave the ship orders to break orbit and approach the moon on the same vector they had used last time. They triggered the same automatic beacon. Barre identified himself and the ship and just as before, he was given clearance to land.

In the very same docking bay Ro had threatened to blow up. That couldn't have been accidental. At least someone had a sense of humor.

The ship landed and docked easily. Barre took a deep breath as the clamps engaged, and slipped his micro into his pocket. Not that he needed it, per se. He could always communicate with Halcyone directly, but it wouldn't do to give away his only advantage. Neurals were still rare enough that they wouldn't assume he had one.

Barre made his way to the airlock and paused with his hand on the release. "Halcyone, override and archive all stored entry parameters."

"Override approved."

Now even Ro couldn't get on board. It was a precaution—a paranoid precaution to be sure—but this ship and her computer were his only backup. And while it was a remote possibility, the station could have hacked their entry credentials from their prior adventure here. Directly through his neural, Barre sent Halcyone a snippet of a melody he'd been working on recently. "Save file 'Charon's Theme'."

"Saved."

"Set new pass-code to musical file 'Charon's Theme'."

"New pass-code set."

"Thanks, Halcyone. Keep your engines warm."

There was a gentle vibration beneath his feet as she prevented the drive from entering its full shutdown state. It wasn't ideal and most docking facilities prohibited it, but Barre wasn't planning on being here long enough for anyone to lodge an environmental complaint.

He released the door, stepped out of the ship, and squared his shoulders. Ada May needed a ferryman, he would be her ferryman. At least for now.

The automated kiosk welcomed him. He paid for twenty-four hours from Micah's accounts. It wasn't as if they didn't know Halcyone was connected to the Rotherwood name. As soon as he confirmed his biometrics, the door from the docking bay opened. The skin on Barre's back crawled as he slipped out and the door shut behind him, sealing him off from the ship.

If this was a trap, there would be no one coming to rescue him.

Someone was expecting him—he followed the glowing path on the floor through the maze of the docking area until he reached the inhabited parts of the station. Just in case they weren't as accommodating when it was time to leave, Barre opened the map Halcyone had traced the last time they were here and set it to continuously update for his current location.

The directions led to a standard nexus design. Only one of the exits opened for him and he kept walking. The comforting background hum of Halcyone's monitoring buzzed through his head. He was more than grateful for the tether.

Barre walked through the empty corridors. Almost all the shops and offices were still shuttered. Smugglers must not be early risers. Even the bar was closed. But it was where Ro and Micah had connected with Larson and since Ada May hadn't given him any other information, it was where Barre would start. The door swung open when he reached it. The interior of the bar glowed under the same night-vision-sparing lights that Halcyone's bridge used. The furniture cast deep shadows in the room.

He took a deep breath before stepping inside.

A bright light shone directly into his eyes. He stopped, squared his shoulders, and tried not to look as rattled as he felt. "Mr. Larson?"

"Who wants to know?"

"Charon."

"I heard he died."

"Don't you know your mythology? The ferryman moves back

and forth across the underworld."

"Fair enough." The light clicked off, leaving Barre blinking away the afterimages. "Can I get you a coffee?"

"I'd appreciate that."

As he adjusted to the dim interior of the silent bar, he made out empty tables dotting the area around the bar and booths lining the wall. A white shadow detached itself from the far side of the room and resolved into a tall man wearing an apron.

"The last time I saw the Ferryman, he wasn't quite as large or young or dark."

"One of the enduring mysteries of the afterlife." Was Taro Odachi the only Ferryman before him? A question for Ada May, to be sure. "I was told I had a soul to escort."

"Sit a moment. It'd be a shame to waste good coffee." Larson gestured to a booth. Barre took the side facing the door, watching as the bartender ducked under the bar and loaded a tray with a carafe and two cups. "What do you take in yours?"

"Sugar, if you have it."

The scent of the earthy brew reached him before Larson did. It was the real stuff.

"Here." Larson slid him a cup and a sugar bowl.

"Thank you."

"So how did the Ferryman come to have possession of Captain Maldonado's ship?"

"You'll have to ask her some time."

"I think I'll pass." Larson laughed a deep and hearty laugh. When he recovered himself, he asked, "Would she really have risked her ship to blow up my station?"

Barre remembered their terse standoff. He could have said something amusing, something to brush Larson off, but the truth was, Ro didn't bluff. It unnerved him and he wanted the bartender to understand in case he crossed her path again. "Yes."

Larson smiled wryly. "I thought so." He paused for a moment, not breaking eye contact with Barre. "I suppose she wouldn't appreciate my condolences on her father's abrupt demise."

"No." Barre drained his coffee and set his hands across the top of the cup. "My passenger?" The longer he and Halcyone were parked here, the greater the chance of something going wrong.

"He's waiting for my confirmation." Larson leaned back in his seat.

"And?" It would have been nice for Ada to have given him a little more intel on this whole deal.

"And I have to wonder who you're working for."

"It's good to cultivate a sense of wonder."

Larson laughed again. "You're fairly confident for a young man without so much as a stunner, no backup, and a forty-year old ship with paper-thin shields."

It wasn't anything Barre hadn't already considered. "Well, my employer knows I'm here and if you even scratch Ro's ship, you'll have one very angry captain on your case."

He wiped his hands on the towel tucked into the apron. "She is rather like her father in that regard."

"Just so."

"Well, then, your passenger has already paid for his exit from my fair establishment and an appropriate sum has arrived from an anonymous source for the handover fee. You'll find you are pre-cleared for takeoff when you return to your ship."

Larson's eyes lit up on "appropriate." Barre wondered how much May had paid for Lowell's passage and what she expected to get from her investment.

"And the passenger?"

"Should already be waiting outside your docking bay. If I am correct, he will be as eager to board as your employer is to receive him."

"And why would that be?" There had to be others looking for Lowell and not all of them wanted him alive.

"Oh, you know. The usual." Larson's laugh was infectious and Barre found himself, if not liking the bartender, then appreciating his candor.

"Well, then, thank you for your hospitality."

"A word of advice. The river Lethe is never easy to cross. Even for the Ferryman. There's always a price. Remember that."

"I know." And Barre did. There was no turning back to the naive musician who had agreed to hide aboard Halcyone to wait out his parents' wrath. Too much had changed since the day the ship made her first panicked burn.

He retraced his path back to Halcyone and arrived safely, though the nape of his neck had tingled with the sensation of being watched. Larson had been true to his word: Lowell was pacing a tight line in front of the door to the docking bay. Barre paused to observe the man who had turned out to be at least a double agent: a smuggler working for the cartels and an informant being paid by the Commonwealth through Targill.

Now Ada May was going to give him sanctuary. Why?

Barre must have made some soft noise because Lowell whirled around. "You! What the hell are you doing here?"

He folded his hands across his chest. "I am your ride."

"You're the Ferryman?"

"Well, if it were up to me, I'd take on Orpheus's role—you know —the musician." Barre smiled to himself. He'd done that already and unlike the Orpheus in the Greek mythologies, he'd been successful. He'd rescued his brother from the underworld and neither of them had looked back. "But we don't always get to choose. Come on. We need to shove off before someone else decides to offer you passage to somewhere you probably don't want to go."

Lowell's eyes narrowed, but he kept his mouth shut.

Barre triggered the door to his docking bay and waved Lowell ahead of him.

"I still can't believe you got this wreck to fly."

"This wreck is Halcyone and she's your ticket out of the mess you made. Be respectful." Barre actively linked his neural with the ship and played the opening notes of the dirge he'd composed for the old Ferryman. Halcyone opened the airlock.

"My apologies." Lowell started down the corridor toward the bridge.

"Let's get some things sorted out," Barre said, stepping in front of him to block his way. "I don't trust you. If it were up to me, I wouldn't be taking you anywhere."

"I wouldn't be in this predicament if it weren't for your brother's illegal data mining."

"Do you really want to go there, Lowell?" Barre stared him down. It wouldn't be all that hard to physically toss him off Halcyone and leave him for any of Larson's other contacts. Except Ada May wanted him. And Lowell wanted Ithaka. "What did you promise her?" He didn't realize he'd said it aloud until Lowell smiled and shook his head.

"I was told I'd have safe passage. Was that a lie?"

Barre held the man's gaze for several long seconds. "If I had a brig, I'd confine you to it. As it is, Halcyone is still a work in progress. When we need to jump, you will take the upper berth in my quarters. Otherwise, you'll be confined to the bridge. You won't have access to any other space, so don't wander."

If he could have kept Lowell off the bridge, he would have, but without functioning doors, it wasn't possible.

"And if you had any ideas about taking over the ship, well, you can try, but Halcyone won't recognize you. She won't even let you pair your micro long enough to make a cup of coffee."

"If it's all the same to you, I'll stay in your quarters for the duration."

It wasn't ideal, but Barre didn't have very many other options. "Fine. Follow me."

He escorted Lowell to the small room crowded with musical instruments that he'd made into his home aboard the ship. Halcyone opened the door at his silent request. "Top's yours."

"You're too generous."

He hoped Ada knew what she was getting into. "Halcyone, seal the door behind our guest. Override authority Charon's Theme."

The door slid shut. Barre counted to five before Lowell pounded on it from the inside.

"You can't lock me in here," Lowell shouted.

"I just did," Barre said to himself as he headed toward the bridge.

*

All through their slow ride back to Midlant and through the quiet dinner he and Dev ate alone in her container apartment,

Micah struggled to find the words to apologize to her. The hell of it was, he wasn't even sure what he needed to apologize for.

Her brothers were nowhere to be found and somehow Micah felt that was his fault. Dev had been unusually quiet, and after they'd cleaned up the meal, had retreated to the small space that had been her room. Though with only curtains for doors, it wasn't much of a retreat.

It had taken Micah a very long time to fall asleep and when he did, he'd dreamed of his parents. For some reason, they were living in the empty shell of the house Dev had taken him to, but it was on the coast instead of landlocked in the middle of the Midlant region, and the water was rising. His mother kept trying to bail it out using a small bucket while his father opened all the doors and windows.

He woke to sunlight streaming in through the window. Symbolism much?

The murmur of low voices drifted in from the kitchen area. Micah rolled out of bed, washed, and changed before joining Dev and whoever she was talking with.

Dev and Giles fell silent when Micah stepped into the common area. Her face was red, but Micah couldn't figure out if she was angry or upset. Maybe both.

"Oi. Morning, hopper." Giles leaned back in his chair and propped his booted feet on the table. Dev glared at him.

"I smell coffee," Micah said. "I'm not hallucinating, am I?"

Dev slid a covered mug across the table to him. "There's some fresh bread on the counter." She lifted her chin. "From Stoltzfus's."

The coffee was lukewarm, but he didn't care. He could feel the withdrawal headache receding with every sip. "Thank you."

"Better with a bit of burn." Giles lifted an unlabeled bottle from where he'd been holding it under the table.

"I'll pass."

"Your loss." He took a huge slug right from the bottle.

"We can leave as soon as you're ready." Dev's voice was tight and brittle.

"Had enough of us deeps?"

Dev swiped the half-empty bottle. Giles overbalanced on his chair and nearly toppled over.

"I would've shared if you asked."

She narrowed her eyes and walked toward the sink.

"You wouldn't," Giles said.

Without a word, Dev emptied the bottle. Micah winced as he remembered doing that with the entire contents of his father's bar on more than one occasion.

Giles let the front feet of his chair come to rest on the floor. He sighed and leaned forward against the table's edge. "When did you turn into Grandmama?"

"When did you turn into an alcoholic?"

"When highsiders like him held us under the water."

Dev opened her mouth to argue, but Giles stood, bracing himself against the table.

"Maybe not your friend here. Not directly. But his father?" Giles's eyes blazed with hatred. "Vray."

Micah drew his breath in sharply.

"Yes, I know whose spawn you are. I'm a drunk, not a fool."

Gone was any trace of his Midlant patois. Gone, too, was the slurred speech and the loose-limbed movement. Giles stood tall and steady, meeting Micah's gaze directly.

Micah faced him and spoke softly into the shocked silence. "I am not my father."

"Pity, that. He could have fetched a heavy pocket to the right people."

That, Micah understood. Was Giles threatening him? How did he figure out who his father was?

Dev whirled toward them, the empty bottle clutched in a white-knuckled hand. "Giles Martingale Morningstar, don't you fucking dare."

Dev's brother's eyes widened and he stepped back before recovering and giving her a wide smile. "All friendly-like, vray?" He turned to Micah. "Fair shake, hopper?"

"How did you find out who I am?" So much for the Commonwealth's promises. But Micah should have realized how empty they were by now.

He glanced at Dev and shrugged. "Little sister isn't as tough as she seems. My brothers and I decided to keep a tail on you while you were here." His folksy Midlant dialect vanished again as quickly as it had returned. And it was clear he wasn't nearly as drunk as he had seemed. "As soon as I realized Dev was taking you to her little hideaway, I borrowed a scooter and beat you there."

"That was you in the woods." Dev slammed the bottle down on the counter.

"Vray. And you have an interesting past, hopper. Seems it's not just us deeps who hide from who we are."

"My father was a drunk son of a bitch who managed to hurt or betray everyone who ever trusted him. I walked away from his name and his legacy." Micah held Giles's gaze for several long seconds. "Vray?"

"And his money?"

"How is that your business?"

"Giles ..." Dev took a step forward as if she wanted to physically keep the two of them separated.

Micah shook her off. "No. I want to know. If you're threatening me, you should know I learned from a master. My father was better at extortion than you'll ever be."

Dev glared, first at her brother and then at Micah, before retreating to the counter. "Oh, joy, a pissing contest. Like I haven't seen enough of them in my lifetime."

That wasn't it. Well, maybe it was on some level, but Micah knew he had to push back against Giles—and push hard—if he was to safeguard his identity. He took a step closer. "What is it that you want? Because that tale you spun about being concerned for Dev? That's bullshit. You saw me as an opportunity from the moment I set foot in this container. Even before you knew my father's name."

"Your hopper has a deep mind," Giles said, smiling at his sister.

She folded her arms across her chest. "Answer him."

Giles looked away from Dev and his face blazed. "We figured you were tight with the highsider. That you would forget where you came from."

Dev drew in a sharp breath.

"We were planning on convincing him deeps don't belong with highsiders."

"Convincing?" Dev's low voice bordered on dangerous.

Giles shrugged.

"Then you figured out who my father was and you saw an opportunity."

"Fill a pocket and scare you away from my sister. Vray."

"And were Tanner and Vic part of this little plan, too?"

Giles shrugged again.

Dev started to laugh—a choked sound as if she was trying to hold it back. Micah stepped to the sink and pumped a cup of water for her. She drained it in a single breath. "So they volunteered you to confront us? Typical. Cowards."

"So now what?" Micah asked.

"That's up to her."

"You have something to say, Giles?" Dev's voice was dangerously polite. "Say it plain. Or has your time with the English changed you?"

Her brother's face burned red, again. "Whoever got through Uni was going to support the rest. That was the shake. You owe us."

"And you decided I couldn't be trusted?" Her cheeks burned crimson.

"We." Vic and Tanner came through the door. Giles slumped in his chair.

Dev stared down her older brothers with her hands on her hips. "Well, at least you didn't leave Giles to face the tide alone."

The images from Micah's dream came back to him in stark clarity: His mother's panicked movements with the leaky bucket, his father's mocking laughter at the open door.

Vic and Tanner took the same seats they'd been sitting in when Dev brought Micah here just a few days earlier.

Dev paced the small open kitchen area. "I'm doing the best I can. It's hard." She fixed Giles with a direct stare. "You of all people should know how hard. I trust Micah. He's my friend. You going to begrudge me that?"

"Your friend nearly got you killed," Tanner said.

Micah dropped his gaze to his feet. "Vray," he whispered.

Tanner glanced at Vic and then back to Micah. "There's something owed, hopper."

"What's owed is on our tab. Micah risked his life to save mine."

Tanner opened his mouth to answer, but Micah interrupted. "He's right, Dev. If it hadn't been for me—for who my father was—you never would have pinged Maldonado's sensors. That's on me."

"That doesn't give them the right to threaten you!"

"But here we are. I want my anonymity. What is it you want?" He was channeling the late senator and the irony was thick enough to choke him.

Vic, silent up until now, leaned forward in his chair. "Hopper is a straight talker. Good."

Micah nodded to himself. Vic was the eldest sibling, the one who seemed to take charge, even over Dev. Now they'd get to the real issue.

"No matter where she ends up, our sister belongs to Midlant. You belong to the void. It's nothing personal, hopper."

"Vic, it's not—"

He cut her off, without even a glance. "Leave her be. For the good of all."

Micah could just about feel Dev vibrating with fury. "And you'll keep my name in confidence?"

"A token of your good faith would not be amiss," Vic said.

Dev grabbed Micah's arm and pulled him to his feet. "I've heard enough of this crap. We're leaving."

Vic stood to block her way. "This is for your safety. Your friend has enemies. Too many already know his secret."

"I am not a child anymore and I don't need your protection."

"Dev—" Vic interrupted. Dev rolled right on as if he hadn't spoken.

"And the truth is, you need me more than I need you. Or you wouldn't be threatening my friend. You're afraid. Afraid I'll leave my past—and all of you—behind." Dev paused, panting to catch her breath as if she'd been running. "And you know what? You should be afraid."

Micah shook his head. She didn't want to lose her family. Not like this. "Dev?"

"You." She poked her index finger into his chest. "Stay out of this."

He couldn't help it—he started laughing. After a moment of shocked silence, Vic and his brothers joined him, leaving Dev sputtering and furious.

While she stomped back to her room, Vic turned to him and spread his arms out in a helpless shrug. "She's deep, deep down, vray?"

"Yeah, I know." Her strength came from Midlant and she should be proud of it.

Without another word, Giles and Tanner slipped from the container, leaving Vic behind. Dev's eldest brother held out a hand. "And hopper, your share's a shake. For her."

Micah clasped Vic's hand, knowing something seismic had just shifted, but not fully understanding what.

"Keep her safe on the highside."

"I promise."

Still gripping Micah's hand, Vic started to speak, paused, shook his head and took a deep breath. "A warning, hopper. Your father's associates are looking for you. Offering a heavy,

heavy pocket for news of your whereabouts."

"And?" Micah's voice was barely a strained whisper.

Vic let go and shrugged. "Morningstars are lazy drunks. All of Midlant knows that. The only thing we can find is the bottom of a bottle, vray?"

Micah nodded.

Dev emerged from the back of the container carrying both of their bags. "You going to stand there while the water rises?"

Vic shook his head. "When the water rises, all swimmers drown."

Her sigh filled the common area. "I thought you'd forgotten."

"Should be able to find a ride at the gate. I'll walk you." Vic hugged her before taking both their bags. Dev let him.

Chapter 16

Barre leaned back in the command chair and propped his legs on the console. "Halcyone, can you pipe in the audio from my room to the bridge? One way only."

The ship's AI played a few bright notes in a major scale and Lowell's deep voice filled the bridge with colorful swearing.

"Volume down by twenty-five percent, please."

Lowell's fury and frustration faded into background noise on the bridge. Barre didn't think the man would take out his anger on the room, but he'd be monitoring, just in case. All his instruments were there.

He considered sending Ada May a message confirming receipt of her "package," but she specifically warned him not to initiate communication while they were underway. Clearly, she didn't trust Lowell or the smugglers either.

Surely there were other places her network controlled. So why risk bringing him to Ithaka? Escorting Lowell there was a risk Barre wouldn't have taken, but it wasn't his choice.

"Halcyone, run the Ithaka program and plot the quickest course keeping the burns under three g's." They were going to need better cushioning at some point—both for acceleration and for temporal damping. Maybe May could help them retrofit the bridge chairs. Cosmos knows it would be a lot more convenient to stay on the bridge during jumps.

The grumbling from his room died down. Perhaps Lowell had bowed to the inevitable. If Ro were here, she'd laugh at Barre's naivete. Halcyone's soft chime interrupted his thoughts and he glanced up at the course she'd displayed on the viewscreen. Three brief stints through interstitial space and two jumps would get them to Ithaka in about six hours of galactic time. Subjective time was a whole other matter.

Barre would still have to make the journey from Ithaka back to Commonwealth space to pick up Ro and Nomi before another series of jumps back to Daedalus. He didn't look forward to the time-lag he'd have to suffer through. Better temporal foam would definitely help.

"Okay, Halcyone, that looks good." He saved the nav program with a musical trigger on a sixty-second delay. It was so much easier for him that way. Everything had a melody—even Lowell's invective had been a kind of percussion—and the briefest musical interlude seemed to carry so much more meaning for him than the same length of words.

"Halcyone, wipe the display."

The screen went dark, accentuating the crack that wandered across it.

"Open a channel to spaceport control."

"Comms open."

"Spaceport control, this is Acting Captain Durbin of the

freighter Halcyone, requesting permission to leave." Barre hoped his voice didn't betray any of his nervousness, given how complicated leaving had gotten the last time he had been here.

"Halcyone, you are cleared to leave. Coordinates for departure window are being transmitted to your ship. Docking clamps will be released on your request."

Halcyone beeped brightly to confirm and Barre's tense shoulders relaxed.

"Thank you, spaceport control. Halcyone out." He waited for the ship to calculate their takeoff trajectory. "Okay. Enable transmission to my quarters."

Another confirmation beep sounded in his mind.

"We're about to leave the docking bay. I suggest you bunk down now."

The sound of rustling filled the bridge. "The conditions here are a little primitive, Mr. Durbin."

"It'll serve and there's a saying about beggars and choosers that I think applies."

Lowell answered with a grunt.

"Don't worry, I'll give you fair warning for any burns or jumps. I did promise to deliver you in one piece."

"Would it insult you to know I'm less than fully reassured?"

Barre laughed. "Fair enough. Are you secure?"

"Yes."

He had Halcyone cut the transmission again and reopened the channel to the spaceport. "Control, we're ready for departure. Release the docking clamps, please." If Larson was true to his word, Halcyone would be free momentarily. Barre wasn't sure what he was going to do if they decided otherwise.

Time seemed to warp in the same way it did during a jump as

Barre waited for them to let the ship go. He was just about to ask Halcyone for the exact elapsed time when the speaker crackled to life again, startling him.

"Stand by, Halcyone."

Barre slammed his hands on the damaged console. Stand by. Stand by for what? For someone to swoop in and grab Lowell? Had Larson double-crossed him? Even if he could send a message, there was no one who could help him. Not Ro, not Gutierrez, not Ada May. It was just him and Halcyone.

He paced the tight confines of the bridge. A slight vibration shimmied the ship and Barre glanced at the dark display as if he could see past it to what was happening.

"Thank you for your patience, Halcyone, docking clamps have been released. Clear skies."

Relief nearly dropped him to his knees and he grabbed the back of the nearest chair. "Halcyone, take us out."

She warbled a cheery tune as the engines ramped up from standby. The ship seemed to leap away from the docking bay with an eagerness that matched Barre's own.

"That's more like it. Let me know as soon as we clear the system." He didn't wait for her confirmation before heading to his quarters. Charon's tune opened the door. Lowell lifted his head from the jump cushioning.

"Do we have a plan, Mr. Durbin?"

"Keep your p-suit on." Barre triggered the nav program before settling into his bunk. "We have one minute before the first burn. Get comfortable. It's a few hours till we get there."

Lowell settled his head back into the foam.

"Ironic, isn't it? All those years looking for Ithaka?"

"Do we have to do this now?"

Barre smiled up at the bunk. "And you still won't know how to find it." Lowell's silence didn't surprise him in the least. He was still smiling when Halcyone's engines kicked off the burn and his suddenly very heavy body pressed down into the foam. The AI communicated a running countdown directly through his neural. Poor Lowell would just have to trust that Barre knew what he was doing and that Halcyone wouldn't fly apart.

She might be old, but Barre trusted her. Numbers flashed in the corner of his mind and ten seconds later, the burn ended, leaving them cruising toward their first wormhole. Barre took pity on Lowell.

"We have twenty-seven minutes on this course before our first jump, so if you want to get up and stretch, now's the time to do it."

"Not a lot of room to stretch here."

Barre rolled out of the lower bunk. "Yeah. Next time, book first class."

Lowell dropped from the top bunk and gave him an apprising look. "All of these yours?"

Over the months he'd lived aboard Halcyone, Barre had figured out how to secure his instruments against acceleration damage, creating temporal foam cradles and webbing for the more delicate ones. "Yes. And before you ask, I play all of them, too. Some more skillfully than others."

He scanned the room. "Impressive. So tell me, how does a musical prodigy get tangled up in the politics of Ithaka?"

"You know, even when you were the comms supervisor, I was never under your jurisdiction, so you can stow the Commonwealth officer act. Now that you're pretty much wanted by all sides of our invisible conflict? I don't think you're in any position to be asking questions." There was a time when Barre would have responded to the habit of command in Lowell's voice, but that was before Halcyone. Before Ithaka.

Lowell spread his arms out. He nearly brushed the walls of the small room. "Can't blame a guy for trying."

"How did you convince Ada to take you in?"

The man laughed. "So she doesn't share much with her lackeys, then."

Barre glared at him. "I may be a lackey, but you're someone with a price on his head and nowhere else to turn."

"Touché." Lowell bowed his head briefly. "I will tell you this— she found me. And made me an offer I found hard to refuse. The rest you'll need to ask her."

There was little chance she would share what she knew, unless it served some larger purpose. Judging by the humor in Lowell's voice, he understood that too. Well, there were other ways of getting information. Lowell should appreciate that, given his present predicament.

Whatever May was doing, she had a plan and Lowell clearly played a role in it. There wasn't much that surprised her, though she had definitely not expected Barre and his music to be able to hack into her personal AI.

"Do you need anything to eat or drink?" Barre consulted the flight plan again. "Oh, and the head is over there." He pointed to the access panel in the wall.

"A full-service cruise, I see."

"Well, water bulbs and meal bars."

"I'll pass."

Barre double-checked his instruments while Lowell used the head. His hand lingered on the neck of the beautiful twelve-string guitar. The strings were lax, so Barre didn't bother trying to play them, but the memory of its lush, resonant voice moved through his mind. He hadn't had enough time to play much of anything these past few months. The only music he'd composed had been the start of Charon's theme and the little snippets of melodic code he used to communicate with Halcyone.

After this business with Lowell was finished, he knew he needed to spend time playing and practicing, immersing himself in the world that had always made sense to him. He did derive a lot of satisfaction from being able to pilot Halcyone, but it wasn't his passion in the way it was Ro's. And playing the part of May's ferryman wasn't his life's ambition either.

When Lowell emerged, Barre checked the time again. "About ten minutes until the first jump."

Lowell eyed the foam-lined bunk with suspicion. "And you're sure this is enough protection?"

"Would you prefer an old jump snug?"

"No."

"Then settle in. I wouldn't risk jumping if it wasn't safe." Halcyone was more than capable of doing the complex math that controlled the dynamic temporal shielding while they slid through the wormholes that connected noncontiguous segments of interstitial space.

The cushioning was an extra level of protection. Without it, they might not feel very well, but any single uncushioned jump was highly unlikely to leave them with a permanent discontinuity between their thoughts and their perceptions. Decades after May and Dauber developed the SIREN code that made jumping almost as safe as traveling through interstitial, medicine still didn't know the precise mechanism of jump-sickness and why not all jumpers had been susceptible.

"If I were you, I'd try to sleep after the next burn."

"Mr. Durbin, I've been hopping through the void since before you were born." He laughed. "Maybe since before your parents were born. I think I know what I'm doing."

"Suit yourself. Five minutes to the first jump."

Above his head, Lowell settled into the foam-lined top bunk in silence. Barre worked on stilling his thoughts. Once they hit the event horizon of the wormhole, there was nothing he or anyone else could do to influence their course. It was all up to Halcyone.

A soft alarm chimed through his neural. Then the ship entered the folding other-space that only existed inside a wormhole and would deposit them, cosmos-willing and in an indeterminate amount of subjective time, on the other side of the galaxy.

Halcyone's background hum vibrated through his mind. It was a kind of music, even if Ro accused him of anthropomorphizing the AI. Using his neural, Barre played a counterpoint to the song Halcyone sang to herself as the ship corkscrewed through the galaxy.

*

Nomi woke, squinting in the bright stream of light. For a moment, she thought that Daedalus had glitched her alarm somehow, before she realized she was home.

"Ro?" Nomi reached out, but she wasn't there. Before she could sit up, the door to her room opened bringing Ro and the scent of fresh coffee. "Ah, thanks!"

"I found something," Ro said, handing her one of the two cups. As Nomi sipped the hot liquid, Ro downed the contents of hers in what seemed like one long swallow. "And I need your help to make sense of it."

"You didn't sleep any last night, did you?"

"Guilty as charged."

Nomi sighed and there was a flash of annoyance in Ro's now muddy green eyes. "I know. You're a big girl. You don't need anyone to take care of you."

Ro winced and turned away.

"I'm sorry. That was out of line."

"It's okay—"

Nomi interrupted her. "No. It's not." She took another slug of her coffee. Normally it was Ro doing the apologizing. "This is a big part of why we came here, so show me."

Ro dropped both their micros on the bed and crawled in beside Nomi. "I knew those pictures weren't just pictures. First off, my father would have never cared enough to keep them. Second, you only safeguard things you love or to hide a secret. Care to guess which one represented the late and unlamented Alain Maldonado?"

Nomi's answer was a quiet sigh.

"It's okay." Ro reached for Nomi's hand. "I can't change my past, but I have you now."

Heat rushed to Nomi's face and she interlaced her fingers with Ro's. "So what did you find?"

Ro set down her empty cup and slipped her other hand free to control the linked micros. "I haven't analyzed it all yet, but the bastard hid all sorts of data in the lower-order bits of the image files. See?"

Virtual windows sprang up all around them. At first, they displayed the photos of Ro and her family. Nomi stared at Ro's mother, wondering what had become of her. Wondering if Ro would ever choose to find out. It wasn't something Nomi felt comfortable asking.

"Here. Look." Ro manipulated the closest display with a blur of her hands and the image shifted to layers of small blocks of eight cells each. She pointed to the lower left-hand corner of the window. "See there? He hijacked the space for his own data."

"There aren't a lot of images in that archive. How much could he have hidden?"

"It's not how much he hid, it's what. Remember all those nonsensical text files?"

"Yeah."

"Well I think what's here in these images is a decryption key. And I'm betting they unlock the secret of the information in those files. I just need to figure out how to assemble it."

"That's an awful lot of layers, Ro. And a lot of trouble to go to for data that was already securely locked. Unless he meant you to have access." It was her DNA that opened the memory cube. What if he was still manipulating her?

"I don't buy it. I'm betting he never figured I'd have the courage to take it from him and he certainly never anticipated becoming elemental particles in space." Ro let her arms fall to her sides and turned to frown at Nomi. "Besides, in what universe do you believe my father had even a micron of sentiment? Those images are a classic smokescreen. The only reason he kept them were to use them, somehow. Like he used everything in his life." She slumped, letting her hair swing forward to cover her face. Her voice dropped to a hoarse whisper. "Do you think she wanted me? Cosmos knows he never did."

Nomi didn't know what to say. Her own interactions with Alain Maldonado had been mercifully brief, but were enough to show her just how abusive he could be. How Ro had survived a lifetime of him spoke to her strength and resilience. "I don't know, sweetie, but you could find out."

She snapped her head up and blinked back the tears she'd been hiding. "I don't ... I can't ... "

"He's gone, now. He can't hurt either you or your mother anymore."

"But I can still hurt him," Ro said, staring through the bright displays. "Or at least destroy whatever his plans were."

Maybe then Ro would find a measure of peace. "Okay. What do you need?"

Ro frowned and turned away. "Well, I already borrowed your house AI for a while. I didn't think it would be a problem. Everyone was asleep, anyway. I know. I should have asked."

While her mother might be miffed, it was good to know that some things didn't change. "Well, as long as you didn't blow it up."

"I'm going to need to use it to analyze the key fragments. And your family will definitely notice the lag once I set my program to run. If we were aboard ship, I could use Halcyone."

"Go ahead. I'll let my folks know."

The relief was evident on Ro's face, but Nomi wasn't sure if it was the permission or the fact that she wouldn't have to confront her girlfriend's parents. Nomi smiled. Probably some of both.

"Can I bring you up some breakfast?" Her father was probably cooking something for them all. Nomi would hate to disappoint him—when Ro was chasing a problem, she'd happily eat food bars as long as they came with a constant infusion of coffee.

"Yeah. Sure. Whatever."

While Ro stared motionless into the displays, already devoured by her father's puzzle, Nomi washed up and changed. She piled their empty cups on the tray Ro had used and headed downstairs to the kitchen. The smell of cinnamon wafted toward her. The sweet rolls were Nomi's favorite. She set down the tray and hugged her father. "You really don't want me to leave again, do you?"

He kissed the top of her head. "I'll send you back with some to store."

"Not the same, but I won't say no."

"Is Rosalen awake?"

Nomi nodded. Ro would need to sleep at some point, but there was no way she'd break from her work now. Not until she either collapsed or bested her father. "She's working. And I've given her access to the house AI. Things may be a little slow."

Her father paused to check the oven. "Let your mother know. I think she was planning on running an analysis later today."

With any luck, Ro would be finished by the time her mother needed the AI's resources. And she wouldn't have blown anything up in the process.

Her father set a timer on his micro and motioned Nomi to the table. "Fifteen minutes. Can you wait?"

"For your cinnamon rolls? I'd leap through a wormhole backward."

He smiled and fell silent for a moment. "How is it on Daedalus? Are you happy there?"

The past few months had been one jump after another into uncharted territory. Everything she thought she had known about the Commonwealth and its history had turned out to be a lie. There was so much she couldn't tell her family. And that was something new, something distinctly uncomfortable.

So, was she happy? Nomi glanced toward the stairs. She loved Ro. Barre, Jem, and Micah had become close friends as well as co-conspirators. She wasn't sure how she felt about that. "Comms is tedious. A first-year student at Uni could do the job." It certainly wasn't using her skills and talents, unless she counted the whole Ithaka situation. But that wasn't anywhere near what Nomi was trained to do. Getting arrested certainly wasn't, either. Yet another thing she couldn't tell her parents. "It's weeks and weeks of routine followed by moments of terror."

"I think that's the reality of life, Konomi-chan."

She smiled sadly—that was what her grandfather had called her.

"Your mother and I, we're proud of you. We only wish we'd been able to afford to pay for your education outright. Then you wouldn't be so far away from home."

And she would never have met Ro or discovered the truth about Ada May and Ithaka. The cosmos had become a much scarier place, but Nomi had no regrets. Maybe someday she could confide in her parents, but for now, their safety relied on her silence. She only hoped that whatever Ro uncovered in her father's files wouldn't put them all at even greater risk.

The lights in the kitchen flickered and the oven alarm blared.

Nomi's father jumped up to check the baking as Daisuke's voice shouted through the house. "Mom! Dad! Who crashed Tetsujin?"

"Konomi?" Her father turned to her, his eyebrows raised.

"I'm on it." She bolted from the kitchen and ran upstairs to her room. As she opened the door, Ro was swearing at their linked micros and the house AI.

"It wasn't my fault!"

"What happened?"

Their words tangled together while the house lights kept flickering.

Ro swung her arms through the air so fast they seemed to blur. Windows all around her blanked and the house lights winked out altogether.

"Um, that didn't help."

"I'm on it!"

A few gestures later and the room returned to its normal illumination. Ro collapsed on the bed, breathing hard.

"Any idea what you triggered?"

"Something big. I think."

Nomi shivered and crossed her arms on her chest. "What do you mean, big?"

Ro gestured at her micro to open a new window.

"Wait. I don't think that's a great idea."

"I'm isolated from your house AI now and it's rebooting. We should be safe."

Should be? Safe? "What if you're wrong?"

"I'm not wrong." Ro paused before swallowing hard. "And I was right about the family pictures. My father chopped up a decryption key and scattered the pieces there. Your house AI helped me extract them. But as soon as I reassembled it, everything locked up. He left a tripwire and I didn't see it. I'm sorry."

"What happened?"

"Whatever he programmed tried to seize all the AI's resources."

"Is that what took it down?"

Ro winced. "No. That was me. I had to crash it and sandbox both our micros to kill his attack."

"What was he trying to do?" Nomi's voice dropped to a whisper.

"Beyond taking control of the AI? I don't know." Ro chewed on the edge of her thumb until she'd drawn blood. "And that's what terrifies me."

"Now what?"

Ro picked up her micro and turned it over and over in her hands. "Whatever I triggered, I've isolated it on this now."

"Are you sure?"

If she hadn't known Ro so well, Nomi wouldn't have noticed the slight pause before her answer. "Yes."

"Then we fit the key to the lock and figure it out."

"Are you sure?" Ro echoed Nomi's own question in a strained whisper.

"This is what we came here for. If you stop now, he wins." Nomi blinked back angry tears. "If that fucker's put my family at risk, I damned well want to know what he was hiding."

Ro canted her head and fixed Nomi with a puzzled stare. "Is that what I sound like?"

"Sometimes?" Ro's look of honest outrage broke the tension and Nomi started laughing. Every time she regained control of her breathing, she'd glance at Ro and lose it again.

"Are you done?" Ro stood, tapping her foot, but she couldn't keep her mouth from curving into a wry smile.

Nomi wiped her eyes and cleared her throat. She hiccupped one more time before nodding. "You're not going to let him win, are you?"

Ro took a deep breath before rebooting her micro and setting it on Nomi's desk. "Not a chance." She frowned at the virtual windows hanging at her eye level. It wasn't a worried expression; it was her focused one. Another window opened in response to her finger flick. One of the text files Nomi had puzzled over earlier shimmered in front of them. Ro zoomed in on the final line of binary they hadn't been able to decipher earlier. "Ready?"

"No. But when has that ever stopped you?"

"Wow. Thanks for the vote of confidence."

Nomi stepped closer and gave Ro's shoulder a gentle squeeze.

Ro gestured at the first window. "That's the decryption routine. If this goes south, the worst it can do is trash my micro."

"Do it."

As Nomi watched, Ro swept the algorithm toward the perplexing file. She held her breath, but the light levels in her room kept steady and there was no sign that their house AI was compromised. For several long minutes, she watched Ro's windows glow silently, but nothing else happened. "Do you think we damaged it somehow?"

"I don't know." Ro chewed her lower lip. "I don't think so. Maybe?"

Slowly the line of numbers at the bottom of the file blurred and triggered yet another window to open.

"Wait. Did you just do that?"

"No."

They were both whispering, as if Ro's dead father would hear them.

"Programs layered within programs. Damn, he was devious."

Nomi glanced between the two displays. "But what was he hiding?"

"Could be anything. Dirt on the smugglers is a good guess."

All the active windows collapsed and before either of them could react, another new one opened and Alain Maldonado's smirking face seemed to be gloating at them from the stored video.

"If you're seeing this, it means two very important things. One, I'm dead." He paused to chuckle, staring out at the camera. "Two, you are now well and truly screwed."

Ro snatched the micro off Nomi's desk, repeating a litany of "Son of a bitch. Son of a bitch. Son of a bitch."

"What does he mean, Ro?"

"I can't turn the damned recording off." She glared at her father's smug face. "Why couldn't you stay dead?"

His deep green eyes seemed to stare right at them, but it was an artifact of the holographic processing on the video. "Whatever he says, he can't hurt you anymore."

Maldonado's face faded from the camera's focus and was replaced by a rapidly expanding stack of plain text files, each glowing in its own window, all while he continued to narrate.

"You underestimated me. The files you're seeing have been broadcast to every major Hub news outlet and every small colony reporter in the cosmos. With each passing second, the data is duplicating itself and using whatever ansible and node it hits as a new repeater."

"Oh, fuck." Nomi moved toward the door. "I have to tell my parents. What if the data gets traced to us?"

The recording window brightened again. "And the best thing is, it's too late. You literally can't stop me."

Both Maldonado's voice and Ro's high, strangled laughter sent chills down Nomi's spine.

"I just did and you, father dear, are a worthless pile of space dust."

"Ro?" Nomi glanced between her and the door, not knowing what to do.

"It's okay. I told you. The micros are sandboxed." She tapped the screen on the little device. "He's trapped in here."

"So nothing got out?"

There was the slightest pause before Ro answered. "No."

Nomi took a deep breath and returned to Ro's side. "I think I need to sit down for this." The two of them sat on the floor, leaning against the bed.

The virtual windows recentered themselves at their eye level under Ro's skilled command, but she couldn't hide the slight tremble in her hands. "Okay. I've shut him up for now. At least we can look through these in peace." She paged through the documents too quickly for Nomi to keep up. "Shit. It looks like he was gathering blackmail material. Going back twenty-five years." Ro pointed at the newest window. All the others darkened and disappeared. A clear-text file slowly came in to focus.

"Blackmail. On who?"

"Everyone. Each of those text files is some dirt on someone, likely high up in the Commonwealth. He'd been building this archive for a long time."

Nomi pulled another file into focus. "Ro, did you read this?"

"I'm little busy."

Leaning closer to the display, Nomi zoomed the tiny text out so Ro could see. "This is an angry screed against the president of UCom-Northwest. From after he got booted out."

"Why am I not surprised," Ro said with a dismissive snort. "My father couldn't manage to keep a single job through an entire contract. Why would his Uni experience be any different? So he held a grudge against the president for all these years. But he kept it all locked away until now. Why? And what could he hope to gain in releasing it all at once?"

If Ro couldn't figure it out, then maybe nobody could. "I don't know. Do you think all of it's like this? Just paranoid rants?"

"He may have been paranoid, but it didn't make him stupid. He had dirt on people. He just never used it." Ro tugged her hands through her hair. "We're going to have to go through all of it. One file at a time."

"And you're certain it didn't get out?"

"Pretty certain." She sighed, her gaze shifting between the window and her micro. "I shut it down pretty quickly. Even if something escaped, it would probably be corrupted."

"We need to make sure. This is my family."

"I know."

Nomi had never seen Ro so paralyzed. Damn Maldonado. He did this to her. Dead and scattered to the cosmos, he still had power over her. Over them all. She snatched up her micro and reconnected to Tetsujin. Using command shortcuts, she navigated to the house's comms subroutines and requested a copy of the logs from the last hour.

"Oh, well done!" Ro said.

They stood side by side reviewing the readout. The only

outgoings seemed to be the expected ones—communications with her mother's lab and her father's school, pings with the colony's array for long-range ansible traffic. Nothing weird. She sighed her relief and turned to give Ro a smile. She was still frowning. "What?"

"Would you think I'm as paranoid as him if I say I'm still worried?"

"No," Nomi said softly. "I'd say you were being careful."

"Can you do a full diagnostic?"

It would take a lot of processor cycles and her family would be annoyed, but they had little choice. Alain Maldonado was nothing if not clever at programming loops within loops, and the barest possibility of some kind of transmission escaping placed the people she loved in danger. Well, Nomi had just been talking to her father about how her skills and talents were being wasted on Daedalus. Now she had a chance to put them to the test.

She clenched her jaw and started setting up the diagnostic. This was all her fault: tempting the cosmic fates was never a wise thing.

Chapter 17

A PULSING LIGHT SLOWLY BRIGHTENED in Jem's mind, bringing him to full wakefulness. He stretched under the covers and yawned before triggering the message waiting for him. It was no surprise that it was from Gutierrez.

/Meet me in my quarters/

He washed and dressed before emerging into the apartment's common area to find his mother sitting slumped at the counter sipping coffee, still in the uniform she'd been wearing last night.

"Mom?"

She quickly straightened up, but not before Jem noted the furrows in her brow and the dark circles beneath her eyes. "You headed off to work with her?"

"Yeah," Jem said, settling the bag filled with prosthetic parts across his shoulder.

"Good."

"Mom?"

One of her eyebrows lifted.

"You should sleep."

She met his gaze with her own fierce one. "I know what I'm doing."

It was an odd answer and it bothered him more than he understood. "Ping me if you need me. I'll be back later."

"Jeremy. Be careful."

He wanted to say the same thing back to her, but held the words back. "Is Dad up?"

"Not yet. But he will be soon."

Whatever was going on between his mom and Targill, Jem hoped she would confide in his father. If the two Doctors Durbin couldn't figure it out together, then whatever problem they had was insoluble. Their extreme competence had always comforted Jem. Until this. Until now.

Jem gave her a quick hug. She startled, then hugged him back.

"Take something to eat," she said.

He grabbed a few plain rolls left over from a dinner-to-go several nights back along with coffee and left before she could criticize his choices. Just outside his quarters, Jem paused to activate the ghost protocol. Better paranoid than sorry. He was starting to get as bad as Ro.

The station bustled with its normal morning activity. Uniformed personnel headed for their first shifts, blissfully unaware of the political currents that swirled around them. It would be a lot easier if Jem could be that oblivious. Sighing, he slipped around them; if anyone greeted him, he didn't notice.

He'd just taken the exit from the north nexus to the corridor that led to the officer's quarters when a voice from behind startled him.

"Now where might the young Jem Durbin be headed with such determination?"

Jerking his head up, Jem whirled around to glare at acting comms supervisor Simon Marchand. The man smiled down at him, looking smug, satisfied. Shit. The ghost program couldn't help when someone was physically looking for him. Had Marchand been following him? Or did he merely happen to find him here? Jem didn't believe in coincidences much these days. "Just walking," he said, shrugging.

"Lieutenant Commander Gutierrez's quarters are here."

"Among others. Sir." His heart pounded and he had to struggle not to clench his hands into fists.

"That's true, Mister Durbin. But irrelevant." He paused to stare directly at Jem. "Let's not play games. Talking in a public corridor is less than optimal."

"Mr. Marchand." The LC's icy voice interrupted them. She stood in the open doorway to her quarters, in uniform, except for the boots.

Jem gazed up at her, trying to convey his apology. She looked away to stare at Marchand, her expression unreadable.

"Both of you, inside."

She retreated and he and Marchand followed. The door sealed behind them. They stood in an uncomfortable silence for a moment until Gutierrez sank into the sofa and propped her bare feet up on the low table that also held her prosthesis. Marchand stared at the partially dismantled and obviously damaged arm before moving to sit across the table from her.

Jem unpacked the contents of his bag, piling the components next to the limb, and took the empty chair. "I didn't bring him here."

"You've been avoiding me, Lieutenant Commander."

"I'm on medical leave. If you have an issue with comms, I recommend you contact Commander Targill." Gutierrez's voice was as colorless as water, but her right eyelid twitched rhythmically.

"You're in uniform, sir."

"I'm still an officer on this station, Acting Supervisor Marchand."

And one that was reminding him of her status. Jem smirked. The LC must have caught it because she threw him a warning glance.

"One who is distancing herself from her commander," Marchand said.

"I'm following my doctor's orders."

Jem snorted. They both ignored him.

Marchand leaned forward in his seat. "I'm not your enemy."

"You have a remarkably boring service record. One could even say generic. Carefully manufactured, perhaps?"

"It's not impossible to hack into Commonwealth systems. As your young friend here can attest to."

"That may be true, but it doesn't help me know who you are."

"I'm not the only one who hides in plain sight."

Gutierrez narrowed her eyes, but otherwise didn't react. Jem wiped his slick hands on his pant legs. His pulse rate rocketed as Marchand spoke. How much did this man know? Who was he working for? The LC never took her gaze off the droll comms officer. She never once glanced down at her sidearm, nor did she move her right arm closer to it, but Jem was very much aware of the weapon. He was betting Marchand was too.

"Look. I didn't need to come here. I'm putting myself at risk as much as you. So let's stop circling the wormhole and commit to the jump. I have as little love for the Commonwealth as you do. I just don't work for the same people."

Jem started, then forced himself to settle back in the chair.

"I'm a decorated Commonwealth officer, Marchand. Where are you going with this?" The edges of Gutierrez's mouth twitched into a half-smile. It seemed more dangerous than her obvious anger.

"That's true, of course. And is that all you are? I think not."

"I'd be interested to know where you get your information."

His eyes twinkled. "I'm sure."

On some level they were enjoying this. Jem wanted to throw up—and for once, it had nothing to do with his head injury. "Why did you help Nomi? You knew she hacked Lowell's records. You could have been charged with treason along with her."

Both Gutierrez and Marchand turned to him. The comms officer smiled. "That's really not how this is done, young man." He jerked his chin toward the LC. "She knows. Listen and learn."

The man's smugness was all on the surface. Below the banter, undertones of fear rang in his voice. Jem folded his arms and snapped his mouth shut. For now, he would listen. If Marchand underestimated him, all the better.

"What I do know is you can't risk disclosing your suspicions to our acting commander. Otherwise, you already would have."

Marchand nodded, conceding the point. "You've triggered my interest. I'm also curious about your friend, here. Interesting that the architect of a particular and very sophisticated illegal data miner is meeting secretly with the station's second in command."

She gestured at the partially dissected prosthesis and its spare parts. "Secretly? No. He's assisting me in the rebuild. There's an advantage not only to having two hands, but having small ones."

"True, but I'm certain that isn't the entire story. Where did he disappear to when he went off to get that neural? There's far more to this young man than exists on the surface."

"He is certainly eminently resourceful. But Jem Durbin isn't the reason you're here today."

"Well, he does factor into my curiosity, but you're the main focus. I have some information you may find valuable. I can assure you, even if we're not exactly on the same side, we share more than you know."

"And what exactly would that be?"

He took a deep breath and let it out before reaching forward to lightly touch the claw of the broken prosthesis. "I know how you lost your arm. I know about Taro."

Gutierrez gasped—a thin, high-pitched sound that was cut off nearly as soon as it started. "How?" Her control snapped back so quickly, Jem almost doubted having seen it slip.

"I served with him. Before he was pulled from the front lines to babysit a certain pair of famous scientists. And I know the story of his death decades ago in your official report was somewhat ... premature."

The LC's face flushed a bright red and her right hand slid down to rest near her holster. A chill moved through Jem.

"I used to be left handed. But I re-qualified as a sharpshooter with my right after my injury." Despite the evidence in her body, her voice remained perfectly calm.

"I have no doubt that you could kill me with a single shot.

But do you really want to have to clean up that kind of mess?"

Jem might have believed Marchand was as cavalier as his answer seemed if it weren't for the strange synesthesia that accompanied his perceptions. Both Marchand and Gutierrez blazed yellow to his senses. He swallowed his unease. They wouldn't let this end in violence. They couldn't.

Gutierrez relaxed her arm. "Point taken. Blood and burns are so hard to get out of the fibers."

Jem exhaled loudly and his two companions laughed.

"I do believe your friend was nervous."

The LC paused just long enough for Marchand to get fidgety. "Jem Durbin is wise beyond his years."

"Point taken," Marchand echoed.

"What do you want?" Gutierrez asked. "You have an intelligence advantage on me, clearly. But you're not here to threaten me. So let's get to it."

"There are things I want, Lieutenant Commander, but I'm here also because of what you need to know." He nodded at Jem. "What he needs to know. And because you're a woman of honor, I'm going to tell you, without any expectation of quid pro quo."

"Fine." The color was still bright on her cheeks.

"If you have the ability to contact Ro and Nomi, you need to warn them."

Jem's head jerked up. "About what? I already told them Targill was here."

"And why do you think he showed up now?"

How much could he tell Marchand? Jem glanced over to Gutierrez. She nodded almost imperceptibly. Okay, then. "Because of the intel we uncovered. You have a copy it. Well, so does Commander Mendez. I think she started poking into it."

"Mendez is irrelevant. She's not even a pawn in this game, but she got swept into it anyway, thanks to you and your friends." Gone was Marchand's Cajun accent and easy humor. "Targill is here to question Nomi and pressure Ro."

"But why?"

"Because Nomi was the one who released your worm and rendered his operative useless, so if he can use her to get Halcyone, so much the better."

"That doesn't make sense. The ship is a barely flying rust bucket that should have been scrapped long ago, and I seriously doubt they can prove anything except that the worm was uploaded during Nomi's shift. Give me five minutes with her micro and I can establish that she was hacked or framed. Whichever looks better." He might need more than five minutes and he'd probably need Ro's help, but it could be done. He should have thought of that sooner.

"Targill is a threat. To all of us. He wants what Ro knows about her father, and that 'barely flying rust bucket' holds the route to Ithaka."

Jem caught a blur out of the corner of his eye and when he blinked, Gutierrez was standing over Marchand, her sidearm drawn, her eyes narrowed, her right hand steady.

Marchand sighed, but didn't move a muscle otherwise. "I told you. I knew Taro Odachi during the war. And after."

Gutierrez drew in a sharp breath.

"By then he was already the Ferryman and he ferried me to Ithaka once, a long time ago. So you see, we used to work for the same team."

"So you know ... You've met ..." Jem could hardly breathe.

"The doctor isn't the hero you think she is." He stared up at

Gutierrez. "I believe you know that."

"She let you walk away. I think that says something." Gutierrez lowered the weapon and stepped back.

"It says she's a fool who can't see past her own old hurts and her need for revenge."

Jem stood with his fisted hands on his hips. "How can you say that? She's the smartest person I've ever met."

"Intelligence doesn't protect you from making the wrong choices." Marchand's voice was gentle, but it cut close to home. Had Jem made the wrong choice to contact the black-market and get his neural? It had healed some of the damage from his brain injury, but it also had ensnared him, his brother, and their friends in a covert war between Ada May's Ithaka and the Commonwealth.

"So if you abandoned Ithaka and you aren't Commonwealth, who are you?" Gutierrez spoke with a quiet intensity that was at least as menacing as her weapon.

"There are a lot of folks scattered through the cosmos who resent the hidden planet. Who supported the independence movement and were left drifting in the void when Ithaka retreated to lick her wounds." He paused to glare at Gutierrez. "Or did you think the reunified Commonwealth of Planets was just one big happy family?"

"But you want the same thing she does," Jem said.

"Do we? I want greater autonomy for the colonies and planets who take all the risks just to feed the Commonwealth and good old mother Earth. I thought that was what Ithaka was fighting for, too." He shrugged. "But I don't see any independent colonies, do you?"

Gutierrez lowered her voice to a deadly rumble. "If you know her at all, you know that's what she has been working toward all these years."

"Even Taro had his doubts. But then again, he always saw you as somewhat naive."

She raised her sidearm again, but this time, her hand trembled. "Get out."

Marchand stood, holding his hands out in front of him. "Tell her there's still a chance to earn back the trust of those who would have followed her. Tell her Targill is more than he appears to be and a greater threat than she realizes. To all of us. Tell her if she's not willing to risk her precious isolation, we'll all drown when the water rises."

Gutierrez didn't move. She didn't even blink as Marchand turned around and left. The only sound in the room was the door as it whooshed closed behind him.

*

Halcyone emerged from the final jump into the system where Ithaka hid, not in a fold of space, but in a part of the cosmos Ada May had literally erased from all the maps. As soon as the ship signaled Barre the all-clear, he rolled out of the cushioned bunk.

"I don't have to remind you to stay here, do I?"

"Your ship, your rules, Mr. Durbin."

Barre didn't doubt for a moment that Lowell would try to take over Halcyone if he had the opportunity. "I'll contact you when we're ready for hand-off."

"I'll be here."

After quickly splashing some cold water on his face, Barre made his way to the bridge. Halcyone was sharing a steady stream of trajectory data with him as they orbited Ithaka. "Send our official greetings."

The bridge's display was blinking for an incoming comms request as Barre stepped through the permanently opened doors. "Put it through, audio only."

The speakers crackled to life. "Welcome home, Halcyone. Proceed to docking bay seven one. Do you require assistance?"

"Negative, Ithaka control."

"Confirmed. See you on the ground, Halcyone."

"Halcyone, out." Barre leaned against the captain's chair. "Ready to take us in?"

The AI warbled her assent.

"Let's see who's there to greet us this time." When he and Ro had bumbled their way here following Jem, they had been met by the late Ferryman. And had been confronted by the truth of Ada May and her quiet insurgency. From that moment on, everything in their lives had been upended.

Halcyone broke orbit, shifting them with perfect precision onto their glide path. There were no other ships entering or leaving Ithaka's system. That was interesting.

They landed with the barest of bumps. The ship clanged softly as the docking clamps engaged. Barre linked to Halcyone and played the main melody of Charon's theme through his neural. "Unlock the door to my quarters and open internal comms, please."

Her confirmation chirp sounded both in his mind and through the bridge.

"Mr. Lowell, we have arrived. Meet me at the airlock, please."

"What? No escort?"

"I think you know the way."

Before he left the bridge, Barre engaged the AI's security protocols. If Ada could manage to reproduce the music Barre had composed for Charon and use it to force Halcyone to respond, then she deserved the ship. He smiled. He'd like to see her try.

Lowell was waiting beside the airlock, his face composed in a neutral expression, his arms clasped behind his back.

"Well, I'm fairly sure they won't execute you out of hand."

"No, they'll probably wait until they've wrung me dry."

Barre wasn't sure if Lowell was joking or not. He didn't think Ada May would condone torture or extra-judicial killings. But it was true that Lowell posed a threat—either by his direct actions or because he was wanted by so many different factions within and without the Commonwealth.

The ferryman conducted souls to the afterlife. A role, were it anything other than metaphorical, that Barre would never be comfortable with. "Well, shall we?" He gestured broadly while requesting Halcyone to cycle the lock.

As soon as the inner door opened, Lowell ducked inside. Barre squeezed in behind him, not wanting to let the man out of his sight until Ada May's agents had him secured. The inner door sealed. The outer door unlocked. Lowell stiffened briefly before stepping into the docking bay. Barre held back and scanned the room.

Three people stepped forward to meet Lowell: two members of Ithaka's security detail and in the middle, the small, limping form of Ada May. All three were dressed in the nondescript jumpsuits that seemed to be the standard uniform of Ithaka. May briefly caught his eye and nodded before turning to the former comms supervisor.

"Cameron Marcus Lowell, welcome to Ithaka."

"Dr. May. A pleasure to meet you." Lowell stepped forward to offer her his hand. Both her security guards stiffened and placed hands on their sidearms.

Barre narrowed his eyes. Security on Ithaka hadn't been armed the last time he was here. Had something changed? Or was this simply a precaution because they didn't trust Lowell?

May shook her head in a tiny gesture Barre would have missed had he not been watching her. The guards returned to their rest position as the tiny scientist took Lowell's hand.

Her other hand whipped forward faster than Barre believed possible and before Lowell could pull away, she'd fastened one of the metal security bracelets around his wrist. The snick of it closing filled the silent docking bay.

"I've given you freedom of the public areas of the station. If you try to access locked sections, Lethe will notify security."

Lowell kept his voice level, but his body stiffened. "And the cuff? What's that all about?"

May slid her sleeve up to reveal hers. "Security, access, and comms, among other purposes. You'll find it is quite robust and quite versatile. Don't try to remove it. Barre? You'll need one for your stay as well."

"Yes, ma'am." He held out his arm. The cuff snapped around his wrist.

"You have full access." She turned to her guards. "Escort our guest to his quarters and see to his comfort."

"I was under the impression that my debriefing was of critical importance, Dr. May."

Debriefing was an interesting word to use. Did it mean Lowell had been working for Ithaka all along? The man was skilled, but was he skilled enough to be juggling that many alliances?

"So it is," she said. "And I'll be with you shortly."

Barre raised an eyebrow as the silent security guards flanked Lowell and marched him out of the bay. The man left without a backward glance, which showed either supreme arrogance or resignation. He was betting on the former.

"Ferryman, you and I need to talk."

That was true, but May was not likely to want to hear what Barre was going to tell her.

"Come on. I have some coffee and lunch waiting."

The doors of the docking bay opened again as she limped toward them. Barre followed, questions streaking through his mind like meteors. The corridors of Ithaka seemed quieter than they had before. Personnel passed by them, greeting Ada May in subdued voices. All of them were now armed.

When they reached May's quarters, she waved her wrist at the sensor plate. The door slid open and Lethe greeted him in a slightly stilted version of Ada's voice.

"Welcome home, Ferryman."

The AI brought the lights up over a small sitting area as he followed May inside. "Hello, Lethe."

"I really appreciate your help." May sat to pour two mugs of coffee from the thermal carafe waiting on the low coffee table. Barre stepped forward to take one.

Not sure where to begin, he paced the distance between the door and the chair, cupping the warm mug in his large hands. "I'm not him. I can't be him." More than that, he didn't want to be Ithaka's ferryman if it meant losing himself.

"How is she?"

Barre sighed. "Still not talking to you?"

"More or less. I got a brief message yesterday, but no response to my reply."

"You're going to drive her away for good if you don't let her be."

May's hand shook, sloshing coffee over the rim of her mug.

"Jem is working with her to restore her prosthesis. Her injuries will heal in time." But would the emotional wounds? Part of him wanted to coax her story from May, but even though Barre wasn't a physician, that felt uncomfortably like an unforgivable breach of privacy.

"Emma knows the resources of Ithaka are at her disposal. I suppose that will have to do for now." She sighed and set her cup down.

It had only been months since Barre had seen the venerable scientist, but in that brief time she seemed to have aged considerably. Her limp was more pronounced, her shoulders more stooped, and her blue eyes seemed tired and dull.

"I'm sorry," Barre said, softly. It wasn't what he had intended to say. He wanted to shake off the mantle of the Ferryman and make sure she understood Halcyone wasn't his to offer even if he had wanted the job. But he thought about what it would be like for Ro if she were to lose any one of them. Taro Odachi and Lieutenant Commander Emmaline Gutierrez were Ada May's "crew" on both a literal and metaphorical level. It had to be devastating.

"I'd like you to observe my interrogation with Lowell."

She had pivoted so quickly, Barre felt dizzy. But he noted that she didn't use the word "debriefing." Interesting. "I'm not sure I can add anything beyond what you already know. You have the data Jem gathered."

"You have good instincts. And you have an ear for patterns. I simply want you to tell me what you hear."

"Isn't he less likely to talk with both of us in the room?"

"Oh, you won't be in the room." She smiled and Barre saw a flash of dangerous humor brighten her blue eyes. "Lethe, lights up, tap into the surveillance feed and display."

The AI illuminated the far end that had been lost to shadow. Ada May's computer lab took up a space larger than Halcyone's bridge. Its large viewscreen spanned one entire wall of her quarters.

Cam Lowell's image sharpened until it looked as if he were pacing the far side of the lab, instead of in some guest space deep within Ithaka. Guest. Barre grinned. Lowell was probably as much of a guest here as he had been on Halcyone.

"Make yourself comfortable. I think I've kept him waiting long enough. If you need anything, ask Lethe." She turned to leave.

"So he's not one of your agents?"

May sighed. "No."

"Why did you bring him here? Surely there were other places you could have questioned him. Hell, we could have set up an interview from Halcyone."

"Lowell required sanctuary as a part of his agreement. This is the most secure spot in the cosmos. For now." She sighed again, her back turned to Barre. "And some conversations need to happen in person and in real time." When she reached the door, she paused. "I haven't left Ithaka in a very long while. Initially that was for security reasons. We couldn't risk anyone recognizing me, discovering I was very much alive. But what started as necessity became habit. With Taro gone and Emma hurt, perhaps it's time to rethink that."

Before he could respond, she'd left her quarters, leaving him alone with her AI and the image of a very irritated Lowell on the large screen.

Lowell would be more than irritated when Ada May was through with him, but Barre doubted the former comms supervisor would be as perplexed as he himself was right now.

So much for refusing Taro's job.

While he waited for May to reach Lowell's quarters, Barre took the opportunity to check his messages, knowing there was no better security in the cosmos. His micro had automatically paired with Lethe at some point, which spoke of a certain level of trust. Barre was sure that trust had its limits, though.

Not that he could blame May. It wasn't just her life she was safeguarding, but the lives of all the people hidden here with her and hidden in plain sight through Commonwealth-controlled space. If he had that many people reliant on him, Barre would be just as paranoid.

His micro buzzed for incoming messages. He ignored the routine traffic—music industry news got delivered every morning along with notifications of downloads of his samples and full tunes. It had been far too long since he'd added anything new to his music server. Junk solicitations got filtered out for the most part, but some always sneaked through. There was a brief note from Jem in the midst of all the spam.

"Holy mother of the cosmos," Barre whispered in the empty lab. Targill as acting commander of Daedalus meant nothing good for any of them. He glanced up at the sudden whoosh of the door to Lowell's quarters opening. As Ada May lurched through them to confront her new guest, a chill slithered down Barre's spine. It couldn't be a coincidence. Not with Targill's former operative here.

Could Lowell have laid down a trail to follow? Barre didn't know the specific technical details of how Ada eliminated Ithaka from Commonwealth maps, but he knew it was a masterful hack. If it weren't for him and Ro stumbling over the hidden nav program in Halcyone's damaged mind, they would never have found their way. His pulse slowed from its panicked pace. If Targill knew how to find them, he'd already be here.

As Lowell and Ada began to speak, Barre asked Lethe to send a copy of the audio directly to his music server. May wanted him to listen? He would listen. And then analyze everything he heard. In the meantime, he sent a message to Jem and Ro.

/Crossed the river Lethe with one soul. Your news complicates delivery. Keep your head down/

He was probably being more cryptic and more careful than he needed to be. And he still felt as if they were all far too exposed. Barre returned his attention to the conversation unfolding in front of him in real time. For now, Ada May needed him to pay attention to her interview with Lowell. Maybe the man would reveal something that would help them understand what Targill was doing and how much of a threat he posed.

Then, regardless of what May said, Barre would rejoin Ro and Nomi. Returning to Daedalus while Targill was at the helm seemed a huge risk, but what choice did they have? If they tried to run, they would only call more attention to themselves. Besides, Nomi belonged to the Commonwealth. Dereliction of duty carried heavy penalties; she was already in enough trouble.

He focused on Cam Lowell. Was he adding to that trouble or giving them a way out?

Chapter 18

"Come on. We need to talk to my parents."

Ro bunched the thin blanket in her hands and stared past Nomi at the closed door. "I have to monitor the diagnostic."

"It's linked to my micro. And hiding here isn't an option." Nomi gave her a measured look.

"I know." Ro stood and picked up an image cube sitting on Nomi's desk. It lit up as soon as she touched it and projected a rotating display of family pictures. It was impossible for her not to compare these to the images her father had used to hide his program. There was even one where the Nakamuras were holding a baby Nomi that was nearly identical to one of Ro with both of her parents. But they were galaxies apart from one another: The Nakamuras were laughing, looking down at the serious-looking, dark-haired Nomi with obvious love and delight.

She set the cube down gently. Nomi's arms circled Ro from behind and Ro leaned against her, sighing. "I know," she repeated. "I fucked up. I'll think of something."

"Would you stop that?"

Ro stiffened and pushed away from Nomi. "Stop what?"

Nomi spun her around and grabbed Ro's arms. "Stop blaming yourself for everything that happens around you. Stop thinking you have to somehow atone for it all, alone."

She was right, which didn't make it any easier for Ro to accept. "Okay, then. What are we going to tell them?"

"Ithaka is out of the question, right?"

"Unfortunately." Ro knew how hard it was for Nomi to keep so much from her family.

"Then we focus it on your father." She winced and her brown eyes narrowed. "Is that going to be okay?"

"You mean, do I have any problem throwing my father under the afterburners?" It was nearly what had happened to him. Literally. "Not for a nanosecond."

"Then let's go."

Ro would have rather faced a gauntlet of smugglers and salvers than deal with Nomi's parents. "How long will it take for your diagnostic?"

"Hard to say. Could be a few hours."

She followed Nomi downstairs, missing the freedom of Halcyone with a sharp ache. Paul and Azuki Nakamura were sitting in the kitchen, picking at the remnants of sad-looking sticky buns on a shared plate.

"They're not much to look at, but they still taste good." Paul smiled and gave them each one. "Coffee?"

Ro nodded as she slid into a seat, feeling guilty, but the fatigue was rapidly catching up with her. "I'm really sorry about the computer. I —" Nomi nodded at her to continue. "I never would have used the AI if I thought my father's data posed a threat."

"A threat? I don't understand." Azuki leaned forward and glanced at Nomi. "I thought he died."

"It's complicated," Ro said. When in the cosmos was her life ever not? "My father was complicated. No. He was more than that. Alain Maldonado was an abusive, nasty man and even after he died, he found ways to interfere with my life." That was all true and saying it out loud was both terrifying and freeing. Especially in front of strangers.

Nomi squeezed her hand under the table.

"He left me a memory cube. Presumably with his will in it. But nothing my father did was ever straightforward, and he'd encrypted it."

Paul reached over to pat Ro on the shoulder, and if not for Nomi holding her hand she would have jumped out of her chair. Her father didn't seem to notice. "Something in his will crashed our house machine?"

If she could be sure that was the extent of it, Ro could leave the lie there. But not if something had gotten out on the comms. "Not exactly."

"So what happened, exactly?" Azuki spoke with Nomi's quiet authority. The intense focus in her expression was eerily similar as well.

Ro glanced toward Nomi, hoping she would answer, but that was the coward's way out. "Apparently, in addition to being a terrible father, he was also a terrible person. He was keeping files on people he considered his enemies. When I unlocked the data, I must have triggered a fail-safe program he'd hidden." She swallowed hard, hoping that Nomi's diagnostic would come back clean. "It tried to take over the house AI."

Azuki pushed away from the table and stood, her eyes open wide.

"I deliberately crashed it to keep it from being hijacked." Ro looked up at Nomi's mother. "I'm sorry. I shouldn't have —" She blinked rapidly to keep the frustrated tears from falling. "I shouldn't have come." Everything she said was far too close to the truth. And she shouldn't have involved Nomi's family. How had she been talked into this?

"Did it work?"

Ro looked down at her folded hands.

Nomi came to her rescue this time. "I'm running a high-level diagnostic on Tetsujin. If he was corrupted in any way, I'll know."

Azuki stood behind her husband and placed her hands on his shoulders. Her face was an unreadable mask—eyes narrowed, lips pressed tightly. Ro had had a lifetime to recognize that kind of anger. She couldn't bear to look at Nomi. It wasn't hard to guess how she would choose if it came down to Ro versus her family.

Paul sighed. Ro stiffened in anticipation, as if for a blow that would be worse for striking her with polite words.

"Konomi, we know there's more you're not telling us."

Ro's pulse pounded in her ears, but nothing could drown out what she knew would come next.

"Your mother and I trust you. We've always trusted you. That's not going to stop now, no matter what trouble you've wandered into."

Blinking in confusion, Ro looked up into Nomi's parents' faces. She hadn't imagined the anger; it was still clearly there, but it wasn't directed at her or Nomi.

"We're here. Whatever help you need. Just ask. Both of you," Paul said.

"But get our machine running again, okay?" When Ro met Azuki's eyes, they held a momentary spark of amusement. "Or Daisuke will come after you."

Ro ducked her head, hating the way her cheeks blazed and betrayed her emotions. Out of the corner of her eye, she saw Nomi stand to hug both of her parents.

"I'm sorry. There are things I —" Nomi glanced at Ro. "Things we can't tell you. It's not a matter of trust." Her voice broke and it took her a few seconds to gather herself. "It's about your safety."

"Nomi —" her mother began.

"Please. Don't ask me anything else." Nomi busied herself checking her micro. By the time she spoke again, her voice was calm and steady. "We should know for sure soon. The quick scan came back clean. That's a good sign."

But not anywhere near as definitive as Ro needed it to be.

"So now what?" Azuki asked.

"Have you considered turning over the data to Commonwealth authorities?"

It was all Ro could do not to snort at Paul Nakamura's naivety. Turn the data over. As if that was the solution to their current problem. The Commonwealth—or at least Commander Mendez—already had the contents of the cube, as much good as it would do them.

"We have," Nomi said. Neither a lie nor the complete truth. Ro hated that Nomi was becoming so skilled at deception.

Ro scrubbed her eyes with her fists. Time to focus on what

was next. "I have to go through all my father's files and figure out which are the ravings of a paranoid man and which are credible, actionable threats. I need to know who his enemies were."

"What you need is sleep," Nomi said.

"When this is over, you can put me in cryosleep for a month, okay?" Ro tried to keep her voice light, but the look Nomi gave her said more than any spoken rebuke.

"Give me your micro."

"Nomi ... "

The rich, bright laughter from Paul was completely unexpected. "She's Azuki's daughter, Ro. Trust me, you won't win this round."

"You've been up for what, thirty hours straight?"

Ro shrugged. It was probably more than that, but who was counting?

"Even you can't run like this for long. If you were one of Halcyone's engines, you'd take yourself off-line."

She hated to admit it but Nomi was right. The fatigue was one of the reasons she'd screwed up and triggered her father's little booby-trap.

"I promise I'll wake you as soon as the diagnostic finishes running. Then, at least, we'll know where we stand."

They were all watching her: Azuki and Paul with curiosity, Nomi with a fierce challenge in her expression.

"At least let me start a basic text crawler. Then I'll have some preliminary sorting to review when I wake up."

"Fine."

"And no more than two hours of sleep."

"Six."

"Four."

"Fine."

Paul smothered his laugh with an obvious cough.

"We'll have dinner for you when you wake," Azuki said.

How could Ro thank these people? How could she live with herself if she'd brought danger to them?

Nomi towed her upstairs to her bedroom and stood, tapping one foot while Ro set up the basic text program. She held out her hand. "Micro."

"You don't trust me."

"Let's say I know you."

Sighing, Ro passed it to her. "Four hours. Not a minute longer. Shorter if your diagnostic finishes earlier."

Nomi tucked Ro's micro in a pocket with her own before stepping forward to hug her.

"And let Barre and Jem know what's going on."

"Hush," Nomi said.

"And Ada."

"We'll tell them when there's something to tell." Nomi moved away a small step and pushed Ro toward the bed. Startled, she lost her balance and fell against the piled blankets and pillows. "Sleep. That's an order."

"Since when am I in your chain of command?"

"Since always." Nomi tried for a serious glare, but the corners of her mouth twitched into a brief smile.

"What would I do without you?"

Panic chased the amusement away and Ro kicked herself for opening her mouth.

"It's going to be okay. Sleep."

Nomi dimmed the lights and opacified the curtains. The late

afternoon turned into night in the small room.

Ro curled up and closed her eyes. Even if she couldn't actually sleep, the rest would do her good, as much as she wasn't going to admit that to Nomi. She fell into a dreamless sleep, hugging Nomi's pillow to her chest.

*

Barre paced in front of the large viewscreen in Ada May's lab as her interrogation proceeded. "Lethe, mute sound, please," he asked. As skilled as he was at hearing the music behind speech, sometimes it was even more useful to watch the body language without the words getting in the way. The AI was cloning the audio recording to his music server; he could analyze it in a number of ways later.

For now, he watched as May crossed her arms and leaned back against a chair that made her look even smaller than she was. Barre would be willing to bet it was calculated to make Lowell feel overconfident. Lowell had stood when May entered the room and he now sat opposite her, his body posture mirroring hers—crossed arms, legs braced on the floor.

Tense. On guard, even.

What Barre had seen of Ithaka confirmed that sense of wariness. Armed guards where there hadn't been weapons before. More security personnel and fewer civilians walking the corridors. Was all that because of Cam Lowell?

What possible threat could one stoop-shouldered, gray-haired officer pose?

Barre laughed in the empty room. A similar description could be applied to Ada May and as far as he knew, she was the

Commonwealth's public enemy number one. At least among those forces in the Commonwealth that knew she was alive.

Was that Targill's game? Had he tasked Lowell with finding her? It made some sense. Lowell had connections with the black-market—connections Targill could disavow if needed. And it would explain Gutierrez's long surveillance of the comms officer.

Lowell leaned back and rubbed his temples. Barre requested the resumption of the audio track.

"... unauthorized freelancing." He shrugged. "I still have no idea how he figured it out. The system was foolproof. Even that hacker kid didn't know about it."

So Lowell was doing some kind of side work Targill didn't approve of. Is that why he'd fled Daedalus? Somehow that seemed like a manufactured excuse.

"No system is foolproof. You should know that by now."

"Not even yours?" Lowell's eyes lit up. "The infamous Dr. Ada May. How have you managed to hide yourself and this little enterprise for so long?"

She leaned forward in her chair and gave him an intense glare. "An imperfect solution but one applied with near perfect care."

"Now you're just being deliberately obtuse."

Smiling, May relaxed again. "Actually, no. But I don't expect you to understand." She glanced up at where one of the AI's sensors must have been because it looked like she was smiling directly at Barre. "It's quite straightforward."

Barre wasn't sure what she meant either. From what he did understand, she had somehow programmed a brilliant hack that altered the Commonwealth star charts to erase all evidence of Ithaka's presence. A place you couldn't get to didn't exist. It seemed like a pretty perfect solution to him.

"However, that has no bearing on why I allowed you to come here. Nor on why you accepted my offer."

"If you already know why I'm here, why don't you tell me, then."

A dangerous amusement danced across Ada May's face. "You're not here because you're worried the Commonwealth will find you." Before he could interrupt, she held out her thin hands. "Well, you are concerned, but that's not your main purpose. For one thing, you're hoping to shake off your pursuers long enough to access your funds and launder them through more acceptable channels. No coincidence, I think, that we happen to have secure side channels into the Commonwealth banking networks."

Lowell sank back against his chair.

"But even that is a sidelight. You were planning on infiltrating our comms systems so you could get a ping-back through the ansible network, essentially doing an end run around my protection. Before selling our location to the highest bidder."

Lowell laughed. "You can't fault a guy for trying."

"Actually, I can. But that's beside the point."

"If you already knew what I was going to do, why did you give me sanctuary?"

"You, Mr. Lowell, are going to be our honey pot." Ada's smile lighted her whole face.

Lowell stood up so abruptly, his chair toppled over behind him. "And who are you trying to catch in your trap?"

Now her eyes were twinkling in their amusement. "Who in the cosmos would most like to make an example of both of us?"

The color left Lowell's face. "Targill."

"Of course."

"You wouldn't." He took a step closer to her, and Barre moved toward the screen as if he could physically protect the frail scientist. But she had Lethe and the resources of Ithaka watching over her. In truth, Lowell posed no direct threat to her and they both knew it.

She looked up at him, her expression calm. Lowell exhaled heavily and sat back down. "Wouldn't what? Turn you over to him? Actually, that's up to you."

"What do you mean?"

"Think about who's the bigger threat here versus who just might be able to save your complicated life. Understand—you don't matter to me, other than as a means to an end. Ithaka isn't some big secret military installation. It's a massive maker space and innovation hub. We value good tools here. The question you have to answer is how useful a tool can you be to us.

"I'm going to give you some time to think, Mr. Lowell. The resources of Lethe, our station AI, are at your disposal, within obvious limits. We'd prefer your cooperation." She stood and limped out of the guest room she'd given him, leaving the former comms officer staring after her with his mouth open.

Barre poured himself another coffee and freshened her cup as he waited for May to return.

"That was quite a show," Barre said as she entered.

May collapsed into her chair and reached for her cup. Her hands shook. "It wasn't a show, Barre. We need Targill. And Lowell is the best way we know to reach him."

Was that why they'd ramped up security on Ithaka? "He's a decorated war hero. You can't disappear him from Commonwealth space and not create an intergalactic incident."

She sighed and remained silent for several long minutes. "We're not terrorists, Barre. I don't want to kill him. We just need to talk. To negotiate."

"Negotiate what?"

"The peaceful reintegration of Ithaka into the Commonwealth."

Barre set his cup down on the coffee table and sat heavily. "Wait. What? You're giving up?"

May sighed again. "Barre, look at me. I'm old. I'm tired. I was older than you are now when I lost my best friend to the madness. The man who killed him became a friend in time, and then I lost him, too. I drove Emma away when I made her pay too high a price for her loyalty for a second time. I'm tired."

Her words burned through him like a solar flare. Charon. She was talking about Charon. Charon killed Charles Dauber. "I don't understand."

She set down her cup with deliberate care as if she was afraid she'd break it otherwise. "The Commonwealth was using us to justify their war. Before Charon became my Ferryman, he was a Commonwealth soldier. With orders he believed he needed to follow."

"Taro Odachi," Barre whispered. He had never known his story. Nor his connection to Gutierrez.

"Taro acted on what he was told was a threat. For a long time, I hated him, but I never blamed him."

"And Gutierrez?"

"Emma never forgave him for what happened that day. But for the sake of the greater good, she agreed to work with us."

"What happened?" Barre asked.

Ada shook her head. "That's not my story to tell."

Different pieces of history and fragments of conversations clicked into place. "It's when she lost her arm, isn't it?"

"Yes."

"And Taro was involved?"

She sighed. "In a way."

"She's still grieving," Barre said, blinking in his confusion. Taro had sacrificed himself to save her life and in the end, that may be what she couldn't forgive more than anything else. "She said she wouldn't mourn him, but she was lying."

"I know. She has every right to be furious with me. Because of me, she lost her arm, her idealism, and her certainty." May's voice dropped to a whisper. "She deserved better. It took losing her and Taro for me to understand. I'm sorry, Barre. I shouldn't have pressured you to take Charon's place. This isn't your fight. It's mine and I can end it."

Not his fight. Truly? Is that what she believed? Barre stood to pace the small sitting area. But it had become his fight, certainly from the moment he and Ro tracked Jem here, or rather had been dragged here by their damaged AI. But maybe even before that.

When he, Micah, Jem, and Ro had been forged into an unwilling crew, they had found a place to fight from, even if what they had been fighting for at first was simply their own survival. "You've sent your people away."

If May was confused by his sudden shift, she didn't show it.

"Yes. All non-essential personnel."

It wasn't that there were more security staff, it was that there was less of anybody else. "This was their home."

May lowered her gaze to the floor. "They have been relocated to safety."

"Are you trying to be found?"

She glanced back up at him quickly before turning away.

"Holy mother of the cosmos. You're going to let them destroy you."

"It's one of the possibilities. Lethe puts it at about a seventy-three percent probability. The odds become better if we can convince Targill to talk first."

"And if you can't?" Barre thought of the tall, dour soldier who had earned his scars in the same conflict that had cost May so much. May had lost so much to.

She spread her hands out. "Then they win."

"You can't mean that."

"I tried to wage a silent war and watched as everything I created got turned into a tool for greed and corruption. I perfected the Underworld as an unhackable communications subsystem and the backbone of a trade community unhindered by the Commonwealth. I thought I'd figured out everything, including the fact that they couldn't shut it down without permanently disabling the ansible network.

"I was an idealistic idiot. Now I can't untangle Ithaka's work from the cartels, the weapons dealers, and the black-market profiteers. Not without shutting down our whole infrastructure and much of the Commonwealth's along with it.

"That was my work. I allowed it to spin out of control. That wasn't supposed to be my legacy. Now I'm going to use it as leverage."

Barre studied her deeply lined face, searching for some assurance and finding only her quiet resolve. His voice dropped to a shocked whisper. "You're going to threaten them with shutting it all down."

"If that's what it takes to get them to talk."

"You can't be serious."

"I've been at this for forty years and practically nothing has changed. The military government is still consolidating its power and actively strangling the colonies. And for what purpose? I was supposed to fight for them—for the people like my parents who died because fixing infrastructure is expensive and their lives were cheap."

"So you're giving up? And how do you think Emma will take that?" Barre deliberately used the LC's first name, though the implied familiarity felt strange.

Ada stared straight at him without flinching. "She will hate me. But she already does a little, I think. And at least it will free her from her ties to Ithaka. Besides, there's a solid chance this will work."

"A twenty-seven percent chance."

"Not exactly. Lethe doesn't have enough data to predict success, but she does know several failure scenarios. There's an eleven percent chance that simply contacting Targill will cause him to be assassinated, which would not bode well for Ithaka."

"You mean open hostilities. War."

"Probably."

"You're going to get everyone here killed."

"Possibly. But by the time that's a reality, I'll be the only one left on Ithaka."

"Dr. May!" Barre whirled around and came to kneel by her chair. "You can't do this."

She patted his shoulder. "Well, of course I can, young man. But there's still a chance it won't have to come to that. And if I'm not willing to take that chance, then I truly have betrayed my ideals.

"I'm sorry to burden you with this. If Charon were here, he would have told me I was being a fool. Go back to Daedalus. Despite what you probably think, this isn't ill-considered. Lethe and I still have a few tricks up our sleeves. And who knows? It might just work." She laughed. Barre wished Jem were here to tell him what colors lived in the sound.

How could he just leave her? Her plan was an elaborate form of suicide. And for what? So she could absolve herself over her guilt for losing Taro to death and Gutierrez to disillusionment?

May leaned over to take Barre's hand. "Everything's going to be all right. You'll see. Have dinner with me later."

Barre blinked unexpected tears from his eyes.

"Are you still creating music?"

He nodded.

"Will you play something for me?"

"Yes," Barre whispered. He'd play Charon's theme for her. As a warning. As a gift.

Chapter 19

Nomi watched as Ro's breathing deepened and slowed. Given other circumstances, she'd like nothing more than to curl up beside her, but for one thing, Nomi didn't want to risk waking her. For another, there was work to be done.

She relinked their micros. While Nomi wasn't the skilled programmer Ro was, she still knew her way around the little computers. She set them on top of her desk. The glow from the virtual windows created a cone of light around her that didn't extend to the bed or the sleeping engineer. In one display, Nomi watched her diagnostic run in real time, not that the raw data would tell her much besides the fact that it was still churning through the AI's systems.

In the second window, Nomi monitored Ro's text analysis. Like everything Ro created, it used small blocks of code to build an effective and elegant little program: one that did exactly what she intended and nothing more. It was an aesthetic Sofu would have admired. Not for the first time, she regretted he and Ro never had the chance to meet.

Nomi glanced at the bed. Ro's hair spread across the pillow like a tangle of gold filament. In sleep, her guarded expression softened. Perhaps, in time, she would be able to express that vulnerability in her waking life, too. But first, they had to break her father's hold on her.

And that meant organizing and understanding his blackmail files.

The diagnostic would notify her when it completed; worrying about what it would or wouldn't show wasn't going to help. Nomi sighed and turned to Ro's program. It had opened a third window where it created a hierarchy out of Maldonado's files.

More than that, it analyzed the contents to form a histogram of sorts, grouping together files that included similar text and weighting them preferentially for review. Within each grouping, it rank ordered data by coherency, flagging files with the highest emotional content and the most keyword repetition.

It was a clever sorting rubric. Nomi was amazed Ro had been able to set it up so quickly, especially given her exhaustion.

Dimming the other two windows, Nomi focused on the rapidly updating results. Examining the partial data-set would slow the sorting down some, but it was a performance hit Nomi was willing to take. Ultimately, even the most brilliant algorithm needed the kind of relevancy a human mind could bring to the assessment process. While Nomi might not have known Maldonado long, she understood him well enough to start to analyze what the program found.

She opened the first file and scanned the text. It was a string of barely coherent phrases strung together with profanity used as a kind of punctuation. Nomi was about to disregard it and go to the next one, when she caught a familiar name: Dominic Targill.

An image of the scarred, silver-haired starship commander filled Nomi's mind. In the span of a heartbeat the memory of his interrogation returned with uncomfortable clarity. Despite the fact that Nomi had been confined to her quarters, interrogation was probably too harsh a word for their conversation. Targill had been utterly polite as he'd asked her questions about Lowell and Ro. Nomi understood him wanting intel on Ro, but his probing about Lowell didn't make a whole lot of sense, given he'd been the comms officer's handler.

Had Targill been looking to trap Nomi in a lie? Or had Lowell kept intel isolated from the hand that fed him?

The only thing that connected Ro to Lowell was Ithaka: He wanted to find it. She knew it existed and how to get there. Or, rather, Halcyone did. And Targill had been overly curious about the ship, too.

Somehow, Targill had incurred the wrath of Alain Maldonado. Nomi shook herself out of her memories and took a closer look at the file. The date-stamp was nearly two decades old.

She leaned back in her chair and brought the window closer, but it didn't force Maldonado's words to make any more sense. She set the file aside and scanned the list, looking for another that contained Targill's name. There were dozens and the program hadn't even remotely finished its sorting routine.

This would have gone faster if they could have used Tetsujin, but the house AI was still working through its high-level diagnostic. Nomi glanced over to check again and this time was rewarded with a blinking green cursor. Holding her breath, she scanned the results. The house AI had not been hacked. Relief flooded through her and dialed down the fear for her family from near-panic to just obsessive worry.

And true to the fast scan, there had been nothing sent through the comms array. Ro had shut it down in time. Nothing could be tracked back to Nomi's family. She whispered a quick prayer to the gods her grandfather had honored even if only out of habit, before turning back to work.

There was more to assess, but now Nomi had other priorities. She cloned a copy of the scan to Ro's micro. Maybe something in the assessment would help them figure out what Maldonado had been trying to accomplish. For the moment, she needed to keep poring though the man's data.

Alain Maldonado and Dominic Targill. Whatever happened between them, it had started decades ago and consumed a lot of Ro's father's processor cycles.

"Huh," she said.

"What?"

Nomi turned, ready to apologize, and found Ro already sitting up at the edge of the bed watching her.

"You're cute when you're working."

"You're supposed to be sleeping."

"I was. Now I'm awake. Show me what you got." Ro stood and padded barefoot over to Nomi's desk.

"Tetsujin's scan came back clean. I copied you on it."

Ro let out a long exhale.

Nomi pointed at the mass of files delineating Maldonado's hatred. "Do you think Targill knew your father was stalking him?" Without waiting for Ro to answer, she shook her head. "He couldn't have. He let Maldonado serve aboard the

Hephaestus when we were searching for Halcyone. Or maybe he did know and it was a matter of keeping his enemies closer." Targill had even asked her about Ro's father and what she thought of him. He'd seemed so concerned for Ro's safety, but maybe that had been a smokescreen, too. "None of this makes sense."

Ro rested her hands on Nomi's tense shoulders. "My father hated everyone and everything. But this seems over the top, even for him."

"I can't precisely identify what triggered his fixation on Targill, but it started when your father was at University." Maybe he'd been connected to Maldonado's expulsion. "Do you think he had any real dirt on him?"

"Or is it just the ravings of a paranoid lunatic?"

"Yeah. Exactly."

"My father was many things, but even at his most unhinged, he didn't rage at shadows. There has to be something."

"We can't exactly track Targill back all those decades without generating a great deal of curiosity and interest from the Commonwealth."

Ro leaned forward to take a closer look at the file Nomi had been looking at. "That's odd."

"What?"

She pointed to two words at the bottom of the screen. "Reaction chamber."

Ro's father was an engineer, but why would he add that to information on a Commonwealth officer? "What do you think it means?"

"No idea. But my father didn't waste words. If he wrote it, it was important." Ro took control of the kinesthetic input. Her hands blurred the virtual windows as she changed the search parameters of her text crawler. A new window opened with a short list of filenames—each for a different person Maldonado had been monitoring.

Nomi scanned down quickly, but Ro was quicker. "Son of a bitch," she whispered, her hands jerking to a stop in mid-air.

They both stared at the name at the bottom of the list: Corwin Rotherwood.

"Open it," Nomi whispered. The late senator's file had a host of additional names associated with it: politicians, Commonwealth officials, and others she didn't recognize. And at the bottom, that same phrase: Reaction Chamber.

"It has to be a code of some kind, but what in the cosmos does it mean?"

"Why bury yet another level of encryption here? Your father already collected enough to incriminate several dozen very important people. What if it means just what it says?"

"That makes no sense. A reaction chamber is where the combustion takes place in an engine or power plant."

But it did make sense. It was about power. Just not the kind Ro was thinking of. All of those people were power brokers of one sort or another. Nomi was willing to bet the names she didn't recognize were part of the black-market and the cartels. And judging by the presence of Targill and Rotherwood, all of them capable of triggering any number of explosions—literal and otherwise.

Nomi's mind raced, finding a logical pattern in what had seemed like ansible nodes, pinging randomly in the darkness. "You couldn't figure out why your father would sit on all this material without acting on it? He wasn't finished yet. He was putting a puzzle together and Rotherwood was one of the pieces.

"What if the weapons smuggling deal and the money were just a smoke screen? Or maybe an added bonus." Ro was frowning at her, her eyebrows drawn together. "Look." Nomi waved at the dozens of windows hanging in the air around them. "All these people? They are the Reaction Chamber. It's a government within the government—the place where all the real power is concentrated and channeled."

"And what? My father wanted to take it down?" Ro snorted. "He's not any kind of hero. Not even an anti-hero."

The nodes were connecting almost faster than Nomi could process. "No. Don't you see? He wanted in. His collection may have started as a revenge fantasy, but at some point he stumbled onto the truth." Now that Maldonado was dead, they might never figure out how, but it wasn't all that surprising given his connections with the black-market and the cartels, and his skill at hacking. "That's why he never acted on those files. Getting to be part of the Reaction Chamber would be a lot bigger than taking Targill and the rest of his targets down. It's why he worked with Micah's father and when Rotherwood died, tried to get access to his money. He figured he'd buy his way in. Be in charge for once. But he didn't count on you. Or Dev."

"Or the pissed-off smugglers."

"But mostly you."

"Son of a bitch. He was going to give them my ship as a peace offering. He must have figured out Halcyone's history. Knew she could access Ithaka." Ro fell silent a moment before swearing softly. "Targill has to know about Halcyone, too. Otherwise why make a salvage claim? She has no value, not even as scrap, at least not to a high-ranking Commonwealth officer."

"We need to get back to Daedalus and warn Mendez. If she goes after Targill with the info we gave her, it'll go critical and blow up in her face."

"Can we trust her?"

"She tried to help me, Ro. Don't you think we owe her something?"

Ro's micro buzzed. The virtual windows winked out as she picked it up and checked the small screen. "Too late." Her space-pale face was as white as Nomi had ever seen it.

"Ro?"

Before she could answer, Nomi's micro also chimed with incoming messages. Notes from Jem and Barre decrypted themselves as she watched. "Holy mother of the cosmos," Nomi whispered. "Are you seeing this?"

Ro nodded. "We have to get back to Daedalus."

"And face Targill? It's too much of a risk." Could they stay here? Nomi glanced around her childhood room, her eyes unblinking. Not without putting her family in even more danger than they already were. "Ithaka. We could go to Ithaka."

Ro shook her head. "Leaving Jem alone at the helm? Not a chance."

"But ..."

"Think, Nomi. You belong to the Commonwealth. What happens if you go AWOL? Oh, and conveniently with me and Barre on Halcyone. Do you think they won't figure it out and find us? Even if we disappeared to Ithaka, we couldn't stay there forever. They have leverage on us. Your family. Jem."

Nomi's face flushed. "But what else can we do?"

"We contact Barre and have him pick us up as soon as he can get here. We head back to Daedalus at the end of your bereavement leave. Like nothing's changed. They can't know what we know. Even if Targill suspects something, he won't go after us directly. He has no evidence. We keep working on my father's files until we find something we can use to protect ourselves."

"And then what?"

"Hope it doesn't explode in our hands."

She shook her head, but knew Ro was right. They couldn't stay here. They couldn't run away. But she wasn't going to leave her family unprotected. Not anymore. She took a deep breath and met Ro's puzzled gaze. "I'm going to tell them what they need to know."

"Okay."

It wasn't the response Nomi expected. "No argument?"

"No static. You're right. Go talk to your folks. I'll message Barre and Jem." She sighed. "I'd better let Micah know what's going on, too. He deserves to know."

Nomi paused at the door and looked back at Ro, lit by the glow of a dozen virtual displays. "I'm scared."

"That makes two of us."

It wasn't the answer Nomi wanted to hear. She opened the door with trembling hands and went to find her parents.

*

"Shall we get to work?"

Jem jerked his head back to Gutierrez from where he'd been staring at the door in Marchand's wake. The LC had a faintly amused expression on her face.

"What the hell are you so happy about?"

"Happy? No. But at least we know where we stand with our Cajun friend."

"Is he?"

"Is he what?"

"Our friend."

Gutierrez's eyes had a distant look to them. "For the most part."

"What's that supposed to mean?"

The LC didn't answer. Jem sighed and sank to the floor near the prosthesis, sifting through the spare parts and tools he'd borrowed from medical.

"Fine. There isn't much I can do, but I can help you fix this. And then maybe you can do the things I don't have the strength and power for." Jem meant with her damaged limb, but it also was true for the political mess they had blundered into.

"Fair enough," Gutierrez said. "Let me know what you need me to do."

"You could sit down for starters." She was pacing the room like a tiger in a cage. "And you could warn Ada."

Gutierrez didn't answer and Jem turned to the pile of components. Most of the work would be plug and play, except for getting the artificial neural network to interface with the remains of the LC's own nervous system.

It was delicate work that would take a steady hand and an acute sense of vision. The steady hand he had. Jem just wasn't sure he'd be able to focus for a long enough time to get the job done. "I'll do the best I can, but I still think ..."

"Leaving isn't an option. Especially not with Targill here."

Jem sighed. She was probably right. Besides, they couldn't get to Ithaka without Halcyone, and the ship and her crew were otherwise occupied. Even if they were here, they couldn't risk taking Gutierrez off-station now. Targill was far too interested in her. And at this point, Jem wasn't so sure Ro, Nomi, and Barre should return anyway.

Fixing Gutierrez's prosthesis was something he could tackle. Once she had two functioning arms, she could actually return to work. Get close to Targill. Discover what he knew. "Fine," Jem said again, though inside he was anything but fine.

He opened both the upper and lower access ports and did a diagnostic on the wiring. The input/output modules were functioning. Both the upstream sensory data and the downstream motor messages passed through the artificial nerves according to specs. Jem suspected that normal specs wouldn't be good enough for Gutierrez, but that was going to be her problem.

She came over to sit next to him, pulling her chair close. With a thought, he transferred the diagnostics' results from his neural to the small screen on his micro. It was getting easier—maybe because of practice and maybe because his brain was healing. Either way, he was grateful.

"The attachment harness needs to be in a nonstandard configuration because of the extent of the damage to the residual tissue." Her words were as matter-of-fact as if she were talking about fixing some piece of generic machinery, and not her own arm.

"I'm on it," Jem answered, keeping his tone as neutral as hers with an effort. "Before we hook you up, I want to replace the kinesthetic stabilizers." They would be the trickiest of the limb's components. It was possible to use a prosthetic without them, but that placed an increased demand on the neural. The performance hit wouldn't be all that noticeable in day-to-day functioning, but Gutierrez had tuned the pre-processing to such an extent it had allowed her left arm to work with exceptional precision. "You're not going to be happy with how it feels initially," he warned.

"You're the one who suggested we go this route."

It was still the best way to get her a functioning arm. "I suspect you'll need to stay right-handed for a while."

She touched the empty space on her right hip where her holster sat. "That's not a problem."

They worked in an easy silence, interrupted by Gutierrez softly making a suggestion or brief comment as Jem swapped and tested components.

"You're good at this," she said.

Jem glanced up at the LC, the microloupes magnifying the lines around her eyes and lips and across her forehead before they automatically adjusted for distance vision. There was a time when Jem might have bristled at the implied surprise of the compliment. Now he simply thanked her. "It's still pretty crude, but it should give you about thirty percent function or so in the limb. Ready to give it a try?"

"Let's go."

Jem felt a flash of orange before she hid her worry behind her usual control. He suppressed the urge to reassure her, not because she didn't need the support, but because she did. In a way, she and Ro were alike. But at least Ro had Nomi. Who did Gutierrez have?

Jem sealed both access ports and watched as the seams vanished. She could have easily matched the color and texture of her intact limb—synthetic skin was that good. But she had opted for the more primitive-looking bare metal along with the claw hand. It sent a definite message; Jem just didn't know who it was meant for.

He slipped off the loupes for a few minutes to let his eyes rest before tackling the complex wiring harness that connected biological nerves to artificial ones, and stood, stretching his spine. The series of pops was satisfying. "You can't stay mad at her forever."

"You don't understand."

"Maybe not, but you're not the only one who's lost something."

Gutierrez's face flushed a deep red before she turned away.

Jem struggled with the urge to apologize; he hadn't meant to shame her, but it was true. It had taken up until this moment for him to realize just how true. The damage from his head injury wasn't ever going to miraculously or fully heal. The nanites that created his neural did a good job bridging the gaps, but he would always struggle with glitches in his cognitive function. The trajectory he had been certain his life would follow was altered for good. He might always need the benzos and the anti-nausea meds.

So be it. Helping the LC had shown him what he could do, working with his brain and the neural. Whining over what he couldn't do wasn't going to make his life any better.

And pressing Gutierrez wasn't going to force her to do what she didn't want to do. "I think you're making a mistake, but it's your choice. When we're done here, I'm going to contact Ada and Ro so I can pass on Marchand's intel."

"Fine." The LC's lips were pressed into a tight line.

Jem picked up the nominally repaired limb, the installation

kit, and his loupes. "This will be easier if you're lying down."

Gutierrez walked across the apartment and opened the door to her bedroom. It was as impeccably furnished as the rest of her quarters. The bed was made to military precision, which couldn't have been easy with one arm. She slipped off her over-shirt to expose the ruined remnant of her shoulder and stretched out on the left edge of the bed.

He placed the prosthesis next to her and opened the proximal access hatch. "It may feel weird until I can modulate the sensory feedback."

She raised an eyebrow and gave him a half-smile. "This isn't my first jump."

Jem pulled over a chair before putting the loupes back on and dialing up the magnification to the highest setting. Under their added light, he could trace the slender nerve filaments that had to be joined to either end of the connecting harness—biological nerves on one side, artificial ones on the other. Once he finished the repair, she'd be able to disconnect and reconnect the harness one-handed without exposing the nerves to further decay. "I have to remove the inhibitory seal on your shoulder."

"Do it."

He unfolded the installation kit, triggering its sterile field to deploy around Gutierrez. Then he pulled out the portable sterilizer and ran it over his hands, the prosthesis, and the wiring harness. "We could do this in medical. It would probably be easier for you."

"Just get it done."

He winced. "It's going to hurt."

"I've dealt with worse."

Jem linked the loupes to his neural and displayed the

schematic like an overlay. A wave of dizziness made his vision blur. He shut his eyes and concentrated on calming his mind. It was easier when all he saw was the schematic. The visual input from the loupes added a layer of complexity that he fought to integrate.

"Jem?"

"Working on it," he said through gritted teeth. Vomiting all over the LC's bedroom was not part of the repair process. He forced himself to relax and the nausea retreated. "Okay." This time when he opened his eyes, the immediate data from the loupes didn't trigger any added dizziness. He rotated and adjusted the magnification of the overlay so it matched the LC's anatomy.

He selected the tiny injector that would dissolve the goop sealing the residual limb's nerves and keeping them from scarring. Wincing on her behalf, he deployed the solution. Gutierrez didn't even twitch. Other than a sip of indrawn breath, she betrayed no reaction, but the sound of that tiny gasp burned through Jem's mind. He pulled his hands away from her shoulder and swallowed hard.

The clock was ticking. Once the seal was gone, her remaining nerves would begin to form tiny vesicles that would scar them to the point of uselessness. He took a deep breath and focused on the proximal end of the wiring harness. It was already prepped with the nerve-growth-factor glue that would allow the artificial nerves to interface with the biological ones. He just had to connect them all. Just.

There wasn't time for doubt. Jem channeled his mother and focused on the work in front of him. Even Gutierrez vanished until all there was were the tiny filaments of nerves and the glowing schematic that showed him which to connect.

Sweat beaded on his forehead and upper lip. He ignored it. By the time he'd joined the last nerve pair, he was breathing as hard as if he'd been working for hours in an EVA suit.

His hands shook. Once he capped the connection, he dropped the tiny forceps back into the sterile field before leaning back in the chair and closing his eyes.

That was the hard part. Connecting the distal end of the harness to the artificial plexus of the prosthesis was simple. Or at least simpler. He didn't have to worry about the nerves scarring. This part wouldn't hurt. After that, the rest would be up to her.

"You okay?" he asked.

"Everything's comets and quasars," she snapped. "Can we get on with it?"

Jem laughed and the tension in his body eased. "Aye, aye, sir." With steady hands, he linked up the artificial nerves to the harness. "Done." The final step was to sheath the proximal end of the prosthesis and Gutierrez's shoulder before enabling full nerve transmission. "Do you want me to do the honors?"

But she had already gotten there. The claw end of her prosthesis opened and shut once with a soft clink. Gutierrez gave a grunt of satisfaction and sat up at the edge of the bed. "Nicely done," she said as she pulled her shirt over her head and newly integrated arm.

"There are a bunch of diagnostics recommended in the schematics."

She stood and laughed. "I've had one of these a hell of a lot longer than you've been alive."

"Point taken." Jem doused the schematic and removed the

loupes before packing up the installation kit. He was looking forward to a long rest in a dark room. "You probably should keep this. Just in case."

His micro buzzed as he handed the kit over. Without conscious thought, he opened the message directly using his neural. It decrypted and displayed instantly and as he read Ro's message, Jem stumbled, falling against Gutierrez.

Poorly integrated micro-servomotors whined as she struggled to catch him. The claw bit into his arm before she was able to modulate its force. Jem swore and regained his balance.

"What?" Gutierrez demanded.

He read the message again. The fear morphed into anger and back to fear again. They were coming back to Daedalus to face Targill and what they knew changed everything. It was worse than Marchand had suspected. Targill was much more dangerous. "You want to continue to feel sorry for yourself? Go ahead. Have fun watching everything you care about, everything you worked for burn. I'm sorry. I can't." His hands shook as he whirled away from the LC and headed to the door.

She caught up with him in the living room, stopping him with her right arm. The warmth of her hand penetrated his light shirt and he stopped short.

"Tell me."

Jem refused to turn around. "You've made your position very clear. You don't want to get involved." He pressed his hands against his thighs. This was big. Bigger even than when he blundered into Ithaka.

She spun him to face her and repeated the demand: "Tell me."

He scanned Ro's message again, hoping he'd read it wrong

somehow, but Targill's secret society was described in terse, blunt words that hadn't changed. "Ro dug into her father's files. There was blackmail material hidden under levels of encryption."

Gutierrez started to interrupt. Jem shook his head.

"Never mind. That's not the important part. Somewhere along the way, Maldonado found something. Something bigger than you or me or even Ada May and Ithaka." He stared right into her dark brown eyes. "You sure you want to know?"

She dropped her hand away from Jem.

"Do you think it's a coincidence Targill is here? Marchand didn't and he didn't know the half of it. Everything orbits around him. We all believed Ithaka was the biggest secret in the cosmos, but we were wrong. Targill has connections to the cartels and smugglers, to movers and shakers in the government. It's all beneath the surface.

"He's been gathering power and influence from within the Commonwealth itself for decades. If he wins, it's war." Jem could hear his voice rise in pitch and volume as the fury shook through him. "But you're out of the game. Why would you care?" After all they had done to safeguard Ithaka, Ada May's loyal guard dog had abandoned her post.

Gutierrez stepped away from Jem. Blinking back tears, he watched her walk across the living room. That was that. He had held onto a tiny hope that she would shake off her self-pity and do the right thing.

"I'm done here. Don't ask me for any help again." He got to the door when her voice stopped him. She wasn't talking to him. Jem leaned against the door, closed his eyes and listened.

"Daedalus, open a channel. Private message to Durbin, Leta.

Official business. Please record."

"Channel opened."

"This is Dr. Durbin."

"This is Lieutenant Commander Gutierrez. My prosthetic arm is functioning at"—she studied the readout for a moment —"forty-three percent efficiency and I request formal clearance to return to duty."

Jem gasped and his eyes sprang open.

"Are you sure, Lieutenant Commander?"

"Yes, Doctor."

"Upload the telemetry. Let me take a look."

As he waited for his mother's response, Jem stole a glance at Gutierrez. She was staring back at him with an unblinking gaze.

"Lieutenant Commander Emmaline Gutierrez, you are cleared to resume light duties. Your firearms rating will be contingent on your marksmanship scores. Durbin, out."

Without a word, Gutierrez checked and tightened her holster before sweeping past him into the corridor.

Jem blinked up at the empty apartment. "Well, space me."

Chapter 20

Aʙᴛᴇʀ ᴛʜᴇʏ'ᴅ ʜᴀɪʟᴇᴅ ᴀ ʀɪᴅᴇ and negotiated passage to the spaceport, Dev retreated into a stony silence Micah didn't know how to break. At least this time the driver didn't try to talk to them. Micah paid the man, grabbed their bags, and headed toward security screening.

As the line snaked closer to the waiting Commonwealth officer, Dev's spine stiffened and her hands balled into fists at her side. The armed woman gave her a withering glance and demanded her ident. Dev handed over her micro without a word.

The soldier gave no signal that Micah could see, but two additional officers appeared and separated Dev from the line. "Excuse me," Micah said, using his father's best official voice, but before any of the security detail could answer, Dev turned to warn him off with a quick shake of her head and a narrowing of her eyes.

"Yes?" The woman in charge of the security station turned to him, her gaze suspicious.

As Dev vanished down a turn in the corridor, he swallowed hard, adopting the bored traveler's stance he'd seen his father use on the rare times he'd flown without official Commonwealth clearance. "How long will this take? I have a transport to catch."

"Ident," she snapped. Micah forced himself to relax before placing it in her hand. His clearance seemed to take significantly longer than it had on the outbound trip. Sweat beaded on his forehead. Had the Morningstar brothers betrayed him? Was his identity invalid? Why had they taken Dev away?

Seconds ticked by in an agonizing slowness until he couldn't measure his subjective time any more than he could during a jump. He glanced back, but there was no sign of Dev.

"Mr. Chase?"

Micah started and looked up into the agent's face.

"My apologies for the delay. You are cleared for reentry." Her former brooding expression had shifted into something more obsequious.

Micah felt his shoulders drop. His Commonwealth-forged identity was still intact. Dev's brothers hadn't lied.

"I'm sorry, but there are a few questions we need to ask before scanning for plant matter."

Plant matter. She had to mean bittergreen. It was a good thing he hadn't tried to smuggle any past entry control.

"Have you visited any farms during your stay?"

"No."

"Contact with any stray animals or livestock?"

"No."

"Do you have any seeds or spores on your person or in your baggage?"

"No."

"Please stand on the marks." She waved him toward the booth beside her counter.

It was a broad spectrum scanner with a decontamination cycle, guaranteed to render any seeds or pollen sterile. But Micah didn't need viable seeds to extract useful information from a plant's DNA. If they weren't going to physically search him, it meant they probably didn't care all that much if people smuggled in small amounts of wild bittergreen for personal use. He couldn't imagine the practice was widespread, given the time, energy, and expense of getting what was a poor relation of a relatively inexpensive drug through security.

He could return and take back a sample after all. Maybe it wasn't fully a lost cause.

The officer returned his micro and passed him through with a bored wave. He waited near the gate, scanning anxiously for Dev. Why had they detained her? She had the right travel authorizations, and her University ident should have given her easy access.

They would be boarding soon and still no Dev.

What would he do if they wouldn't release her? What could he do? He had no political power, nor could he call on his father's name.

The gate agent had made the last call announcement for their flight and still Micah waited. There was no way he'd go back without Dev. He was about to look for the security officer who'd screened him when Dev emerged from a previously hidden door, adjusting the buttons on her shirt with shaking hands.

Relief surged through him as he waved her over to the gate. "Our flight's about to leave. What happened?"

"Nothing. Just the normal exit interview." Her voice was

hollow, but her eyes burned with barely controlled fury.

"Dev?"

She stared past him. "Everything's fine."

Micah took a step closer, but before he could say anything else, she strode toward the gate. "We need to board now."

She closed her eyes and pretended to be asleep during the entire flight. Micah tried to break her silence again after they'd landed in the New Chicago Spaceport and had secured a transport back to campus.

"What happened back there?"

"Random secondary screening." She turned away trying to hide the shame and fury in her expression.

"The hell it was. Tell me that happens every time you try to leave Midlant."

Dev shrugged. "You can't shout the water down."

"We're both students. You have the same rights as I do."

"Really? Not in my world." Dev fell silent again and Micah sat stiffly beside her, fuming on her behalf. "I'm sorry about my brothers." Her voice was hoarse and barely filled the back of the small transport.

He sighed. "Don't be. It's not your fault. My father was a complete bastard. But here's the thing: he was also a smart bastard. They wouldn't have stood a chance." But in the end, the senator's survival instincts and his savvy hadn't saved him. Not when he'd been sold out by his own son.

"You have every right to be furious."

Their transport slowed to a stop in front of their dorm building. Micah waved his micro over the sensor and the doors opened.

The Morningstar brothers had only done what they thought

they needed to for their family's survival. Micah might have done the same in their place. Besides, Dev was the one who should be angry. Angry at the lives her brothers had to lead. Angry at the intrusive search she'd had to endure just because she'd been born in Midlant.

After unlocking their apartment door, Micah dumped his bag inside and shuffled over to the sofa in the dark. Dev sat opposite him. Neither of them triggered the lights.

"So what now?" Her voice was quiet and small, still.

"I have no idea." Did it even make sense to stay at Uni and earn his botany degree? With a decent sample of wild bittergreen and the primitive lab he'd had on Halcyone, he could probably hybridize a new strain. And then what? "I've been so focused on cracking the sterile seed problem, I honestly never planned much further."

A bunch of messages scrolled across the screen as his micro logged itself in to the University network. He ignored the memos from his adviser and saw that most of the other mail was department related. It would wait. An encrypted message from Ro caught his eye. His hands shook as he raced through what she sent. "Fuck. Holy fuck," he whispered.

"Micah?"

He tossed his micro over to her. "You need to read this."

She scanned Ro's message, her eyes widening. "Did you know?"

"That my father was part of a secret cabal working to wrest control from the Commonwealth?" His choking laugh filled the room. "Not so much." How much of his father's public face had been a mask he slipped on? Had any of the man's supposed humiliation been real? It could all have been a cover. All the moves, the isolation, being blackmailed by the cartels, just part of an elaborate act.

Which meant it had never been Micah's fault. All those wasted years he'd carried the guilt for ruining his father's career. He stood and walked blindly until the wall stopped him. Without thinking, he kicked the faux plaster surface and howled as pain spiked through his foot.

"Micah?"

Stupid. Stupid. Stupid. He crumpled to the ground.

"Come on. Let me help you."

She boosted him up and he leaned on her as he hopped to the sofa.

"How could she have loved him?" he whispered. "Everything my father did was a lie. Everything."

"I'm sorry."

"I'm not. Bastard's dead because of me and you know what? He fucking deserved it. I'm just glad my mother died before she discovered the truth."

"What will you do now?"

Micah didn't have a word for the strange mix of emotions swirling through him. "All those wasted years," he thought, shaking his head. He eased his throbbing foot out of the protective shoe. "I don't know. Even if I could reverse engineer the sterile bittergreen and flood the market with a strain the cartels couldn't control, what would it get me? It's not going to bring my mother back."

"It would inconvenience the cartels."

"There's that." Micah shrugged. "And then what? There's nothing useful for me here anymore. I guess I could go anywhere. I have my father's money." He blinked past her, seeing instead the smuggler's space station and the surprise on the bartender's face when Micah had revealed his name. That was something more valuable than all of the senator's hidden accounts. And far more powerful.

A new jump path suddenly opened up before him and Micah struggled to map out the branching possibilities. He must have made a noise because Dev turned to him, her brow furrowed.

"What?"

He shook his head, but couldn't push the idea away. "Maybe there's a seat in the Chamber for another Rotherwood."

The sound of Dev's indrawn breath filled the room.

"No. Really. Think about it." Micah's own thoughts spun like an out-of-control flitter. "Targill's been playing a massive game of 'nought and shuttle with us. We just didn't realize."

"Your father tried to run with the big dogs. Look where it got him."

"What are you saying?"

"Maybe you should take advantage of your anonymity. Stay out of this, Micah. Live your life. A life your mother would have wanted for you."

Micah canted his head and stared at Dev. "And just let some secret organization roll over us? I thought you'd be on board. The power contained by the Chamber could blow the settlements apart."

She shrugged. "The Commonwealth. The Reaction Chamber. The cartels. Even Ithaka. None of them would as much as throw a float if a deep was drowning. It doesn't matter who's at the controls. Not to us."

"It should matter. It has to matter." Micah couldn't believe he was defending either the Commonwealth or Ithaka, but at least it was a status quo he understood. "I've told you enough about my father. Do you really think an organization made up of people just like him is going to do anything but aggressively pursue its own self-interest?"

She laughed, and it was a harsh, bitter sound. "And that's different from the way it is now? I knew you were naive. I didn't think you were that naive."

"And what will you do, Dev? Return to your coursework? Get your degree and act like nothing in the cosmos has changed?" He wanted to ask her how getting her diploma was going to make Midlant better, but the pained expression in her eyes told him she'd already gone there. "Tell me you're not tired of being treated like a potential terrorist every time you move in and out of Midlant. I saw the look in your eyes at the spaceport. I'm not stupid."

"I promised my brothers I wouldn't abandon them and I won't."

"I could siphon off some of my father's money for them. Then you would be free —"

"No." Her arms were folded across her chest, and her eyes blazed. "We're not your charity. Keep your blood money." She sighed. Her shoulders relaxed. "Get your degree or not. Go back to Daedalus. Stay on Earth. It doesn't matter. You have a chance at a life, free from your past. Why would you throw all that away?"

Micah swallowed hard. Running away was his father's course. "Ro, Nomi, Barre, and Jem—they're like my family. No. They are my family now. I can't let them fight alone. Not when I can help them. Not when I'm probably the only one who could."

And there was Dev. He wouldn't abandon her. He stared at

her. She was the first to break eye contact.

"Vray. That I understand. But Micah, if you dive into that current, you'll surely drown."

"Maybe. Maybe not. Vic warned me before we left. The cartels are already looking for me." Micah had known using the Rotherwood name had been a risk when they were tracking Maldonado, but they hadn't had many other options. "Which means the Chamber knows who I am." Hell, it had been Targill who'd given him his new identity. "I have a way in and it may be the only way I make it out alive."

The Rotherwood name would give him access. And he was enough of his father's son to know just how to put Maldonado's intel to work for their advantage.

Dev took a deep breath and smiled fiercely. "So what are we going to do next?"

"We?" His eyebrows lifted.

"Your share's a shake, hopper. A deep's word counts for all. Besides, they've kept us under water for too long. Maybe they forgot some of us learned to swim."

∗

Barre retreated to Halcyone, leaving the unnatural quiet of Ithaka behind. The ship greeted him with a fanfare that played directly through his neural. Despite the fact that he had taught her how to "sing," the degree of nuance and meaning she could imbue in just a few measures of music continued to amaze him. Without using any other language than melody, Halcyone managed to convey a welcome and a question.

"We'll head back to pick up Ro and Nomi in the morning

before returning directly back to Daedalus. Pass me the flight plan and I'll approve it after dinner."

Halcyone answered with a confirmation tone.

Being part of a ship's crew had never been among Barre's ambitions. Neither had uncovering a galactic conspiracy. All he'd ever wanted was his music. Halcyone opened the door to his quarters before he even had the chance to ask. He patted the sensor embedded in the bulkhead as he went inside.

There was barely room to walk past the bed, but Barre didn't mind. What he needed was here. He had collected and mastered these instruments over the course of his life, and even though most of what he composed was written through his neural, there was still a joy in the discipline of playing.

The twelve-string guitar called to him. Pushing the netting aside, he lifted it out of its case, sat on the edge of his bed, and began to tune its slack strings. The fingers of his left hand found familiar chords with unconscious ease, but he'd pay for his lack of practice with cracked and sore fingertips later. Layered sound filled the small room.

He triggered his neural to play back the opening section of the melody he had written for Charon as he continued to strum the guitar. Like the man himself, the music was complex, discordant. It trailed off, ending on a single note, repeating and echoing. He flattened his right hand to still the guitar strings.

A single note continued to sound in his head before shifting into the music Barre had always associated with Jem.

His brother worshiped Ada May. How in the cosmos was he going to tell him what she was planning?

He let Jem's theme swell in his mind, and somehow it found a strange resonance and harmony with Charon's elegy. All their lives had become entwined with Ithaka. What May chose would affect them all.

Barre lay back on his bed, the guitar across his chest. He closed his eyes.

"Barre?"

Jem's voice floated between the notes of melody, jarring him out of the song. He gripped the neck of the guitar tighter.

"Barre? Can you hear me?"

He let the music die away before answering his brother. *"I'm here."* He sat up and settled the guitar in his lap, letting his left hand shape silent chords.

"I keep trying to reach you, but it's like there's always a barrier in the way. I finally took a neo-benzo. I didn't know what else to do."

It seemed like the connection was always easier when Jem's mind was drifting and his was lost in music. It was still maddeningly random. *"What's wrong?"* Jem's fear floated on the surface of his words. Barre didn't know how much of his own emotion would be carried on this strangely intimate connection.

"Didn't you get Ro's message?"

"About Targill? I got yours. What's going on with Ro? Is she okay?"

"It's complicated. Here."

Jem pushed a message across their link before retreating to the back of Barre's mind. He read and re-read Ro's note. It was brief, but it had the power to shake the cosmos apart. Shock reverberated across the link with his brother, breaking it. Barre struck the guitar's strings over and over until his right hand throbbed. When the sound died, he stood.

Halcyone opened doors for him as he strode through the ship

and into the hangar bay. Ithaka's security system recognized the access granted through the cuff and let him through until he stood at Ada May's door. He glanced down in surprise at the guitar he still gripped in his right hand.

The door slid open. The small, stooped scientist stood just inside, smiling a greeting. Then she glanced up at his face and the smile died.

"Barre?"

"Targill isn't who you think he is."

Frowning, May ushered him inside. The door swooped shut behind them. "Sit. You look gray. Tell me."

They took the same seats they had been in earlier. Two covered trays sat on the table between them. Barre set his guitar down carefully on the floor.

"You have a copy of the data Ro stole from her father. Well, there were more layers of encryption on it. She cracked them all. Maldonado had been collating and collecting blackmail files on dozens of his supposed enemies.

"At some point, he stumbled across something worth more than any simple extortion plan." Barre shook his head, struggling with the enormity of what she had uncovered. "There's a secret cabal made up of Commonwealth leaders, politicians, and cartel heads working to consolidate power and influence across the cosmos. Our friend Micah's father was on it. Alain Maldonado wanted in."

"And Targill?"

"Ro thinks he's the head."

May leaned back into her chair. "Is she certain?"

"This is Ro we're talking about."

"Well, then, I'd best get ready to meet the man."

Barre shot up from his seat and nearly tripped over his guitar. "You contacted him."

"Not directly, but I set some things in motion."

"Then unset them."

"That's not how these things work, Barre. I made some inquiries, sent out some less than secure messages. I expect to be contacted at some point fairly soon."

"You have to evacuate with the rest of Ithaka. Send Lowell somewhere far away. Somewhere unconnected to you. Come with me."

"No."

"What do you mean no?" Barre's voice resonated through the room and set his guitar strings humming.

"This changes nothing. I need to negotiate with someone in a position of power. That's still Targill, no matter how you look at it."

"This is crazy! Dr. May, you can't do this. They don't want to negotiate. They want to destroy you and everything you stand for."

"That's a distinct possibility, but not inevitable, at least according to Lethe's latest projections."

How could she be so calm? "And you can't trust Lowell, no matter what he tells you. No matter what security protocols you put in place. Hell, Targill probably engineered this to get to you!"

May stood and placed a gentle hand on Barre's arm. "And if he did? No, I've preparing for this day for a long time. Charon's death just hastened it a bit."

"What about all the people who depend on you?" Barre shook her off and folded his arms across his chest.

"Ithaka was supposed to be so much more than what we

became. For that, I blame my anger. My selfishness. I wasn't the only one who lost something, and I pulled away when I should have pushed forward. I have a chance to fix that now."

"You're really going to sacrifice yourself?"

"Well, it depends on how you define sacrifice." Her eyes twinkled with a fresh defiance. "There is such a thing as a Pyrrhic victory."

"If you're dead, then they win." The Reaction Chamber already had control of the Commonwealth and the political process, as well as access to the black-market and the cartels. If Ithaka fell, who would stand against them?

May fell silent for a moment. "It's not a game. It's never been a game. I thought I understood that, but I've still spent the past forty years playing by their rules. There comes a time to put the pieces away and upend the board."

"Gutierrez dedicated her life to you. Charon trusted you."

She winced. "I know. And I'm asking you to trust me, too. It may not feel like it, but I know exactly what I'm doing."

Barre struggled to find something to say that would change her mind.

She nodded at his guitar. "Did you bring that to trip over or to play?"

He had forgotten about the instrument. He picked it up gingerly, as if it were suddenly alien and dangerous. What use was music now?

"Please. Play something you love."

Barre slipped the strap over his head and settled it across his shoulder. The guitar felt heavy. He tuned the strings, listening as he played a few test chords before adjusting the knobs again. His hands followed the chord progression for Charon's theme and he filled the room with the elegy.

May sat and closed her eyes. The tension in her shoulders eased as she relaxed in her chair. Barre sent a request to Lethe through his neural as easily as he connected with Halcyone. An electronic keyboard melody played through the AI's speakers to accompany Charon's theme.

Barre's hands stilled on the strings, but the music played on. It shifted as he poured out his hope and his fear for Ada May and the idea she had built in the language he knew best.

The song he didn't know he was composing ended and the last notes faded into silence. May sighed.

"Thank you. That was lovely."

He listened to the room hum, the different subtle sounds of life support and air handling and computer equipment making their own music. It had been a long time since he had played for anyone but himself.

Was there even room for a musician in the universe he had fallen into? "If you need me, I'll come for you."

She let the silence lengthen so long, Barre was sure she wouldn't answer. "I won't require a ferryman for this journey. It's one I planned a long time ago. Go back to your friends. They need you. I promise, I'll do what I can to keep you safe."

Barre nodded—not in agreement, but because there was nothing left to say.

Chapter 21

Aꜰᴛᴇʀ ᴀ ʀᴇsᴛʟᴇss ɴɪɢʜᴛ, Nomi sat in the kitchen with her mother, drinking coffee in silence. She'd left Ro sleeping upstairs. It was a mark of the woman's exhaustion that she hadn't even stirred when Nomi got up.

She'd have to wake her soon. Barre had sent them his flight plan and he would be landing at the spaceport within the hour.

"I don't want you to go back."

Nomi sighed. They had been through this all last evening. "You know I have no choice." And even if she didn't owe the next several years to the Commonwealth, Nomi wouldn't abandon Ro and the others. Not now. Not ever.

"I know." Her mother blinked back tears. "I hope she understands how lucky she is."

"She does." Ro's soft voice drifted into the kitchen from the doorway. "Trust me, I tried to talk her into staying, too."

That had been a bigger argument than the one with her parents.

"She's a lot fiercer than she appears."

"I'm starting to appreciate that, Mrs. Nakamura."

"Azuki, please."

Ro joined them at the table. "Azuki."

Nomi pushed over a coffee and studied her girlfriend. Ro's green eyes were dull with fatigue. The circles beneath them, puffy and bruised. She resisted the urge to smooth the hair out of her face.

"Are you ready to go?" Ro asked.

Nomi sighed and nodded.

A brief grimace of pain flashed across her mother's face before she schooled her expression. "Can I pack anything for you to take?"

He father had already given her a container of leftover cinnamon rolls and she'd taken some of her grandfather's last spicy pickles. "No. We're all set." There was nothing more Nomi could give her family. The warnings she'd been able to articulate felt generic and pointless this morning. How could they guard against a threat composed of rumors, secrets, and lies? In the end, she had told them that Ithaka existed. That they had uncovered a conspiracy hidden within the heart of the Commonwealth. That they didn't know who to trust.

Nomi was shocked her parents even believed her. It sounded like the plot of one of the ansible thriller serials Daisuke watched. "I'm sorry," she whispered.

Her mother clamped her hand over Nomi's. "Don't do that. We raised you to fight for what you believed in."

"At any cost?"

Her mother's hand shook.

"At least now we know what we're buying," her father said.

He stood just inside the kitchen doorway, his mouth down-turned, his knuckles white against the counter's edge. Nomi patted her mother's hand before jumping up to hug her dad. He enveloped her in his wiry arms.

"I dropped Daisuke at his friend's house for the day. Are you ready to go?"

"Mom, are you coming to the spaceport?"

She shook her head. "I need to review the security protocols Ro installed on Tetsujin."

At least they were taking steps to protect themselves. Nomi would be able to communicate safely with them. It wasn't nearly enough, but it had to be. She stepped away from her father and took her mother's hands. "Be careful."

"I'm not the one traveling into danger, Konomi." Her mother stood. "Be careful, both of you." Nomi released her hands so they could hug. There was a strength in both her parents. A strength they would have to rely on.

Ro brooded all the way to the spaceport as Nomi's father tried to keep up a semblance of casual conversation. Nomi stared out the transport's window at a familiar landscape that already felt like a distant memory. Her father pulled in to the short-term parking lot. The rumble of distant engines shook the transport as they sat in an uneasy silence.

"We're here," he said softly.

Nomi hugged her father fiercely, neither of them acknowledging their fear for the other. Long after he drove away, she stared into the distance blinking back tears.

"We can't stay here," Ro said quietly. "Barre's waiting."

She nodded and followed Ro into departures.

They cleared customs and Nomi wondered how much data on them was being collected, scrutinized, assessed. Were they on a list somewhere? Did the bored Commonwealth officer who processed their exit even know a shadow government lurked inside the massive military bureaucracy that had existed since before the Drowning?

Both of their micros pinged simultaneously as Barre checked in from the hangar. The ship was already in the queue for departure. Ro's sigh filled the entire bay when she saw Halcyone opening her airlock doors.

"Welcome back, Captain Maldonado, Konomi Nakamura."

Nomi nodded absently before boarding.

Barre leaned against the bulkhead just inside the ship. "Thought I'd run off with her and strand you?"

Ro lifted a single golden eyebrow. "Smart ass. Do you want me to take us out of here or do you already have it dialed in?"

The ship cycled the airlock behind them.

"Halcyone has it programmed." He sighed. "We need to talk. Before we get back to Daedalus. It's important."

Nomi gripped Ro's arm. The longer they delayed, the harder leaving her family was going to be.

"After liftoff," Ro said.

"Aye, aye, Cap," Barre answered. "I'll be on the bridge."

"Go on ahead." Ro patted Nomi's hand. "I'll drop our bags and meet you."

She gave Ro's arm a quick squeeze and hurried after the tall musician. "Hey!" Nomi caught up with him at the threshold to the bridge.

Barre strapped himself into the navigator's chair. "Better get tight. As soon as Ro's here, we'll blast off."

Nomi took comms. "Barre? Are you okay?"

"No. I don't think that I am."

A crackle through the speakers startled her.

"Halcyone, you are number one for departure. Stand by."

Ro jogged through the door and took the command chair as Barre answered. "Control, we are ready for departure."

"Outer bay door retracting."

Barre whistled what sounded like a random collection of notes and Halcyone's interstitial engines fired up. The thrum beneath their feet began to build.

"Halcyone, you are cleared for departure. Docking clamps released."

"Thank you, control. Halcyone out." Barre must have signaled the ship through his neural because she leaped out of the docking bay with a caged animal's eagerness.

They powered through the atmosphere and pierced its thin skin, entering the vacuum just beyond before orbiting Nomi's home planet. The familiar contours of clustered archipelagos and wide seas spun beneath them in patterns of blues and greens. Nearly everything she loved lived down there.

She glanced at Ro and Barre before wiping her eyes. Tears would be inconvenient now.

The ship's engines growled. Nomi was pressed back into the padding of her chair and started a count-up in her head. She should have asked Barre how long and how deep the burn would be, but it was too late now.

She got to a hundred and seventy-three seconds before the burn ended and the added g-forces faded.

Ro was the first to unbuckle her harness. "So. What gives, music man? What does the great Ada May want from you now besides my ship?" There was a real fear beneath the sarcasm.

By the time Nomi shrugged out of the restraints, Barre was already pacing the outer ring of the bridge. "It's not that. She's busy trying to get herself killed."

Ro slammed her fist on the command station and Nomi started. "Is she jump-sick?"

"We can't let her do this," Nomi said. Of all of them, she was the only one who'd never met May. She'd helped Taro Odachi, Ithaka's loyal ferryman. The compact man who had laughed at Gutierrez's anger and had bled on Nomi's sofa. Who died saving Gutierrez under May's orders. If anything happened to May, the LC would go ballistic.

"And how do you propose we stop her?" Barre asked. "She keeps insisting she has a plan, but it just sounds like suicide to me. Hell, she's done everything except broadcast her coordinates on all ansible frequencies."

"What in the bloody cosmos does she think she can accomplish by being a martyr?" Ro asked.

Barre sighed. "I pretty much asked her that and I think she figures if things go sour, she can take some of the threat with her."

"She's a fool."

"She reminds me of a certain engineer," Nomi said softly.

Halcyone signaled for an incoming video message, cutting off Ro's angry retort.

"Pass it through, Halcyone," Barre said.

Micah's face appeared in a corner of the viewscreen, frozen with his mouth partly open.

"Play it," Ro said.

"I figured this was easier than trying to write it all out. I'm also going to go on the assumption that Ro and our esteemed friend do in fact know what they're doing and this is actually secure. Otherwise, we're already drifting in the void which means nothing I say here will matter anyway."

"Thanks for the vote of confidence," Ro muttered.

"You're not going to like this, but I know what to do with Ro's father's intel. And I'm probably the only one who can pull it off."

Micah smiled. It reminded Nomi of vids she had watched of his late father. The Rotherwood charm lived in that smile. A chill made her shudder.

"I'm going to make this short. I've already initiated contact, so it's not up for debate. I'm sorry, but I know you guys would try to stop me."

Ro stepped closer to the screen and gripped the back of the command chair tight enough that the composite creaked in complaint. "What have you done?" she whispered.

Nomi reached for her hand.

"I'm going to claim my father's seat in the Chamber."

"What?" Barre's and Ro's voices rose together in outraged protest. Nomi gasped as Micah kept speaking.

"... from the inside. I have the name. I just have to convince them I'm my father's son." He smirked. "That shouldn't be too hard, right? Don't worry, Dev thinks I'm out of my head. She could be right. Well, too late to worry about that now. I'll contact you again when I've gotten into the bad guys' underground lair."

His video stopped. The image jumped back to the opening frame.

Ro was swearing methodically and Barre looked like someone had just spaced all his musical instruments. Nomi stared up into Micah's frozen face and saw the fear written there.

*

Jem woke up disoriented. It gave him a little sympathy for

what a bittergreen hangover must feel like. He smiled to himself, thinking of Barre. Maybe more than a little sympathy. Yawning, he stretched and moved his head side to side experimentally.

No dizziness. He could get used to that.

"Daedalus, lights up, forty percent." Maybe someday, he'd be able to use his neural effortlessly for all of that, but for now, some things were still easier to navigate with voice commands. "Time check?"

"Twelve hundred hours, eighteen minutes."

Jem drew in his breath sharply—he'd slept nearly fourteen hours. There were no messages on his micro from either Ro, Barre, or Gutierrez. Not that he'd expected to hear from the LC, but after all they'd done together, he'd hoped. At least Halcyone would be back here soon. Too much was happening too quickly and he was just a kid. As much as he hated to admit it—even to himself—he needed his big brother.

He washed and dressed quickly, hoping he could score something to eat and some coffee in their quarters before heading out into the station to see what had blown up while he was asleep.

His mother and father were waiting for him in the living room. Their faces were grim, drawn.

"What's wrong?" Jem backed up against the now closed door to his room. A wave of cold swept through him, raising gooseflesh on his arms and lifting the hair on the back of his neck.

"Sit down," his father said. "We have—"

His mother hushed him with a look. "I have something I need to tell you."

Jem took a seat opposite the two of them. The last time they had faced one another like this, it was after he'd returned from

Ithaka and Barre had been sitting beside him. He called out his brother's name in his mind, but he couldn't focus through the worry. There was no answer through his neural.

"I'm sorry your brother isn't here."

His mother's words surprised him and not just because it mirrored what he'd just been thinking.

"But this can't wait. Can I count on you to make a record and share it with him?"

"He'll be home soon. Why can't you tell him yourself?" His mother's face was gray. Her gaze looked past Jem to something he couldn't see.

Jem's father reached over to take her hand. As she started to speak, Jem held his breath, wanting to be anywhere but here. But he'd owed her his attention. He set his neural to record.

"Your father and I were both given full scholarships to Uni and med school from the Commonwealth. When we finished our training, we owed back six years in service."

He nodded even as he frowned. This wasn't something he didn't already know.

"It didn't matter that we had gotten married. They split us up." She shrugged. "You go where you're assigned. Your father was sent off Earth to a mining colony. I was assigned to one of the settlements."

Orange and red streaks colored her voice. Shame. Fear. "It's okay. You don't have to—"

"Yes. Yes I do. I owe it to you and to Barre." Her voice caught on his brother's name. "And you owe it to me to listen."

He and his father shared a brief wry smile. Generations of medical trainees had been reduced to near tears by that tone. "Mom? Does this have something to do with Targill?"

She didn't directly answer, only sighed and continued as if Jem hadn't interrupted. "Cairngorms."

"What?"

"The Cairngorms Settlement. Where I'd been raised."

Jem had known his mother had lived in one of the European settlements, but that was about all he knew. She never spoke about her childhood.

"It wasn't any kind of joyous homecoming, if that's what you're wondering." Jem's father squeezed her hand again as if reminding her he was still there, still with her. She squeezed back and smiled sadly at him. "Your father has been telling me for decades that it wasn't my fault. That it was the perfect storm and I just got caught by it.

"But I know better. I wasn't strong enough. I made mistakes and those mistakes cost innocent lives. Nothing I can do will make up for that."

Jem wanted to get up, cross the room, and hug her, but he was paralyzed by the look in her eyes and the quiet self-loathing in her voice.

"I was isolated in a place I had sworn I'd never go back to. My old friends, my family, they all scorned me as a Commonwealth sellout. A 'highsider.' Then there was an outbreak of pyrexemia."

She sat motionless, staring straight ahead as she told her story. Jem had seen a blood-fever outbreak when he'd been a child and still had nightmares about the deadly hemorrhagic disease.

"I'd run through nearly all the supplies I had in my tiny infirmary. People were dying faster than I could get to them. The authorities kept promising help and meds, but nothing came.

Not in the first twelve hours. Not in the first twenty-four. There was just me and a handful of inexperienced trainees. I lost three of them within a day.

"An old soldier brought in his grandson. It was too late to save the boy. But the old man offered me canisters of decades-old battlefield boost. So I could keep fighting, he said." She closed her eyes. Jem could only imagine what she was reliving—the dead and the dying, the sickly sweet smell of fever-sweat and blood.

"It was another four days before the authorities got around to sending in an infection control team. I probably slept an hour or two each one of those days total.

"When they took control, I kept working. Until I collapsed. By then, the outbreak was finally over. I woke up in my own infirmary in full withdrawal. The team had gone. The bodies had been hauled away. Four hundred and seventy-two people had died including all my staff. And my parents. My brother. His wife. Their baby."

She'd never mentioned her family. Ever. "What was the baby's name?"

"Bernard," she whispered.

Jem's stomach heaved. The smell of death lingered in the back of his throat. Through it all, his mother hadn't moved a muscle or cried. "It wasn't—"

"My fault?" Her head snapped up. "I didn't kill them, if that's what you mean. But I kept taking the boost. Then moved on to purer stimulants when they were all gone. I kept telling myself it was because they needed me. There wasn't anyone else. But the truth is, I liked the rush. The feeling that I could do more, think faster, be better.

"And there was the added benefit of avoiding the nightmares." She shook her head before Jem or his father could interrupt. "It doesn't matter why. I was a junkie. I stole some kinds of meds to trade for what I needed. Others I synthesized using the infirmary's lab. No one knew. Not the new trainees they provided me, not my patients." Slipping her hand from Jem's father's, she stood and smiled down sadly at him. "Not my husband."

Jem wished he could connect to Barre. He needed to hear this now—not as a recording. It explained so much. But would it be enough for Barre to forgive her? Jem already had—it was that moment in medical when she had stood up to Targill, and her vulnerability afterward. He stood, wanting to go over to her, wanting to hug her, but she waved him off.

"I had everything under control. Until I killed someone."

"Leta, it was an accident." His father's gentle reply was almost masked by Jem's sharp intake of breath.

"An accident that would never have been fatal if I'd been sober." She turned to Jem. "You need to know the truth. All of it. No matter what you think of me after."

"Mom, I—"

She shook her head again and Jem fell silent. Tears gathered in his eyes. Hers were dry and dull. He wanted her to cry, or for her voice to break. The terrible matter-of-fact tone in her voice terrified him.

"A patient was rushed to the infirmary in cardiac arrest. I ran him through the code protocol. It should have been idiot-proof."

Jem and his brother had been trained in managing cardiac events by their parents practically as soon as they could read and handle the auto-injectors.

"I injected him with the nano-release anti-coagulant. The dosage was wrong. I didn't notice. By the time I realized his brain was hemorrhaging, it was too late."

"Leta, the root cause hearing implicated the drug manufacturer. They were using damaged nanites. You couldn't have known he would get the full dose in one bolus."

She glared at him. "If I hadn't been using, I would have noticed. I could have saved him. Instead I killed him."

Jem stared down at the floor. How many years had she been torturing herself over this? No wonder she'd freaked out when Barre started using bittergreen. No wonder she'd been so difficult over Jem's sedatives.

"You were exonerated, Leta. And you went through rehab. Think of how many lives you've saved since then. How many lives that would have been lost if not for you. How much longer will you carry this?"

She lifted her head and gave him a weak smile. "Until I die."

"Mom?" Jem's voice cracked and he cleared his throat. "Can Targill do what he said?"

"Legally, no. The root cause analysis transcript was sealed as was my rehab documentation." His mother shrugged. "But the reality is, anything can be hacked with enough determination, skill, or money."

"What will you do?"

She smiled and this time the fierce fire was back in her eyes. "Your father and I have been talking about our options. We have more than enough experience to get a good placement wherever we wish."

Cold coiled in Jem's belly. How could he leave Daedalus? Barre wouldn't follow where his parents went. Jem didn't have that choice. Besides, Ro and Nomi were here. Halcyone was here. He had a responsibility to his friends and to Ithaka. "You can't!"

"Your mother and I agree that working under Targill presents a constant threat. And we've long since paid our dues to the Commonwealth. A private hospital would give us the kind of stability we've never had."

But it would be without Barre. And Jem would be trapped. "Leaving means he's won."

His father shook his head. "This isn't a game, Jem. And it isn't up for debate. We need to do what's best for our family."

If what Ro had uncovered was true, then it was a game. A long running and powerful one, where Targill held nearly all the pieces on the board. Except Ithaka. But how could he convince his folks without betraying what he knew? "There's more at stake here. Why else would Targill threaten Mom? And all these years later? It doesn't make sense." Jem lowered his voice and looked into his mother's eyes. "I thought you didn't like bullies."

His father took a long breath. Jem was about to get the "how could you understand, you're a child" speech. He wasn't in the mood for it today.

"Don't you think it's strange for the acting commander to suddenly blackmail the station's doctor over a medical decision?" Jem swallowed hard. Targill wanted the LC released to active duty. Why? Did he suspect her connection to Ithaka? "And if he's willing to do that, what else might he do?"

Jem's father's face blanched. "That's dangerously close to treason."

"No. It's just an observation." Jem kept his face blank. "I thought you didn't like bullies," he repeated, softly, still looking at his mother.

She blinked and pressed her lips together for an instant. "I've stood up to more powerful men than our acting commander and I'm not about to start backing down now."

"Leta ..."

"Jem's right. If we leave now, it sets a dangerous precedent. It lets them manipulate us." The color was back in her cheeks and they shone a deep bronze. "I'm sorry."

Jem drew breath to speak, but she kept going.

"I'm sorry I didn't trust you. And I'm sorry I was so harsh with your brother. I made threats when I should have listened. But I was afraid. I was so afraid."

This time, Jem didn't let her keep him back. He wrapped his arms around her in a fierce hug. She stiffened, but Jem didn't let go. Her quiet sob was muffled in his shoulder as she hugged him back. His father joined them, holding them both as his mother cried.

Chapter 22

To prepare for his role, Micah forced himself to watch holos of his father. Since he had long deleted anything of the senator's from his personal server, it meant searching on the public net where there was a wealth of footage. There were victory and concession speeches, policy talks, and interviews. Micah even found video of their whole family from when he was a boy, along with the public spectacle of his mother's funeral. His father had never been one for wasting a good photo op.

He propped his feet up on the coffee table. There was nothing in the recordings to even hint that Rotherwood wasn't simply the charming con-man Micah had thought he was. Had he always been manipulating them? Even before his mother had died?

The irony wasn't lost on Micah: it was more than likely the senator was only playing the oh-so-slightly-smarmy politician. He would be imitating an imitation.

"Damn, he was smooth." Dev leaned over the back of the sofa and pointed. "You have his smile."

"And my mother's moral compass."

"The Chamber will be looking for the former. And you'd best hide the latter."

"Then let's hope I have enough of him in me."

"I still think this is a mistake."

"Been talking to Ro lately?"

Dev shrugged. "In my experience, if everyone around you tells you the same thing, it's usually a good idea to consider what they're saying."

"I have considered it." Micah slid his feet off the table and stood to face her. At least he didn't wince. Not from her direct gaze nor from the familiar pain of weight-bearing. "And you're all probably right. But it doesn't really matter. We need information. We need someone on the inside. The only someone who can do that is me." He turned back to the coffee table and swiped at the virtual screen above his micro, consigning all his father's images to the trash. "Time to go to work."

Settling back into the chair, Micah searched through old mail until he found the diplomatic headers he'd used the last time he'd contacted Targill. That had been long before he knew the scope of his father's betrayal. Before his feet had been nearly destroyed, though that was only tangentially his father's fault. "Son of a bitch knew all along."

"Who? Your father?"

"No. Targill."

Dev dropped into the seat beside him. "What did Targill know?"

"When Halcyone took off with all of us, Targill was the one who came looking. We thought it was a rescue mission." Micah sighed. "It's complicated. I knew my father was working with Maldonado. I wanted a way out. I wanted my own life. So I offered Targill proof of my father's involvement in the weapons smuggling in return for immunity and legal adult status.

"And he took the bargain. Even though he must have already known my father had forged the diplomatic seals on the weapons crates. Hell, Targill had probably orchestrated it. I don't understand. Why would he let me throw my father under the afterburners like that?"

"You're thinking like a voidhopper. Not a deep," Dev said softly.

Micah raised an eyebrow.

"What if Targill had nothing to do with the smuggling operation? Maybe your father had taken the job on the side. Not one sanctioned by the Reaction Chamber."

"Why would he do that? Why risk his position of power for a payday?" He shook his head. "He had plenty of money in the accounts he left me. It couldn't have been that. I thought he'd been blackmailed into it by the cartels. But he was never in danger from them, either. That was all smokescreen."

Dev drummed her callused fingers on the arm of the sofa, her soft brown eyes narrowed in thought. "Then this is even more dangerous than I thought."

"What do you mean?"

"Think, Micah. If Ro's intel is right, your father and Targill were working together. So say the smuggling operation was sanctioned by the Chamber. Maybe it started out as a setup—a way to eliminate Maldonado."

Given what Ro had unearthed, that made sense. "But it backfired. On my father."

"After you blew their plans. After you contacted Targill. You came along at the right time and provided the perfect excuse to get rid of a rival and salvage a lost operation at the same time."

"Space me, I didn't think of that."

"This is the man you're going to play games with."

Micah glanced down at his micro and then back up at Dev. She was probably right. No, she was certainly right, but that didn't matter either. "Well, I was always pretty good at 'nought and shuttle." Before she had a chance to respond, Micah quickly drafted a note to Commander Targill. "How does this sound?"

Dev scowled as he read it back to her.

"When my father met his unfortunate end, I, as sole heir, inherited his estate. In addition to a comfortable sum of money, it contained quite a bit of documentation I think you will find interesting. Given your past involvement in my father's affairs, I think a meeting would be mutually beneficial. Sincerely, Michael Rotherwood."

"I think it sounds like you're an ass."

"Then it's perfect."

Dev snorted in response to his wide smile.

"My aim is to rattle some cages. I know it's risky, but it's the only way." His finger hesitated over the send button as he glanced at her.

"Vray," she said, softly. "Whatever you choose, I think the water will only rise."

"Then I'd better not wait until it gets over my head." With a broad gesture—mostly for Dev's benefit—he sent the message. "Well, that wasn't too bad."

"Now what?"

"We wait. It shouldn't take long for the message to reach him on Daedalus. If we're right, he can't afford to ignore it. Not if he thinks I might pose the same kind of threat my father did."

Dev frowned and stared out the living room window to the

campus grounds below. Micah joined her. Uni looked like it always did—students walking across the well-manicured green. A blur of wings passed close to the glass—there was a version of 'nought and shuttle being played with drones just outside their dorm. The shuttle pilot was good and the small craft darted and swooped like a mechanical dragonfly, forcing the dreadnought to take huge risks just to keep up.

They watched in silence as the shuttle took a steep dive. The dreadnought followed even though it likely didn't have the maneuverability to change course in time to avoid crashing. It was a rookie move. Micah waited for the inevitable—a smashed dreadnought and the shuttle taking a victory lap over the loser's remains.

But the dreadnought's pilot must have anticipated the instant when the shuttle would need to pull up. Instead of trying to save the larger ship, the pilot made the smallest of corrections, slamming its bulk into the rising shuttle. Both drones hit the ground and disintegrated.

Dev stared at the wreckage. "Well, that certainly wasn't metaphorical in any way."

The message alert from Micah's micro startled them both. The reply from Targill had no identifiers, save for the diplomatic headers Micah had used. The commander hadn't even signed it, but there was no doubt who it had come from. He read it several times, wondering if he'd just made the biggest mistake in his life.

*

Ro was still furious with Micah hours after receiving his message. Hours where her replies went unanswered as Halcyone raced them back to Daedalus under their revised course. When the AI finally signaled the all-clear, Ro rolled out of the bunk she shared with Nomi and paused to splash her face with some cold water before heading up to the bridge.

"Hey," Nomi said.

Ro stopped at the door.

"Breathe."

She slammed her palm into a bulkhead. "He's going to get himself killed. And maybe all of us in the process. I should never have dragged you into this."

Nomi's harsh laugh startled her and gave Ro a new target for her worry. She whirled around to face her girlfriend, but her angry words were silenced by the grim look on Nomi's face.

Without breaking eye contact, Nomi slowly came to sit on the edge of the bunk. Their shared blanket slid into a pile on her lap. "You didn't drag me into anything. I'm here because I love you. Because what we're fighting for is important."

"But Micah—"

"Stop. It's not about Micah and you know it."

Ro pressed her lips together.

"He's not doing anything you wouldn't do in his place."

Nomi was right and Ro hated to admit it. But it didn't do anything to quell the rising fear that made it hard to breathe. Hard to think.

"Targill is down there and we're going to have to face him as if we didn't know any of this. Are you going to be able to do that?"

"Do I have a choice?" Ro forced a smile for Nomi's benefit.

"No."

Ro closed her eyes briefly. When she opened them again,

Nomi was standing in front of her. She took the girl's slender hands in her own work-scarred ones. "There's no safe place, is there?"

Nomi sighed. "No," she repeated.

Barre's scratchy voice broke in on the room's speaker. "We're in orbit around Daedalus. Still no reply from Micah. Do you want me to take us in?"

"Give me a nano. I'll meet you on the bridge."

"I have coffee."

"Thank the cosmos."

The comms connection closed. Ro looked down. She was still clutching Nomi's hands.

"I'm not going to tell you it'll all be fine," Nomi said. "Because nothing about this is remotely fine. But you're not alone."

"I know." That was what she was afraid of.

With a final gentle squeeze, Nomi slipped her hands free. "Ready?"

Ro nodded. Hiding here on Halcyone wouldn't change anything.

When they stepped through the permanent opening to the bridge, Barre handed them each a thermos of insti-synth. It was hot and caffeinated, and she slurped it down gratefully. Below them, on the forward viewscreen, the misshapen asteroid that housed Daedalus waited.

"Halcyone, request clearance to dock."

"Incoming private message for Maldonado, Rosalyn."

Ro glanced at Barre and Nomi and they both shrugged. "Patch it through."

Commander Targill appeared on their screen. The crack gave

his face an additional line like another scar to match his old wounds. "Captain Maldonado."

Ro kept her face expressionless.

"During Commander Mendez's absence, I have been given charge of Daedalus Station. Please report to command as soon as you are docked."

"Yes, sir."

His image winked out. The display showed the station again.

"What the hell?" Barre slammed his cup down on the nav console.

"Do you think he knows?" Nomi asked.

Ro shook her head and laughed until she started choking. She took a long drink from her thermos, welcoming the scald of the hot liquid on her tongue. There was too much to know and no way to find out what intel he had.

"This is a bad idea," Barre said.

Ro tugged through the tangles in her hair. "What could possibly go wrong?" Manic laughter threatened to overwhelm her again.

Nomi reached for her hands. "We're not alone. Gutierrez is down there. Marchand is too."

But the LC was still dealing with her injuries, and Marchand was a puzzle. The truth was, without Ada May and the silent support of Ithaka, they didn't have any protection from the power Targill controlled. What they discovered from decrypting her father's data had only made life significantly more dangerous for all of them. Especially if Targill suspected they knew about the Chamber.

Ro walked forward to the command console and rested her hand against the slightly warm work surface.

"Halcyone's yours, free and clear."

She knew Nomi meant well and in a simpler universe, that would be true. But Targill wanted the ship because he wanted Ithaka. And he wouldn't confine himself to legal channels to get it. "Halcyone, do we have clearance?"

"Yes, Captain."

"Then set a glide path and bring us in." Ro gripped the edge of the console. Regardless of what Targill tried to do, this wasn't going to be her last flight on this ship.

Halcyone nestled them into their familiar docking spot and they waited as the clamps locked the ship down. "Airlock paired with Daedalus Station. Switching to station power."

There was a brief flicker of the bridge lights before Halcyone's engines cut out. The sudden silence filled Ro with dread, even though she knew it was just a normal docking. And if it came to it, Halcyone had already wrenched herself free of the station once before.

She squared her shoulders and pushed the hair from her face. "Okay. Barre—get in touch with Jem. I want to know what's been going on over the past few days. Nomi?" Ro hated to put her anywhere near harm's way, but that ship had jumped a long time ago.

"Yup. Marchand. On it."

Barre frowned at her.

"What's wrong?"

"Your coverall. You should change it."

Ro glanced down. It was her work gear. She'd changed into it as soon as they boarded Halcyone. Grease stained the chest and the material around the pockets was shiny with wear. She could change back to civvies, but that didn't feel right. "I'm the station's acting chief engineer. Not a politician." That would be Micah. Never Ro. "Targill's going to have to cope."

Nomi nodded. "He knew your father. If he underestimates you, so much the better."

Ro hoped she was right. "Regroup back here at eighteen hundred?"

"Aye, aye, Captain." The two of them said it in unison and for the first time in a long time, Ro's laugh wasn't strained.

After giving each of them a brief hug, she smoothed her coverall and headed to the airlock. The clang as the Halcyone sealed the door behind her felt uncomfortably final.

Station personnel nodded to her as she entered the north nexus. No one was overly friendly, but no one was hostile either. They had been openly hostile to her father. Or at least disdainful. Quiet acceptance might not be the same as enthusiastic support, but she did have a place here. Targill couldn't make her disappear. Could he?

Would any of the station staff protest? Mendez had gone. What had Targill told them about their commander? Not enough data. Garbage in, garbage out: an old programmer truism that was even more true than ever.

Ro paused at the entrance to command to take a steadying breath. As far as anyone knew, she had been out of station contact during Nomi's bereavement leave. She should act surprised, but not alarmed at Targill's presence here. Everything else she knew needed to stay locked away in her mind. Whatever Targill said, Ro couldn't react. "Okay, then," she whispered, before triggering the door release.

"Chief Engineer Maldonado, take a seat. The commander will be with your shortly."

Ro barely held back her gasp at seeing Gutierrez at her desk. The LC's face looked ashen, but her prosthesis was reconnected and working. She clearly wasn't at a hundred percent, but it was a far cry from how the old soldier had looked aboard Halcyone after Dev's rescue.

"Good to see you upright, sir." Ro hadn't always gotten along with the LC, but there was no doubting the woman's strength and resilience. And her rigid sense of honor.

Gutierrez returned to the multiple displays open on her desk. Ro sat. Waited. Every few moments, she felt the LC's gaze on her, but when she looked up, Gutierrez was focused elsewhere. The door to Mendez's office remained shut. Gutierrez continued to pretend to work.

The rigid chair back pressed into Ro's spine. She wanted to check in with Nomi or Barre, but it would be poor form to be on her micro when Targill called for her. This was a power play. He was telling her his time was more valuable than hers. Gutierrez sighed and doused all the virtual displays, her agitation visible in her short, staccato movements and the sharp clicking of her claw-like artificial hand.

Even though she'd been watching the door, Ro started when it finally slid open.

"Maldonado, please come in." Targill stood, backlit in the open doorway to the commander's office, his dark ship-suit in contrast to Gutierrez's gray and silver station uniform.

Gutierrez stood.

"I won't be needing you for this, Emmaline."

His familiar use of the LC's first name bothered Ro almost as much as his very presence here.

The LC nodded and sat, her spine stiff. Her claw hand

gripped the edge of the desk hard enough to make the polymer creak.

Ro followed as Targill turned and stepped back into Mendez's office. The room had always been stark—Mendez wasn't one for ornament—but in the past few days, Targill had stripped away any evidence of its former occupant. The tiny lit ship's sculpture that had once sat on Mendez's translucent smart-desk was missing. A single chair sat in front of the desk, a larger chair behind. Gone were the small table and sitting area in the far alcove.

Targill stood beside the desk and gestured for Ro to sit. Thoughts whirled through her head: where was Mendez? Had she been transferred? Was she under arrest? Did her absence connect back to Halcyone or Ithaka?

Ro struggled with her silence. There was no legitimate way she could ask about where Mendez was or how long she would be away without casting suspicion on herself or her friends. Targill seemed ready to out-wait her for as long as it took for Ro to say something.

She pressed her spine into the chair back and pushed her feet into the floor to steady herself before meeting Targill's ice-blue gaze. "Commander, how can I help you?"

He kept still for a moment longer—long enough for cold to wash through Ro's body. Then he leaned against Mendez's desk. "Ms. Maldonado."

Ms. Not captain. Not chief engineer. Ro swallowed back a wave of nausea. Her standing here on Daedalus was at Mendez's discretion. She held no official Commonwealth rank. Had neither the Uni degree nor the job experience to claim the engineer's position she'd been assigned to fill.

"I have been reviewing your records."

Another long pause. The corner of Targill's mouth twitched so briefly, Ro wasn't even certain she'd seen it. She kept her breathing steady, refusing to break eye contact or show any sign of weakness. This was no different from her father's bullshit. Ro would be space dust before she let someone play petty power games with her life again.

The anger smothered the fear. Anger was an old comfort, but one she couldn't let cloud her judgment. This man was far more dangerous than her father, partly because it wasn't at all personal. He had power. It was as simple and as deadly as that.

"Commander Mendez has appended several commendations to your file."

Ro jerked her head up.

"I see that surprises you."

"I'm pleased she found my work worthy of merit." Ro's thoughts continued to race. Was he trying to make some kind of accusation here of collusion between her and Mendez? For what purpose?

"Your position on-station is unorthodox."

Again a distinct pause. If he'd intended for her to fill it, he'd be waiting a long time.

"It appears Mendez made some concessions and promises to you that violate Commonwealth practices."

Her hands began to sweat. He couldn't mean Halcyone. If nothing else, the ship was hers, by right of salvage. That was law that preceded the Commonwealth. And the agreements she'd signed in lieu of compensation for her testimony had been approved by legal counsel. "I don't understand, sir." At least her voice was steady.

"Halcyone."

Ro swallowed hard, but otherwise kept perfectly still. It felt as if her life depended on it.

"It is illegal to dock a privately owned vessel on a Commonwealth military base."

"What?" That's what he had? No proof of conspiracy? Nothing connected to Mendez or Ithaka? Nothing about Nomi's and Jem's hacking?

"This is not a commercial spaceport. Remove your ship or it will be impounded."

Could that be all he had?

"In light of your service to the station, you have one standard day to make other arrangements for your ship."

"Yes, sir."

"Dismissed."

As Ro left Mendez's office, she knew Targill was staring at her. As soon as the door slid shut behind her, she started to tremble.

"Chief Engineer?" Gutierrez nodded to her from behind the anteroom desk, part acknowledgment, part warning.

Ro took a steadying breath, nodded back, and forced herself to walk normally back to Halcyone. There had to be a bigger threat here. There had to be.

*

Barre paced the empty bridge after both Ro and Nomi had headed back to the station. He knew he needed to do the same. Events were slipping out of their control. It felt like everything was happening at once, both slowly and far too quickly, in the way wormhole jumps distorted time.

How in the cosmos was he going to explain to Jem what Ada May had done?

"Barre. We need to talk."

He glanced up, startled, as if his thoughts had conjured his little brother. Jem's face wore a grave expression. There had been a time when his goofy smile would make everyone around him laugh. Even their mother. But that was before Halcyone. Before Jem's head injury. Before Ithaka. Shit. How much did he know? "I know. I'm sorry. I should have messaged you, but you deserved to hear it in person. I just wish I could be sure she knew what she was doing."

"Wait. She told you? I thought —"

"I guess she and Gutierrez are talking again."

"Mom and the LC?" Jem furrowed his dark eyebrows. "What are you talking about?"

"No. Ada May."

"What about Ada?"

Shit. He sat heavily at the nearest console. "You first. Ro got called to Targill's office and Nomi is making contact with Marchand. If they're in danger, I need to know now." Jem tried to interrupt, but Barre shook him off. "There's shit happening with Ada and Ithaka. I promise, I'll tell you everything. But what the hell is going on with Mom?"

Sitting at the workstation across the aisle, Jem watched him, his eyes dark and serious. "Okay. You need to listen to this." He must have hooked his micro to Halcyone's larger speakers: their mother's voice crackled through the bridge.

Barre drew in a sharp breath and held it as the haughty and unyielding Leta Durbin told the story of her secret shame. Her words struck him like energy bursts. Like defibrillator pulses. *"I'm sorry I didn't trust you. And I'm sorry I was so harsh with your brother. I made threats when I should have listened. But I was afraid. I was so afraid."*

His hands balled into fists. Anger and confusion warred for control. The recording looped back to the start and Barre shook his head. His words emerged in a low growl. "Turn it off. Turn it off now." He couldn't stand to hear the pain in her voice. That descant had always been there; he just hadn't recognized it for what it was. Or had refused to hear the truth of it when he'd been too busy wallowing in his own self-pity.

He blinked away unexpected tears and saw them reflected in Jem's eyes as well. "Can Targill do that? Can he unseal the records?" Another reason to fear the man.

Jem rubbed at the scar hidden by his regrown hair. A nervous habit he probably wasn't even aware of. "I don't think he makes empty threats, Barre. Maybe I shouldn't have told her to fight back. He could get her medical license revoked."

"She's stronger than that." She'd been fighting a silent war with her own failure for a lifetime. At least this would give her a different target. "And she's not alone."

Jem blinked up at Barre.

"She may not think she needs our help, but this is bigger than her. It's bigger than all of us." He reached out for his brother's smaller hands. "Ada's done something incredibly stupid. Or at least incredibly risky. And if she's wrong, I think it'll make a supernova feel like a burst of static."

All the color drained out of Jem's cheeks when Barre told him about Ithaka, about May's plan to use herself as bait to force the Commonwealth to negotiate some kind of detente.

"But Targill isn't just some war hero. He's the power within the power. There's no way he'd let May live."

"I know. I tried to tell her, but she wouldn't listen." No. It wasn't that she didn't listen as much as it didn't seem to matter to her. And it also didn't matter what odds Lethe quoted: Ada May was going to martyr herself one way or another. Either to the Commonwealth or to the Reaction Chamber.

"What do we do now?" Jem wiped his hands absently over and over on the fabric of his pants.

"Halcyone. Query Daedalus for the location of Durbin, Leta and Durbin, Kristoff."

"Are you sure?" Jem whispered.

After a brief pause, the ship's AI spoke. "The Doctors Durbin are in their quarters."

"No. But when has that ever mattered?" Grabbing Jem's hand, Barre tugged him out of the chair. "It's time we had a serious talk with Mom and Dad." Jem's dark brown eyes got very big and wide, but he didn't resist as Barre towed him off Halcyone and into the station. Barre strode through Daedalus's corridors seeing only the weariness in Ada May's stooped frame. It matched the weariness in his mother's voice. Then they were in front of the place Barre had called home until his recent emancipation. Would he even be welcome here? He took a deep breath and thought of his mother's confession. If she could take a risk, so could he.

He signaled. The door slid open.

His father and his mother stood just inside. His mother's face was flushed and her eyes red-rimmed. She met his gaze briefly before staring down at the ground. They all waited as if frozen in mid-jump until Jem pushed Barre into their quarters and the door slid shut behind them.

Barre clasped his hands together because he didn't know what else to do with them. "Mom?" His voice rose in pitch and broke as if he were Jem's age again. He cleared his throat and tried again. "What you said. That took a lot of strength."

Her head tipped up until she was looking at him, her body trembling. He'd never seen her shake. Ever. Not in an emergency. Not during a procedure. Not in a confrontation. He wanted to hold her hands to help still them, but was afraid to move.

"You're the strongest person I've ever known. Stronger than Dad." He glanced up at his father and gave him an apologetic smile. "Sorry, Dad."

His father shrugged and gave a half-smile in return.

"Whatever happened in Cairngorms, that was in the past." Barre swallowed hard. If she could let go of her anger, so could he. "What happened between us, that's over, too. I made my own share of bad choices. They were no one's fault but my own. I can't change them, but I can work harder moving forward. Which is what you've always done. What you're doing now."

His mother took a ragged breath. Her hands stilled. "I'm sorry. I can't erase what I've said and done. I wish I could."

Barre hated to hear the raw fear and vulnerability in her voice. He wondered how much worse it must be for Jem with his short-circuited senses. As if his brief thought were a conduit, his mind opened to Jem's in a rush of shared anxiety and resolve. It was carried on a current of music weaving elements of Jem's theme and the melody he'd created for Ada May out of Charon's elegy.

He nodded to his brother and turned to face his parents

again. "I want you to know. I haven't used bittergreen since I took that tainted dose." It seemed like a lifetime ago, but it was just a few months. "It was stupid. I was angry. I probably wanted to be caught just so I could prove something to you. Which doesn't make any sense. I know." He gave a short, sharp, bitter laugh. What he wouldn't give to have that Barre's problems now.

His father drew breath to speak, but Barre stopped him with a glance.

"Look. None of that matters anymore. That's what we came here to tell you. You're in a war zone you didn't even know about, and Targill is a more powerful enemy than you realize." Barre felt a tinge of dizziness coming through from Jem. "Look, this may take a while. Can we sit?"

His mother took his hands in hers. They were void-cold, but steady. "Welcome home."

Chapter 23

After leaving Halcyone, Nomi wandered into hydroponics, hoping to find a moment of peace before she searched out Marchand. The green-space was quiet, though not empty. Off-duty personnel sat on the benches scattered through the artificial garden or walked along its paths. No matter what the shift, there were always visitors here.

She rested on an empty bench and checked station time. It was well into second, but she had no idea if Marchand would be working in comms or not. The schedule had been upended during her brief leave. Synchronizing her micro with Daedalus, she waited as the comms assignments updated.

He'd been on first shift today. Nomi let out a breath she hadn't realized she was holding. She drafted a quick text message and sent it to Marchand.

/My parents sent me back with some pickled radishes. Happy to share./

If they were monitoring her communications, she wished

them luck in scrutinizing this one. Anyone who knew either her or Marchand knew their shared passion for pungent food. She didn't think radishes could be taken as code for anything.

/Perfect timing! Was getting a snack together. Come on over./

Nomi glanced around her but no one was paying her any attention. Why would they? She was just a low-ranking comms officer on an out-of-the-way monitoring station. And anyone who suspected otherwise wasn't going to risk exposing any one of the multiple plots weaving around all of them. No, the smart move would be to wait until someone screwed up. Someone without any experience in covert politics. Someone like her.

She squared her shoulders and stood. Meeting with Marchand was her job. She was the only one of them that could do it without arousing unhealthy curiosity. Besides, Ro was dealing with Targill and that was far more dangerous than sharing snacks with her comms supervisor.

Nodding to her fellow staff, Nomi left hydroponics and headed to the residence ring. All the way there, she felt as if she was being watched, but other than a smile or a brief greeting, no one paid her any unusual attention. Daedalus's red oculars glowed at regular intervals at the intersection of the corridor's walls and ceiling. The AI was always watching to some extent, and Nomi had always trusted in its programmed disinterest. But now, its impartial eye felt somehow menacing.

If the Commonwealth was being manipulated from the inside, how could she trust in its guarantees? How could anyone?

Marchand's door slid open to her request. The jolly New Cajun stood in his usual spot in the galley, a well-worn apron over his crisp uniform. "Come in! Come in! I have a surprise for you."

If his good humor was for any monitors, she couldn't tell. He seemed genuinely happy to see her. And it was hard not to respond to the wide smile that sent a spiderweb of lines outward from the corners of his eyes. From the moment she had met him, Marchand had made her feel welcome. She wanted to trust him. The reality was, she had to trust him. They all had to.

Nomi reached into her bag and pulled out the small sealed container she'd grabbed from her parents' house. The pickled radishes were the remnants of the last ferment her grandfather had started before he'd died. She wanted to keep them stored away and hoard them, but that wouldn't bring her grandfather back. Besides, he always enjoyed feeding others. "I think Sofu would have liked your cooking."

Marchand handed her a glass of wine. Nomi raised an eyebrow. "I'm off duty and you're not on until tomorrow."

She took the glass, admiring the deep red liquid. It must have cost a fortune to bring it on-station.

"To the memories of those we love," he said. His eyes were solemn.

"And to those who have loved us," Nomi answered.

Marchand nodded before tossing back the wine in one long draw. Nomi sipped at hers, wondering what to say next. They needed his help. They needed to tell him everything. She set her glass down with shaking hands.

He pulled out his micro. With a grace and confidence she had only seen Ro employ, he filled the air around him with sparkling windows, then grunted in approval before wiping them out of existence.

"We have about fifteen minutes of absolute privacy. I'll set a timer for ten."

Nomi swallowed hard. Then she swiped her glass again and this time finished her wine. She didn't need fifteen minutes. Or even ten. Ever since they broke through Alain Maldonado's final level of encryption, Nomi had been organizing what she'd needed to say.

"All right, Marchand, whatever your issues with Ada May, get over them. What you told Jem and Gutierrez? You were right, but it's even bigger than you imagined. And our acting commander is at the heart of it."

"Simon. It's Simon." His voice was hushed, nearly reverent in the silent room.

"Well, Simon, things are about to get very messy. Lots of noise to scramble the signal. I'll make it as clear as I possibly can." She glanced at the empty wine glass, wishing it had magically refilled itself, before she counted off the salient details on the fingers of her right hand. "One: Targill is the head of the Reaction Chamber, a secret group operating within the Commonwealth and setting its course for their own personal gain. Likely going back decades. And with involvement from the cartels." That might have been more than one point, but they were all related. "Two: Ada May has cleared out all nonessential personnel from Ithaka and is attempting to use our friend Lowell as bait, but Barre believes she's in the process of playing some kind of galactic martyr. Probably out of guilt. Three: She's convinced herself that she can negotiate with Targill for the future of Ithaka, even at the cost of her own life. Four: He'll probably get himself killed in the process, but Micah Rotherwood is going to trade on his father's name and infiltrate

Targill's group. Oh, and four and a half: The late senator was part of the cabal."

She deliberately didn't look at Simon for his reaction, but casually waggled her fingers. "I think that's about it."

There was a long moment of silence broken by the sound of Simon refilling both their glasses.

The timer was counting down, but still Simon didn't respond. Nomi frowned at him. She wasn't sure what she'd expected, but this wasn't it. When just a few minutes remained on their original ten, Simon leaned in toward her.

"You're wrong."

"What?" Nomi's heart rate galloped. Had she just made a catastrophic mistake?

"My people have known about the Chamber for some time now. But it was just rumors. We didn't know for sure Targill was its leader, though we've long suspected. We've just never had any way to get close to it. At least not successfully." His eyes widened. "But now? Your friend Micah —"

"You knew? You knew and you didn't say anything?"

He glanced at the timer. "I've lost friends and family to this fight. Every piece of intel we've collected has had a blood price. Going back decades. When Ada refused to let us use Ithaka's resources to fight back, we knew we had only ourselves to rely on. Then you and your friends show up and Ithaka is suddenly relevant again. What a coincidence. Of course I didn't trust you. Would you have, in my place?"

"But you helped me." Her hands trembled. She gazed at the wine sloshing against the glass. He had sent her a hidden message when she'd been under house arrest, or whatever Mendez had considered her detention after Jem's hack had been discovered. "Why?"

He spread his hands wide. "Because you shared your family's food with me. Because you didn't deserve to get caught up in a war as old as your grandfather without the resources to protect yourself. And even though you and your associates are late to the party, at least you're finally here and it's going to take all of us if we're going to get through this." He fell silent again and for a long moment, Nomi didn't think he'd say anything more. "Because you remind me of someone I lost a long time ago, and I couldn't stand to see Ro go through what I did."

The timer rang shrilly through the small galley kitchen, startling both of them. When Nomi searched Simon's face, she was shocked to see his eyes glittering with tears.

He wiped them away with a deliberately casual gesture. "You could have warned me. Those radishes are spicy!"

Nomi set her empty glass down and gave Simon a quick hug. "Come have dinner with us on Halcyone. We can see how Ro can handle the heat."

Simon's eyes widened briefly before he hugged her back. "I think I have some left over gumbo I can bring." He nodded toward the counter where several more bottles sat. "And some more wine. We'll probably need it."

"No doubt."

*

Ro had been the first to arrive back on Halcyone. The silent corridors of her ship were a soothing counterpoint to the anger roiling through her mind. She walked the length of the stubby vessel, from the aft storage bays where her father had once hidden illegal weapons, past the retrofitted quarters that had transported troops during the war, past the small staterooms she and Barre had claimed as their own, past engineering, and finally to the bridge.

The sound of voices startled her and she turned to face the wreckage of the doors Micah had broken through what seemed like a lifetime ago.

Barre and Jem had identical expressions of worry and resolve on their faces.

"Hey," Jem said.

"Well, you're not under arrest. That's a good sign. Right?" Barre took the nav officer's station and propped his legs on the console.

"I hope you're okay with this, but I messaged the LC to meet us." He glanced around the bridge. "It's going to be a little tight in here."

"We can meet in engineering."

The scent of something spicy wafted through the bridge. "Better make that the crew barracks." Nomi stepped through the doorway with Marchand in tow.

"Since when did I authorize a party?"

"And here I went ahead and brought the booze." Marchand pulled a bottle of red wine from a box he was carrying.

"Fine." But it was anything but fine. They had a lot to discuss, and Marchand and Gutierrez were still interlopers on Ro's ship. She nodded at Jem. "Let Gutierrez know. We can't afford to wait until she shows up. I'm going to assume she knows how to mask her location signature, but remind her anyway."

"I will."

She turned to Marchand. "Will anyone be curious as to your

whereabouts?"

"I'm having dinner with my good friend Nomi. Nothing unusual about that."

Ro glared at him for a moment before leading them all to the large room filled with stacked bunks. It wasn't the most conducive to having a conversation, but at least they'd all have places to sit. And something to eat, judging by the pot of food Marchand unpacked.

"I'll get bowls and spoons." Barre headed to their tiny commissary. Were there even enough spares there for all of them?

"Bring cups, too," she said.

Jem lifted the lid of Marchand's pot and inhaled deep. "That smells amazing. Way better than meal bars."

Ro managed to snag Nomi's gaze and frowned.

"I trust him," Nomi said, answering her unanswered question.

The LC sauntered in just as Barre returned with dinnerware. "Captain. Thank you for inviting me on board."

Ro glanced over at Barre who smiled and shrugged. He'd been the one to tell Halcyone to let the LC in. Okay, then. Barre, Jem, and Nomi were all looking at her, waiting for her to start. The only one missing from their original "crew" was Micah. She cleared her throat. "Well, I guess we all know why we're here, then."

Marchand lifted a bottle and waggled it in the air. "Aside from cleaning out my personal stash?" Ro accepted the mug he poured her. The cups still smelled vaguely of insti-synth coffee, which would probably annoy the New Cajun, but that was the best they had.

Gutierrez accepted the wine with a gracious thank-you and what seemed like a genuine smile. It was the most friendly Ro had ever seen the LC. Jem waved off the wine and so did Barre.

Ro raised an eyebrow and the musician shrugged. While waiting for her shipmates and guests to serve themselves some of Marchand's gumbo, Ro sat on one of the lower bunks that still had more or less intact padding. "Let's get started. We have some immediate term issues in addition to the threat posed by the Reaction Chamber."

Marchand started and wine sloshed over the rim of his mug.

"We're as secure here as we can be. I've isolated our comms from the station and there's an interference filter on outgoings from our micros. Incomings aren't affected, so if one of you gets a ping you need to answer, let me know."

He nodded and sat on a bunk across the aisle from her.

"So I'm going to start with what we all know and move on from there. Okay?"

No one objected.

"For decades, my father had been collecting information and blackmail materials on movers and shakers in the Commonwealth and the cartels. Somewhere along the way, he figured out that the Reaction Chamber was the power behind the power and that Dominic Targill was its current leader."

"And Senator Rotherwood had been a high-ranking member," Marchand said. There was an eager light in his eyes.

"Micah has concocted an insane plan to take his father's place. My father had been doing his level best to worm his way into the Chamber when he met his fiery and well-deserved end, but I was able to hack his data. Maybe it will do Micah some good."

"Is that why Targill dragged you into his office?" Marchand asked.

"Not quite." She turned to the LC. "I take it you had no idea what Targill was meeting with me about."

"None," Gutierrez said. "But I could hazard a guess that he presented you with some kind of veiled threat."

"Correct in one." She took another sip. "He so very generously gave me a full day to find another place to keep Halcyone. Accused Mendez of acting inappropriately for agreeing to let us dock on station."

"He knows I won't leave Daedalus. Not with Nomi here. And he's got to know I won't sell or scrap my ship." Even if Halcyone hadn't been their link to Ithaka, Ro wouldn't give it up. Not after she'd fought so hard to resurrect the damaged AI. Not after what they had all been through on board and off. "So. Options?"

"I take it giving Targill control of the ship is off the table." Marchand had finished one of the bottles and had opened a second.

"Even if I wanted to, I made a promise to Ada May."

"Which she seems intent on breaking all on her own. She's mad if she thinks she can trust Targill." Jem's voice cracked.

"What are you talking about?" Gutierrez asked.

Jem and Barre started to speak simultaneously, but Jem's higher-pitched voice rang the room with outrage. Ro gestured for him to wait. "Let Barre walk her through this. He's the one who was there."

Barre winced, but didn't shy away from telling Gutierrez what had happened on Ithaka. "I smuggled Cam Lowell to her. He'd requested sanctuary. She had other ideas."

The LC stood. Her claw hand opened and closed, clicking in

the room's silence. "Take me there."

"You can't save her from herself," Barre said softly.

"The hell I can't." Gutierrez turned to Ro, the desperation clear in her eyes. "Please. Take me there."

Barre stood and gently touched her artificial hand to still its restless motion. "Hasn't she lost enough? Taro's gone. I think it would kill her to lose you, too."

"Besides, I think we have more immediate concerns."

Everyone turned to Marchand. He had set down his wine and was manipulating his micro with both hands. "Targill has had a flurry of priority communications in the past few hours. Including a narrow band transmission under diplomatic headers to someone in North America. That's about as close as I can localize it, but you want to hazard a guess as to who the man has been talking to?"

Micah. Shit.

"And Hephaestus just broke orbit. Targill is aboard. His flight plan is taking him to the Hub."

"How do you know?"

"I have an ally on his ship." Marchand put up his hand. "And no, I won't tell you who it is. For everyone's protection."

Ro shifted her gaze back and forth between Marchand and Gutierrez. The LC looked like she wanted to use her claw hand on whatever soft part of him would hurt most.

"If Targill's headed to Earth, that means that for the moment he's deemed Micah a greater prize than Ada May," Barre said.

"Or a greater threat." Ro hoped Micah knew what in the cosmos he was doing.

"Either way, it means she's in the clear for a little while longer." There was a desperate hope burning in Barre's eyes. Ro hated to douse it.

"Unless Targill sends his minions after her."

Gutierrez shook herself out of her fury and paced between the bunks. "He won't. If what you've uncovered about the Reaction Chamber is true, Targill will want to bring her down himself. It's what he's wanted for too many years. He won't be satisfied with anything less. Besides, can you imagine the power he'll command as the Commonwealth war hero who brought down the leader of the rebels?"

"Then we still have some time left." Nomi's soft voice was hesitant, but it cut through the emotion in the room and captured everyone's attention.

"Time for what?" Ro asked.

"To rescue Ada," Nomi said.

"How? I can't take Halcyone there. That would just make Targill's job that much simpler." It might have been what he wanted anyway. Spook her enough and she'd run away to Ithaka, with his agents following right behind.

"Charon's ship. Micah still has it."

"And then what? We swoop in and take her by force? Even if she'd let us land, she won't come," Barre said. "I tried to get her to leave with me on Halcyone. She refused."

"She'll listen to me." Gutierrez spoke quietly, looking down at the ground.

Ro's thoughts raced. How quickly could they get to Earth and back? "If Targill returns and we're all gone—"

"I can monitor Hephaestus. Give you plenty of warning. But to be on the safe side, I think you're going to have to sit this trip out." Marchand nodded to Gutierrez.

Ro waited for the inevitable explosion. It didn't come.

Instead Gutierrez's face turned thoughtful. "Can you pilot Odachi's ship, Barre?"

"I think so. We can have Halcyone calculate the course and lock it in for me."

"Okay, then. Get back as fast as you can. I'll leave from here."

Ro shook her head. "Fine. Assume we recover Charon's ship. Assume you go to Ithaka. How are you going to cover your absence from Daedalus? You're the lieutenant commander. You can't just disappear."

"I'll figure something out by the time you get back." Her eyes glittered fiercely in the harsh overhead light.

"What are you going to do about Halcyone?" Nomi asked.

"I can put her in a parking orbit outside of Targill's control. Charon's ship looks like a flitter. Barre can ferry us to the commercial hangar. We still have access to Micah's money, right?"

It meant she'd be separated from the ship until Gutierrez got back. If she got back. Without ready access to Halcyone, Ro would be trapped on-station. It made her feel as helpless as she'd ever been under her father's control.

She pointed at Marchand. "You. I want to know the nanosecond something changes on Hephaestus. Tell Nomi. She'll be able to reach me." Turning to Gutierrez, she softened her tone. "And keep trying to reach Ada. If you can convince her to leave, then you won't need to go and kidnap her."

Gutierrez spun on her heel and left the barracks room.

"I'll keep an eye on the LC," Jem said.

"Go."

"Good luck, guys. If you see Micah, tell him ... tell him not to be some kind of hero, okay?" Then Jem sprinted after the LC.

"I think you have things well in hand." Marchand packed up his box. The empty bottles clinked softly against one another.

"When we get back, you and I need to talk."

He glanced at her without changing his slightly amused expression.

"I'm serious. You know all of us. We only know you have someone on Hephaestus. That's not good enough."

"Sorry, it's the best I've got."

Ro lightly grabbed his arm. "That's not going to fly. Not when everyone I care about in the cosmos is at risk."

He opened his mouth as if he had a smart comeback, glanced at Nomi, and shook his head before leaving the large compartment.

Ro turned to follow him.

"Let him be. It's all right." Nomi's touch stopped Ro in her tracks. "The quicker you guys leave, the quicker you'll be back."

"Nomi, can you get a message to Micah?"

"Yes."

"Let him know we're coming?"

"Yes."

"We need Gutierrez to clear our arrival with the New Chicago Spaceport."

"I'll take care of it, Ro."

"Nomi ..."

She gave Ro a fierce hug. "Just go. I'll be waiting. And I'll keep an eye on Simon."

"Who's going to keep an eye on you?" But Nomi had already gone, leaving her alone with Barre. "Fuck."

Chapter 24

"Come on. Let's get a course laid in."

Ro was staring down the corridor where Nomi had gone. She didn't react, even when Barre put his hand on her shoulder.

"Ro?"

"We don't have a flight plan. We don't even have clearance from Daedalus to leave. This is crazy."

"It'll be okay."

She whirled on him. "We could get ourselves killed."

"You heard Marchand. Hephaestus is on her way to Earth. That means Gutierrez is officially in charge on Daedalus. If I know the LC, she's already figured out our clearances. We need to get moving. Now."

"Do you know how vulnerable we are out there? We have no weapons. Barely enough shielding against space dust and radiation and we're chasing one of the Commonwealth's top-of-the-line cruisers with arguably its single most powerful person at her helm. What part of this makes sense?"

Barre sighed. "The part where we're trying to save our friends. And the cosmos. And doing the right thing."

"You're a fucking musician and I'm a hacker. We shouldn't even be here."

"I know." He started walking to the bridge. Behind him, Ro swore and followed him. "But we are here." They got to the blasted doors. "Micah's out there about to do something as jump-sick crazy as pointing that blaster at the restraints on his own feet. At the very least, we owe him our support." Not to mention what they owed Ada May.

"We're jumping blind. I can't see any kind of clear path."

The fear in Ro's voice chilled him. He was the one who was uncertain. The risk averse one. Ro was the one who jumped first and balanced the equations after. He needed that Ro to take Halcyone's helm. "And that's different than any other time we've taken this ship out in the void?"

She crossed the threshold into the bridge next to him and paused just inside. "No. But I still don't like it."

"Yeah, well, me neither." There was a time when his world consisted of retreating to his music and fighting with his parents. Funny to be nostalgic for how miserable he'd been then.

He stifled a yawn. As safe as jumps had been made by temporal damping and dynamic shielding under an AI's control, they still took a toll on the body. Between the round trip to Nomi's home-world and the side jaunt to pick up Lowell and deliver him to Ithaka, he'd been traveling for nearly four days.

Ro shot him a concerned look. "How deep a burn can you handle?"

It wasn't the acceleration that he found wearing, but at least with more shallow burns, they had more time between jumps.

Unfortunately, time wasn't their friend just now. Though there was a limit to how high was reasonable, even accounting for safety. They had to calculate both acceleration and deceleration, and there were occasions where a shallow burn got you to the wormhole faster, using less fuel and with less wear and tear on the body. "I'll cope with whatever Halcyone ends up figuring, given the shortest possible transit time. We can use sedatives if it comes to that."

Not ideal, but nothing about this trip was going to be ideal. At least they had a year's supply of insti-synth. They were going to need it.

Ro set her micro down on the command console and interfaced with Halcyone. Her hands moved in a blur as she communicated through gestures in a way that always seemed like dance to Barre. She would probably mock him for saying that.

"I'd recommend those sedatives. It's going to be a rough ride." Ro shuffled through her virtual windows, closing some, recentering others. "But it'll get us there in about seven hours of elapsed time."

Barre whistled long and low. "How far did you degrade the safeties for that?"

Ro's cheeks brightened, but she didn't look away. "About seventeen percent."

So deep burns and quick turnovers. From his parents' instruction, he knew that military personnel were trained for much worse, but then military ships had state-of-the-art protective gear. "All right, then. Send it directly to Gutierrez." If she couldn't figure out how to shield them from Commonwealth curiosity, no one could—and in that case they were spaced before they'd begun.

"Are you sure?"

"What choice do we have?" Barre ran down to the storage locker where he'd been laying in medical supplies. Some Jem had liberated for him; some they'd purchased from Daedalus's stores with Micah's father's money; some had come from Ada May. It still was a long way from appropriate, but it was what they had to work with. He grabbed several doses of the mild sedatives, enough for both him and Ro to get through the next seven hours.

They paused for a check in the corridor outside their rooms.

"Do you have your micro handy?"

Barre handed it over. She bumped it with hers.

"I've passed along the entire flight sequence. Can you check it over and set a musical trigger for Halcyone?"

Nodding, Barre reviewed the parameters. She must also be exhausted—she'd even programmed Halcyone to take them from the asteroid's surface to the approach to the small wormhole Daedalus controlled. He quickly scanned the combinations of burns and jumps that would take them through to the hub. The trip would be as brutal as he'd suspected, but they'd be okay. They had to be.

He had a little program already prepared that would act as the countdown mechanism and trigger—he'd learned that from the way Ro programmed. "Sixty-second delay?"

"Yeah."

The time for doubts and second thoughts was long past. He handed her a blister pack of sedatives. "Set your micro for elapsed objective time. Take two of these every two hours. They'll dissolve and hit your bloodstream instantaneously."

Barre entered his room and checked the restraints on his instruments before taking the first sedative dose and getting himself as comfortable as he could in the bunk's jump padding. It was going to be a long seven hours.

The ship-wide speakers crackled. "Halcyone, you are cleared for departure."

Ro's voice sounded muffled. "Thank you, Daedalus Station."

"Ro? Triggering program Nav One now. Sixty seconds to take off."

"See you on the other side."

Halcyone played a soft repeating series of notes Barre thought of as waiting music. His neural monitored the sixty-second countdown. The docking clamps disengaged with a loud clang, and the interstitial engines thrummed beneath him. Halcyone leaped up into space with her usual eagerness. Barre hardly felt the increased weight as the foam absorbed the tiny g-force. The first jump followed; it was a familiar strangeness. As wormholes went, this one was short, old, and very stable. Still, Barre was glad he'd taken the sedative first.

It felt like he'd been trapped in a kinesthetic hallucination for an endless, timeless now, but he knew that somewhere in normal space, his micro was measuring how long he had to wait to take another dose. Then came the first deep burn and as the seconds ticked by, he was sure the tiny capillaries in his eyes and the alveoli of his lungs were going to burst with the pressure.

There was only enough time for Barre to take several full inhales and exhales before Halcyone decelerated them just as severely so they would hit the right approach vector at the right speed for their second jump.

By the time Halcyone signaled the all-clear, Barre decided

he'd rather space himself without a p-suit than ever make a trip like that again. "Ro?" His voice wobbled. His whole body felt like it was made of an overcooked polymer. "You alive?"

"Fuck no."

"Where in the cosmos are we?"

"Orbiting just outside the hub traffic control zone. I thought we'd need some recovery time before dealing with spaceport authorities."

"Thanks. That ... That was not optimal."

Her weak laugh triggered one of his own. "But we made it. I need to shower and change. I'm laying in a puddle of sweat. At least I hope it's sweat."

"Meet me on the bridge when you can manage to stand." Barre groaned as he rolled out of the damp foam. His hair was matted to his head and his legs didn't want to support his weight. It took another ten minutes before the room stopped spinning and he was willing to risk getting up. Even then, he walked holding on to the free-fall handrails just in case.

Sitting in the compact head, he stripped, and let hot water sluice away what felt like fever-sweat until he felt halfway to being human again. He left his dirty clothes in a wet pile on the floor and changed. His dreads lay damp against his back. Their coolness was refreshing.

A pale and shaken Ro met him on the bridge holding two mugs of insti-synth.

Barre reached for the one she held out to him. "I don't care what they say, you are the best captain in the cosmos."

"How many captains do you actually know besides me?"

"That's totally not the point." Barre drank deeply and could practically feel the caffeine spreading throughout his grateful body.

"Okay. Let's see if we can reach Micah."

"Halcyone, what's local time, North American central zone?"

"Zero four hundred and thirteen."

Micah was definitely not a morning person. Barre smirked. "Well, then, let's wake our friend, shall we?"

Ro pulled out her micro, but before she could compose a message, Halcyone's alert tone rang through the bridge.

"Commonwealth registry Epsilon Delta niner seven niner, this is New Chicago Spaceport control. You are cleared for landing in the transient small vessel hangar. Stand by for coordinates and optimal glide path."

Gutierrez must have pulled strings. "New Chicago Spaceport control, this is Commonwealth registry Epsilon Delta niner seven niner. Landing instructions received. Thank you."

"Can you take us in? I'll let Micah know to meet us at the spaceport."

"Aye, aye, Captain." Barre finished the insti-synth and linked his neural to Halcyone as Ro's hands waved through virtual screens in an intricate pattern. The AI hummed her readiness for work. They made a good team, but given what they were going up against, that might not be enough.

*

If Dev hadn't already been awake, she would have missed Micah's soft knock on her door. She slid back the security latch and opened it to find him dressed in dark clothing, a travel mug of coffee in hand.

"I need to run an errand. I didn't want you to find me gone."

"You're not going alone, Micah. I thought we'd already settled this." If he was going to be foolish enough to go through with contacting the Reaction Chamber, she was at least going to know about it. Someone had to.

"It's not Targill. Not yet, anyway. It's Ro and Barre. They need Charon's ship. It's complicated."

"More complicated than your father being one of the secret power brokers of the cosmos?"

He winced. "Actually? Yes."

She pushed past him into the common area. "You have more of that coffee? Because if you don't, I may have to hurt you."

He blinked at her in the dim light. "You're dressed."

"Of course I'm dressed. I didn't trust you."

"Oh."

She rummaged around the kitchen until she found another clean thermos and poured herself the hot drink. "Let's go."

They took an automated transport to the private long-term hangar where Micah had stashed Charon's little ship. From the outside, it didn't look much different than a family-sized flitter, but it was jump capable.

In the predawn darkness, everything was silent and still. Micah unlocked the hangar door with a wave of his micro and exhaled a long, deep breath when the automatic lights illuminated the battered ship.

It opened for his credentials, and interior lights lit as they stepped on board. There was only enough room for them to walk single file down the corridor to the cramped bridge.

It was hard for Dev not to see the wounded Emmaline Gutierrez slumping in the captain's seat.

"Buckle up. We're going to take the short hop to the

spaceport."

"Is it safe?"

"Is anything? It's got a brand new top-of-the-line black-market transponder, and there's nothing that links it to Ithaka."

At least they wouldn't be traveling out of Earth's atmo. The ship had gotten them there, but she didn't trust it. Dev untangled the webbing on the navigator's chair and strapped herself in. Micah seemed to know what he was doing, but then again, he'd spent a lifetime in the void.

"Hangar Control, this is the private craft Obolus, outbound to the New Chicago Spaceport, transient docks. What is my flight lane?"

An inflectionless automated voice answered. "Obolus, you are clear for flight lane two two alpha. Be advised there is a fog advisory. Instruments landing only."

"Roger that, Hangar Control. Obolus out."

"Who in their right mind would attempt a manual landing at New Chicago Spaceport?"

"Not me. But the fog means at least no one will see us glide in."

The sun rose as they short-hopped over to the spaceport, but all it did was brighten the glare around them. Micah had the autopilot land them at the bay where Halcyone waited.

Barre greeted them at the airlock, first giving Micah a big hug and then wrapping his arms around Dev, as if she were a long-lost friend. She stiffened and then relaxed. "Come on. Ro needs to talk to you."

He led them into Halcyone.

"Welcome back, Micah Rotherwood. Welcome, Devorah Martingale Morningstar."

"Um, it's just Dev. Dev Morningstar." There weren't a lot of

AIs in her life. It was odd to hear her full name in its slightly atonal voice.

"Correction. Welcome Dev Morningstar."

"Thanks."

"Come on. Ro's on the bridge."

They followed him through the central corridor to the fore of the ship and she stopped short, eyeing the damaged doors. "What the hell happened here?"

Micah hung back, looking down at the ground. "I did."

"Oh." He'd told her the story of how he burned his own feet rescuing his friends. The blistered door made it all too real.

Ro was standing with her back toward the large forward viewscreen. Dev followed the crack that meandered across its expanse. Halcyone wasn't in much better shape than Taro's battered little ship.

"We think Targill's on his way. You still going through with this meeting?"

"What choice do we have?"

"Not very many good ones." Ro sighed. "May's gone and made herself a very tempting target for the Reaction Chamber. With you on the inside, at least we'll have some idea what's going on." She turned to Dev. "Give me your micro."

She shoved her hand in her pocket and gripped the small device tight. Ro didn't seem to notice.

"Yours too, Micah."

He handed his over without as much as a peep. Slowly, Dev drew hers out and rested it on the console next to Ro.

Ro placed hers next to Micah's and with a flurry of short, sharp hand motions, pulled up dozens of virtual windows and cloned them over to his machine. "That's everything Nomi and I got from my father's data. There are files on dozens of people. We think most—if not all—are part of the Chamber. That'll give you at least some edge." She shot him a look that was clearly disapproval and worry. But it didn't stop her from giving him the data.

"And I'll need root access on yours," she said, nodding toward Dev.

"Why?" She glanced at her micro and then at Micah.

"Just do it. She'll hack in anyway. This just saves us all time."

"Way to get your friend to trust me. Thanks." Ro gave her a brief smile. "I have a secure messaging program. Its backbone is something Ithaka developed. That way you can keep in contact with us. Especially if Micah does something monumentally stupid."

Dev picked up her micro, unlocked it, and handed it directly to Ro.

"What do you need Obolus for?"

Barre raised an eyebrow. "Obolus?"

"It needed a name. It means coin in some long-dead language." Micah shrugged. "Thought it was appropriate, being the Ferryman's ship and all."

"Gutierrez is going to take it and try to rescue May before everything blows up in her face. Halcyone is too conspicuous."

"Are you sure that's wise?" Micah asked.

It still gave Dev a thrill to know Ada May was alive and Ithaka truly existed.

"You idiot. I could say the same to you. Even Jem thinks you're being reckless—and that's saying something."

Micah's micro buzzed for an incoming message and they all started.

"I should check that." Micah picked it up off Ro's console and opened the message. As he read and reread it, his frown deepened. "You better fold space and time getting back. I don't think Targill's actually coming to Earth."

"What do you mean?" Ro's face paled to a pearly gray.

"He's agreed to a virtual meeting with me. Probably between jumps. Which means he's already got a trail to follow to Ithaka."

"That's not possible," Ro whispered.

"It is if May's the one who laid out the breadcrumbs," Barre said. "I didn't think she'd go through with it. Not really. Fuck."

Ro tossed Dev back her micro. "Get the hell out of here. Both of you. I want to know everything Targill says. And what he doesn't say."

"Aye, aye, Cap." Micah saluted her.

"And don't you dare get yourself killed in the process!"

"Yes, sir, Captain, sir!"

"Micah, I'm serious." Ro's cheeks had bloomed with bright red patches.

Dev took a deep breath and stepped into what felt like an intimacy she wasn't really a part of. "I'll keep an eye on him."

She wasn't sure what she expected when Ro walked up to her, but the fierce hug from the petite woman wasn't it. "I'm sorry you got dragged into this, but for Micah's sake, I'm glad he has you on his side."

Dev shrugged. "A handshake counts for all." There was nothing else to say.

*

They took a transport back to campus from the spaceport. Dev didn't ask a single question. Every time Micah glanced at her, she was staring down at her micro. He wished he knew what she was thinking. Sighing, he dug into the documents Ro had given him.

The files on Reaction Chamber members read like a who's who of industrial wealth, criminal enterprise, and political connections. No wonder Ro's father had hoarded all of this. He gave a low whistle.

"What?" she finally asked, breaking her silence.

"Look."

She scanned the names on the preliminary list he'd put together. "We're in over our heads."

If she expected Micah to argue with her, she was going to be disappointed. "Tell me something I don't know."

There was a long pause before she spoke again. "Do you think they'll get to her in time?"

He'd never even met Ada May. Had never been to the fabled Ithaka, but just knowing they were both out there had made him feel some weird measure of safety. "I don't know. She's supposed to be the smart one." But Barre and Ro were both worried. That wasn't a good sign.

They reached their dorm building just as the morning sun had burned off the fog.

"He said to expect his call at zero eight thirty." It was just shy of eight. Micah glanced up at their building. "I don't want to be here when we talk."

"The biodome."

Micah nodded. Security through obscurity. Besides, the same factors that isolated each shielded habitat would make it harder to trace his signal. He started walking toward the dome farm.

Dev matched him stride for stride.

"What?"

"I'm coming with you."

"So it seems."

"You're not going to talk me out of it?"

"Would it do any good?"

"Well, no, but you could at least try."

That made him laugh. "Don't you have classes this morning?"

Dev snorted. "Don't you?"

As if any of that mattered anymore. Not for him. But for her? He wanted to say something, but her choices weren't up to him. If she was going to stand by his stupid decisions, he would stand by hers. "You're the most remarkable person I've ever met."

She fell silent again as the campus walkways gave way to the lush biodomes and their unique and precious diversity. Rain fell softly in the dome nearest them, creating a fine mist. Next to it was an arid environment where prickly plants struggled in a sandy soil. Past all the carefully cultivated spaces, through overgrown hedges, was the abandoned dome Dev had shared with Micah.

The airlock hissed open and Micah carefully walked around the one raised bed where a broken pressure transducer made it fountain water for eleven minutes four times a day. He wondered if he'd ever have the chance to fix that now.

"Here. There's a bench that's out of the splash zone."

"Thanks."

"Now what?"

Micah checked the time. Zero eight twenty-three. "We wait. Seven minutes."

"Micah?"

"Hmm?"

"If this goes bad, we can retreat. To Midlant."

"Where your brothers were ready to sell me to the highest bidder?"

Her cheeks flushed a dark pink. "My brothers have no idea how close they came to defenestration."

Micah smiled. Certainly she was strong enough to toss any of them out the window of their second-floor container home.

"I'm serious. It's a place people come to vanish. No one would be able to find you there."

"Thank you." He reached over to squeeze her hand.

"Sometimes knowing you have an out gives you the freedom not to use it."

Then his micro signaled and it was time to embody everything he loathed about Senator Corwin Rotherwood. He set the tiny computer beside him on the bench, tilting it upward so only his torso and head would be in the image it broadcast.

A virtual window opened between him and Dev, showing Targill in his immaculate ship's uniform. If Micah hadn't have known he was on Hephaestus, there would have been no way to tell he wasn't simply broadcasting from Daedalus. The lighting hid whatever was in the background in deep shadow.

"Micah, I hope your studies are going well."

"It's fair to say I've found more fertile ground in other areas."

Targill nodded thoughtfully. "What is it you think I can do for you, young man? As I recall, I fulfilled my part of the bargain. New identity, emancipation, University admittance."

"My father —"

"Your father is devalued currency."

Micah raised an eyebrow and waited exactly five seconds. It was something his father used to do that had driven him crazy when he was younger. He was betting it would annoy Targill, too. He let a half-smile play across his face before he answered. "I think you'll find what my father left me has made him extremely relevant again."

"I sincerely hope you're not wasting my time. I've been more than generous with you, but even the Commonwealth's largess has its limits."

"Commander Targill, I trust we're on a secured line?"

He sighed, theatrically. "Yes, son, we're on a secured line."

Son. He would have to go there. It was time for Micah to flip the polarity on him. He stared right into Targill's eyes and used his low voice to its best effect. "Commander. I am not your son. If we were friends, Micah would do, but for now, I think Mr. Rotherwood is the way to go. And, by the way, I asked about security for your benefit. Not mine. I have little to lose if word of our conversation were to leak."

He waited another several seconds. Targill showed no outward signs of the anger and annoyance Micah knew had to be building inside him.

"Fine. I'll lay it out for you. My father's seat in the Reaction Chamber. I'm claiming it."

When Targill did react, it wasn't what Micah had expected. The silver-haired man laughed. His eyes flashed with dangerous amusement. "You should know I never bluff. Not in battle. Not in negotiations. And I don't take kindly to a virtual child trying to bluff me. I don't know where you heard that term, but I assure you, you don't want to be playing in this weight class. Go back to your plants, Micah, and be grateful for the deal you got." He leaned forward as if to close the comms channel.

Micah felt his pulse race. Adrenaline surged though him and

he wanted to laugh right back at the old soldier. Instead he quietly recited a name. "Jasper Finnegan." He was a high-ranking member of the Commonwealth Senate and the chair of the Appropriations Committee. And a member of the Chamber.

Targill halted instantly, still leaning forward.

"Iona Pearson-Eddy and Ramon Salazar." Those were the next two names on Ro's father's list. Both industry moguls. Micah smiled and sat back. "Shall I continue?"

"Where did you get those names?" Targill's voice was a fierce whisper.

"Names? No. Not just names. Events, payments, communications—my father was resourceful." He paused. "I learned from the best."

"What do you want?"

"I told you. I'm claiming his seat in the Chamber. No more, no less."

"You have a lot of confidence for the child of a disgraced politician. Wasn't it you who not so long ago begged to have your name changed?"

"You and I both know that 'disgrace' was manufactured. What I can't figure out is whose idea it was—my father's or yours." He paused for another brief beat. "But, you know what? That's in the past. What matters now is what you choose to do next. You know how to find me. Oh, and you should know: I have a dead-man's switch programmed to leak all sorts of fascinating details should I inconveniently disappear." He gestured at his micro to drop the connection. Targill's window winked out, taking the man and his anger with it.

Micah threw his head back and laughed and laughed until he couldn't breathe.

Chapter 25

AFTER LEAVING HALCYONE, Jem had raced through Daedalus's corridors, but Gutierrez had retreated to her quarters and didn't answer his chime. He'd stayed as long as he dared, but there was absolutely no reason he had to be camped out by her door.

He'd sent a private message to the LC before heading back to the residence ring. His parents were both gone—probably in medical—and for once, he was disappointed to be alone.

Ada was probably alone in an empty Ithaka. This wasn't the future Jem had imagined when he first met the brilliant scientist. Growing up to work with her had been a dream he'd barely even admitted to himself, and now it was gone before he was even healed enough for it to be a possibility.

With tears blurring his vision, he set up several messages, each to repeat every hour through the night. One to Gutierrez, one to Ada May. Jem had little hope either of them would answer him.

He collapsed into bed without changing his clothes and

slipped his micro under his pillow.

The automated room lights woke him from fragmented and disorienting dreams of endless shiny corridors that twisted into mazes and a series of dead ends. He sighed. No symbolism there.

A tiny blinking light in his visual field made his heart race. He opened the reply with a shift of his attention, but it wasn't the answer he'd hoped for.

/You may as well work on some of the arm tweaks while we're waiting./

So May hadn't answered Gutierrez either. He washed and changed before heading out by way of the commissary. The LC was in uniform when he arrived, but had removed her prosthesis. It was lying on the low table. Jem put his coffee cup beside the claw hand. "Still life with caffeine and metal."

Gutierrez gave him a sour look.

"Either something's wrong with the messaging protocol or she's ignoring both of us."

"Barre had better get back here with that ship." The LC's voice was an angry growl.

A round trip to the hub and back in under a day of elapsed time would be brutal, and she knew it. "What do you want me to focus on?" Jem gestured at the limb.

She sighed. "I did some programming tweaks, but the kinesthetic stabilizers are still sluggish. There are some micro-switches on the units themselves. I'd like to try a different configuration."

Slipping on the microloupes, Jem crouched beside the limb and triggered the releases. The access ports slid back, revealing the mass of components inside. Gutierrez paced as he followed the wiring to the stabilizers. "Will you stop that!"

She halted, mid-stride, casting Jem and the arm in shadow.

"Just sit down. She's not going to answer any faster if you make this harder." Which totally didn't made sense, but she sighed and sat anyway.

"I swore I wouldn't set foot on Ithaka while Taro was there. That I would kill him if I ever saw him again."

Jem remembered her claw hand on Taro's throat, her sidearm pointed at his chest. She had very nearly killed the man right here on Daedalus. He swallowed hard and glanced at the exposed prosthetic arm. "Did he do this?"

She didn't answer for the longest time. When she did, her voice was shot through with shades of yellow and orange. Pain. Fear. Shame. "No. I did."

"Oh."

"It was a long time ago." She sat with her head cradled in her right hand.

It was hard for Jem not to get up and give her a hug. He blinked back tears and focused on the tiny switches instead. "You should talk to Micah some time." It wasn't what he'd planned to say, but it was true. Jem couldn't imagine the strength and desperation it must have taken for either of them to do what they had done to themselves. He wasn't sure he could have, no matter how terrible the circumstances. "What will you do if she doesn't answer?"

"Carry her out of there kicking and screaming." Gutierrez's words were heavy and edged in a dark, fierce determination.

She most certainly could. Ada May probably weighed about what Jem did, and Gutierrez was both strong and singularly focused. And yet, he wasn't about to give the LC more than low odds of being able to force Ada to do anything she didn't want to do.

Jem hesitated before flipping the first switch. "Do you think she knows what she's doing?" She had to have a plan. She was Ada May.

"She's not infallible, Jem. Just a tired old woman. And I'm a tired old soldier doing what she convinced me to do a long time ago: protect her. No matter what." All the color leached out of her words.

Checking the schematic against what he was seeing, Jem shifted the configuration of the stabilizers. With the tweaks Gutierrez had programmed, it should help with the responsiveness. He sealed the access hatches and handed her the limb. With practiced ease, she clicked in the wiring harness and seated the arm one-handed. Once she rolled her sleeve down and stood, the only sign that she'd lost the arm was the shiny metal claw she'd refused to replace.

Jem removed the loupes and let his vision readjust before checking for messages. Ro and Barre were probably on their way back. He'd hoped Micah was okay. The blinking light of an incoming response surprised him. Gutierrez's micro beeped its alert tone simultaneously, startling them both.

She waved her hand over the small computer and Ada May's voice emerged from its tinny on-board speaker.

"Emma, I'm not in any danger. But you will be, if you persist in this senseless rescue mission."

Jem jerked upright. "Ada!"

"Oh, good, Jem's with you. That saves me having to do this twice."

"Shut up and let me do my job." Gutierrez's barely restrained fury pressed on Jem like heavy g-forces.

"Wait," Jem said, looking around the room wildly. "Are we secure?"

Gutierrez shot him a withering look. "I think we know what we're doing."

Jem shut up. Of course they did. They'd been communicating under the noses and sensors of the Commonwealth for decades.

"Your job is to trust me."

"My job is to protect you from yourself!" Gutierrez was pacing again.

"Emma, it's going to be okay. I know what I'm doing."

The LC fell silent for a moment. When she spoke again, her voice was under control, low and steady. "From where I stand, what you're doing is suicide. And I can't let you destroy everything you've built over the last forty years."

"I promise you, it isn't what it looks like."

"Then what is it?" Gutierrez's voice was tinged with red again. "This can't be what Chaz or Taro would have wanted! Think. There are lives depending on you."

It was Ada's time to fall silent. When she finally did answer, Jem could taste the fear and resolve even through the distortion of the under-powered micro speaker. "I'm doing this for them. For you. I can't tell you any more. You're just going to have to trust—"

The connection dropped. Jem drew in a sharp breath. Gutierrez pulled up a window and sent a series of commands.

Silence.

She rebooted her micro and repeated the process two more times before throwing the device across the room. She had used her prosthetic arm. The micro bounced off the wall, leaving a dent three or four centimeters deep in the metal surface and tumbled across the floor.

"Daedalus, locate Acting Comms Supervisor Marchand."

"Acting Comms Supervisor Marchand is in his quarters."

"Jem, give me your micro."

"You're not going to throw it, are you?"

She exhaled heavily. "Fine. Use the secure text program. Message Marchand for me. I need an update on Hephaestus."

The utter calm in her body belied the emotion blazing in her voice. Without his synesthesia, he'd never have known.

"Now."

/Any word from your friend?/ Secure or not, Jem didn't dare risk being more explicit than that.

He stared at the tiny screen, waiting for an answer. It didn't take long.

/No. Looks like their holiday plans changed. Waiting for a post card./

Gutierrez snatched Jem's micro out of his hands. He waited for the inevitable explosion that would send it careening to join hers, but it didn't happen. She quickly typed her own reply.

/Alert me the instant you hear—EG/

"Thank you for your assistance, Jem. I think I have it from here." She handed him back his micro and went to retrieve hers from across the room.

Jem wasn't sure what unnerved him more: her earlier outburst or the cold calm that had settled over her afterward. He wanted to reassure her, to tell her Ada was going to be all right. That Ro and Barre would be back soon.

Gutierrez had a distant look in her eyes. Her claw hand flexed rhythmically.

He retreated to the safety of his quarters.

*

"Shit." Barre paced the bridge on Halcyone, checking his messages, hoping for something from Jem or, better yet, from May, but it was only the usual junk. He glanced at Ro. "Now what?"

"Change of plans. Take Charon's ship. Go directly to Ithaka. Contact me when you have Ada."

"Gutierrez will go critical."

"Gutierrez isn't here and we don't have time to stop and get her."

"But —"

"She'll live, Barre. Ada might not. Do you want to explain that to the LC?"

"You know there's a good chance she'll refuse to come." It wasn't just that Barre didn't want to force her, but with the control she had over Lethe, she could easily prevent him from landing. Even if he could set the ship down somewhere, she might keep the station sealed against him.

"Just do your best."

Barre nodded. "Can you set up the link with the ship's computer while I grab some things from my room?"

"Go. I'm on it."

He ran down Halcyone's corridor to his quarters. There was no way of knowing how long he'd be away. To be on the safe side, he tossed several changes of clothes in a bag. He glanced at the array of instruments crammed in his room. This wasn't a pleasure trip and he wasn't planning on moving in to Obolus permanently, but he'd never been without something to play. Well, except on that first unexpected trip on Halcyone. Before she was Halcyone.

A flute wouldn't take up too much space. And the echoes would be interesting. Maybe Ada would enjoy it. He nestled the small instrument in a layer of clothing. His kit bag came next, along with the sedatives he had left. Anything else he needed he hoped he could grab on Ithaka, or wherever they would bring May.

He stopped short at the door. It couldn't be to Daedalus. They had to find some place free of Commonwealth control for her to be safe. Which meant Barre wasn't coming home for the foreseeable future.

Home. It had been a long time since he'd thought of any place as home. He hoped his parents would understand what he was doing and why.

"Barre? All set. Halcyone has established communications with Obolus's AI. It's at root level. Nonverbal."

"Why the hell would Charon have such a primitive AI?"

"Space me, I don't know. But you should be able to pair directly from your micro, if not from your neural. And I pushed over the authentication tokens."

But he wouldn't be able to sing to it and understand its nuance the way he could with Halcyone. It would make control harder. He wasn't the natural with computers that Ro or his brother was. And while he was a competent small-craft pilot, navigation didn't come easily to him and he was glad Ro would be able to help.

Navigation. Shit. "Does it have the Ithaka program in memory?"

"Wouldn't it have to? I mean, otherwise Charon couldn't have been the Ferryman."

First things first. He would have to get clearance to leave Earth's flight space. Then take at least one jump outbound from the hub before he would risk engaging the nav protocol that allowed them to actually find Ithaka. And time was slipping away.

"Okay. I'm leaving Halcyone now." He reached the airlock and whistled a few notes. The AI cycled the lock for him. "Ro?" He paused before stepping from the corridor. "You should have full access without my musical interface. But if you run into any problems, I created a library with all the programs and triggers."

"So I don't need you after all."

He smiled at the real affection and teasing in her voice. "Don't be so sure of that. Maybe I forgot one or two. By accident."

"Hey, music man. Be careful."

"Right back at you, Cap. You're the one who's going to have to face the wrath of Gutierrez."

Barre stepped through the ship's side of the airlock and waited as it cycled through. Then he jogged over to the small vessel Taro Odachi had once captained as Ithaka's Ferryman. It opened to his micro and he stepped aboard, ducking his head to avoid hitting it on the low hatch. He was going to have to remember that, or it was going to be a very uncomfortable trip.

"Hello, Obolus." It didn't matter that the AI wasn't able to answer him verbally. Just because something sentient couldn't speak didn't mean it didn't communicate. He wondered how it liked the name Micah had given it.

"Barre?" Ro's voice came through the small speaker on his micro. "How's it look?"

He triggered the airlock to close behind him. Ship's lights

illuminated the interior. "As beat up as it was when I came in here to rescue Gutierrez." Random panels were missing all up and down the narrow corridor. A few jump berths had been built into the bulkheads in lieu of cargo space. Hell of a way to travel. Barre peered inside. He wouldn't even fit in one.

The bridge was in better shape. State-of-the-art seats for a pilot and co-pilot had integrated temporal-damping foam and would contain the g-forces of interstitial engine burns. And they were big enough for his frame. "I'm all set here. Give me a minute to figure out my access."

"Halcyone's got clearance to leave in thirty minutes. A ship as small as Obolus shouldn't have any issues."

He set his micro on the captain's console and pondered the simple AI. Maybe not simple, but direct. Elegant and resourceful. Like Charon was. Or rather Taro Odachi, the man he had been before the title. He must have been extraordinary to have had Ada May's trust for so long.

Ada wouldn't have let him fly a ship that was as ramshackle as this one appeared to be. Therefore, its appearance was a distraction. And its AI was probably every bit as sophisticated as Lethe, and probably a hell of a lot more so than Halcyone.

He smirked. That would piss Ro off.

But for now he needed to access the ship and its computer. Gloating would come later. If there was a later.

"Obolus—I hope you don't mind the new name—Ada May once asked me to be her Ferryman." He glanced at the lights blinking on the console and smiled. It was definitely listening to him. "I turned her down. I thought it was a choice. But it wasn't really just up to me. Now I find I need to take one very precious soul to safety. I need your help." He accessed the part of his neural that allowed him to connect with Halcyone or his micro and waited.

The calm voice reverberated in his mind. *"Welcome, Ferryman."*

"Barre? Everything good to go?"

"Aye, aye, Cap. I've got full access." He flicked his attention to the AI and queried it quickly. He needed one quick jump out of the hub so he could calibrate the nav and access the maps to Ithaka.

"Do you need me to rendezvous with you?" Ro's worried voice echoed in the small cockpit.

A star map unfolded in his mind with a schematic of the hub's solar system. Around a minor wormhole was a circle.

"Nope. I got it. Obolus has the Ithaka program."

"Affirmative." The ship's voice sounded both confident and smug.

"Then light up your engines. Send word when you can."

"I will. Keep your eyes sharp. Just because Targill's off Daedalus doesn't mean you're in the clear."

"I know. Now get the hell out of here."

Barre tucked his micro back into a pocket. He wasn't going to need it. As he buckled the webbing and dogged it down, he requested Obolus open a comms channel to Spaceport control.

A green light flared on the main console.

"Spaceport control, this is private vessel Obolus, Commonwealth registration—" He fumbled for the micro he actually did need, since it had Micah's data on it, but before he could pull it out, the AI fed the numbers to him.

"Seven four four eight delta one one three"

"Commonwealth registration seven four four eight delta one

one three requesting outbound travel lane to wormhole foxtrot nine one seven."

"Good day, Obolus, please stand by." That was the spaceport AI. Several seconds ticked by before a different voice answered.

"Seven four four eight delta one one three, you are cleared for takeoff lane epsilon. We have a high volume of outbound traffic this morning. Set your autopilot for station override. You are number four for departure. Estimated wait time is eleven minutes."

Ro would definitely not be happy to relinquish Halcyone to the port, even for just take off. "Roger control."

By the time Barre had glanced down at the main console, Obolus had already set them for automated flight. "Sweet." Halcyone was getting better at anticipating their commands, but she would probably never get to the level of syntactic skill as this AI. Partly because she was first-gen and there was a limit to what they could do, even with upgrades. Partly because of the damage she had taken from the virus. Barre patted Obolus's console, feeling more than a little disloyal to Halcyone.

They updated his departure time once per minute and by the time Obolus's engines started purring, Barre was already sick of the spaceport's overly enthusiastic AI interface.

Several other small vessels took off ahead of him, passing uncomfortably close to Obolus. Closer than he would risk on manual, but the spaceport AI had the timing down to the nanosecond. Then it was their turn. His body pressed into the seat, but he hardly felt the increased weight as the high-tech foam dispersed the added g-forces. Obolus leaped into the sky and smoothly through the atmosphere, the ship's shielding clearly better than it appeared from the outside.

"Standby for resumption of local control in ten seconds, Obolus."

"Roger that, Spaceport." He glanced at the small viewscreen as the curve of Earth appeared with its precious ring of atmosphere. "Ready, Obolus?"

"Affirmative, Ferryman."

"Enable the Ithaka program and take the jump when ready. Thirty-second countdown, please." It was likely easier and faster for the AI to access Barre's thoughts, but it was harder for a human mind to communicate with a constructed one without all sorts of extraneous thoughts and emotional content confusing the message. Besides, it felt less lonely hearing his own voice on the ship.

"Affirmative."

As much as he was proud of the musical language he'd crafted for Halcyone, this was incredibly easy. It was much like speaking with Jem worked, when it worked. Again, Barre wondered how he and his brother were able to connect. Maybe he'd be able to talk it over with Ada.

If he got there in time.

If she agreed to go with him.

Obolus started his countdown. His. The voice did seem male in Barre's mind, though AIs didn't really have gender. Barre fumbled with a sedative pack and slipped the tablets under his tongue.

The half minute passed under a brief acceleration before the ship reversed thrust to drift to its approach vector. As jumps went, it wasn't terrible. Just the normal misery of traveling outside of normal space-time and having no temporal or visual spatial referents to rely on. The integrated padding was several generations more advanced than what they had on Halcyone and while the jump was still wearing and wearying, it wasn't incapacitating.

"Okay, Obolus, how does local space look?" This region was typically pretty quiet. Not a lot of trade or routine traffic since newer and larger wormholes had been discovered that acted as a bypass. Fewer jumps meant faster transit times and better profit margins for traders. The only ships that typically ended up here were traveling through interstitial space on their way home.

"Traffic is within normal parameters for this region of space."

"Anyone follow us from Earth?"

"Negative."

"Okay, then. Plot a course from here to Ithaka. Parameters: minimize transit time. Push safeties to one hundred and twenty percent of baseline."

"State authorization for safety override."

Barre swore softly. There was no way to know what Charon or May had programmed in. Unless they hadn't changed the defaults. "One zero one zero one zero."

"Override denied."

Well, that would have been too easy. How in the cosmos was he going to convince Obolus that pushing the safeties was warranted? It wasn't like you could out-logic a machine. And it wasn't susceptible to emotional arguments. Barre could feel the seconds fly by. Seconds he was sure Ada didn't have.

"Obolus, this is an emergency situation."

"Describe the nature of your emergency."

It sounded like the med-bay's emergency protocol when his parents were unavailable. The artificial voice had the same calmly infuriating tone as every other AI installation in the cosmos and for a brief moment, Barre imagined telling the sentient machine exactly what it could do with its emergency.

Then he smiled. A medical emergency. Those overrides never got changed. It was a matter of common sense and safety. "Obolus, emergency medical override alpha alpha alpha. Calculate minimal transit time to Ithaka, push safeties to one hundred and twenty percent."

There was a brief pause and Barre worried that Charon had disabled the medical override.

"Affirmative. Official objection will be entered into the medical record of Durbin, Bernard, designation Ferryman."

Barre hadn't thought it was possible for an AI to sound annoyed and passive-aggressive. Obolus complied. The forward window turned into an opaque display where the ship previewed the course: several jumps, each with some steep burns between, but none as bad as the ones Halcyone had made getting to Earth. And his protection was better.

"Save course as May One. Create ten-second delay and countdown."

"Affirmative."

He took a moment to check his restraints. "All right, Obolus. Execute May One."

Chapter 26

Going back to work in comms as if nothing at all had changed was one of the hardest things Nomi had ever done. She had slept through her alarm and had to sprint through the station to make turnover. It wasn't an auspicious start.

Marchand sauntered in his usual few minutes late. Nomi didn't even spare him a glance, worried that if she did, her concern would be apparent to any casual observer. If he'd heard from his person on Hephaestus, surely he would have contacted her.

The shift passed in a blur of routine ansible traffic just busy enough to keep her from checking her private messages but not busy enough to quell her rising anxiety. She'd heard nothing from Ro and Barre.

She didn't even remember which of the comms staff she handed over her station to after shift.

"Nakamura!"

Nomi stopped short in the corridor outside comms and was

nearly run over by several crew headed to the commissary. They mumbled apologies. She waved them off. A hand grabbed her shoulder.

"Nomi."

Turning, she blinked up into Simon Marchand's face.

"Rough day at the office?" He smiled and it was only because she'd spent so much time with him lately that she saw through its brittleness. "You look like you need a drink."

Her stomach gurgled. She'd been too rushed to eat breakfast and by the time her break had rolled around, had been too wound up to eat lunch. "How about I buy you dinner?"

It was an ideal time to be in the commissary. Most folks on first or third would wait until later to have their meal and those on second would just be settling in to their shifts. When they arrived, it was practically empty. Nomi moved through the line, choosing some broth and a small loaf of crusty bread. It was all her queasy stomach would be able to handle.

By the time she'd picked up her cutlery, Simon had chosen a table in the back corner of the room, close to the air vent. The soft hiss of life support would mask any quiet conversation.

"Any news?"

Simon shook his head and frowned. "You?"

"No." Nomi swirled the spoon around in her soup and watched the miniature whirlpool form and settle. She had slept poorly last night and if she didn't hear from Ro by tonight, figured on a repeat performance. For the hundredth time, she checked her messages, even though her micro would notify her. "Your turn."

As he pushed his tray aside to make room for his micro, it beeped. Nomi dropped her spoon and it landed in the soup, splashing warm liquid across her tray and on her clothing.

She quickly blotted herself dry and stared at him as he read whatever he'd received, trying to parse any meaning from his rigid expression and rapidly scanning eyes. He closed those eyes briefly before handing her his micro.

"You need to see this." His voice was devoid of its thick, casual drawl, devoid of any emotion. Nomi shivered. She took the device from his hands.

Before she could read whatever he'd been sent, Simon placed a hand on her wrist. "If you reveal his existence to anyone, you put his safety in extreme peril. I'm trusting you with this. With a man's life."

Her throat was so tight, all she could do was nod.

Simon withdrew his hand. Nomi started to read.

He's vanished with the target. Ship's in chaos. Our XO has taken command and put us on lock-down. No one leaves, no one boards. Priority comms only. Future messages risky. Preparing to break orbit. Destination classified.

That was it. Nomi read it several more times, but it didn't make much more sense. "What does that mean, vanished?"

His eyes were wide. "I have no idea. With the target. Did he abandon his ship and take her with him? That makes no sense. He wouldn't jeopardize his position. Not even for that."

The message wasn't signed, which wasn't a surprise. It had no headers, which was. That could only mean one thing: Simon Marchand's man on the inside was a comms officer. She had worked with most of the comms staff during the search for Halcyone. She'd even been dressed down by the comms supervisor, Lieutenant Odoyo. It wasn't her—Simon had said "him."

She'd worked closely with Leon Jenkins during her time aboard. He was a thickset, jovial man who reminded her a little of Simon. He even had a trace of Simon's New Cajun accent, now that she thought about it.

"Can you send a reply?"

Simon shook his head. "Too risky. You need to get in touch with Ro. The quicker she gets back here the better. Especially if Hephaestus is returning."

"Without Targill? Do you think they will?"

"I have no idea."

Nomi reached for her micro and halted with her hand halfway to the device. "Space me, we have to tell Gutierrez."

Simon's face paled. "I'll do it. She's going to want to talk to me about my intel. And no one will think it noteworthy that she meets with her comms chief."

"I don't envy you." She squeezed Simon's forearm. "Good luck."

He pushed his untouched food away. "Just get in touch with Ro. I'll check in with you later."

Nomi walked blindly through the station until she stumbled into her silent quarters. She eyed the empty bed, but didn't want to be there without Ro. Instead, Nomi grabbed Ro's worn quilt, wrapped it around herself, and curled up on the sofa. She hesitated before writing a note to Ro, but she wasn't the only one who needed to know. "Space me," she muttered again, and copied the message to Jem.

Despite her exhaustion, she knew there was no way she'd be able to sleep now. She stared at her micro's screen with bleary eyes, waiting for a response. The one she got wasn't what she'd been hoping for. Her door chimed and the AI announced one

Durbin, Jeremy.

Sighing, she triggered the door release and he practically fell inside her quarters.

Nomi held up her hands to keep him from speaking. "I don't know any more than what I've already told you. So don't ask."

"What are we going to do?" His voice was thick with emotion, and he looked very much like the young boy he was.

She patted the sofa. "Come on. We can wait together." It was just like when Daisuke had been afraid of thunderstorms, but didn't want to tell their parents. Nomi had always comforted him by convincing him that it was she who was nervous in storms.

Jem curled his compact body next to hers. Nomi tucked the quilt around them both.

"I take it you haven't heard from Barre."

He shook his head.

"Not even ..." She tapped her temple, unable to imagine being able to speak directly, mind to mind, with Ro. Maybe that was a good thing. It was sometimes hard enough communicating face to face. For all her stoic appearance, Ro's emotions ran raw and fierce.

"I got flashes of color and light a little while ago and some waves of vertigo. But different from the head injury stuff. I think they're from Barre. Probably from inside a jump. But nothing any more coherent than that."

Communications in a wormhole was supposed to be impossible because of the way time ran differently between jump space and interstitial space. "So they're on their way back."

"I think." Jem fell silent for a few minutes. "Do you think they hurt her?"

"I don't know. But it seems like whatever happened at Ithaka wasn't what Hephaestus expected to happen, so that's a good thing." At least Nomi hoped so. Maybe Targill had planned this all along and they were on their way to some hidden stronghold controlled by the Reaction Chamber. She shivered and burrowed more deeply into the quilt. If Targill had abandoned his post, it meant either the Chamber was confident in its position or that it had nothing left to lose.

Neither position worked in Ada's favor.

Jem frowned before looking away. He might be young, but he wasn't stupid.

"Whatever happens, we're going to try to find her. To help her."

They both started when Nomi's micro buzzed. She fumbled for the device and held it where Jem could see the screen also. Ro's message scrolled across.

/Targill never went to Earth. Suspect he went after May. Sent Barre to Ithaka in Charon's ship. Halcyone's ETA zero two hundred hours. Don't wait up./

Jem's eyes opened wide. "No. He can't. What if there are Commonwealth ships waiting for him there? Nomi, what do we do?"

She took his hands and gently squeezed them. "We try to warn them. I'll use my way. You use yours. Okay?"

He blinked back tears. "Okay."

*

Obolus's engines quieted to a gentle grumble.

"Destination: Ithaka. Geosynchronous orbit achieved. Gravity at Earth standard."

Barre extricated himself from the chair's webbing, stood, and cracked his spine. It wasn't as brutal a trip as the outbound one had been on Halcyone, but it was still too many jumps and too many burns in far too short a time and he was exhausted.

"Open a channel and hail Dr. May."

"Unable to comply. Station comms off-line."

He wasn't surprised. She'd sidelined all of them so she could make her grand and ultimately doomed gesture without interference. Well, there were other ways of reaching her. He pulled out his micro and crafted a brief message.

/You wanted a Ferryman, well you have one now. And he's here to row you to safety./

The minutes ticked by and there was no response. Barre sighed. Fine. He'd knock on the front door then. "Obolus, take us down."

"Unable to comply."

"Why the hell not?"

"Docking bays unavailable."

"What does that mean?"

"Unavailable. Not able to be used or obtained."

Barre let his frustration out in a low growl. Damned literal machines. He'd have to land manually. He glanced up at the small window that also functioned as a nav screen. It was currently still opaque and still showing their prior course. "Obolus, clear screen and display external view."

There was a brief blink of light in the bridge and the window cleared. The small maker space and space station lay on the tiny colony planet below them, but a thick blanket of fog obscured the buildings.

"Magnify and center image around the docking bays."

The viewscreen shifted. Barre staggered back, banging his legs against the captain's seat.

Ithaka was burning.

What he had taken for fog was a thick, oily smoke arising from where the docking bays had been. There were several other fires flaring across the compound.

He gripped the chair arms to keep from collapsing and swore.

"Scan for life signs."

"There are no life signs on Ithaka."

"What in the cosmos happened here?" Barre hadn't realized he'd asked the question aloud until the AI started answering him.

"The docking bays show evidence of close-range medium munitions fire. Commonwealth design, typically carried on the following ship classes:"

"Obolus, stop report!" Fuck. He didn't care what kind of ship had destroyed Ithaka. Had Ada been there when they'd rained down destruction? Were they still here? Cold washed through his body and this time his knees did give out. He fell heavily into the command chair. "Scan local space. Report on any vehicles or surveillance satellites."

The fact that no one had shot at them didn't comfort him. Obolus had no weapons and no shielding. Nothing that would protect them if whoever had firebombed Ithaka had stayed to do cleanup.

"Local space contains no other ships at this time. There are no unidentified satellites in orbit around Ithaka. Local ansibles are functional but unresponsive."

His heart slowed down to its normal rhythm, but his hands

still gripped the chair's arms. What the hell was he supposed to do now? He could take the ship planet-side under manual control, but without a functioning dock, he'd need a p-suit and have to find a station airlock that he could force open. And then what? He didn't have any fire suppression and given the extent of the burning below, neither did the station. He also wasn't equipped to transport any bodies, even if he could find them.

Bodies. Was Ada May down there? Had she guessed wrong? What was it she'd said? That Lethe had anticipated a number of failure scenarios. Barre wondered if this one was one of them.

He sagged against the chair. He should have forced her to go with him on Halcyone. Hell, he should never have agreed to bring Lowell to her. He wondered if the former comms chief had died in the attack. It would have served him right.

There was nothing left to do but return to Daedalus. He hung his head in his hands. It shielded him from the sight of the burning station below, but not from his guilt and his anger.

He had to tell everyone back on Daedalus. Jem was going to be devastated and he couldn't even begin to predict what Gutierrez's reaction was going to be. But first he needed to tell Ro. She'd be waiting for some message from him. He lifted his head and pushed his dreads back. Maybe he could use Ithaka's ansibles. It would get the message through faster than Obolus could from transit. The ship's AI should have the codes to access them.

"Obolus, can you ping the ansibles? I need to get a message to Ro on Halcyone. Let me know when comms are on line."

"*Affirmative.*"

Several moments of silence followed. Barre couldn't look away from the burning below.

It seemed to be taking an inordinate amount of time and Barre was starting to worry that the ansibles had been disabled somehow, even though Obolus had reported them functional. He was just about to check in with the AI when every light in the bridge flickered out and every alarm blared in a cacophony of fear.

"What the fuck?" The ship shimmied under him, its inertial stabilizers sluggish. Barre lurched for manual controls before they lost their stable orbit and were captured by the planetoid's gravity well. "Obolus, respond!"

He fought to break orbit and set the ship on a course—any course—outbound from Ithaka. He'd figure out where in the cosmos he was later. "This is going to be a very unpleasant ride if you don't wake up." Unpleasant and potentially lethal. "Any time now. And do we really need the fucking alarms?"

They continued to play their panicked symphony. Barre growled and reached for the controls. They were essentially the same as the ones on a large flitter—at least on the interstitial side of the engines. That would have to do for now. He played the console the way he'd play a complex keyboard, but instead of music, he was composing his own safe passage.

The ship settled. Ithaka receded on the viewscreen as they hurtled through unfamiliar space.

"It could be worse, I guess. We have life support and thrust, right?"

The ship's AI remained unresponsive. He sighed and kept talking. Maybe Obolus was listening on some level.

"Okay. Let's see about locking in this course so I can shut down these damned alarms!" Autopilot was usually under the AI's control, but with Obolus missing in action, he'd have to try something more basic. Ro had said he should be able to link his micro to the ship. That was how Micah had controlled it, so it had to be possible.

It was hard to concentrate over the noise, but it wasn't like Barre had any other choice. He pulled out his micro and set it to pair with the ship's basic functions. This would be a lot simpler if Ro had been here. But she was either racing back to Daedalus or already there.

"Come on, come on," he muttered. His micro still showed itself in pairing mode, though nothing changed on the ship. "This is definitely not good ..."

The alarms cut out so suddenly, Barre's ears rang. The sound of the ship's engines filled the bridge instead. It was sweeter than any music he'd ever composed.

"Okay. Obolus, you there?"

"Good afternoon, Ferryman." A slightly flat and mechanical version of Ada May's voice filled the bridge.

"Lethe? What the hell?"

"Course laid in. Please review."

The window turned opaque and was replaced by a schematic of a star map. "Wait. What? Where are we going?"

"Prepare for three-g burn in thirty seconds."

His micro chimed. Lethe had pushed their new heading through. Barre blinked down at the small device and then up at the star chart.

"Burn commencing in twenty seconds."

He scrambled for the webbing and strapped himself in. "Lethe, how did you get here and where is Obolus?"

Instead of answering him, Lethe counted down to zero. The small ship smoothly accelerated away from the system where

Ithaka smoldered. Neither Lethe nor Obolus broke the silence and the ship maintained its course for several minutes. Three g's wasn't an impossible burn, but it made getting up and moving around difficult.

Barre let the chair support his added weight and linked his neural to his micro, hoping the tunneled text protocol would be able to reach a functioning ansible.

/I don't know how to say this, so I'll just say it. Ithaka's been destroyed. There's no signs of survivors. I'm sorry. I didn't get here soon enough. What the hell do we do now?/

"Ferryman, your message has been locked and placed on a time delay."

It was hard to talk under acceleration, so Barre didn't bother. He reached out with his neural. *"Lethe, what are you doing? We're your allies. We're trying to help. Ada needs our help."*

"Please stand by, Ferryman."

Stand by. What else could he do? He was strapped into a ship with potentially dueling AIs, no idea where he was, and no way to retake control.

"Deceleration starting in ten seconds."

To where? The course she had shared with him contained no familiar landmarks or referents. He braced himself for the turnover where the forward thrust would shift to braking thrust, but the AI handled it smoothly.

"Initial jump in seven minutes."

"Are you talking me to where Ada is?"

"Negative. Dr. May is currently outside of known space."

Did AIs have a conception of death? Certainly they understood that organic life ended. But why would Lethe use a metaphor? That didn't make any sense. *"Lethe, did Dr. May survive the attack on Ithaka? Is she still alive?"*

"Dr. May is currently outside of known space."

Barre tried multiple variations of his question and the AI would only repeat that same infuriating answer. Finally, he gave up and asked a different one. *"Where are you taking me?"*

"Ithaka."

Chapter 27

WHEN THE CONFIRMATION CAME, Micah nearly ignored it. It hadn't arrived concealed beneath diplomatic headers; it wasn't anything official-seeming at all. It was simply a series of numbers.

Numbers that translated into a time and a place.

So Targill had blinked first. And more quickly than Micah had anticipated. He forwarded the message to Dev. She'd gone to Dr. Sellen's lab—the one class she'd decided not to risk skipping. When she got home to find him gone, she'd be furious. There wasn't anything Micah could do about that. At least she'd finally agreed to stay behind and be his dead-man switch in case Targill had set a trap.

But Micah doubted that. Targill would be curious about the son of his Reaction Chamber rival. He'd want to know what intel Micah had. What's more, he'd probably believe he could use Micah for his advantage.

Let him think so. His own father and Ro's had

underestimated Micah, and that hadn't ended well for either man.

The meeting was in two hours, in greater New Chicago. Micah chose his clothes carefully. Well-tailored, but not too formal—the kind of clothes his father had worn when he'd needed to appear casual, comfortable, and in complete control. Black slacks; a gray shirt with a subtle pattern of red threads woven through it. Red and gray striped socks that would show a flash of color when he sat and crossed his legs.

He frowned as he glanced down at the custom shoes he wore to cushion his feet. They spoiled the image, but then again, what he'd done was likely no secret and it might even work to his advantage.

The last thing Micah did before heading back out of his dorm was send an encrypted message to Ro. With any luck, she and the others would reach May in time and he'd have new intel to pass along.

He rented a high-end-model flitter. When it arrived, he programmed its autopilot for the coordinates Targill had sent. It wasn't as if Micah wasn't a competent pilot, but that's not how the game of appearances was played. He doubted there were eyes on him yet, but the performance always started long before the curtain was raised.

Relaxing against the flitter's plush passenger seat, it bothered him how easy it was to play this role. Dev would be angry with him for looking at it that way. He tried to explain it to her, but all politicians had ever given the settlements were institutional misery and more reasons to distrust the political process. At least the cartels had given them money and temporary respite from the dreariness of their lives. And a sense that getting ahead was a constant battle against those with the power.

Now Micah was going to embrace that power. No wonder Dev's brothers had hated him.

His micro vibrated with a new message from Dev.

/Be careful./

Careful was not part of this game, but he tried to reassure her. /I will be./

/Liar./

Well, she certainly understood Micah. */I'll be fine. Watch your back./*

They had to know about Dev. Micah felt uncomfortable leaving her, but the reality was, she knew how to protect herself better than he ever could. She had proved that many times over —not just with her survival as Alain Maldonado's prisoner, but in Midlant.

/Always./

They'd agreed on radio silence until Micah contacted her again. And if he didn't, she'd contact Ro, head back to Midlant, and release Maldonado's files to the public net.

Micah didn't think it would come to that, but better to plan for a galactic clusterfuck than get caught in one.

He triggered the windows to clear and watched as they flew over the massive New Chicago skyline. Stark high-rises thrust upward into a hazy late afternoon sky, dark parallel lines where the wealthy and the connected lived lives that would never intersect with those who had been trapped for generations in the settlements.

Most of the highsiders had never set foot in one. Those who had only saw their own privilege reinforced and normalized. That divide was one his father and those like him kept in place as ruthlessly as the old caste system in nations like pre-Drowning India or the post-industrial inner city ghettos.

The Commonwealth's famous new prosperity had eliminated the last vestiges of visible poverty and swept the flotsam and jetsam of the Drowning into settlements, away from the society it had so carefully crafted.

Micah was quietly furious at the lies he had believed. And at the systematic denial that allowed this new stratification to thrive. The settlements deserved better. Dev deserved better.

He laughed—a short, bitter bark of a laugh—and hoped his father was rolling over in his grave. Though that expression made little sense in a cosmos where bodies were cremated and the ashes jettisoned into space.

Then there was no more time to lose himself in thought. The flitter signaled it was starting its glide path to landing. It swooped lower toward the city. Blue lights flicked on, indicating a private flitter bay on the roof of the building right below them.

"Showtime," he said softly.

They touched down with barely a jolt. A small jetway attached itself to the flitter's door. Micah stood and smoothed his pants. The door opened to his touch. No one was waiting to escort him. That wasn't any kind of surprise. They knew that was a deliberate snub. And they knew he'd know it, too.

An open doorway into the building beckoned at the end of the jetway. Okay then. Micah strode down the translucent corridor, ignoring the city glowing all around him in the twilight. He'd seen the cosmos, floating from a tether in an EVA suit. A cityscape didn't impress him.

Once he stepped inside, the door shut behind him and he lost his balance briefly as the elevator dropped through the floors of the skyscraper without any warning. Another message. Micah linked his hands behind his back and smiled. He was sure he was being watched, so he'd send a message, too.

He counted silently and subtly braced himself as the elevator decelerated, again without warning. When the doors opened, he stepped into the corridor in front of him with a self-assurance he almost believed himself.

This time, there was someone waiting. An armed guard. He wore no uniform, but Micah had no doubt this was someone career military. The guard started walking. In his father's endless reframing, this was an escort, not security, and Micah followed without a word.

The guard led him on a serpentine path through generic hallways that Micah didn't even bother to study. If he had to make a hasty retreat, he would have already lost. But then again, so would they.

They reached a set of wide double doors. The guard stopped and signaled. Micah's pulse raced, not with fear, but with excitement. He wondered what Dev would make of that.

The doors opened outward to a large, windowless room dominated by a massive oval conference table, made out of honest-to-goodness real wood. It was worth a small fortune. Chairs, only about a third of them filled, encircled the table. A few of the ten men and women were people Micah recognized, either from his father's illustrious career, or from the news. The rest were unknowns. He wondered which files went with which faces.

One face was conspicuously missing: Targill. Micah stepped inside the room and it fell silent. Ten sets of eyes turned to face him. Micah didn't miss a step. The only thing that differentiated this from any of his father's interminable press conferences was the lack of bright lights from the cameras and vids.

"Gentlemen. Ladies." He bowed toward the assembled group. "It's an honor." He strode to the far side of the room and took an empty seat, not at the table's head, but just to its left.

"Michael Evan Rotherwood." The woman who addressed him looked familiar, but he couldn't place her. "So we're inviting children, now."

He lifted an eyebrow. "I would say fresh perspectives."

"You are your father's son."

He snapped his gaze back to the old white woman with a frizz of gray hair framing her face. The last time he'd seen her, she'd had dark brown hair, but the disapproving scowl was the same. "Judge Saltonstall." Micah had been a child when she had disbarred and publicly humiliated his father.

She tried for a smile, but it was far too insincere on her face. "I hope you don't hold grudges."

"Apparently my father did." Micah was going to let them think his blackmail material came from the late senator. It did more than keep suspicion from Ro; it also forced them all to doubt one another.

"Laurel, we have far more important issues to discuss."

Senator Jasper Finnegan looked exactly the way his vids appeared, likely courtesy of nanorepair and plastic surgery. His father had always mocked Finnegan as a shallow womanizer. At least that hadn't been one of Rotherwood's faults.

Micah nodded to the empty chair next to him. "I appreciate that this meeting was called on short notice, but I expected Commander Targill to be doing my formal introduction." And most likely choking on it. That he wasn't here raised concerns about Ithaka and Ada May, but he couldn't focus on that now.

Finnegan raised his eyebrows and glanced at a few of the members near him. Ramon Salazar was another familiar figure, though not one Micah had ever met before. The dark-eyed, dark-haired man had made his fortune manufacturing the short-haul craft that transported goods to and from the colonies. They were inelegant, but efficient, little more than a cargo bay with a bridge, and could operate with a single crew member. Likely his position in the Chamber gave him a considerable advantage against his competitors.

Saltonstall glared at him. "There is no one here who didn't know your father. And we all know that you've followed in his footsteps in more ways than one."

That was interesting. Had his father blackmailed his way into the Chamber too? No wonder they weren't surprised by Micah's appearance.

"The question is, have you taken up his old rivalries?" Salazar's voice carried a slight lilt, similar to some of the accents he'd heard in Midlant. Interesting as well.

"I'm not so foolish as to think I can take over the Chamber where my father failed." He paused and smiled for effect. "At least not for another six months or so."

No one laughed. A small flutter of nerves made Micah's hands shake, but they were beneath the table, hidden.

Why were there so few people here? What in the cosmos had happened in the scant hours since Micah had spoken with the confident and annoyed leader of this merry band? He wished he could check his micro or speak with Dev, but he was on his own here.

He might was well try for a little sincere confusion. "I'm

sorry, I don't understand what's going on."

"You want us to believe this is a coincidence?" Saltonstall asked. He was really beginning to loathe this woman.

"I'm not sure what 'this' you're referring to. I'm here because of my father. Because I was groomed my entire life to continue his legacy. I only recently discovered what that legacy was. That's when I contacted Targill. He arranged for my introduction."

"Well, Mr. Rotherwood, there's something you need to see. Maybe then you'll understand why we're somewhat doubtful." Finnegan triggered his micro. An entire section of the wall became a large viewscreen.

"Are you sure?" One of the women he hadn't recognized glanced at Finnegan and then at Micah. Her voice held weariness rather than anger. For some reason, that increased his jitters more than Saltonstall's outright hostility.

Finnegan didn't answer. He only gestured toward the screen. It flickered to life showing a view of what looked like a standard planet-side station installation.

"What am I looking at?"

Finnegan glanced at him, disbelief in his expression, but he answered calmly. "Ithaka."

Micah forced his body to stay relaxed. "Ah. The fabled hidden planet."

"This is recorded footage from Hephaestus. From fifteen hundred hours, Commonwealth standard time. Today."

His heart pounding triple-time, Micah watched as Ithaka got larger and larger. Details filled in: the dual-ringed design was nearly identical to Daedalus. The docking bays were empty, except for one small ship that was about the size of Charon's vessel. A second small craft—this one military—glided in to land and docked itself to the first ship.

A flash on the recording startled him. He blinked and leaned forward to stare at the emptiness where both ships had just been. "Wait. Replay that. What just happened?"

Finnegan paused the playback. "Well, that answers at least one of our questions."

Micah pulled himself away from the frozen image and looked around the table. Everyone else in the room was looking at him, gauging his reaction. He turned back to the screen. "The ships. Where did they go?" The flash was definitely not weapons fire, and the crew on Hephaestus wouldn't shoot their own captain.

"There's several minutes where it appears nothing happens during which Hephaestus is frantically trying to locate Targill. There's no answer on comms." Finnegan fast-forwarded the recording. "They reported the mission's failure to Commonwealth command and were given orders to destroy the station before returning to Earth."

Over the course of the next few minutes, Hephaestus methodically fired on the docking bays and the power plant, effectively destroying Ithaka as a viable base.

"I don't understand. Ships can't just disappear."

"It appears we underestimated Dr. May, because now they can."

*

All through Sellen's class, Dev kept a hand in her pocket, feeling for the vibration that meant she'd gotten a message from Micah. She was grateful Sellen had other students to torture today. Although Sellen got more student complaints than all the other professors in the materials science program put together, Dev was grateful for the woman's unconventional and often brutal teaching methods.

Without them and without the little photo-active cube Sellen had given Dev to puzzle through a few weeks ago, she might not have been able to survive, to escape from Alain Maldonado. Dev only regretted having to turn it in.

"Devorah?" Dev's head jerked up. The rest of the students were filing out of lab quickly, only too happy to leave before they were put on the spot again.

"Yes, Professor?" Dev braced herself for a critique or an extra assignment. Neither would be unexpected.

"Don't miss another class or I'll be forced to fail you."

Dev swallowed hard and nodded. Most of her attention was still on her silent micro and her worry for Micah, so she missed the first few words that followed.

" ... impressed by the thoroughness of your report, but it doesn't make up for skipping the lab. You have promise. Don't squander it."

The professor didn't add the "for a settlement student" part, but the unsaid words stung nonetheless. Dev wondered if there would ever be a time when they wouldn't.

"And Devorah? Where you're from matters far less to me than where you end up. No additional absences."

Heat warmed her cheeks, but Sellen had already turned away to leave the lab. Dev packed her bag before returning to the dorm. Where she was headed was to an uncertain future. In a way, her brothers had been right—meeting Micah had thrown her plans into a tailspin. Getting her degree, landing a high-paying highside job, and supporting her brothers had been driving her on since childhood. None of that would change the brutal truth of life in the settlements, life that the rich and the powerful had manufactured and deliberately maintained for decades.

What she'd told Micah earlier was true. It didn't matter which organization came out on top—the Commonwealth was no different than the Reaction Chamber or the Cartels as far as the settlements were concerned. And Ithaka was mostly a figment of lost hopes, now more than ever if May was truly planning to sacrifice herself.

Something had to change. Micah didn't know it yet, but he just might be in the perfect position to help her make that change.

If everything went according to plan. If the Reaction Chamber accepted him.

The apartment she shared with him felt uncomfortably empty. She paced in front of the large window. Below her, groups of students crossed the residential quad, blissfully unaware of the secret society that controlled their lives and their futures.

In a way, being from Midlant was a blessing: it was all too easy to accept how little control she had over her life. It would be a rude awakening for her fellow students when they realized their privilege was largely an illusion.

She sat on the sofa with her legs propped up on the coffee table, the way Micah had so often sat, and waited as late afternoon faded into dusk and then true sunset. Still she made no move to trigger the lights. Her micro lay in her lap, silent. Micah and Ro hadn't specified how long she should wait to release the files, only that if Micah didn't contact her, she needed to use her discretion.

The waiting gave her a sense of what Micah must have gone through when Maldonado had kidnapped her. Now it was her turn to worry.

There were so many points of failure in Micah's plan; the only fail-safe he had was the information duplicated on her micro and Ro's. That certainly protected the data. It didn't help him any.

Dev slid her legs off the table and stood. More than enough time had gone by for Micah to worm his way into the Reaction Chamber. He should have contacted her by now. For all their sakes, she couldn't afford to wait any longer.

Using the messaging program Ro had added to her micro, she initiated the first step of the fail-safe.

/Micah has been out of contact for nearly six hours. Have you heard from him?/

No answer. She waited another fifteen minutes and tried again.

After forty-five minutes and two more attempts, she called it. She would retreat to Midlant and if Micah was safe, he would try to reach her there, either by comms or in person. If she didn't hear from him by tomorrow at this time, she would release the data to the net. Maybe she could leverage the resulting chaos and find something to help Midlant along with all the other settlements.

It was past twenty hundred hours and there would be no commercial transport to anywhere near Midlant until the morning. She should be able to make it home before tomorrow night.

Dev packed her meager belongings. So much for Sellen's predictions of her future. She sighed and almost missed the soft click of the door. Pulling out the knife she had honed on Maldonado's stolen ship, Dev crept back into the common room without triggering the lights. She knew every centimeter of the apartment the way she had learned every space she'd ever explored in the abandoned neighborhoods and towns near Midlant.

She smelled the stale alcohol before she sighted the silhouette of a large body in shadow slipping into the apartment. Cursing silently as her heart raced, Dev crept forward, her knife securely gripped in her right hand. Her would-be assailant was clumsy and loud and more than covered up the sound of Dev's soft footfalls.

Coming up next to the intruder, Dev grabbed their arm and kicked out, sweeping their legs from under them. The body went down with a loud grunt and muffled curses. Dev straddled it, pressing the knife against the soft skin at their throat.

"What the fuck?"

"Micah?" Dev snatched the knife away as she scrambled back and tripped over his custom shoes.

"Lights up," he said.

The two of them sat blinking at one another on the floor.

"I could have killed you!" Dev's hands shook and she dropped the knife.

"It would have made an interesting end to my day," he said quietly.

His eyes were clear and there was no slurring in his voice. "Why do you smell like a distillery? And why the hell didn't you contact me?"

"I was being surveilled. The alcohol was a smokescreen. I thought they would tire of following me on my bar hop." He shook his head. "Never mind. That's not important. I need to show you something."

Dev sheathed her knife and scrambled to her feet. Reaching a hand down, she helped Micah up.

"You are a one-woman strike force."

"Who very nearly killed her best friend. Next time, turn the fucking lights on."

He held on to her hand for several long seconds before tugging her to the sofa. As they watched the video, Micah summarized his meeting with the Reaction Chamber. His words barely penetrated her shock.

"It's a copy of a copy—the best I could do under the circumstances. Maybe Ro can enhance it. Have you heard back from her?"

"No."

"Shit."

Both of their micros simultaneously signaled an incoming message.

/May and Targill are gone./

Micah glanced at Dev. She tossed him his micro. "Go on. You should answer her."

He appended a copy of the bootlegged video to her message. */We know. You need to see this. It's from the RC. They're in a panic. No one knows where Targill or May went. Stay clear of Ithaka./*

/Too late. Stay in touch and be careful./

Dev reached in her pocket for the security of her knife. It was stupid—a blade wasn't going to protect her from this. "Head back to Midlant with me. I promise my brothers won't —"

"I can't." Micah's face was pale, his blue eyes wide and staring at something past her. "Not now. I'm sorry I dragged you into this. Go home. I need to stay and see it through. I have a seat in the Chamber now. And that may be the only advantage we have."

"Micah ..."

"If you're in Midlant, they can't use you to get to me."

She gripped the knife tighter. "I'm not going anywhere, voidhopper."

Chapter 28

By the time Halcyone had taken the final jump into the system where Daedalus orbited, exhaustion had finally driven out Ro's fear.

If it was that bad for her, it had to have been even worse for Barre. She just hoped he'd been able to escape the chaos on Ithaka. There had been no hint of Obolus on the recording Micah had sent her. And no evidence of wreckage, either. That had to be a good sign. Holding on to hope, she checked her micro for about the hundredth time, but there wasn't anything from him. He was probably racing back here at a brutal pace, too.

"Halcyone, open a channel to Daedalus. Request clearance to land." Ro was betting that Targill hadn't officially forbidden her from linking with the station. Now that he was gone, and until the Commonwealth saw fit to reinstate Mendez or bring someone else in, Gutierrez was in charge.

"Channel open."

"Welcome home, Halcyone. You are cleared to land."

"Thank you, Daedalus Station."

Well, that was easy. At least something was. She had a feeling that very little would be simple ever again. The pull of her quarters and the bed she shared with Nomi had gravitational attraction, but the information Micah had given her was more important than sleep. She pinged Nomi and wasn't surprised to find her awake.

/*I'm on approach to Daedalus. Too much to tell over messaging. Get Jem, Marchand, and Gutierrez—wake them if you have to. Meet me in engineering.*/

/*Did you find May?*/

Ro exhaled heavily. /*No.*/

After Halcyone glided them in and set the airlock, Ro sat in the silence of the empty bridge. There had been a time she'd dreamed of this—on her own, in control of her ship, but it felt lonely and hollow without her crew. "Come on, Barre, fire up those rockets," she muttered.

She took a sip of the now lukewarm insti-synth and her stomach nearly heaved. Any more wouldn't help at this point. She set the thermos down and left the bridge.

Once she reached engineering, Ro collapsed into the nearest seat, dropped her head in her hands, and wished she were nearly anywhere but here.

Jem raced in and looked around as if his brother would jump into view at any moment. "Is Barre landing Charon's ship?"

Nomi followed and all Ro wanted to do was to curl up and sleep next to her. Even the floor in engineering would do. Ro sighed as Marchand and Gutierrez entered close behind.

Ro waited until they all settled. There was no easy way to tell them, so she just blurted it out. "May is missing. Along with Targill. No one knows where. The Commonwealth took their ire out on Ithaka and as far as I know, it's still a smoldering wreck. And Barre is somewhere out there on Charon's ship."

Gutierrez launched herself from the seat she'd just taken. Her claw hand opened and closed compulsively. "What happened?" Her voice was a dangerous low growl.

"I don't know."

The LC turned to glower at Ro.

"Micah smuggled this to me. He's infiltrated the Reaction Chamber." Ro held up her hand when both Gutierrez and Marchand started to speak over one another. "But it doesn't really explain anything. Or at least raises more questions than it answers." Pulling up an empty window from her micro, Ro sent the video capture to it. The five of them watched in tense silence as Targill's ship blocked May's before a bright flash briefly obscured both. When the light levels stabilized, there was nothing where the two small craft had been. No debris. No wreckage. Nothing but an empty bay. She let the video play on through the bombing of Ithaka.

Other than the clack of her prosthetic hand, Gutierrez didn't make a sound.

"Can you enhance the quality?" Marchand asked.

"Not by much. I'll try." Ro quickly riffled through her toolbox looking for video tools. Noise and artifact reduction would help, but there weren't a lot of pixels to work with. If she had access to the original source, maybe.

At least she could align it better. Then she ran it through several filters and managed to sharpen the image by about fifteen percent. It was as good as it was going to get. "Okay. Let's look at that again."

Gutierrez stepped close to the screen. "Slow it down just before the flash."

Ro nodded and started the recording again. The ships' outlines were crisper now and they could make out the Commonwealth seal on Targill's craft. May's had no markings. At the point where Targill landed, Ro slowed the playback until it was advancing frame by frame.

A splotch of light bloomed on May's ship and quickly grew to encompass both. The next frame showed an empty docking bay again.

"Reverse. Frame by frame."

Ro played the recording backward. The ships reappeared, a starburst of light dazzling the space around the entire docking bay area. Then it shrank to a tiny pinpoint before winking out altogether.

"Stop." Gutierrez waved at the screen. "Forward again. Freeze on my mark."

She ran it again.

"Stop." Gutierrez stared at the image of the tiny light gleaming from the nose of May's ship.

Jem stood up and joined her. "I know what that is," he said. "That's the unfurling of a quantum shield."

"They jumped?" Nomi stared at the frozen image, frowning. "That doesn't make sense. How could they jump? There's no wormhole there."

"Not one we can see." Jem pointed to what Ro thought was more artifact she hadn't been able to clean up. "But that's the spillover effect of a wormhole pushing into interstitial space. Look."

Ro peered closer and noticed the telltale striations she had missed before. Spatial stretch marks, the quantum engineers called them. "It's not possible. There aren't wormholes that close to planets."

"There are now," Gutierrez said. "At least one. Or there was when this recording was made."

"Holy mother of the cosmos." Marchand leaned forward looking at each of them in turn. Ro had forgotten he was there "Do you have any idea what this means?"

"That Ada May is alive," Jem said, smiling broadly.

"Yes, but that's irrelevant." Marchand glanced up at Gutierrez who was staring, unblinking at the still image. "Shall I tell them or do you want to?"

The LC kept silent. A muscle in her jaw twitched.

"So who else knows about this recording?" Marchand asked.

Ro ticked them off on her fingers. "Micah and Dev. The Reaction Chamber. Hephaestus's crew and whoever they report to in the chain of command."

"So basically everyone." Marchand sighed. "Then your Dr. May has just done something very, very unwise. She's upended the balance of power in the entire Commonwealth."

Ro started to say she didn't understand. And then she did. Somehow May had discovered a way to open a tiny transient wormhole anywhere she wanted. But was it stable enough to traverse?

"Control the wormholes, control the galaxy," Nomi whispered.

That was what the entire Commonwealth's power base relied on. But what happened when you could travel from anywhere to anywhere at will? The Commonwealth managed traffic through all known wormholes. It's how they controlled commerce, the colonies, and galactic travel. Want to punish a world? Blockade its nearest wormhole. Want to control the price of trade goods? Set tariffs for jump access.

Ro walked up to the LC. "Did you know May had this tech?"

Gutierrez shook her head. "There wasn't even a whisper of a rumor."

"So now what?"

"Do you think Barre got sucked in to wherever she went?" Jem searched the still image with wide eyes.

Ro had watched that recording dozens and dozens of times aboard Halcyone. There was no sign of Barre's ship either before or after May and Targill had vanished. "I don't think so. I think he's just trying to get back here as fast as he can."

"I'm sorry, but we have bigger problems than your brother or Dr. May or even Commander Targill, though his disappearance will create ripples through both the Commonwealth and the Reaction Chamber." Marchand rubbed the stubble of his shaved head.

Ro closed her eyes briefly, imagining the destruction someone like her father could have caused being able to deliver the weapons he'd been smuggling directly to one side or another in a conflict. No playing 'nought and shuttle with Commonwealth patrollers. No needing to rendezvous with other ships to offload contraband. No way to safeguard a planet from a direct attack. The resulting chaos would make the war Gutierrez had fought in look like a minor skirmish. "So what do we do?" She felt the warmth of Nomi's hand on her shoulder.

Halcyone played a brief fanfare, startling them. Just as she recognized the melody, Ro glanced up to find Barre slumped against the doorway. His eyes were bloodshot and his face had a grayish cast to it. She had never been as glad to see him.

"We hope that May comes back from her jump to nowhere or that somehow we figure out her magic trick before anyone else does."

"Barre!" Jem barreled into his much larger brother with enough force to rock him back on his heels.

"You look like crap."

"Hey, Ro, nice to see you, too." He frowned down at his rumpled clothes. "Look, I can't remember the last time I wasn't traveling. I'm tired, hungry, and just about every part of me aches. Can we skip to the part where I tell you I know about Ada and her vanishing act?"

"You were there. Did you see her?" Gutierrez nearly pushed Jem aside in her eagerness to get answers.

"Not exactly." He put up his hands to keep her from barraging him with questions. "I arrived after Hephaestus destroyed Ithaka. At that point, I thought Ada was dead. I tried to access the station's ansibles to send word back and I must have triggered a program she'd left for me. Lethe downloaded herself into the Ferryman's ship's AI.

"She took me for quite a ride before I could persuade her the safest and best course for both Ithaka's future and Ada May's survival was to let me come back here."

"But Ithaka is gone," Gutierrez whispered.

"Not exactly. It's just distributed in little hidden pockets across the galaxy. Along with all the personnel she evacuated. Lethe has the master map. It seems that Ada has been preparing for this for a long time. I think Charon's death just advanced her planning some."

"And the wormhole tech? How do we find her?"

"I don't think we can. When I asked Lethe where she was, the AI kept repeating that she was outside of known space."

"With Targill," Ro reminded him. "She'd better hope no one can track them, or both the Commonwealth and the Reaction Chamber will be gunning for her."

Gutierrez cocked her head, staring at Barre. "She knew you'd be back for her. And Lethe was more than just the station AI— she was a repository for all of Ada's notes and research. She wanted you to have that data."

"Then I guess we have work to do," Ro said, nodding toward Jem, before looking at Barre. "And so do you."

"Was she always this good at getting her way, Lieutenant Commander?" Barre asked.

Gutierrez had a distant look in her eyes, but when she turned back to him, a wry smile transformed her severe face. "Always. And Ferryman? I suspect we're going to be working together for some time. It's Emma."

Ro took Nomi's hand and held it gently. "Can you establish some kind of regular check in with Micah?"

"I think it might be better to go through his friend Dev. I'm betting Micah's comms traffic is going to be closely monitored. Can your messaging program stand up to that degree of scrutiny?"

It was as robust as both Ro's and Ada May's talents could make it. "Probably? But you're right. It's not worth the risk."

"And what's my part in this cozy little conspiracy?" Marchand's eyes twinkled when he smiled.

Eagerness? Sarcasm? Irony? Ro didn't know him well enough to interpret. How far could they trust him? He knew enough to get them all arrested or worse. Before Ro could answer, Gutierrez did.

"You and I need to work on the rift between our groups. Neither one of us will survive without the other. Not now. And I'm willing to bet this was part of Ada's plan, too."

"Throw the galaxy into a frenzy of entropy and then walk away? Great plan."

Nomi squeezed Ro's hand. "Actually, it's not the worst plan. The status quo wasn't helping, so she took herself and Targill out of the equation."

"And expected us to balance everything? Look around." A kid with a wonky brain, a musician, a young comms officer, a politician's son with father issues, and an emotionally stunted hacker. "We're not a very impressive group."

Jem looked up at her and laughed. "Don't underestimate the power of being underestimated."

Jem was right. Look at what he had accomplished—his desperation had led him and them to Ithaka when no one else in the cosmos could find it. Ada May surely hadn't anticipated that. Or that Ro would crack her father's encrypted data and uncover the Reaction Chamber. She nodded at each of her crew, including Marchand and Gutierrez. And they were a crew, even if they didn't all stay aboard Halcyone. "Halcyone, grant unlimited access to Marchand, Simon and Gutierrez, Emmaline."

"Access granted. Welcome aboard."

"I appreciate the gesture, but I think it will be best if the acting commander of Daedalus Station doesn't take you up on your hospitality."

"So no word from Mendez?"

Gutierrez shook her head. "And no answer from my official inquiries. At least until I hear otherwise, Halcyone can stay where she is."

"Thank you."

"If there aren't any more revelations, it's past time I returned to my quarters. Where Daedalus will corroborate I have been all evening. Asleep."

"I'm on first shift in a few hours." Marchand nodded at Nomi. "And so are you." He stood, yawned, and followed the LC back to the station.

That left Ro, Nomi, Jem, and Barre, and they were all pretty much dead on their feet. "I think we've had enough bombshells for one night." Ro's last word was almost swallowed by her yawn. It wasn't over, and May's gambit had made their lives even more complicated than they had already been, but Jem was definitely right. Each of them had been underestimated and each of them had proven over and over again that there was no better crew in the cosmos. "We all need to get some rest. I promise, there'll be plenty of conspiracy left for tomorrow."

Epilogue

THEY POPPED OUT OF THE WORMHOLE and back into interstitial space exactly where her theoretical models had predicted. They were orbiting a small, uninhabited planet in a system no one had bothered naming before Ada had removed it, along with dozens of other obscure places, from the maps when she'd hidden Ithaka. "Lethe, open a channel to our companion, please."

"Channel open."

"Commander Targill, I've instructed the ship to grant you access. Please come aboard at your convenience. I am unarmed."

He didn't reply. She hadn't expected him to. And she wasn't at all surprised when he thundered onto her ship, weapon drawn, aimed at her heart.

She didn't stand. Moving would only convert her from potential threat to actual threat in his eyes. And besides, she was weary. The past few days had taken more out of her than she'd anticipated. She kept her voice calm. "I wouldn't recommend killing me before you understand our situation, Commander."

Their unexpected jaunt must have left him shaken, but there was no way of knowing that from his impeccable uniform, steady hand, and solid stance.

"Then I recommend you start talking."

"Please, sit down."

He simply reset his stance.

That, too, was predictable. "Charles Dauber and I long believed there had to be a way to create metastable micro wormholes. It took almost forty years to prove our initial theoretical models. We've just traveled through one."

He didn't react.

"If you don't believe me, look at the viewscreen. We're not in any known space. No one will find us here. If you try to send comms traffic, it won't go anywhere. There are no ansibles. Nor are there conventional wormholes within reach of our short-range crafts."

May had chosen this particular system because of its perfect isolation.

"So I recommend you make yourself comfortable, because we're not leaving any time soon."

Targill's expressionless face never changed, but his scar reddened against his space-pale skin. "There are ways of encouraging cooperation short of using lethal force."

"I'm not fond of euphemisms. You're threatening to torture me." She fought to keep her own voice level and her body relaxed. "As you can see, I'm alone. I have no weapons and I certainly don't have the strength or the training to resist. But other than venting your frustration, it won't do you any good. Lethe has locked us here. Even I can't override her. The cosmos is just going to have to figure out how to live without us for the time being."

He stepped closer. The muzzle of his weapon suddenly looked a lot larger and more lethal. "You're bluffing."

"I'm tired. I'm old. And I'm cranky. What I don't do is bluff. I have enough supplies on board for both of us to live comfortably until Lethe decides to let us return home. Which she won't do if I'm dead."

He took another step. May swallowed hard. Forced a smile. She'd run the probabilities a thousand times. This was a risk, but doing nothing would have led to open war. It had been a virtual certainty, given how powerful the Reaction Chamber had become. The return of Halcyone had given her no choice, but she didn't blame Ro and her crew. This would have happened eventually, with or without them.

Removing her and Targill created a power vacuum that might also lead to war, but there were other possibilities now. Ro and her friends had added some unexpected—and much needed—entropy to the system. It was a thin thread of hope, but Ada had grasped it and started planning.

She ignored Targill's steady hand and the weapon that at this distance couldn't possibly miss her and looked directly into her adversary's eyes instead. They were the blue of glaciers and just as cold. Taking a deep breath, she forced her shoulders to relax.

Over the months that had led her here, she'd arranged for every contingency, even her own death, but what happened next was up to him.

* * *

Acknowledgments

It has now been five years since I blundered my way into the initial ideas of what has become the universe of Halcyone Space. When I first drafted Derelict, I had no idea Ro and company would continue their journey across multiple novels. Nor did I anticipate the way their story would twist and expand.

Perhaps I should have: they do travel via wormholes, after all.

This fourth installment of the series could not have happened without the support and encouragement of a whole host of folks–family, friends, readers, and writers–the crew without which this ship couldn't fly.

To the readers who have followed me through the series, my sincere thanks. Any creation is a collaboration between the artist and the audience. Without you, the stories have no life.

I owe a debt of gratitude to my loyal beta readers, some of whom have been reading for me through the series. It's easy to get so close to a project you lose sight of it. Having critical readers who are willing to tell me what works and doesn't work in the draft manuscript is a gift. Roland Boykin, Miaka Kirino, Laura Swanson, Richard Durham, Nightwing Whitehead, Jillian Henning, Sam Henning, Cass M., Paul Jean, Ellie Hussey, Anthony Miller, Bryce Alexander, and Bobbi Fox: You each gave me valuable feedback in the service of making the story better. I sincerely appreciate the gifts of your time and your honesty. The improvements are thanks to you. Any errors that remain are my own.

The SSC is a community of friends that provides support, encouragement, distraction, mayhem, and silliness; each in the right measure and at the right time. Thank you, one and all.

I am also part of a rich community of writers scattered across the globe, connected by a shared passion for the written word and through the magic of the internet. There are so many who have been my support network through this novel's lifetime. I will call out just a few of you here: Nathan Lowell (your namesake is causing trouble again!), Rick Wayne (who needed me to finish this one so I could focus on our joint project), Lynn Viehl (for more than I could mention in a book full of thank-yous), and KB Wagers (thank you for Indrana and Hail and your kind words).

To my family: Neil, Philip, and Eric. You continue to push me to write more, write faster, and write better. Your belief in me keeps me moving forward. Philip, I can say for certain that Dev's scenes in the Midlant Settlement would never have come to life without your help and your insights. The politics in this series are richer because of our conversations.

Chris Howard has created a masterful image for this cover, highlighting the strength and vulnerability of Emmaline Gutierrez. Thank you for bringing her and this world to such stunning, vivid life.

And finally, thank you, Karen Conlin, for your careful and thorough editing. Knowing you have my back for all those pesky subjunctive conditional clauses, the finer points of punctuation, and continuity in small ways and large makes my job so much easier. Again, any errors that remain are mine.

The crew of Halcyone will return.

Best regards,

LJ

(June, 2017)

Read More

DERELICT (Halcyone Space, book 1)
When Rosalen Maldonado tinkers with the derelict space ship, she doesn't count on waking its damaged AI or having three stowaways on board. If the accidental crew can't figure out how to work together, they'll die together, victims of a computer that doesn't realize the war ended decades before any of them were even born.

ITHAKA RISING (Halcyone Space, book 2)
When Barre's brother Jem disappears, Barre and Ro race to find him before he sells his future and risks his mind for a black market neural implant. But locating The Underworld along with its rogue planet Ithaka has political consequences far beyond what Halcyone's crew imagine, pitting Jem's life against deadly secrets from a war that should have ended forty years ago.

DREADNOUGHT AND SHUTTLE (Halcyone Space, book 3)
Charged with protecting Ithaka and its covert rebellion from

discovery, Ro and the members of Halcyone's crew learn to lead double lives within the Commonwealth. Their plans to hide in plain sight disintegrate when Alain Maldonado — Ro's father — returns seeking revenge and takes a hostage to ensure their cooperation. As the former shipmates track Maldonado down, each course they plot endangers the life of his hostage, threatens to reveal Ithaka, and uncovers conspiracies that could brand them all traitors.

THE BETWEEN (Changeling's Choice, book 1)
When Oberon and Titania vie for the allegiance of their long-hidden changeling, Lydia Hawthorne, the one thing they didn't anticipate was her stubborn humanity.

TIME AND TITHE (Changeling's Choice, book 2)
Lydia's victory over the Fae came with a bitter price - her baby sister Taylor grew up without her, aging more than a decade in the mere weeks that have passed in Faerie. When Aeon's madness threatens both realms, the sisters are forced to fight the powerful Fae who was once friend to each of them.

FUTURE TENSE
17 year-old Matt Garrison sees the future. When he has a vision of himself hurting a girl he barely knows, he's willing to do whatever it takes to avoid their shared, violent fate. But where can a kid in foster care go to escape from himself?

STRANGER WORLDS THAN THESE (short story collection - eBook only)

About the Author

LJ Cohen is the writing persona of Lisa Janice Cohen, poet, novelist, blogger, ceramics artist, local food enthusiast, Doctor Who fan, and relentless optimist. After almost twenty-five years as a physical therapist, she now uses her anatomical knowledge and myriad clinical skills to injure characters in her science fiction and fantasy novels. Lisa lives just outside of Boston with her family, two dogs (only one of which actually ever listens to her) and the occasional international student. When not doing battle with a stubborn Jack Russell Terrier mix, Lisa can be found working on the next novel, which often looks a lot like daydreaming.

Connect with LJ online:

Homepage: http://www.ljcohen.net/
Blog: http://ljcbluemuse.blogspot.com/
Facebook: http://www.facebook.com/ljcohen
Twitter: @lisajanicecohen
Tumblr: http://www.ljcohen.tumblr.com
Google+: https://www.google.com/+LisaCohen
email LJ: lisa@ljcohen.net

Sign up for Blue Musings, an occasional email newsletter complete with free, original, short fiction offered in a variety of drm-free formats. (www.ljcohen.net/contact.html)